THE CITIZEN

CHAWTON HOUSE LIBRARY SERIES:
WOMEN'S NOVELS

Series Editors: Stephen Bending
Stephen Bygrave

TITLES IN THIS SERIES

1 *The Histories of Some of the Penitents in the Magdalen-House*
edited by Jennie Batchelor and Megan Hiatt

2 Stéphanie-Félicité de Genlis, *Adelaide and Theodore, or Letters on Education*
edited by Gillian Dow

3 E. M. Foster, *The Corinna of England*
edited by Sylvia Bordoni

4 Sarah Harriet Burney, *The Romance of Private Life*
edited by Lorna J. Clark

5 Alicia LeFanu, *Strathallan*
edited by Anna M. Fitzer

6 Elizabeth Sophia Tomlins, *The Victim of Fancy*
edited by Daniel Cook

7 Helen Maria Williams, *Julia*
edited by Natasha Duquette

8 Elizabeth Hervey, *The History of Ned Evans*
edited by Helena Kelly

9 Sarah Green, *Romance Readers and Romance Writers*
edited by Christopher Goulding

10 Mrs Costello, *The Soldier's Orphan*
edited by Clare Broome Saunders

11 Sarah Green, *The Private History of the Court of England*
edited by Fiona Price

12 *Translations and Continuations: Riccoboni and Brooke,*
Graffigny and Roberts
edited by Marijn S. Kaplan

13 Sydney Owenson, *Florence McCarthy: An Irish Tale*
edited by Jenny McAuley

14 Frances Brooke, *The History of Lady Julia Mandeville*
edited by Enit Karafili Steiner

FORTHCOMING TITLES

Eliza Haywood, *The Rash Resolve and Life's Progress*
edited by Carol Stewart

Isabelle de Montolieu, *Caroline of Lichtfield*
edited by Laura Kirkley

Mrs S. C. Hall, *Sketches of Irish Character*
edited by Marion Durnin

Ann Gomersall,
The Citizen

EDITED BY

Margaret S. Yoon

Routledge
Taylor & Francis Group
LONDON AND NEW YORK

First published 2013 by Pickering & Chatto (Publishers) Limited

Published 2016 by Routledge
2 Park Square, Milton Park, Abingdon, Oxfordshire OX14 4RN
711 Third Avenue, New York, NY 10017, USA

First issued in paperback 2016

Routledge is an imprint of the Taylor & Francis Group, an informa business

BRITISH LIBRARY CATALOGUING IN PUBLICATION DATA

Gomersall, A.
The citizen. – (Chawton House library series. Women's novels)
1. Epistolary fiction.
I. Title II. Series III. Yoon, Margaret S.
823.6-dc22

ISBN 13: 978-1-138-23539-7 (pbk)
ISBN 13: 978-1-8489-3109-1 (hbk)

Typeset by Pickering & Chatto (Publishers) Limited

CONTENTS

Introduction   ix
Works Cited   xxv
Note on the Text   xxix

Ann Gomersall, *The Citizen*   15

Editorial Notes   167

There is no Place in the Town which I so much love to frequent as the *Royal Exchange*. It gives me a secret Satisfaction, and, in some measure gratifies my Vanity, as I am an *Englishman*, to see so rich an Assembly of Country-men and Foreigners consulting together upon the private Business of Mankind, and making this Metropolis a kind of *Emporium* for the whole Earth .... Nature seems to have taken a particular Care to disseminate her Blessings among the different Regions of the World, with an Eye to this mutual Intercourse and Traffick among Mankind, that the Natives of several Parts of the Globe might have a kind of Dependance upon one another, and be united together by their common Interest. (p. 268–9)

~Joseph Addison, *Spectator*, 69 (19 May 1729)

Introduction: Commerce, Community and the Circulation of Benevolence[1]

In September 1829, Thomas Binney, the minister of Newport on the Isle of Wight, wrote to Earl Spencer on behalf of Ann Gomersall (1750–1835).[2] Binney had successfully solicited his aid in recommending Gomersall's case to the Literary Fund Committee twice before: due to Lord Spencer's 'prompt and benevolent interest in her favor', Binney acknowledges, Mrs Gomersall 'has at both times received £10 from the Literary Fund'.[3] Soliciting Spencer's aid yet again, Binney wrote: 'It might be thought, indeed, that to have succeeded <u>twice</u> ought really, to content us – but alas! as life and poverty equally continue, the same necessity remains for something to be done – and I am sure I shall find the same, unchanged benevolence in your Lordship, and, I hope, the same beneficent disposition in the committee of the Institution to which I have referred'. Binney's plea was partially successful. The Committee voted to grant Gomersall £5, half the amount they had previously granted to her. Yet Gomersall's circumstances – evoked so poignantly in Binney's phrase that 'life and poverty equally continue' – were dire. Aged seventy-nine in 1829, she was partially paralysed due to a stroke and was barely subsisting, aided by the grants from the Literary Fund.[4] Her plight, similar to that of many female writers during this period, helps inform our picture of women's experiences during the effort to professionalize writing as legitimate labour in the early part of the nineteenth century.[5]

What was notable about Ann Gomersall's initial petition to the Literary Fund Committee was its silence about her three published novels as proof that she was an author and therefore eligible for a grant from the Fund. In her initial application, Gomersall cited only her 1824 poem, *Creation*, which was her last published work.[6] The omission of any reference to her novels – all of which fit the sentimental mode – points, perhaps, to the public debate surrounding sensibility and the sentimental novel that took place in a series of essays published in the 1780s, a debate that continued throughout the 1790s.[7] One of the central issues of the debate was the power of sentimental literature to stir the emotions of its readers. By 1796, Samuel Taylor Coleridge, in his periodical the *Watchman*, had sardonically observed 'The fine lady ... sips a beverage sweetened with human blood, even while she is weeping over the refined sorrow of [Goethe's] Werter or of [Richardson's] Clementina. Sensibility is not Benevolence'.[8] Coleridge's comments point to the dubious nature of sentimental literature to raise sympathetic responses to fictional characters and situations, which might cause a reader to feel morally elevated. One of the questions that persisted was centred on how real such feelings of moral elevation and virtue were if they did not stir the readers into benevolent action.

Gomersall had, in fact, achieved minor acclaim with her three novels: *Eleonora: A Novel, In a Series of Letters* (1789), *The Citizen: A Novel* (1790) and *The Disappointed Heir: or, Memoirs of the Ormond Family: A Novel* (1796). The *Monthly Review* noted of *Eleonora*: 'These volumes are rendered interesting by a great variety of natural incidents, and are enlivened by an easy and often humourous delineation of characters'.[9] The reviews of *The Citizen* confirmed Gomersall's reputation: 'The favourable idea which we formed of this female writer, from her Eleonora ... is confirmed by this second attempt ... [S]he represents the manners of middle life with great exactness, and has a happy facility in sketching familiar conversations. Her *citizen*, the hero of the piece, is an excellent character, and well supported'.[10] The *Critical Review* finds the novel's humorous quality to be most interesting, and the character of the citizen, though too obviously borrowed from the 'English Merchant', is well drawn and supported.[11] Gomersall's contemporary reviewers gave due notice to the distinctive character of the 'citizen'. James Raven has observed that Gomersall's novels are unusual in that they 'were a defence of the merchant and the values of commerce' and 'that she explicitly differentiates between types of businessmen and their respective social and moral worth'. Raven is particularly struck by her distinction between the established merchant and 'the upstart merchant-manufacturer and petty trader'.[12] Gomersall's distinction between these types can be traced to the underlying philosophies and cultural issues prevalent in the late eighteenth century, particularly in the anxieties related to Britain's tremendous military and mercantile successes and the subsequent gain in wealth and power.[13] Gomersall must be granted a place in literary history for her novels, particularly *The Citizen*, because the plot of this epistolary work reveals a rich convergence of eighteenth-century debates about sensibility, commerce and masculinity in a period when Britain had emerged as a formidable international power.

When eighteenth-century moral philosophers such as David Hume turned to economic questions, they focused on the public benefit to be gained from private enterprise. In his essay 'Of Commerce', Hume declared that:

> The greatness of a state, and the happiness of its subjects, how independent soever they may be supposed in some respects, are commonly allowed to be inseparable with regard to commerce; and as private men receive greater security, in the possession of their trade and riches, from the power of the public, so the public becomes powerful in proportion to the opulence and extensive commerce of private men.[14]

In this essay and in 'Of the Refinement in the Arts', Hume particularly emphasized the importance of the circulation of both goods and responsibilities throughout all levels of society so that men and women 'must feel an increase of humanity, from the very habit of conversing together ... Thus *industry, knowledge* and *humanity*, are linked together by an indissoluble chain, and are found, from experience as well as reason, to be peculiar to the more polished, and, what are commonly denominated, the more luxurious ages'.[15] Hume's emphasis on industry, knowledge and humanity can be translated to commerce, education and community in Gomersall's novel, issues of central importance to *The Citizen*.

The Citizen thus addresses the problem of how to move its readers from sympathetic feeling to benevolent action by using the merchant as a role model. In the tradition of novels such as Henry Mackenzie's *The Man of the World* (1773) and Clara Reeve's *The Two Mentors* (1783), *The Citizen* focuses on the hero, rather than the heroine, and on the role of the mentor in guiding the hero. Gomersall's novel is distinct in that she raises the merchant to the role of moral guide, and in particular, she associates the industrious activity of the merchant with a Christian practice of benevolence. With *The Citizen*, Gomersall engages in the same social and political debates that were central to Henry Brooke's *The Fool of Quality* (1765–70), a novel in which the younger son of an earl is raised in rural obscurity and becomes a moral and prominent man of business. Echoes of *The Fool of Quality* appear in Gomersall's work, especially in the way 'the major debates and concepts of eighteenth-century political discourse' were marshalled 'under two opposing banners': 'under the banner of manners and of sentiment, the properties of feeling, politeness and taste are aligned with industry and commerce; opposing these are the forces of worldliness and corruption associated with aristocratic landed wealth, fashion and city society'.[16] The conflict between these two forces emerges in the choice that faces the young characters in *The Citizen*, particularly Charles Montgomery.

Following the events of a typical courtship novel, *The Citizen* follows the romantic plot of three couples through their correspondence. Their letters, however, are concerned not only with romance but also with making the right choice of learning to reject the frivolous ambitions of 'making a great figure in life, with

respect to *dress, house, furniture, equipage, and a suitable number of servants'* to an
understanding of the role a 'benevolent mind' has in 'the pleasing satisfaction of
performing the necessary duties of humanity'.[17] The practices of the London merchant and 'citizen' of the title, Mr Philip Bertills, become the model that educates
and guides the activity of the country gentleman, Charles Montgomery, in managing his land and wealth. Rather than emphasizing the importance of personal
gain – the popular misconception of merchants' ambitions – Mr Bertills mentors
Charles in the importance of properly and benevolently circulating resources to
aid those who are needy within the community. The novel particularly emphasizes the importance of making the right moral choice between industry and
commerce and fashion and pleasure, through Charles's search for identity and
purpose in life after his father dies, when he discovers that he is illegitimate and
has no legal claim to his father's wealth or estates. Through the story of how a
young man must redefine himself as he enters adulthood, *The Citizen* promotes
an idea of the proper education of gentlemen, and in raising the merchant to the
role of moral guide and mentor, the novel not only defends and validates the commercial activities of merchants, but also powerfully joins that commercial activity
with a communal humanity.[18] Indeed, in partnering Charles's work as a benevolent landowner with Mr Bertills's mercantile practices, the novel more than hints
that Charles has discovered a 'profession', a topic of growing concern during this
period. In fact, one of the most famous inhabitants of Leeds during the period
in which Gomersall lived in that city and wrote her first two novels was Joseph
Priestley, who wrote *An Essay on a Course of Liberal Education* (1765), pinpoint-
ing some of the crucial defects of a gentleman's education.[19]

Directed to the dissenting Warrington Academy, Priestley's essay addresses
a concern for educating those gentlemen who will be 'engaging in those higher
spheres of active life', which

> comprehended all those stations in which a man's conduct will considerably affect
> the liberty and the property of his countrymen, and the riches, the strength, and the
> security of his country; the first and most important ranks of which are filled by gen-
> tlemen of large property.[20]

Here, Priestley identifies a chief fault in the traditional education programmes of
the universities: they were designed for training the clergy and hence only subjects such as rhetoric, logic and 'School-Divinity' are taught.[21] In order to redress
the faults of this narrow view of education, Priestley recommends instruction in
subjects such as civil history, particularly civil policy: the theory of laws, government, manufacture, commerce, naval force, etc. – topics that can serve to benefit
any gentleman in his *active* roles. What Priestley emphasizes, however, is a focus
for gentlemen who have no financial need to embark on a professional career.
Priestley, in fact, recognizes the need and desirability for men of substance to
be educated properly so that they can responsibly fulfil their roles as landowners
and men of influence.

Hence, Priestley's concern is to equip gentlemen and those in the professions to understand and manage the fast-paced, modern world of the late eighteenth century, in which the realm of gentlemanly concerns has expanded beyond the confines of a country estate or a single nation. Aware of the responsibilities as well as benefits of Britain's massive increase in wealth and power, Priestley urges that an educational programme be developed that will help maintain Britain's status against competitor nations:

> so thoroughly awakened are all the states of Europe to a sense of their true interests, that we are convinced, the same supine inattention with which affairs were formerly conducted is no longer safe; and that, without superior degrees of wisdom and vigour in political measures, every thing we have hitherto gained will infallibly be lost, and be quickly transferred to our more intelligent and vigilant neighbours.[22]

In this new international world, Priestley recognizes the need for what he calls 'more lights and superior industry': a 'different and a better furniture of mind' is necessary not only for ministers of state but for anyone who has 'influence in schemes of public and national advantage'.[23] In this growing, global economy in which Britain is the dominant power, the role of a landed country gentlemen now carries more responsibilities, and the ripple effects from one estate can develop into a mighty national wave.

The novel opens at a crucial point in which Charles has fallen into the snare of an immoral, social-climbing beauty from Leeds, Fanny Elwood, the daughter of a wool-stapler. She desires Charles for his wealth and the estates he will inherit from his father, a fact recognized by Charles's father and friends, who see Fanny in her true colours. Much of Volume I centres on the circulation of letters urging Charles to recognize Fanny's moral faults. Charles, however, although well educated and guided by an excellent father, is governed by impetuous passions. As his friend, Sir Edward Melworth cautions, 'take care what you are about; you are on the brink of a dangerous precipice; another step may plunge you into irretrievable misery! Do not suffer your rashness to be the destruction of all your prospects of felicity'.[24] Even in the face of incontrovertible evidence that Fanny has been the mistress of Major Herbert, with whom she has had a child, Charles persists in his devotion to Fanny, ignoring all the dictates of reason and remaining enthralled by his passions. In the end, he is saved only by his father's death, when knowledge of his illegitimate birth emerges. Unable to inherit, he loses his estates, his income and his beloved simultaneously, for Fanny transfers her attention to another man, Mr Wilkins. Thus the death of his father throws Charles into a crisis of identity in which he must 'devise some expedient for the means of sustaining my existence'.[25] Having been educated as a gentleman and knowing no other path, Charles is in a quandary about his future:

> At present, I know not what course to take: trade I am wholly a stranger to, nor do I think I could ever bring my mind to submit to all the servile situations which the trader must necessarily be thrown into very frequently. The army seems to me the only resource I have left. How little did my late honored parent imagine that his darling son would ever be reduced to the necessity of living by his industry! yet it *must* be by the exertion of that, in some way or other, by which alone I *can* live. I can never support the idea of submitting to be a dependent upon the bounty of another.[26]

Charles, an educated gentleman with no practical skills or abilities that will enable him to live by his own means, presents here the two options typically open to the younger sons of landed gentry: trade or the army (and increasingly, the navy).[27] Charles is, in fact, in precisely the position that Priestley had identified in his essay.

It is at this point, at the end of Volume I, that *The Citizen* makes a dramatic turn. The novel's focus shifts away from the courtship plot to the 'apprenticeship' of Charles Montgomery to the merchant, Mr Bertills, as he mentors Charles into a new understanding of the responsibilities of a gentleman of substance. Charles's passions – his ability to feel deeply – characterizes him as a 'man of feeling'. Part of his apprenticeship to Mr Bertills involves governing his impetuous passions – the kind of self-love against which Alexander Pope had written about in his *Essay on Man* earlier in the century – with a rational and sensible humanity. In actively pairing the issues of benevolence and manly action, *The Citizen* tackles one of the paradoxes inherent in the 'man of feeling': that such a virtuous man's feelings often were too overwhelming to result in effective and *manly* action. Henry Mackenzie's Harley from *The Man of Feeling* (1771) famously embodies this paradox, raising questions about what constitutes proper manliness.[28] Charles's passions allow him to shed tears of genuine sympathy, but his training in learning how to act with compassionate humanity (along with his social status and wealth) enables him to render effective aid, rather than merely weeping in helpless sympathy. As a man of substance *and* a man of feeling, Charles embodies the sentimental hero first envisioned by Samuel Richardson's *Sir Charles Grandison* (1753), with the crucial difference that the moral guide of the sentimental hero is not a vicar or a tutor, but a merchant.

Mr Bertills begins his mentorship by having Charles witness several acts of benevolence, in which deeply Christian ideas of trust and faith emerge and are coupled with the prevailing moral philosophy of the period. Mr Bertills personally introduces Charles to those in need, urging him to visit the sorrowful, which parallels Adam Smith's statements about what motivates virtuous duty in *The Theory of Moral Sentiments* (1759). In a powerful statement about the human condition, Smith speculates on the responses of 'a man of humanity' to the knowledge that the 'great empire of China ... was suddenly swallowed up by an earthquake'.[29] Smith imagines that such a person would 'express strongly his sorrow for the misfortune of that unhappy people', but after some 'fine philosophy' on the nature of disasters, he would return to his daily business and cares, 'provided he never saw them'.[30] Although he continues to make a larger point about reason and duty, Smith recognizes here the deep influence of calamities that are witnessed first-hand. In a similar way, Mr Bertills urges Charles to practice a personal kind of benevolence. The emphasis on the personal is reinforced by the epistolary form, in which the stories of those in need are recounted as a personal testimony, or a witnessing, of how sympathy inspires benevolent action as Charles recounts his experiences to his friends. After only a few days spent with Mr Bertills and witnessing his transactions with others, Charles exclaims, 'What a man is Mr. Bertills! how noble, how generous, how exalted is his conduct! In the amiable qualities of the heart *no one* ever surpassed him, and *few* ever equalled him. Every day displays to my view some excellency in his character unseen before'.[31]

This deeply personal touch was an important aspect not only of the communities of sympathy and benevolence promoted by Hume and Smith, but also of the competitive mercantile world of the City of London. Early in their correspondence, Mr Bertills tells Charles, 'remember I have assured you of my friendship; let that satisfy you till we meet; and do not forget that the *word* of a British merchant is as sacred as his *oath*; *I* dare not violate *mine*'.[32] London merchants relied heavily on personal meetings and much of their success in business was based on the strength of their reputation, or their 'public face'.[33] In essence, their business rested on their word. To these philosophical and commercial meanings can be added Christian significance to the merchant's 'word', which emerges in Mr Bertills's first actions regarding the estates he has inherited from his friend.

Mr Bertills chides those who are worried for not trusting that he would act as he should. In the cases of Mrs Ellis, the old butler and the tenant farmers, Mr Bertills gently rebukes all of them for worrying about the future now that he has inherited. As the intimate friend of Mr Montgomery, Mr Bertills has known all of them for many years. Hence, Mr Bertills chides them for not trusting in their knowledge of Mr Bertills and for not trusting in their faith in God that their futures are secure even though Mr Montgomery has died intestate. Mr Bertills reminds all who are concerned that they should 'contentedly leave that affair in the hands of providence' and that all they must do is 'to endeavour to perform [their] duty to God and man'.[34] For Mr Bertills, to worry about the future is to lack faith not only in God, but also in those Christian individuals who have the responsibility of ownership.

In the case of Mr Clements, Mr Bertills extends this Christian philosophy of trust and faith to business dealings. He chides Mr Clements for not explaining about his inability to repay the loan, and also for not trusting in the knowledge that not only could he ask for an extension to repay the loan, but also that he could apply for an additional loan to help him through a difficult period. In

Mr Clements's situation can be seen a microcosm of the larger society, for Mr Clements puts himself in financial peril by promising to help others who are in desperate trouble as well. If Mr Bertills had demanded the immediate repayment of his loan, Mr Clements would have been ruined and along with him all those who were indebted to him. Hence a chain of devastation would have been wrought by the lack of understanding shown to one person.

Charles, however, has already learned to trust Mr Bertills. In a rapid reversal of his earlier prejudices, Charles *does* have faith in Mr Bertills after spending just a few days with him, remarking that 'my heart is at ease, from a certainty that he has too elevated a turn of mind to entertain a thought of reducing me to indigence by taking the utmost advantage that the law allows him ... I have, therefore, dismissed all my fears, and in his hands I think myself safe'.[35] In trusting Mr Bertills, Charles passes a 'test' and learns a valuable lesson. During the interview in which Charles receives the deed for the estates, Mr Bertills explains: 'It has been the will of God to try your patience, for a short time, by divesting you apparently of every *human* support; that you might thereby be compelled to place your dependence upon him alone'.[36] As a man of feeling, Charles knows to trust in his feelings. What he subsequently learns from his apprenticeship to Mr Bertills is how to trust in God as well, and to act on those feelings with a true understanding of his responsibilities as a man of wealth. When Mr Bertills hands over the estates and inheritance that belonged to his father, he impresses on Charles the need to think of 'the *use* of what is committed to your charge: – ever bearing upon your mind that *to whom much is given of him will much be required*'.[37] In receiving his inheritance from the hands of Mr Bertills, Charles is inducted into the philosophy of Mr Bertills.

As a merchant, Mr Bertills represents a contested figure of authority within the novel, with Charles initially voicing fairly typical prejudices against the profession. Charles assumes at first that Mr Bertills 'must, of course, have imbibed opinions and sentiments despicably narrow and contracted' as a result of his occupation as a London merchant. Furthermore, he is certain that Mr Bertills must have a 'love of money' because 'notwithstanding he has only one child to inherit his wealth, he pursues business now with as much avidity as he did in the days of his youth'.[38] As a matter of historical fact, however, the distance between the landed gentry and city merchant is not as great as Charles's prejudice would imply. Many younger sons of landed families were apprenticed to merchants throughout the eighteenth century.[39] Significantly, the character in *The Citizen* who vouches for the integrity and nobility of Mr Bertills and of other merchants like him is Sir Edward Melworth, an example of the English country gentlemen whose knowledge of the world is broad and informed. He and his sister, along with their friend, the Hon. Augustus Fitzmaurice (the son of a peer), spend much of Volume II in France visiting friends. When Charles finally understands the true worth of Mr Bertills, Sir Edward writes, 'I imagine you have now discarded all narrow prejudices against citizens and traders; and, in future, will judge of persons only by their sentiments and conduct',[40] an important lesson of the novel for its readers.

In raising the merchant to the level of hero, the moral voice of the novel, Gomersall actively engages in the social issues of her day, joining the company of other popular novelists who similarly sought to rescue the merchant from his early roots as a figure of scorn and ridicule. The merchant as a literary character gradually metamorphoses over the course of the eighteenth century from a figure of comedy and the focus of satire to a character who grows into the role of hero, and eventually becomes 'justified by a bourgeois ideal of gentlemanliness, based upon ideas of responsibility and service'.[41] The writings of Daniel Defoe and George Lillo served to praise the responsible and productive character of the merchant early in the century, and later, virtuous and admirable merchants appear in popular works such as *The Fool of Quality* and Richard Cumberland's play, *The West-Indian* (1771). Nonetheless, the stock figure of the 'cit' – ridiculed, critiqued and satirized – persisted in eighteenth-century literature.[42] The persistence of this negative portrayal may lie in what has been identified as the merchants' paradoxical place in British society: 'The wealth of the merchant may have been feared in some gentle circles as a threat to the landed order, but their riches were likely to engender conservatism and loyalty to the existing regime. If well-managed, London's merchants could be a key force for stability in a very uncertain age'.[43] The threat of social upheaval depicted in eighteenth-century fiction was not, in fact, a reflection of reality, particularly since most merchants did not actually retire to an estate in the country, but rather continued to work until they died and lived close to their warehouses, remaining confined within the City.[44]

Mr Bertills emphatically defuses any threat of social encroachment when he renounces his legal status as heir to Mr Montgomery's estates and deeds them to Charles. Contrary to Charles's expectations, Mr Bertills states that he 'considered all the property both *real* and *personal* as [Charles's] *natural and equitable right*, and myself [Mr Bertills] as a guardian to *secure* that right to you firmly'.[45] Mr Bertills recognizes that Charles has been educated as a gentleman and cannot conceive how he could be transformed or trained into another profession. He thus emphatically vetoes Charles's initial desire to enter the army, informing Charles: 'Under the idea of being a *gentleman* by profession you would condescend to the very worst slavery, and let yourself out as a *mark to be shot at for so much per diem*'.[46] Nor does he have any intention of attempting to transform Charles into a merchant: 'I shall have employment for you; not in my counting-house, for *that* would not suit your taste, and you would only do mischief there: I mean to place you in your proper sphere, in which every person appears to most advantage'.[47] Here, Mr Bertills gently teases Charles in asking him to accompany

Rhoda to London, by giving him the task of being escort to his daughter and her friend as they go shopping and visiting. Underlying this teasing humour is the serious point that each person does, indeed, have a proper sphere, a place appropriate to his gifts, training and character.

In between the shopping trips Mr Bertills continues to enlighten Charles in his role as an active benefactor by asking him to meet with Mrs Brown, a woman who had applied to a charity aiding poor female orphans that Mr Bertills supports. Rather than asking Charles to join the committee as a regular member, he asks Mrs Brown to visit Charles and Rhoda on a personal visit in order to tell her story, in the hopes of transferring her to their care. Mr Bertills's hopes are fulfilled, and as a result of hearing Mrs Brown's story – a story that moves Charles to tears of sympathy – Charles 'proposes to place her and her family in a small farm, now vacant, upon his estate in Sussex' and is determined that her family 'shall suffer no more from pecuniary distresses'.[48] Thus, Mr Bertills reinforces Charles's social standing, but adds a purposeful and charitable industry, and a broader knowledge of his responsibilities to it.

In his understanding and sympathetic management of business transactions, Mr Bertills promotes not only the circulation of money but also the circulation of benevolence, both of which are necessary for the maintenance of a strong and productive community. Those who inhibit this circulation are deeply criticized. Hence, Fanny, a daughter of a merchant, is treated quite severely in the novel, which may be surprising given that Gomersall married a merchant and created a title character who is a merchant.[49] Yet Fanny follows a disastrous and wretched trajectory in the course of the novel; she is the fallen woman whose eager ambitions drive her to ruin rather than success. She stands in marked contrast to the virtuous daughter of Mr Bertills, Rhoda, and certainly shows Gomersall's awareness of the sharp distinctions that existed in the merchant class, between the London merchant with his international concerns and the petty trader intent on personal gain. The account of Fanny's 'horrid' death while 'in a state of insensibility and intoxication' ends the novel, warning readers about the mortal dangers related to a selfish ambition that blocks the circulation of wealth and charity necessary for a vital and prosperous society. Fanny serves as an example of an extreme private selfishness that runs directly counter to the lessons that Mr Bertills teaches Charles. Her marriage to Mr Wilkins is based on the selfish desire for gain – she wants a secure financial position and her future husband needs her £1,000 dowry to save his failing business – and so is doomed, along with the business.

Gomersall does not restrict her criticisms to petty traders, but also includes the dissipated members of the nobility, represented by Lady Gertrude Carruther, Lady Bab Stansfield and the Duke. These characters who should be leaders of society are focused solely on personal pleasure and have no regard for the larger community. They stand in marked contrast to the more responsible and benevolent peers represented by Lord and Lady Lucan, and the Earl and Countess of Castleton. In the broad array of characters presented in *The Citizen*, Gomersall makes her readers aware of the universally negative effects of self-centred behaviour, contrasting them starkly to the virtuous characters.

By the end of the novel, Charles has learned the true value of his inheritance and understood the responsibilities that accompany his wealth. Mr Bertills, in blessing the marriage of his daughter to Charles – a union that symbolically joins the opposing forces of landed wealth and mercantile industry – gives his benediction to them as they begin 'to act [their] part in the great theatre of the world' and reminds them that: 'You are blest with affluence; let it not be a snare to draw you into indolence, but rather consider it as a loud call upon you to exercise industry in using it properly. Visit the abodes of sorrow; dispense your bounty, with a liberal hand, to the indigent'.[50] In urging his daughter and son-in-law to be the 'delegates of heaven' who are blessed by the Almighty, Mr Bertills combines Hume's three virtues, 'industry, knowledge, and humanity', with Christian ideas of blessings and rewards.

The Citizen envisions a society where industry and commerce are harmoniously allied with landed wealth, and humanitarian benevolence circulates as freely as material goods. In many ways, eighteenth-century England did embody such a society, prompting Joseph Addison at the start of the century to exult in the bustle and activity of the Royal Exchange and the blessings of the English in living at the centre of an international community united by 'common interest'. Historically, the nation did feel that the period was an 'age of benevolence' and an 'age of charity', statements that were given ample weight by the number of charitable organizations that were founded during the century.[51] And yet, as her own experience showed, Gomersall's depiction of the 'Citizen' and his example of benevolent commercial practices was, in many ways, still an idealistic vision. The advertisement announcing the proposal for subscriptions to her first two novels stated that Gomersall had turned to writing in the hope of raising enough funds 'to enable her husband again to enter into business'.[52] In 1788, Leeds experienced a commercial crisis that resulted in a series of bankruptcies, which felled the Gomersalls.[53] While these novels received favourable reviews in both the *Critical Review* and the *Monthly Review*, neither sold enough to give Ann Gomersall a profit and, in fact, the subscriptions did not even cover the printing costs.[54] Unlike Mr and Mrs Clements, the fictional couple in *The Citizen* who are rescued from mercantile troubles by the generous benevolence of Mr Bertills, the Gomersalls never recovered from their financial troubles. By the mid-1790s, the Gomersalls had left Leeds and moved to south-west England, 'from where Mrs. Gomersall's family seems to have originated'.[55] They eventually moved to Newport on the Isle of Wight, where her husband died in 1814, leaving her with little or no money and obliging her to 'labour with her hands'.[56] As her petitions to the

Literary Fund Committee attest, Ann Gomersall's plight was severe. Unlike the characters in her novel, the circulation of resources never fully reached her, but *The Citizen* presents her hope for an ideal society in which the moral philosophies of Hume and Smith can work hand in hand with Christian principles in managing the great wealth of the new empire for the benefit of all.

Notes

1. Deep thanks go to Karen Edwards and Jane Spencer for reading drafts of this introduction, and to Adeline Johns-Putra for generously sharing her knowledge of Ann Gomersall. Thanks also go to the Chawton House Library for granting a fellowship to research this project.

2. James Raven notes only the records of Gomersall's death (17 June 1835), but the *Orlando Project* authors list both dates of birth and death. Her birth date (24 January 1750) may not be accurate since the *Orlando Project* entry also states that 'Gomersall died at Newport in the Isle of Wight, aged just past eighty'. If the dates are correct, Gomersall died well past the age of eighty, at the age of eighty-five. See J. Raven, *Judging New Wealth: Popular Publishing and Responses to Commerce in England, 1750–1800* (Oxford: Clarendon Press, 1992) ftn. 11, pp. 114–5; and S. Brown, P. Clements and I. Grundy (eds), 'Ann Gomersall', in *Orlando: Women's Writing in the British Isles from the Beginnings to the Present* (Cambridge: Cambridge University Press Online, 2006).

3. Letters to the Literary Fund Committee, 1815–1834, Loan Ms. 96 RLF 1/332 (British Library, London) letter 10. This archive contains letters from Ann Gomersall to the Literary Fund Committee, as well as letters from Lord Spencer, the Duke of Somerset, and citizens of Newport writing on behalf of Gomersall.

4. 'The Literary Fund (later the Royal Literary Fund) was established in 1790. Its primary goal was to offer monetary support to financially distressed authors and their dependants. Its secondary aim was more ambitious; to restore literature and authorship to the cultural pre-eminence the charity claimed they had all but lost as the eighteenth century drew to a close' (J. Batchelor, *Women's Work: Labour, Gender, Authorship, 1750–1830* (Manchester: Manchester University Press, 2010), pp. 144–5).

5. Batchelor's work offers an important reading of how literary women's 'labours' were marginalized even as organisations such as the Literary Fund were founded to justify writing as productive labour and legitimize writers as part of a profession. Alongside letters from lesser-known women writers, Batchelor notes that Samuel Taylor Coleridge and Thomas Love Peacock also petitioned the Literary Fund Committee for aid.

6. *Creation* has not received much attention, either from Gomersall's contemporaries or from modern scholars. A catalogue search of the major research libraries in the US and the UK uncovered only one copy, at the British Library. Adeline Johns-Putra finds the poem interesting in light of its epic qualities and, in particular, the radical stance Gomersall takes in representing Eve as Adam's 'intellectual equal': 'Woman she shall be call'd – her proper name / From man she sprang, her nature is the same'. See A. Johns-Putra, *Heroes and Housewives: Women's Epic Poetry and Domestic Ideology in the Romantic Age (1770–1835)* (Berlin: Peter Lang AG, 2001), p. 115.

7. Markman Ellis discusses the 'new criticism of the novel in the 1780s' and 'the controversy of sentimentalism' of which both writers and readers were aware, in *The Politics of Sensibility: Race, Gender and Commerce in the Sentimental Novel* (Cambridge: Cambridge University Press, 1996), ch. 6. Paul Goring argues that it was the questionable

sincerity of sentiment, given its performative qualities, which made critics such as Hannah More deeply suspicious of sensibility's 'counterfeit' signs (*The Rhetoric of Sensibility in Eighteenth-Century Culture* (Cambridge: Cambridge University Press, 2005), p. 181). Other scholars argue that the debate about sensibility arises from its association with political movements, and particularly Jacobin ideas. See C. Jones, *Radical Sensibility: Literature and Ideas in the 1790s* (London: Routledge, 1993); and G. Kelly, *The English Jacobin Novel, 1780–1805* (Oxford: Clarendon Press, 1976).

8. *Watchman*, 4 (25 March 1796), quoted in J. Mullan, 'Psychology', *Jane Austen in Context*, in J. Todd (ed.), *The Cambridge Edition of the Works of Jane Austen* (Cambridge: Cambridge University Press, 2005), p. 382.

9. *Monthly Review*, 80 (June 1789), p. 552.

10. *Monthly Review*, 3 (October 1790), p. 223.

11. *Critical Review, or, Annals of Literature*, 2 (July 1791), p. 255. The 'English merchant' refers to George Lillo's *The London Merchant*, which was a reworking of the ballad of George Barnwell; first produced and published in 1731, it remained popular throughout the eighteenth century. See Raven, *Judging New Wealth*, p. 85.

12. Raven, *Judging New Wealth*, p. 115. In England the term 'merchant' and 'cit', short for 'citizen', typically referred to those engaged in international trade (and hence, most likely to be based in London) 'whereby they are vastly differenced from ordinary shopkeepers and retailers; our merchant is a person of bulk and [a] considerable figure in the commonweal' (*The Character and Qualification of an Honest, Loyal Merchant* (London, 1686) p. 6, quoted in P. Gauci, *Emporium of the World: The Merchants of London, 1660–1800* (London: Hambledon-Continuum, 2007), p. 79).

13. Throughout the eighteenth century, Britain was involved in a series of wars: King William's War/War of English Succession (1688–97); the War of Spanish Succession (1702–13); the War of Jenkins's Ear/War of Austrian Succession (1739–48); the Seven Years War (1756–63); the American War of Independence (1775–83); and the French Revolutionary and Napoleonic Wars (1793–1815). 'The Seven Years War was the most dramatically successful war the British ever fought. They conquered Canada. They drove the French out of most of their Indian, West African and West Indian possessions. They tore Manila and Havana from the Spanish. Their navy devastated its European rivals. And they assumed for themselves the reputation of being the most aggressive, the most affluent and the most swiftly expanding power in the world' (L. Colley, *Britons: Forging the Nation, 1707–1837* (New Haven, CT: Yale University Press, 1992), p. 101).

14. D. Hume, 'Of Commerce', in *Essays, Moral, Political, and Literary*, 1752, ed. E. F. Miller, rev. ed. (Indianapolis: Liberty Fund, 1987), p. 255. As Eugene F. Miller notes in the Foreword, 'Hume's essays were received warmly in Britain' (p. xv) and 'continued to be read widely for more than a century after his death' (p. xvi). Sixteen editions of his essays appeared between 1777 and 1894. Unlike his *Treatise of Human Nature*, Hume's *Essays* and his *History of England* made him famous in his own lifetime.

15. D. Hume, 'Of the Refinement in the Arts', in *Essays, Moral, Political, and Literary*, p. 271.

16. Ellis, *The Politics of Sensibility*, p. 136. Chapter 4 of Ellis's book gives a detailed reading of *The Fool of Quality* and is particularly enlightening about the ways sentimentalism always involves economics.

17. *The Citizen*, p. 138–9.

18. Thomas L. Haskell argues convincingly that 'substructural developments like the rise of capitalism might have influenced superstructural developments like humanitarianism'

('Capitalism and the Origins of the Humanitarian Sensibility: Part I', *American Historical Review*, 90:2 (1985), pp. 339-361, on p. 341).

19. 'Leeds boasted a lively intellectual community during Mrs. Gomersall's residence. Joseph Priestley had been incumbent at the Mill Hill Chapel between 1763 and 1777, and Dr Hey's medical dissertations had won international recognition' (Raven, *Judging New Wealth*, p. 113).

20. J. Priestley, *An Essay on a Course of Liberal Education* (London: C. Henderson, T. Becket and J. Johnson, 1765), *Eighteenth-Century Collections Online*, p. 9.

21. Offering specific case studies of the landed gentry, Henry French and Mark Rothery track some of the crucial changes happening in the universities during this period in *Man's Estate: Landed Gentry Masculinities, 1600–1900* (Oxford: Oxford University Press, 2012), ch. 2.

22. Priestley, *An Essay on a Course of Liberal Education*, p. 4.

23. Ibid., pp. 4–5.

24. *The Citizen*, p. 23.

25. Ibid., p. 57.

26. Ibid., p. 57.

27. Much has been researched about the professions open to gentlemen, particularly in relation to Jane Austen's novels. During the late eighteenth century, the acceptable professions open to gentlemen were the clergy, the law and medicine, but only as one of the Fellows of the Royal College of Physicians (B. Southam, 'Professions', *Jane Austen in Context*, ed. J. Todd, *The Cambridge Edition of the Works of Jane Austen*, pp. 366–76). See also B. Southam, *Jane Austen and the Navy*, 2nd edn (London: Hambledon and London Ltd., 2000; Greenwich, London: National Maritime Museum, 2005); T. Fulford, 'Sighing for a Soldier: Jane Austen and Military Pride and Prejudice', *Nineteenth-Century Literature*, 57:2 (2002), pp. 153–78; and A. Drum, 'Pride and Prestige: Jane Austen and the Professions', *College Literature*, 36:3 (2009), pp. 92–115.

28. Scholars of sensibility have long noted the dangers of effeminacy for 'feeling' men. See the Works Cited section for works on sensibility and sentiment. For topics on masculinity and manhood in the eighteenth century, several sources have been listed in Works Cited that not only shed new light on this topic, but also provide extensive bibliographies. In particular, the *Journal of British Studies* (2005) devoted the entirety of volume 44 specifically to the topic of masculinity.

29. A. Smith, *The Theory of Moral Sentiments*, ed. D. D. Raphael and A. L. Macfie (Oxford: Clarendon Press, 1976; Indianapolis: Liberty Fund, Inc., 1982), p. 136.

30. Ibid.

31. *The Citizen*, p. 115.

32. Ibid., p. 67.

33. Gauci, *Emporium of the World*, p. 47. In fact, the key location for all mercantile dealings in London occurred at the Royal Exchange, where the physical 'layout emphatically recognized that its main role was to act as a meeting-place for merchants, customers and suppliers. In essence, the structure was a piazza a mere forty yards by fifty, ringed by a colonnade whose pillars marked a "walk" devoted to a particular type of commerce, enabling any trader to navigate easily within the enormous diversity of international trade. This compressed arena prevented the exposure of large quantities of goods for sale but facilitated personal interaction, and its cloistered character stressed its role as an arena for face-to-face dealing, as well as supplying some shelter against the caprices of the British weather' (Gauci, *Emporium of the World*, p. 41).

34. *The Citizen*, p. 114.
35. Ibid., p. 99.
36. Ibid., p. 177.
37. Ibid., p. 23. Mr Bertills quotes from the Bible, Luke 12:48.
38. *The Citizen*, p. 57.
39. French and Rothery, *Man's Estate*, ch. 2: 'Entering into the World: University and Apprenticeships'; also Gauci, *Emporium of the World*, ch. 5.
40. *The Citizen*, p. 125.
41. Raven, *Judging New Wealth*, p. 110. See also L. J. Bree, '"Cits and Traders": Commerce and Industry in the British Novel, 1700–1832' (PhD dissertation, University of London, 1991); and E. M. McGirr, *Eighteenth-Century Characters: A Guide to the Literature of the Age* (Basingstoke: Palgrave Macmillan, 2007), ch. 5.
42. *The Fool of Quality* was published in five volumes, from 1765 to 1770, and ran through 'twenty-eight editions before 1822' (Ellis, *The Politics of Sensibility*, p. 130). Cumberland's play was also phenomenally successful, and was produced at Drury Lane, directed by David Garrick (see *ODNB*). Linda Bree offers a wide-ranging study of the literary portrayal of merchants, from the second half of the eighteenth century into the early decades of the nineteenth century ('Cits and Traders').
43. Gauci, *Emporium of the World*, p. 167. In fact, London's 'cits' expressed a powerful response to the threat of Revolutionary France in 1792, 'when a declaration of loyalty to the constitution was issued by a mass meeting of 8,000 merchants, bankers and other traders assembled at Merchant Taylor's Hall' (Gauci, *Emporium of the World*, p. 198). Yet as Elaine McGirr writes: 'The successful cit, with his ready money and good credit, threatened the social order because he could buy the trappings of gentility, even aristocracy' (*Eighteenth-Century Characters*, p. 67).
44. Gauci, *Emporium of the World*, ch. 5: 'The Profession'.
45. *The Citizen*, p. 117.
46. *The Citizen*, p. 66. Henry French and Mark Rothery give historical evidence that young men felt exactly the lack of independence and sense of servitude upon entering the army (*Man's Estate*, ch. 2: 'Entering into the World: University and Apprenticeships').
47. *The Citizen*, p. 130.
48. Ibid, p. 154.
49. In a similar situation, Adam Smith expresses a paradoxically deep hostility toward businessmen in his *Wealth of Nations*. D. C. Coleman attributes this hostility to Smith's suspicion of businessmen's pursuits of monopolies ('Adam Smith, Businessmen, and the Mercantile System in England', *History of European Ideas*, 9:2 (1988), pp. 161–70). This reading makes sense given Smith's promotion of the kind of benevolent circulation expressed in the *Theory of Moral Sentiments*.
50. *The Citizen*, p. 161.
51. P. Langford, *A Polite and Commercial People: England, 1727–1783* (Oxford: Clarendon Press, 1998), ch. 10: 'The Birth of Sensibility'. Many hospitals opened during the eighteenth century, including the Foundling Hospital and the Magdalen House, an institute founded for the relief of penitent prostitutes. Many of these charitable institutions were founded by the generosity of London merchants.
52. From the *Leeds Mercury*, 20 January 1789, quoted in Raven, *Judging New Wealth*, p. 113. Advertisements also appeared in the *Leeds Intelligencer*, 3 February 1789, and the *York Courant*, 24 February 1789 (Raven, *Judging New Wealth*, p. 132).
53. Raven, *Judging New Wealth*, p. 130.

54. The total subscription to *Eleonora* was £66 while the subscription to *The Citizen* was £73.16s (Raven, *Judging New Wealth*, p. 133).
55. Ibid., pp. 114–15
56. See Brown, Clements and Grundy (eds), 'Ann Gomersall'.

WORKS CITED

Barker-Benfield, G. J., *The Culture of Sensibility: Sex and Society in Eighteenth-Century Britain* (Chicago: The University of Chicago Press, 1992).

Batchelor, J., '"Industry in Distress": Reconfiguring Femininity and Labor in the Magdalen House', *Eighteenth-Century Life*, 28:1 (2004), pp. 1–20.

—, *Women's Work: Labour, Gender, Authorship, 1750–1830*. Manchester: Manchester University Press, 2010.]

Boswell, J., *Life of Johnson* (1789), ed. R. W. Chapman, intro P. Rogers (Oxford: World's Classics, 1998).

Bree, L. J., '"Cits and Traders": Commerce and Industry in the British Novel, 1700–1832' (PhD dissertation, University of London, 1991).

Brewer, J., *The Pleasure of the Imagination: English Culture in the Eighteenth Century* (New York: Farrar, Straus and Giroux, 1997).

Brown, S., Clements, P. and Grundy, I., (eds), 'Ann Gomersall', in *Orlando: Women's Writing in the British Isles from the Beginnings to the Present* (Cambridge: Cambridge University Press Online, 2006 [accessed 31 August 2011]).

Cohen, M., *Fashioning Masculinity: National Identity and Language in the Eighteenth Century* (London: Routledge, 1996).

—, '"Manners" Make the Man: Politeness, Chivalry, and the Construction of Masculinity, 1750–1830', *Journal of British Studies*, 44 (2005), pp. 312–29.

Coleman, D. C., 'Adam Smith, Businessmen, and the Mercantile System in England', *History of European Ideas*, 9:2 (1988), pp. 161–70.

Colley, L., Britons: *Forging the Nation, 1707–1837* (New Haven, CT: Yale University Press, 1992).

Drum, A., 'Pride and Prestige: Jane Austen and the Professions', *College Literature*, 36:3 (2009), pp. 92–115.

Ellis, M., *The Politics of Sensibility: Race, Gender and Commerce in the Sentimental Novel* (Cambridge: Cambridge University Press, 1996).

Fergus, J., 'The Literary Marketplace', in C. Johnson and C. Tuite (eds), *A Companion to Jane Austen* (Oxford: Blackwell Publishing, 2009).

French, H. and Rothery, M., *Man's Estate: Landed Gentry Masculinities, c. 1660–c. 1900* (Oxford: Oxford University Press, 2012).

Fulford, T., *Romanticism and Masculinity: Gender, Politics and Poetics in the Writings of Burke, Coleridge, Cobbett, Wordsworth, De Quincey, and Hazlitt* (Basingstoke: Macmillan, 1999).

—, 'Sighing for a Soldier: Jane Austen and Military Pride and Prejudice', *Nineteenth-Century Literature*, 57:2 (2002), pp. 153–78.

Gauci, P., *Emporium of the World: The Merchants of London, 1660–1800* (London: Hambledon Continuum, 2007).

Gomersall, A., *Eleonora, A Novel, in a Series of Letters* (London: J. Walter and W. Richardson, 1789. *Eighteenth-Century Collections Online* [accessed 10 April 2010]).

—, *The Citizen: A Novel, in Two Volumes* (London: Scatcherd & Whitaker, 1790).

—, *The Disappointed Heir: or, Memoirs of the Ormond Family, A Novel* (Exeter: J. McKenzie and Son; London: W. Richardson, 1796. *Eighteenth-Century Collections Online*, [accessed 10 April 2010].

—, Letters to the Literary Fund Committee, 1815–1834. Loan Ms. 96 RLF 1/332. British Library, London.

Goring, P., *The Rhetoric of Sensibility in Eighteenth-Century Culture* (Cambridge: Cambridge University Press, 2005).

Greene, D. *The Age of Exuberance: Backgrounds to Eighteenth-Century Literature* (New York: Random House, 1970).

Harris, J., 'Protean Lovelace', in D. Blewett (ed.), *Passion and Virtue: Essays on the Novels of Samuel Richardson* (Toronto: University of Toronto Press, 2001).

Haskell, T. L., 'Capitalism and the Origins of the Humanitarian Sensibility: Part I', *American Historical Review*, 90:2 (1985), pp. 339–361.

Hilton, B., *A Mad, Bad & Dangerous People? England 1783–1846* (Oxford: Clarendon Press, 2006).

Hume, D., *A Treatise of Human Nature* (1739–40), ed. D. F. Norton and M. J. Norton (Oxford: Oxford University Press, 2004).

Hume, D., *Essays, Moral, Political, and Literary* (1752), ed. E. F. Miller, rev. ed. (Indianapolis: Liberty Fund, 1987).

Johns-Putra, A., *Heroes and Housewives: Women's Epic Poetry and Domestic Ideology in the Romantic Age (1770–1835)* (Berlin: Peter Lang AG, 2001).

Jones, C., *Radical Sensibility: Literature and Ideas in the 1790s* (London: Routledge, 1993).

Jones, V., *Women in the Eighteenth Century: Constructions of Femininity* (London: Routledge, 1990).

Kelly, G. *The English Jacobin Novel, 1780–1805* (Oxford: Clarendon Press, 1976).

Langford, P., *A Polite and Commercial People: England, 1727–1783* (Oxford: Clarendon Press, 1998).

Mayer, M. Z., 'The Price for Austria's Security: Part 1. Joseph II, the Russian Alliance, and the Ottoman War, 1787–1789', *International History Review* 26:2 (2004), pp. 257–299.

McGirr, E. M., *Eighteenth-Century Characters: A Guide to the Literature of the Age* (Basingstoke: Palgrave Macmillan, 2007).

Mitchell, L. G., *Charles James Fox* (Oxford: Oxford University Press, 1992).

Mullan, J., *Sentiment and Sociability: The Language of Feeling in the Eighteenth Century* (Oxford: Clarendon Press, 1988).

Mullan, J., 'Psychology', *Jane Austen in Context*, in J. Todd (ed.), *The Cambridge Edition of the Works of Jane Austen* (Cambridge: Cambridge University Press, 2005).

Newman, C., 'John Coakley Lettsom', *British Medical Journal*, 2 (1975), pp. 282–3.

Porter, R., *Bodies Politic: Disease, Death and Doctors in Britain, 1650–1900* (London: Reaktion Books Ltd, 2001).

Priestley, J., *An Essay on a Course of Liberal Education for Civil and Active Life* (London: C. Henderson, T. Becket and J. Johnson, 1765. *Eighteenth-Century Collections Online* [accessed 24 July 2012]).

Raistrick, A., *Quakers in Science and Industry* (London: The Bannisdale Press, 1950).

Raven, J., *Judging New Wealth: Popular Publishing and Responses to Commerce in England, 1750–1800* (Oxford: Clarendon Press, 1992).

Root, R. K., 'Introduction', *Lord Chesterfield's Letters to His Son* (London: J. M. Dent & Sons; Everyman Library, 1963).

Southam, B., *Jane Austen and the Navy*, 2nd edn (London: Hambledon and London Ltd., 2000; Greenwich, London: National Maritime Museum, 2005).

—, 'Professions', in *Jane Austen in Context*, ed. J. Todd, *The Cambridge Edition of Works of Jane Austen* (Cambridge: Cambridge University Press, 2005).

Smith, A., *An Inquiry into the Nature and Causes of the Wealth of Nations* (1776), ed. and intro. K. Sutherland (Oxford: Oxford World's Classics, 2008).

—, *The Theory of Moral Sentiments* (1759), ed. D. D. Raphael and A. L. Macfie (Oxford: Clarendon Press, 1976; Indianapolis: Liberty Fund, Inc., 1982).

Van Reyk, W., 'Christian Ideals of Manliness in the Eighteenth and Early Nineteenth Centuries', *Historical Journal* 52:4 (2009), pp. 1053–73.

Wagner, P., 'Introduction', *The Life and Adventures of Sir Launcelot Greaves* (London: Penguin Books, 1988), pp. 7–28.

Woodworth, M. A., *Eighteenth-Century Women Writers and the Gentleman's Liberation Movement: Independence, War, Masculinity, and the Novel, 1778–1818.* (Farnham, Surrey: Ashgate Publishing Ltd., 2011).

NOTE ON THE TEXT

The Citizen was published by subscription in two volumes in 1790. Only one edition was printed for Scatcherd & Whitaker, on Ave-Maria-Lane, London. The novel was sold by Binns, Leeds, and Edwards and Son, Halifax. The text for this edition was taken from the copy held in the Chawton House Library, Hampshire. For this edition, spelling has been corrected and modernized and a few editorial changes were made, mostly in the cases of missing letters or words.

THE CITIZEN,

PRICE SIX SHILLINGS./

THE

CITIZEN,

A Novel,

IN TWO VOLUMES,

BY MRS. GOMERSALL,[1]

OF LEEDS,

Author of Eleonora.

VOLUME FIRST.

LONDON,
PRINTED FOR SCATCHERD & WHITAKER,
Ave-Maria-lane;
and sold by
Binns, Leeds, and Edwards and Son, Halifax

1790./

AS

A MARK

of

that esteem due to distinguished merit,

THIS WORK

is most respectfully inscribed
to

THE RIGHT HONORABLE

VISCOUNTESS IRWIN,[2]

by
her ladyship's much obliged,
most humble, and
most obedient servant,

A. Gomersall./

SUBSCRIBERS' NAMES.[3]

H.

RIGHT HON. LORD HAWKE.
RIGHT HON. LADY HAWKE.[4]
HON. MISS HAWKE.
H. H. *Gracechurch-street.*
Miss Eliza Horne, *Clapham.*
Mr. A. Harman.
Mr. Humphrey, *Stroud-green.*

J.

Mr. Jeffries, *Dover-street.*
Mrs. Jeffries.
Miss Jenkins, *Clapham.*
G. J.
Mrs. I. Jones, *Holborn-hill.*
Mr. W. Albin Jones.
Mr. Edward Jones, *Mark-lane.*
Miss Jones, *Hatton-street.*
Miss Jones, *Edmonton.*
Mr. J—n.
Mr. Jacklyn.

K.

Mr. Klein.
Newman Knowlys, Esq.
Mr. Knowlys.
Mrs. Knowlys.
Mr. W. C. Knowlys.
Mr. J. Knowlys.

Miss Knowlys./

L.

HON LADY ELIZABETH LEE, *Hartwell-brooks.*
HON. MRS. LEIGH, *Addlestrop.*
Dr. Lettsom.[5]
Colonel Lawrie.
Mr. Lockier.
Mr. Lobb, *Kennington.*
Miss Lockman, *Clapham.*
Miss Laurence, *High-street, Mary-la-bonne.*
Mrs. Lowrie, *Holloway.*
Mrs. Lawford, *Peckham.*
J. L.
R. L.
Miss Lodwick.

M.

William Meade, Esq. *High Wycom.*
James M' Auley, Esq. *Bristol.*
T. M.
R. M.
Mr. Meniton, *Southwark.*
Miss Margerum, *Hackney.*
Mrs. Martin.
Mr. Thomas Milne.
Mrs. Matthew, *Rathbone-place.*

N.

J. N. Esq.
Mrs. Newland, *Clapham.*
Miss Newsom, *Barbican.*/

P.

Mrs. Powell, *Peckham.*
J. P.
Mr. Phillips, *Tower-street.*
Mrs. Phillips.
Mr. Edward Pryce, *Bucklersbury.*

Mr. T. Pryce.
Mrs. Pryce.
Mr. Pue, *Peckham.*
Mrs. A. Porter, *Titchfield, Hants.*
Mr. William Peart.
Mrs. Powell, *Taoting, Surry.*
Miss Peirce.
Mr. Thomas Pellatt, *St. John-street.*

R.

Mrs. Richardson.
Mrs. Read, *Chatham.*
Miss Raitt, *Clapham.*
Miss Rich.
Mr. Roberts, *Hackney.*
T. R.
F. R.
Mr. John Roper.
Mr. Richardson, *Hampstead.*
Mrs. Richardson.
Master Richardson.
Miss Richardson./

S.

RIGHT HON. LADY SOUTHAMPTON.
Mrs. Scurlock, *Love-hill, Langley, Bucks.*
Mrs. Fenton Scott, *Woodhall.*
Miss Scott, *Park-row, Leeds.*
Mr. E. Stark.
Mr. Skelton.
Miss Stone, *Hartwell-brooks.*
Mrs. Sharpe, *Clapham.*
Mrs. Shrimpton, *Clapham-common.*
Rev. Neville Stow, *Dulwich-College.*
Rev. Thomas Jennings Smith, *Chaplain of Dulwich-College.*
Mr. Slater, *Stoke-Newington.*
Mrs. Stock, *Highbury-place, Islington.*
E. S.
I. S.
J. S.

James Smith, Esq. *Tooting, Surry.*
I. S.
T. P. S.
J. S.
E. P.S.
Mrs. Spencer, *Tooting, Surry.*
Mr. Joseph Street, jun. *Mark-lane.*
W. S.
C. S.
T. S.
I. S.
Miss Scrivenor, *Tooting, Surry.*
Mr. Seale, *Tower-street.*
Mrs. Seale./

T.

Rev. Mr. Townsend.
Miss Mary Toms, *Hadleigh.*
Mr. T—n.
Mrs. Taylor, *Titchfield, Hants.*
Mrs. Townsend, *Hackney.*
Miss Todd, *Stoke-Newington.*
Miss Tute, *Clement's-lane.*
Mr. John Tennant, *Water-lane.*
— Tyler, Esq. *Stockwell, Surry.*

V.

Miss Vertue.
Miss Vincent, *Clapham.*
Miss Vanderstegen, *Care-end*, near *Reading.*
Major Valotton.

W.

Lady Waldo, *Clapham.*
Miss Waldo, *South Lambeth.*
Mr. Josiah Walley.
Miss Wilkie, *Clapham.*
Miss Wolff, *Balham, Surry.*
Mrs. Wood, *Kennington-lane.*

Miss Wood, *Clapham.*
Mrs. Walter, *Portsmouth.*
Mrs. Willis, *Tooting, Surry.*
Miss Winter, *Tooting, Surry.*
Mrs. Wright, *Stoke-Newington.*
Miss Weatherall, *Tooting, Surry./*
G. W.
E. W.
Mr. George Weston.
Mrs. Whitear, *Tooting, Surry.*
J. Y. Esq.
Mr. J. Y.
X. Y.

JAMAICA SUBSCRIBERS.

HON. ALEX. FULLERTON, *Costos and member of Assembly.*
Thomas Jenkins, Esq. *St. Anns.*
John Blagrove, Esq. *member of Assembly.*
William Robertson, Esq. *Colonel of the St. Ann's Militia.*
Rev. David Fullerton, *Rector of the parish of St. Ann.*
Rev. Thomas Rees, *Rector of the parish of Kingston.*
Mrs. Rees.
Isaac Lascelles Winn, Esq. *St. Ann's.*
Adam Anderson, Esq. M. D. *St. Ann's.*
Alex. Weir, Esq. *Surgeon of St. Ann's.*
Richard Wollaston, Esq. *Surgeon of St. Ann's.*
Samuel Betton, Esq. *Surgeon, St. Ann's.*
John Anguin, Esq. *St. Ann's.*
John Johnson, Esq. *St. Ann's.*
John Willox Macgregor, Esq. *St. Ann's.*
Donold, Macdonold, Esq. *St. Ann's.*
William Smith, Esq. *St. Ann's.*
Mr. Thomas Ashmead, *St. Ann's.*
Capt. George Kitson, *St. Ann's.*
Capt. Robert Ward, *St. Ann's.*
Peter Comrie, Esq. *Surgeon, St. Ann's./*

LIST OF SUBSCRIBERS.[6]

A.

HON. MRS. ASTON.
James Allen, Esq.
Mr. Thomas Adderley, *Doctors-Commons.*
Miss Ashburner, *Clapham.*
Miss Agutter, *Aldermanbury,*
— Anderson, Esq. *Tichfield, Hants.*
P. A.
Mrs. Atkinson, *Gosport, Hants.*
William Allen, Esq. *Warden of Dulwich College.*

B.

Mrs. Brooke./
James Bartlet, Esq.
Thomas Bettesworth, Esq. *Mark-lane.*
Mrs. Bettesworth, *Mark-lane.*
Mrs. Bellamy, *Southwark.*
Mrs. Brogden, *Clapham.*
Mrs. Bowermaster, *Tichfield, Hants.*
Mrs. Brett, *Tichfield, Hants.*
Mr. W. B. *Bath.*
Mrs. Banks.
Miss Banks.
Mr. John Bowman, *Water-lane.*
F. D. B.

R. B.
J. B.
William Barr, Esq. *Southwark.*

C.

I. C. Esq.
T. C.
J. C.
Mrs. H, Caslon, *Hackney.*
Mr. Cooke, *Bristol.*
Mr. Campbell.
Mrs. Crane, *Canterbury.*
Mrs. Crabb, *Islington.*
Mrs. Cunliffe, *Colne.*
Mr. Chapman, *Whitby.*
Miss Chapman, *Whitby.*/

D.

— Dyer, Esq. *Hoxton.*
Mrs. Dyer.
Mr. J. Dyer.
Miss Dyer.
W. D.
D. D.
John Deschamps, Esq. *Bucklersbury.*
Mr. Delignon, *Spitalfields.*
Mr. Darkin.
Mr. Dutton.
Mrs. Dunning, *Clapham.*
Miss Dickson, *Clapham.*
James Dickson, Esq.
Mrs. Daman, *Portsmouth.*
Mrs. Dalby, *Clapham.*
Mrs. Dalton, *Stanmore, Middlesex.*
Mr. John Davies.
Mrs. Dixon.

E.

Joseph Edwards, Esq. *Northowram.*
T. F. E.

S. E.
Miss Eyre, *Clapham.*
Miss Eames, *Alverstoke, Hants.*
Mrs. Eade, *Stoke-Newington.*
Mrs. E—t, *Hackney.*
Mr. Edwards, *Camomile-street.*/
Mrs. Eamer, *Wood-street.*

F.

William Fountayne, Esq. *Guisborne.*
M. F.
Simon Frazer, Esq. *Quebec.*
Mr. Fauntleroy, *Stepney-green.*
Mrs. Fauntleroy.
Mrs. Faulkner, *Tichfield, Hants.*
Miss Fanshaw.
Mrs. Folston, *Great Portland-street.*

G.

RIGHT HONORABLE LADY W. GORDON.
Thomas Grant, Esq. *Portsmouth Dock-yard.*
Mr. Thomas Grant.
Mr. William Grant.
Miss Grant.
Miss Mary Grant.
Miss Esther Grant.
Miss Catherine Grant.
Mr. Gardner.
Mrs. Graham.
Miss Graham.
W. G.
Mrs. A. Gardner, *Park-street, Grosvenor-square.*
Mrs. M. G. *Hackney.*
J. G. Esq. *Herts.*
J. G./

THE CITIZEN.

LETTER I.

Charles Montgomery, Esq. to Sir Edward Melworth.

FIR-GROVE.

A REQUEST from my father to return to him immediately has not only brought me from Bath sooner than I intended, but has prevented me from fulfilling my promise to pass a few days with you, in my way home. I had, as usual, travelled with such speed, that when I reached Ferrybridge, yesterday, at three o'clock, I absolutely found myself too much exhausted to go any farther without refreshment, tho' within eight miles of the end of my journey. I therefore stopped at the/ Angel, where I had not been more than five minutes when I perceived my father driving past the window – he saw me instantly, and alighted, and we took a chearful meal together – that ended, we both got into his carriage and pursued our way hither. On the road he said to me,

'When I last wrote to you, Charles, I was just returned from Westbrook-lodge, where I had been spending the day with my worthy friend Lord Lucan, who informed me that he intended, in a few weeks, to visit the Continent[7] in quality of a tutor to his son, whom he wished to acquire every advantage that could be gained by travelling, without any of those *dis*advantages which youth too often receives from being placed under the direction of an hireling. His Lordship then painted to me the benefit *you* might derive from making the tour under similar circumstances; and so earnestly persuaded me to join their party with you, that I consented, and wrote for your return to Fir-grove to consult you upon it and give you time to make such preparation as you may think necessary./

He stopped, in expectation of my answer; but I could not, *instantly*, bring myself to acquiesce in a measure so subversive of my plan of happiness. My father had never before proposed any thing to which my heart did not yield a willing assent; but now, Edward, it formed the most powerful objections; yet of *such* a nature as would, I was sensible, have no weight with him, since they were founded on the only circumstance that had induced him to determine on this tour. I therefore renounced every idea of opposing his will by the slightest remonstrance, and, at length, not without some degree of hesitation, replied,

'Hitherto, sir, it has been my highest pleasure to submit to whatever your inclination dictated, – I see the kindness of your motive in making this proposal, and will hold myself in readiness to attend you; but pray, my dear sir,' I added, 'how long do you and Lord Lucan purpose staying abroad?'

'We shall not be absent more than two years,' returned he, 'in which time, Augustus and you will, doubtless, make every improvement we can wish, as you will both have every/ opportunity for that purpose. The *pleasures* you will, I hope, enjoy, tho' I speak of *them* but as a secondary pursuit, you will find greatly heightened by participating with your friend.'

'Undoubtedly,' said I, 'the participation of friendship heightens every enjoyment of life.'

My father appeared satisfied with my compliance, and turned the discourse on indifferent subjects. I was not very capable of joining in it, my thoughts being engrossed by the painful idea of bidding a long adieu to the idol of my heart, – my beloved, my amiable Fanny. Oh my friend, how shall I support this severe, too fast approaching trial? It is indeed an affliction, that appears to me, now, almost *in*supportable; but I *must*, I *will*, endeavour to obtain a proper degree of manly fortitude for the occasion. Yet, when I reflect on what that dear girl will suffer in my absence from her apprehensions for my health and safety, I am nearly distracted. Alas! why has not fortune placed us on an equality? we might then be happy in each other without/ incurring the guilt of filial disobedience! I have not, at present, any intention of erring in that point, nor do I believe I could persuade my Fanny to consent to such an act; her whole soul would shudder at the proposal, did I dare to make it; but I declare to you that my affections are so firmly fixed that I must either make her irrevocably mine, or be miserable for the rest of my life. I am, therefore, resolved on trying to effect my wishes by the most respectful entreaties, and every endeavour to convince my father how much my future felicity depends on his compliance with my inclinations in this instance. Time may favor my desires, and I must wait the event with patience. Strange! that my father, who in all *other* respects has distinguished himself by the most noble and exalted sentiments, should in *this* descend to a level with men of common minds! While paternal tenderness makes him truly solicitous for my happiness, pride prevents his agreeing to that which alone can promote it, and dictates to him the sordid ambition of uniting me to wealth and greatness. Yet, I verily believe, he is himself deceived in the motive that actuates/ his conduct; for he totally disavows being influenced by Miss Elwood's want of fortune. His objections to my marrying her, he says, are founded on his dislike to her *mind* and *manners*. How astonishing is this! is it possible there can be any thing more captivating? Surely no. Her manners are decorated by the graces, and her mind is, in my opinion, the seat of all perfection: but my father views her with the eye of prejudice; and, of course, is blind to every charm she possesses. Yet why do I complain to *you*, who, influenced by the very high respect you entertain for *his* judgment, view her, likewise, thro' his optics,[8] and not with the eye of unprejudiced reason. I, therefore, disclaim all hope of consolation, or pity, from you. Accustomed, however, as I am, by the habits of early friendship, to communicate to you my thoughts without reserve, I must still maintain the privilege, and consider you as the confidant of all my concerns, notwithstanding the difference of our sentiments in a point of so much importance to my peace. But I hope, my friend, yet to see the time when every prejudice against my Fanny will be removed from the minds of my father/ and you; when you shall be constrained to acknowledge the injustice done her by your mistaken opinions. You will, perhaps, be displeased with the suggestion; but I cannot help saying, that I think the lovely girl would appear to you both, in a different point of view, were her fortune *twenty* thousand instead of *one* thousand pounds. All-powerful gold is esteemed, in general, a better foundation for matrimonial happiness than intrinsic merit; the latter being often totally obscured by a want of the former.

I must, however, drop the disagreeable subject, for the present, and conclude my letter. My servant has brought the horses under my window, which reminds me of the distance to Leeds, whither I am now going, upon the wings of love, to visit my charming, my angelic Fanny: but I will not mar either her delight in the unexpected interview, or my own, by communicating the mortifying intelligence of the tortures preparing for us both, in the approaching horrid separation. Adieu!

I am yours, sincerely,

CHARLES MONTGOMERY./

LETTER II.

The same to the same.

FIR-GROVE.

THO' your disapprobation of the object which my heart has made choice of, deprives me of the pleasure I have received heretofore from your participating in my concerns; yet, I must still continue my usual communications, in the pleasing hope that I shall be able to convince you that your judgment of Miss Elwood is erroneous. I set out for Leeds immediately after concluding my last, and put the poor beasts into a foam, and myself into a situation something similar, by my eagerness to get thither; but my hurry was unnecessary; for, to my extreme mortification, I found my Fanny surrounded by a room full of company, of both sexes, which obliged me to put a curb upon my joy at seeing her, – delicacy prohibiting any particular expression of my feelings in the presence of so many witnesses. I was, therefore, forced to wear the appearance of/ ease and content, while, in reality, I was full of impatience and anxiety. I talked politics with Mr. Elwood, without knowing which of us was for the ministry, or which for the opposition. I heard from Mrs. Elwood the *very best* way of making cowslip-wine and preserving gooseberries, without feeling the least degree of curiosity respecting either; and I sometimes joined the visitors in the dull, unmeaning, uninteresting, common-place topics: viz. weather, public amusements, dress, weddings, &c. &c. In this uncomfortable state was I held from six till half past nine o'clock, when the company took their leave. Mr. Elwood went out to join his bottle-companions, and Mrs. Elwood retiring to undress, I was, at length, left alone with my dear Fanny, when I gave way to the effusions of my fond heart without reserve, and confessed the painful restraint I had been under the preceding part of the evening. The sweet girl, however, made me ample compensation by the kindness of her behaviour, wholly free from the smallest tincture of affectation or prudery. She acknowledged, with all the warmth of *real* tenderness,/ that the hours had been no less irksome to *her*. In short, her conversation filled me with inexpressible delight. It is needless to dwell upon the particulars of it; but I *discovered* – indeed she attempted not to *conceal*, on the contrary, she frankly *avowed* – her affection; declaring, candidly, that her whole happiness centered in *me*; and should she be so unfortunate as to lose the pleasing prospect of uniting her fate with mine, life would have no longer any charms for her.

In the midst of this sweet intercourse of souls, we were interrupted by a summons to supper; but upon my observing how very inferior I should think *that* repast to what I was then enjoying, particularly as I had so little time to devote to her, having promised to return to the Grove to breakfast, she very kindly declined partaking of the supper, and Mrs. Elwood concluding, I suppose, that a second summons would be as much in vain as the first, interrupted us no farther than to send in some wine and cake, which satisfied us; and, in the converse of my Fanny, the hours fled away with such rapidity, that, to our mutual/ astonishment, it was five in the morning before either of us, I believe, thought that the midnight hour had arrived. This discovery alarmed me exceedingly, and I severely reproached myself for my imprudence in subjecting her spotless character to the risk of being sullied by the breath of scandal, issuing from the lips of every servant in the house; but the sweet creature laughed away my fears upon that head, and assured me she entertained no uneasiness whatever about it.

'Really, Montgomery,' cried she, 'I am as cautious to preserve my character from censure as you can be; therefore, notwithstanding I have been so pleasingly engaged, be assured, I should not have been so totally inattentive to the time, had I not known myself perfectly safe in *every* respect. In London, and in many other parts, I know the case would be widely different; my character would be effectually blasted by such an inadvertency; but, in most parts of this county *custom* authorizes it; nothing being more common *here* than for lovers to sit together, *tête-à-tête*, the whole night thro'; nor/ did I ever, in my life, hear any one presume to censure a woman for it; and now,' added she, 'I hope your fears will cease.'

I expressed my satisfaction at the information; and, ruminating upon the circumstance, on my way home, I felt great pleasure in reflecting that the Yorkshire people must, in general, possess excellent hearts; this directs their judgment on the conduct of others, and forms the basis of that liberality of sentiment existing among them: – but for *that* my angel's *reputation* might have been lost, from her excess of kindness to me, while her mind and person were both pure as from the hands of her Creator. I own, I cannot help thinking that many virtuous young women are unjustly injured in their characters, and have a reproachful stigma affixed to them for life, by a censorious ill-judging set of beings, who from one trifling inadvertent action, are ever ready to extract a *crime* as the unavoidable consequence of it: for instance, my Fanny and I know that the hours we were together passed so innocently that Virtue herself could not have disdained a smile of approbation. – Yet/ how very different a construction might *malice* put upon our lengthened interview. I tremble at the idea, even while I rejoice in the certainty of having nothing to apprehend from her baneful influence. When we seriously consider the matter, my friend, how very natural is it for two young persons, passionately enamoured of each other, to protract every interval allowed them for private converse to the longest period in their power! and should they even break in upon the *time* allotted for rest, to enjoy a satisfaction far more pleasing, is it absolutely necessary to suppose it utterly impossible they should have spent it in a manner consistent with innocence and virtue? Surely, candor does not require this. – I am confident, however, that the *honor* of a woman is always safe, at all hours, and in all places, when in company with the man who truly loves her: the purity of his affection will not suffer him to admit a thought injurious to her present or future repose; *her* peace and happiness are infinitely dearer to him than *his own*; and he feels, sensibly, the dignity of her virtues,/ – which, to use an expression from Milton's most celebrated poem,

> – 'Create an awe
> About her, as a guard angelic plac'd.'[9]

My father sends to desire my company in the garden; – I go to him, immediately. Farewell.

Yours, ever,
CHARLES MONTGOMERY.

LETTER III.

Miss Bertills, to Miss Melworth.

C— HOUSE.

'Tis a pleasing idea, Harriet, that tho' distance separates the persons of friends, it has not power to deprive them of the enjoyment of intellectual intercourse with each other. – Happiness must be communicated, or it cannot be complete; scarce, indeed, can it be properly *felt*: and were I deprived of the pleasure of imparting mine to you, the delightful sensations I experience, at this moment,/ would be changed into repining at the severity of my fate. This preface tells you I am about to be the herald of some pleasing event; I will, therefore, keep you no longer in suspense.

This letter informs you that I am now in that dear mansion, where first our friendship grew. I came hither three days ago, purposing to stay a week; Mrs. Martinius having, on *that* condition, promised to indulge me by permitting Miss Delaporte to return, and spend a few weeks with me in town. Of that pleasure, however, I am, for the present, disappointed. – Providence has disposed of our friend in a different way – a way far more agreeable and advantageous to herself. You, my Harriet, love Louisa; she is as dear to *you*, as to *me*; consequently, you will be equally interested in her story; the particulars of which she was not acquainted with herself, till this day. You know that she was placed at the school, some time before either of us; but *how* she came hither, by *whom* brought, or to whom she belonged, were matters into which we did not speculate; nor do I recollect ever having made/ particular observation of her remaining constantly at school during the vacations; nor of her never being visited there by her relations or friends, as the rest of us were. These two latter circumstances happened, I know not how, to occur at once to my ideas, as we were sitting together yesterday evening; and without waiting to consider the propriety of my speech, I inadvertently said,

'I imagine, my dear Louisa, that both your parents died when you were very young, – too young to be sensible of their loss: – for I do not remember having ever once heard you mention either of them'.

I had scarce uttered the sentence, before I deeply regretted that curiosity, which had impelled me to wound, tho' involuntarily, the feelings of my friend; whose fine countenance spoke the strong emotions of her mind. She was pale and red, alternately; her lips quivered, with a half suppressed sigh. – She rose hastily from her seat; and, with her handkerchief, wiped away the big tear that had descended on her cheek; then, assuming a degree of ease, which I am convinced she did not feel, she replied,/

'I wonder not at your curiosity, my dear Rhoda, it is perfectly natural; would to heaven it were in my *power* to gratify it! but, –'

'My dear Louisa!' cried I, interrupting her, 'talk not of such gratification; only pardon the wound I have undesignedly given to your sensibility, and let us drop the subject *for ever.*'

'You are mistaken, my friend,' returned she, 'in imagining that you have either offended, or hurt me. I confess that, till lately, this subject was a painful one, and thence arose my reserve; for I would be a *miser* of my griefs; but time aided by the powers of reason and religion, has, at length, reconciled me to the awkwardness of my situation; and endued me with sufficient strength of mind to converse upon it, without discovering any of those painful emotions, which so rapidly enter into the bosom of friendship; and, by communicating, increase our sorrow.

'From the treatment I have always met from Mrs. Martinius,' continued she, 'you/ have, doubtless, been led to suppose I belong to some family of consequence. Whether that *is* or *is not* really the case, is a profound secret to both her and me. All I know of myself is, that I am descended from the first parents of all; but as to any other parent, relation, friend, or protector, I know none except Mrs. Martinius: with her I was placed, almost in my infancy, by persons who, it seems, assured her I belonged to a family of great respectability. The rectitude of her own heart would not suffer her to doubt their veracity; nor has the strange inattention shewn to me, for many years past, been able yet to shake her confidence. She still believes me to be what I was at first represented to her; and persists in the opinion that the period is approaching, when I shall be acknowledged with pride and pleasure, by the authors of my being. *I*, however, dare not cherish so pleasing an idea; nor, indeed, am I so solicitous to discover my family connections, as I should be, were I not afraid, sorely afraid of feeling the sting of illegitimacy. At present, my uncertainty/ respecting that circumstance, affords me some small degree of consolation, as it leaves room for hope.'

Mrs. Martinius, who had joined us a few minutes before, now took part in the conversation by saying,

'It is really astonishing to me, my love, that you can ever, for a moment, admit so degrading an idea to take possession of your mind; you have not the least foundation for it: but you are determined, I see, to torment yourself with *imaginary* evils; and I tremble to think, my dear, that, by so doing, you may provoke the Almighty to afflict you with *real* ones. As I should be very sorry that Miss Bertills should enter into your idea of illegitimacy, I must be permitted to relate every circumstance I know concerning you, as it really happened; after which, I have no doubt but her opinion will coincide with mine.

'Miss Delaporte,' she continued, 'was hardly three years of age, when she was brought hither, in a plain chariot, unattended by any but a young gentleman and lady,/ whose elegance of manners spoke the dignity of their minds. There was a delicacy in their tenderness towards each other, and in their unrestrained caresses of the child, sufficiently convincing of the *nature* and *propriety* of their connection. After having settled every thing respecting terms, they politely and feelingly requested my tender attention to the little innocent who was, they added, of a respectable family, tho' some unhappy domestic occurrences obliged her parents immediately to quit the kingdom, and also rendered it necessary to conceal the child's *real* name; instead of which she was to be called by that of Louisa Delaporte. – They did not acknowledge themselves to be her parents, but the pangs they evidently felt at separating, were, to me, proofs nearly equal to demonstration. After several severe struggles, they tore themselves away; and I have never seen them since. During the first five years, I was paid very regularly, every six months, by an old gentleman, who came frequently to see Miss Delaporte; and used, at those times, to call her his little/ adopted, and to express great satisfaction at her appearance, and growing improvements; but he was always too reserved to speak of her connections, and too cautious to mention either *her real* name, or *his own*. – Equally ignorant of that, and of his place of abode, it was utterly impossible for me to make any enquiry about him, when his visits ceased; which they suddenly did, near nine years ago; and, putting all circumstances together, I conclude the old gentleman is dead: for, I am certain, he was too fond of Miss Delaporte, and too anxious for her being kindly treated, to let so many years elapse without payment, had he been alive; and, as we are not in any real want of the money, but can do very well without it, we have no right to be displeased. – Let us wait the event, with patience and resignation; and I have no doubt but the termination of the affair will amply reward us.'

'I wish it may, madam,' cried Louisa, with a sigh. 'That expression,' said the good Mrs. Martinius, 'implies a doubt, 'which, for *your* sake, I would be glad to remove,/ but know not how. Let us, therefore, dismiss the subject, and compose our spirits with a little sacred music. *You*, Miss Bertills, must be the instrumental performer; while Miss Delaporte obliges us by singing her favorite air in the oratorio of the Messiah.'[10]

This proposal being immediately agreed to, the conversation dropped: but when I retired to rest, the subject powerfully engrossed my thoughts; as, I imagine, it did those of Louisa, who appeared, in the morning, more than usually thoughtful. When breakfast was ended, and Mrs. Martinius engaged with her pupils in another room, Louisa attracted my sole attention. She continued silent; she sighed; she was evidently unhappy; and her unhappiness distressed me infinitely. I was meditating what plan to form for her amusement, when we were both suddenly roused out of our reverie, and drawn, almost instinctively, to the window; from whence we beheld a coach and four, attended by two servants, on horseback, in rich liveries, driving, with full speed, towards the house. It stopped at the gate; and/ a very handsome young man put down the glass, to speak to a servant. In that

moment we caught his attention; he drew back; and a lady, who was sitting opposite to him, bent forward and met the eye of Louisa, who immediately sunk down
on the seat, pale, and almost breathless. I eagerly asked the cause of her emotion;
but she was only able to reply, – 'Retire with me, *this instant*, dear Rhoda, or the
next destroys me quite!' I took her directly by the arm, and led her, thro' the music
room, to her own apartment; where she gave free vent to her tears, and was, for
some time, utterly unable to speak: during which, my amazement at the cause was
beyond what I can express. At length she said,

'Oh, my dear Rhoda! in that carriage I saw my nearest relations! – Emotions,
unfelt till then, convinced me of –'

Here she was interrupted by the entrance of Mrs. Martinius, who came to
prepare her cautiously for an event, she imagined, totally unexpected: but, being
informed by me of what had passed, she was agreeably surprised, and proposed
accompanying Louisa to the/ drawing-room immediately. They were just going,
when Mrs. Fitzallan, Louisa's mother, too impatient to wait the delay of a formal
introduction, entered the room, followed by her son. And now, my Harriet, I
must refer you to your own feeling mind for an idea of the scene which ensued;
since I am utterly unable to describe it in any other way than by saying, all was
surprise, joy, and rapturous incoherency.

I have encroached so far on my night's rest, that I must conclude, after telling
you Louisa is happy. She has not to blush for the authors of her being. – But I
will give you the story of her parents by the next post. Adieu.

Yours, affectionately,
RHODA BERTILLS./

LETTER IV.

Sir Edward Melworth, to Charles Montgomery, Esq.

MELWORTH-HALL.

THE concern I feel for your happiness is so strong as almost to obliterate, at times,
the remembrance of my own sorrows. You will, perhaps, think me ungrateful in
condemning your conduct, since the particulars you communicate of it have so
happy an effect; but I would, most willingly, submit to that reproach, could any
exertion of my friendship prove instrumental in disentangling you from the web
which Fanny Elwood's *art*, assisted by the impetuosity of your passion, is preparing for you. Oh! Charles! Charles! take care what you are about; you are on the
brink of a dangerous precipice; another step may plunge you into irretrievable
misery! Do not suffer your rashness to be the destruction of all your prospects
of felicity. Depend upon it, you are deceived in the idea your imagination/ has
formed of Fanny Elwood's *mind*: – you may remember, I told you so, when I first

saw her. I liked not her behavior at the concert: I liked it less the day following. *You* were charmed with her face and person; and, having no leasure to examine her mental qualifications, contentedly *supposed* the *two former* to be a clear index of the latter. – With me it was different, quite; – I regarded every *look, motion*, and *word*, with a scrutinizing eye; and, on the result of my observations, my judgment pronounced her wholly unworthy to be ranked even amongst your common acquaintance. With the sincerity of *true* friendship, I told you my opinion immediately as we quitted her presence; and, I think, you must allow me to have been *then* totally unprejudiced by any knowledge of her situation and circumstances. Ineffectual, however, was all I could urge in opposition to your farther pursuit of her; she had spread her snare with success.

On our return to Fir-grove you talked of her with rapture, and delineated her, to your father, as superior to all the rest of her/ sex. I wondered at your infatuation, but was silent on the subject. Mr. Montgomery took an opportunity to draw me aside, when he asked *my* opinion of the lady: I begged leave to decline giving any; and, adopting a thought of yours, pleaded my being too strongly attached to the memory of one much-loved and much lamented object, to be a proper judge of the merits of any other female character. I then hinted to him a wish that he would see her speedily, and judge both for you and himself. In pursuance of that hint, he proposed accompanying you on your next visit to her. You know the rest, Charles, therefore I need not repeat it; but I must be permitted to add, that I was then convinced, by her behaviour, she was a perfect female Proteus.[11] – Yet Mr. Montgomery's penetration was not to be deceived; and his sentiments of her, which exactly coincided with mine, he spoke very openly in the carriage, directly after we left the house; and here I must remind you, my friend, that, upon our return from *that* visit too, we were *all* equally strangers to her circumstances: but it is the common consequence/ of an ill-placed passion to misconstrue the motives of those friends who, with no other view than the benevolent purpose of rescuing from destruction, venture to oppose it; and thus you are led to judge harshly of the conduct of one of the best and most affectionate of parents, who has ever, hitherto, studied your happiness more than his own; or, to speak more properly, makes *his* felicity center in *yours*. As one proof of it, he joins an instructive and pleasing party to travel with you; he even accompanies you himself; and limits the term of your exile to two years; in which you will have every opportunity to gain improvement: – reasonably conceiving that the knowledge you will, in that time, acquire of the world, but more particularly of your own mind, and of the requisites to constitute its happiness, will enable you to act with a proper degree of caution, in a matter of such importance; and that, on your return to your native land, you will be far better qualified to judge, with propriety, of the *excellencies* of Miss Elwood, and observe wherein *they* distinguish her from the rest of her sex. You will know, too, whether the passion she/

has inspired is a *real* affection, or an imaginary one. As to your concern for the distressing apprehensions she may endure upon *your* account, during the separation, I think I may safely venture to pronounce it quite unnecessary. She may, very possibly, force a few tears into her eyes when you bid her adieu; but before you have got to the distance of an hundred yards from her, she will laugh at your folly, in supposing her possessed of those tender sensibilities she knows herself to be utterly *incapable* of feeling.

She loves you *not*, Charles. – I startle you with such an assertion, but I repeat it, she loves you not: your last letter which I am now going to animadvert upon, convinces me of it. I there see her the artful designing character I suspected her to be. The estate you are heir to is the principal magnet which attracts her, and to secure it she is cunningly endeavouring to gain your affections, by practising on your generous, unsuspecting disposition, all the little arts of hypocrisy. She is duping you by a pretended affection, to which your *gratitude*, not your *reason*, dictates an ardent/ return; and, at the same time, blinds you to the indelicacy of her conduct. She overacts her part finely, and I am flattered with a hope that she will soon satiate you; for, in my opinion, nothing can be more disgusting than such violent fondness from a woman; it must make a man feel himself in a situation truly ridiculous. He cannot, possibly, help considering himself, on such an occasion, as inverting the whole order of nature, who never intended *men* to be stuck up as objects to be *courted*. Trust me, my friend, the woman, who *feels* a *virtuous* affection, will never make those warm professions of it to its object, till marriage sanctions them; but, on the contrary, the fear of losing his esteem will operate powerfully upon her delicacy, and actuate her endeavors to *hide* those feelings she finds it impossible entirely to suppress. This veil of modesty, thro' which the discerning eye of a lover easily penetrates, renders her infinitely more captivating than the finest complexion, or the most regular set of features; it increases his esteem, and creates, in his deportment to her, that tenderness and respect which gratifies, at once, her affection/ and her pride. But an attachment of this refined nature, Fanny Elwood is a total stranger to; her conduct is diametrically opposite to that of a virtuous young woman; she seeks not to heighten your respect to her by any attempt to secure your esteem; for, in opposition to all the laws of delicacy and decorum, regardless of the censures of the world, she permits, nay she encourages you, to remain in her company, without any witness to your conduct, from *nine* at night, till *five* in the morning; and then *laughs* away your fears for the stigma it may fix upon her character, and tells you, 'Custom authorizes it.' Did she, indeed, tell you the truth, I should say in reply, 'Custom is the law of fools;' and nothing would more strongly verify the adage than such a practice: but be assured, my dear Charles, she deceives you. – I have lived more in Yorkshire than any where else, and *you* have spent the greatest part of your days in the county, yet neither of us ever, before, heard of such a custom. Amongst all the families *I* have the honour to be acquainted with, I declare, I cannot point out *one* that would not think itself everlastingly/ disgraced by a single instance of so great an indecorum. I will allow that it may possibly be practised by the vulgar, amongst them, and the consequences are natural; but is it for Charles Montgomery, a young man, possessed of every advantage of birth, fortune, and education, to govern his conduct by those rules which are laid down by the vulgar and the vicious? surely not; exert, then, that superiority of spirit which you *ought* to possess, and free yourself, ot once, from the snares of your enchantress; who, I doubt not, entertains a design upon you, too gross to mention.

Let it never be said that the woman whom you honor with your affections, who is to bear your *name*, and be the means of transmitting it to your posterity, has *degraded* it by her want of prudence and delicacy, in having given you her company, alone, for one whole night, before you had a legal title to demand such a proof of her regard. You are, I admit, a warm advocate in her favor; but you argue very sophistically upon the subject, and your reasoning is of no weight in the scale of my opinion: – it only serves to shew me that you are/ able to defend, tolerably, the wrong side of an argument; and the pains you bestow upon it, convince me, likewise, that you are *conscious* of reasoning upon wrong principles. I have not, therefore, entered upon a full refutation of the whole, nor do I intend it; but I must go on to observe, that the honor of a woman is no longer safe in the company of her lover, than while her own actions are consistent with the strictest rules of propriety. The moment she deviates from that which forms the most solid foundation for the *purity* as well as the *permanency* of his passion, that moment both are placed in a dangerous situation, and, in general, the consequences are fatal to their future peace. Admitting, however, that this is not always absolutely the case, but that *imprudence* is the utmost extent of their guilt; yet if the imprudence is of such a magnitude, as the instance in debate between us, it is sufficient to prove, to every one, that the *mind* of the female cannot be chaste, tho' a variety of circumstances may have concurred to keep her *person* so; and this, to be plain with you, is my idea of your Fanny. You assert the innocence of her/ and your actions and intentions on this occasion. *I* am ready to credit your veracity on that point, but to the major part of the world it would signify little; they judge from appearance; – in such matters, it is the only clue they have to guide them, and, you must allow, appearance speaks loudly against you both.

Do not fail to present my respectful remembrances to Mr. Montgomery; he would oblige me much by accompanying you hither, to spend a week, at the hall, previous to your departure for the Continent. Lord Lucan and Augustus Fitzmorice, I hope, will join you in the visit; for I must positively see you *all* before you go.

A domestic duty, alone, prevents my attending you on your tour. – You know my father's will nominates me the guardian of my sister, who had not left school at the time of his decease; when she did leave it, I was solicited, by my aunt,

Lady Milbourne, to let Harriet reside with her. As I looked upon it to be both a pleasing situation and a desirable protection for a girl of her age, I readily complied/ with their united wishes, and she went from school to Lady Milbourne's house, in Hampshire, where her ladyship constantly resided, and where Harriet was perfectly happy; till a few weeks ago, when death deprived her of her friend. She then wrote to me, and expressed a wish to live at the Hall; my wishes were in unison with hers, and I determined to go, immediately, and fetch her hither: but, recollecting her sensibility, and dreading lest the depression which hung upon *my* spirits should infect *hers*, I altered my plan of proceedings, and went first to an elderly relation of my mother's, a widow lady, and requested the favor of her to indulge us with her company for a few months. She chearfully complied, and I went forwards to Hampshire; brought my sister to her house; staid there a few days; and then returned hither, accompanied by Mrs. Horton and Harriet. They have now been with me near three weeks, in which time, I have found their company an agreeable solace: they kindly unite their best efforts to dispel my sorrows; but, I fear, they will never succeed to their wish; for time, tho'/ it is said to have the power of blunting the edge of the most severe affliction, takes no effect upon mine yet: but reason and religion teach me the impropriety of indulging it. I have scarce reached my twenty-fifth year; I enjoy an ample fortune, which enables me to gratify the impulses of benevolence; and I consider that society has a claim upon my best services. Harriet, too, is arrived at that age when a brother's protection is most necessary. – She is near nineteen. These are considerations which call upon me to use every means for the preservation of my life and health, and not to suffer myself to fall a voluntary sacrifice to unavailing grief. I therefore studiously endeavor to dissipate it, by every means in my power. I devote much of my time to social converse; which, if I followed the dictates of inclination, would be given up to solitary reflections. In reality, I experience no happiness equal to that which arises from contemplating the blissful period which I trust will reunite me, everlastingly, to my beloved Matilda; whose memory will be ever dear to my heart. With her I was blessed beyond the/ common lot of mortality; for she was not only lovely in her person, but enchantingly amiable in her mind and manners. – She was the center of my earthly felicity, and each succeeding day brought with it some new addition to my joys. I *gloried* in the title of husband; but ah! how short was the time I enjoyed it, scarce conferred ere taken from me! at the end of poor six weeks, all my joy was changed into mourning: – a putrid fever robbed me, at once, of the delight of my eyes; and in exchange for the title of happy husband, gave me that of an afflicted widower. But I beg your pardon, Charles, for this repetition of circumstances with which you were before so well acquainted. I can add no more than that

    I am, sincerely,
      your friend,
        EDWARD MELWORTH./

LETTER V.

Miss Bertills, to Miss Melworth.

CHATHAM-PLACE.[12]

THE unexpected arrival of some particular friends of my father's, from Jamaica,[13] obliged me, my dear Harriet, to leave Mrs. Martinius the day after I wrote to you last; and to the necessary attention which the laws of hospitality give our visitants a right to expect, must be attributed my breach of promise, in suffering two posts to pass, without transmitting to you the continuation of our friend Louisa's history; for which, I doubt not, you are become very impatient. To enjoy the pleasure of gratifying your wishes, I have declined joining a party to a masquerade, at the Opera-house,[14] this evening. Do not, however, imagine yourself under any obligation on that account, since I can assure you, very sincerely, that I am not making any sacrifice; masquerades being by no means my favorite amusements. But to return to the subject of my last. –/

When the first effusions of joy were over, and some degree of composure restored, I had leisure to observe Mrs. Fitzallan, who appears to me to be near fifty years of age. When I add that Louisa is a striking resemblance of her, both in form and face, I need say no more to convince you that she is an elegant, lovely woman. Mr. Henry Fitzallan, so strongly resembles them both, that it is totally unnecessary for him to tell the world that he is son to the one, or brother to the other. At the request of Mrs. Martinius, they spent the rest of the day at C— house. When dinner was over, and the attendants withdrawn, Mrs. Fitzallan, taking Mrs. Martinius affectionately by the hand, said,

'It is impossible, my dear madam, for words to express the sense I entertain of your benevolence, in having, thro' so many years, extended such unremitting maternal tenderness to my beloved daughter. – My gratitude to you can only end with my existence; but as both Mr. Fitzallan and myself, must, undoubtedly have suffered much in your good opinion, from the ambiguous circumstances/ which attended her being placed with you; and also from the last nine years apparent neglect of her; – permit me to account for the whole, in a brief history of our circumstances and situation; after which, I think you will readily acquit us.

'Sir George Fitzallan, and Mr. Ethelbert, my father, had been intimate friends from their youth. They both married much about the same time, and their ladies did not long survive each other. Lady Fitzallan died in giving birth to her first child; and, in less than six months after *her* decease my mother was carried off by a consumption,[15] leaving no other child than me. As neither Sir George nor my father ever married after, Henry Fitzallan and I were, of course, heirs to very considerable property. The intimacy between our fathers, was productive of a friendly intercourse between us; which, as we grew up, ripened into a strong and mutual attachment. Sir George and my father gave it the sanction of their warmest approbation. Every preparation was made; a day was fixed for our union; and was near at/ hand, when an unexpected event threatened total destruction to our happiness. A dispute, upon a political subject, caused a quarrel between Sir George and my father; in consequence of which, the treaty of alliance was instantly broken off, and we received positive orders never to see nor to think more of each other, on pain of their perpetual displeasure. This command we found it utterly impossible to obey; nor could we avoid deeming it an act of great cruelty and injustice. A few days afterwards, I was, in the most peremptory terms, ordered to receive the addresses of a Mr. H—; a man who had nothing but the gifts of fortune to recommend him. My remonstrances against this proceeding were ineffectual, and my implicit obedience resolutely insisted upon. Determined, however, not to comply, I found means to make Mr. Fitzallan acquainted with my situation; he proposed, as the only alternative, an immediate private marriage. – I consented; and being both of age, a licence was easily obtained, and the ceremony was performed at the parish/ church of St. George's, Hanover-square.

'Our next step was, to write to our respective parents, who were equally offended, and refused to see us. We, therefore, retired to a village, about forty miles from London; where Henry possessed an estate of two hundred per annum, which had been left to him by a distant relation. This, with economy, was sufficient to support us in a very comfortable manner, tho' not equal to the manner in which we had been accustomed to live, and we were more than content; – we were happy. Our time glided away without any thing to disturb our tranquility; except, sometimes, the painful remembrance of having incurred the displeasure of our parents: but we consoled ourselves with the hope that time, and the mediation of friends would produce a reconciliation. In a year after our marriage, my son Henry was born; and we hoped he would have been the band to reunite all parties. But, alas! neither of his grandfathers would be prevailed upon to see him. This was a severe disappointment, and to that succeeded,/ almost immediately, a much weightier trouble; – a suit in chancery was instituted, to recover from Mr. Fitzallan that estate which was all we had for our support. Henry, having little knowledge of the law, became too easily a dupe to the unprincipled part of its professors; who encouraged him with hopes, which they knew had no foundation, and he defended the suit near five years; when, after an heavy expence, a verdict was obtained against him. This was a stroke, dreadful beyond imagination. We had now two children; – destitute of an habitation to shelter them or ourselves; – indebted for large sums, borrowed to defend the suit, and no means of paying them, or of gaining future support, poverty and imprisonment were the only prospects that now opened to our view. In the deepest distress, we quitted our late peaceful abode; and set out in the stage-coach for London. At the door of an inn, where we stopped to dine, stood a gentleman who immediately recognized us; – it was Mr. Delaporte. We had no other acquaintance with him, than/ having been a few times in his company, at the house of a friend, in the village we had just left. He, however, appeared delighted to see us, and insisted on our partaking of the dinner that he had ordered for himself. Then, observing that it must be both inconvenient and unpleasant to travel so far, with our two children, in such an uneasy vehicle, – he added, that, as he was going our road, and was entirely alone, we should oblige him much by occupying the vacant seats in his coach, for the rest of the journey. We wanted very little persuasion to accept an offer so agreeable as this. On the way he said to us,

'It gives me more pain than I can express, to see you, both, so much dejected; – I ask not from what cause that dejection proceeds; I already know it all, and am determined to serve you with my best abilities: but in what manner to do it requires time for consideration. You must, therefore, take up your residence, for this night, in my house. Tho' I am an old batchelor, you will find tolerable accomodation, and we/ can then confer together upon the measures to be pursued in future.' 'We were elevated with his kindness, and accepted it with gratitude. In the morning, this worthy man, whose memory will be ever dear to me, undertook, as Sir George Fitzallan and Mr. Ethelbert were both in town, to wait upon them, and represent our situation. He did so, and was much chagrined at proving an unsuccessful advocate. Convinced, however, of the absurdity of placing any farther dependence upon either of them, he advised my Henry to accept of an appointment, then in *his* power to obtain, in the service of the East India company,[16] and to take his son and me over with him. We consented to it at once, and he generously supplied us with cash to provide whatever we stood in need of. As he judged it both imprudent and dangerous, on account of the debts Mr. Fitzallen owed, for us to continue publicly in London, he proposed our placing Louisa here for education, and then retiring, immediately, to the Isle of Wight, and there wait for the ship, in which we were to be conveyed/ from England. The necessity for Louisa's change of name, arose from a rich maiden aunt of mine, who, by being educated in a convent, had early imbibed the principles of the Romish religion, and was, then, one of its most zealous adherents, having been frequently heard to declare an intention of using every strategem she could devise, to get one or both of the children into her power, that she might bring them up in the religion she professed. Mr. Delaporte, on that account, recommended Louisa's being called by *his* name, and the most profound secrecy observed with respect to her connections. We did as he directed in every respect; and, with sorrowful hearts, committed her to the care of Mrs. Martinius. The letters of recomendation with which we were furnished by Mr. Delaporte, procured us a large circle of acquaintance amongst families of the first distinction, then resident at Bengal; – our circumstances became easy, and we soon remitted to our creditors in England, both principal and interest./

'During the first five years of our stay there, Mr. Delaporte kept our minds easy, by sending frequent intelligence of the health and improvements of our daughter. He had insisted on adopting her, and also supporting all her expences; so that we had no reason to doubt of the regular payments being made for her board, &c. In the sixth year we received, to our inexpressible concern, a letter from an attorney, informing us of the decease of our valuable friend; of whose will he enclosed a copy. – In it he had bequeathed ten thousand pounds to Louisa Fitzallan, daughter of Henry Fitzallan, of Bengal; and one thousand pounds to Mrs. Martinius; adding, that the sealed letter, addressed to that lady, which would be found in his cabinet, would sufficiently inform her to what purpose the said sum of one thousand pounds was to be applied. Having no doubt of that letter and the legacy being both received, we were not uneasy about Louisa; tho' we ardently longed to hear of her – But foreseeing great danger in letting her real name be known to any/ one, we determined to refrain from making any enquiry, till three years ago, when a gentleman, whom we could confide in, was coming over to England. Him we trusted with the knowledge of every circumstance, and he promised to see our child, and send us the earliest intelligence he possibly could. 'Unhappily, however, we were disappointed by his death; which happened a few days previous to the ship he was on board of reaching England. Our anxiety, of course, increased; yet still we flattered ourselves, that all was right; till Miss Curtis arrived at Bengal: when, on learning that she had left C— house but a very short time before her embarkation, I eagerly enquired of her after Louisa Delaporte, and was made extremely unhappy by being informed of the true state of things. How to account for your never hearing of Mr. Delaporte's death, madam, nor of the legacy he bequeathed to you, I confess myself totally at a loss; but I will give you a direction to the executor, and I think the demand for it should be made without delay.'/

Mrs. Martinius acquiesced in this opinion, and Mrs. Fitzallan proceeded as follows.

'Miss Curtis, madam, did not omit to do justice to your excellent disposition, by expatiating largely on the mingled tenderness and respect, with which you had constantly behaved to my child, notwithstanding her dependent situation. Tho' this account was well calculated to ease our minds, yet we could not be happy night nor day; we had been putting every thing in a train for quitting India long before, but Mr. Fitzallan finding it impossible to complete the whole of his business in less than four months, so earnestly persuaded me to depart in the first ship bound for England, that I consented, and brought my son as my protector. After an agreeable voyage, we landed safe at Falmouth; from whence we set off post for London; which place we reached yesterday evening. We drove immediately to Cavendish-square, to the house of some of our Asiatic friends, lately settled there. They expressed much pleasure at seeing us, and observing that I did not appear/ too much fatigued for company, desired to introduce me to the drawing-room, which I found pretty well filled. In a few minutes, a very communicative lady, attracted by my name, came and seated herself on the sopha by me, purposely to make inquiries into my pedigree. I had no motive to dictate concealment, therefore satisfied her inquiries very readily, and soon found that she knew my whole history, together with all my family, and the family of Sir George Fitzallan. From her I learned that the latter was then at Bath, with a female companion, who had lived with him several years, and kept him in perfect submission to her will. I also learned that my Roman catholic aunt had been dead near three years, and had left her whole fortune to her confessor, and two favorite servants. She farther added, that the temper of Mr. Ethelbert was much softened towards me, and from what she herself had heard him say, she had no doubt but he would now *rejoice* to be reconciled. In consequence of this information, I directly left the room, wrote/ a short letter to my father, and dispatched a messenger express with it, to his seat in Oxfordshire; and, if his answer to it does not prohibit me, I shall introduce his two grandchildren to him to-morrow; after which, my dear children, we must turn our attention to providing an habitation fit for the reception of your father, who, I suppose, we shall soon begin to be in anxious expectation of.'

Mrs. Fitzallan now concluded with a warm expression of thanks to Mrs. Martinius, and to all who had been friendly to Louisa; adding, that it would give her a very sensible pleasure to have it in her power to testify her esteem for them.

The young man shewed his affection for his sister, not merely by little tender fraternal endearments, but also by expressions of regard for all who had honoured her with their friendship. You, my Harriet, were mentioned by Louisa in terms that did you honor; a vote of thanks for your kindness passed the house *nem con*;[17] and I was chosen secretary, to convey them to you. It was really pleasing to see the brother and sister together. – The former/ is a great observer; nothing is lost upon him; things apparently trivial in themselves, he makes matters of importance, if in any degree connected with her happiness. He warmly expressed his admiration of her person and manners; commended her taste in the little simple ornaments of her dress; and, then, complimented Mrs. Martinius, very elegantly, on the noble confidence, which the superior style of his sister's habiliments, demonstrated her having placed in his parents. The good lady was evidently pleased with his remark, but was prevented replying to it by Mrs. Fitzallan saying, with a smile,

'Henry, you anticipate me in speech tho' not in thought; for I had noticed the circumstance, and was much struck with it.' –

Then addressing Mrs. Martinius, added, 'The obligations, madam, you have conferred upon me, are such as renders it impossible for me to mention the word settlement; since it will never be in my power to make you a compensation that will set us upon *equal* terms. – I shall ever consider myself/ your debtor; but, as a small testimony of my esteem, you must do me the honor to accept this' – presenting her with an elegant pocket-book, in which were inclosed bank-notes to a considerable amount. The carriage being now ready, they rose to depart; and, after an affectionate farewell, left us.

Let me now tell you, my dear, that in compliance with the wishes of Mrs. Fitzallan, Mrs. Martinius came with me to town, to demand her legacy; when she learned, that Mr. Green, the nephew whom Mr. Delaporte had made his heir and the executor to his will, being in a bad state of health, had been ordered by his physician to try the air of Lisbon, whither he went within six weeks after the decease of his uncle; but a four month's residence there producing no change for the better, he returned home and died, in a few days, intesate; in consequence of which, his brother, Mr. Thomas Green, a dissipated, thoughtless young man, came immediately into the possession of all his fortune. The attorney employed by the first Mr. Green, died shortly after dispatching his letter to Mr. Fitzallan; and the sickness of/ his client preventing his employing any other, all business respecting Mr. Delaporte's will was suspended; and when Mr. Thomas Green came into possession he was totally ignorant what legacies were paid and what were not, and too thoughtless to make the inquiry: but he has, nevertheless, both good-nature and honesty; for, on the application of Mrs. Martinius, he behaved very politely; and, after being satisfied in a few particulars, readily admitted her claim, and paid both principal and interest. On her mentioning the letter, he laughingly said, that perhaps he might find some valuable treasure in that cabinet, when he looked into it, for he knew not what it contained, as his curiosity had never yet been excited to open it. He however did it then, – found the letter, and delivered it to her. It contained an assurance that Miss Delaporte would sooner or later be claimed by her parents, but that as it possibly might be a few years first, he had bequeathed one thousand pounds, for the purpose of defraying the dear child's expences: if she was claimed before that sum was expended, as he hoped and expected/ she would, then it was his desire that Mrs. Martinius would accept of the residue, be it what it might, as a token of his esteem for her character and conduct. Adieu.

    I am,

        yours, affectionately,

        RHODA BERTILLS.

LETTER VI.

Charles Montgomery, Esq. to Sir Edward Melworth.

FIR-GROVE.

YOUR letter has just come to my hand, and forgive me if I say it is the *least* welcome of any I ever yet received from you. Were I not disarmed of all resentment by the deep distress with which your heart is evidently surcharged, and which gives you an irresistible claim to the most sympathetic tenderness, I fear I should discover more real displeasure than you could ever draw from me on any occasion wherein my lovely Fanny is not concerned;/ in every *other* point I will, most readily, allow the superiority of your judgment; – but in *this* I must claim the privilege of *free agency*, and beg leave to judge for myself. Believe me, my dear Edward, it is only the cruel melancholy by which your spirits are depressed that shuts out my Fanny's virtues from your view, and gives to your portrait of her character those dark deforming shades that are not to be found in the original. Twelve months back your generous nature would have spurned at the idea of injuring a female character by such illiberal and unjust censures; but it frequently happens that affliction has the power of changing the most amiable disposition; and I am now convinced it has done so by yours, and made you as sour and morose as old age and its train of infirmities could have done. You are really, my friend, most cuttingly severe upon an innocent lovely girl, whose only fault is her excess of tenderness towards me. I hope, however, to repair the injury your injustice does her, by making it the principal study of my life to promote her happiness. Yet, notwithstanding all you have/ said, I must tell you, I had far rather endure the severity with which you treat the subject, than renounce your friendly correspondence, or let it dwindle into mere formality, by withholding my accustomed communications; therefore, like it or dislike it, I shall still continue to persecute you with a recital of every important occurrence, and in pursuance of this resolution am now going to relate the conversation that passed between my father and me, after concluding my last.

'My dear Charles,' – said he, as I advanced towards him, – 'I am really grieved at observing that your compliance with my wishes in accompanying me abroad, tho' in a manner highly advantageous to yourself, is not a voluntary one. – Till now, you have never, in a single instance, given me occasion to put any disagreeable restraint upon your inclinations; I am, therefore, particularly hurt at the necessity for doing it now. I know my conduct wears, to you, at present, the appearance of great unkindness; yet, do me the justice to believe, it is only my ardent desire for your future happiness/ that compels me to adopt it. – But when I see you in danger of becoming a slave to your passions,[18] and burying all the nobler faculties of your mind in a mistaken attachment to a young woman, *every* way unworthy of being your wife; and –'

'Oh, my dear sir,' interrupted I, 'wound not my feelings, I beseech you, by speaking in those strong terms; nor suffer your partiality to your son to occasion your depreciating the merits of Miss Elwood, by contrasting them with those you imagine him possessed of. Permit me to say, you are mistaken in the idea you have formed of her. – *I* know of but *one* point in which she can possibly be deemed unworthy of being allied to me. – I mean her deficiency in riches: – and you, I am sure, sir, entertain more elevated sentiments than to impute to her as a *crime*, what, to say the worst of it, can only be termed her *misfortune*; and that is amply compensated by her intrinsic excellence, which is sufficiently conspicuous to add dignity to a throne.'/

'You are, really, quite *eloquent* upon the subject, Charles,' – returned my father, with a smile, – 'and I perceive love has drawn his bandage so close over your eyes that you will not easily be convinced your judgment errs: – but I yet trust time and experience will do that for you which my best counsels find ineffectual.'

'I will not flatter you with a hope that your wish of *detaching* my affections,' resumed I, 'may be effected by *time* or *experience*; for, on the contrary, my dear sir, I rather expect the operations of both will tend to *strengthen* the attachment on both sides: – but I look forward with pleasing expectation of their effect upon you, as I do not doubt but a short period will convince you of your mistake, by discovering my Fanny's amiable properties to your view.'

'Well, Charles,' said he, 'I will not contend that matter any longer; but allow me to say, that even admitting I may be mistaken in my opinion of Fanny Elwood, and that she is *good* tho' not *great*; yet, my son, I am confident she is not calculated to/ make you happy. – Her family connections would wound your pride; you have not been accustomed to such associates; and would find it difficult to level your manners and conversation to theirs, without which *they* would feel uncomfortably aukward in your presence, and amongst themselves would make *you* the constant subject of their ridicule; for –'

'I grant you *that*, my dear sir,' interrupted I, 'and am ready to confess, candidly, that I could never think of *Fanny's* connections as *mine*; but I am very certain her affection for me will render it an easy matter to her to detach herself entirely from them, in a short time.'

'And what happiness,' – resumed my father, gravely, – 'can you promise yourself with a woman whom you believe capable of such a renunciation? – Trust me, Charles, she who feels so little *natural* affection as voluntarily to resign the social, endearing intercourse of those to whom the tie of nature and consanguinity ought to bind her; or, to gratify the pride or caprice of a husband,/ will be deficient in the performance of any of the little offices of tender kindness

towards them, will not be very exact in the observance of her conjugal duties. -
No, my son, even *I* will not think so hardly of Fanny Elwood, as to suppose she
would easily be brought to detach herself from her relations, who cannot appear
to her in the light they do to you or me. - Her parents, for instance, must have
testified, in their conduct to her, that tender partiality which is usually felt for an
only child; and, if she is not destitute of all the virtues of humanity, their unre-
mitted indulgence must, undoubtedly, have engaged her warmest gratitude and
tenderest filial affection; of course, it must be impossible *she* should see a single
defect in *either* of them, tho' neither you nor I can avoid perceiving in *both* many
so glaring as totally to unfit them for polite circles. - Nor is it to be wondered
at, if we consider their situation a few years back, when Mr. Elwood lived in an
house not many degrees superior to a cottage; his occupation that of a working
manufacturer. –/ By the exertions of his own and his wife's industry he, at length,
realized a sum sufficient to purchase a tolerable quantity of wool; part of which
he used in his business, and the rest he sold amongst those who could only buy
a small quantity at a time: this, by degrees, increased his property, and the death
of a relation in London, who bequeathed him five hundred, and his daughter a
thousand pounds, enabled him to remove, with his family, to Leeds – commence
the business of a wool-stapler –[19] and rise into a style of more gentility. – Yet,
his want of education will for ever preclude his claim to the title of *gentleman.*'

'Permit me, sir,' - said I, with surprise, - 'to ask, where or how you gained all
this information concerning them?'

'That is a question,' replied he, 'which, at present, I must decline answering;
but, be assured, I had it from undoubted authority.'

'I do not dispute that, sir,' said I, 'nor yet the authenticity of what you have
heard; on the contrary, I acknowledge my belief in/ the truth of it: for, tho' I
never before heard the family history so fully as you have now related it, yet
many things which have at different times dropped from the lips of Mr. Elwood
in conversation, convince me you have not been deceived. – But do these circumstances render him the less *estimable*? Surely, the man who raises himself by
honest industry has a claim to general respect, and deserves to be esteemed as a
valuable member of the community.'

'I admit it, Charles,' replied my father, and no one entertains a higher respect
for the character of honest industry than myself: but give me leave to observe,
at the same time, that tho' we respect the man for his useful qualities, and the
propriety with which he conducts himself, in that sphere wherein it has pleased
providence to place him, yet those who possess the superior advantages of birth,
fortune, and education united, cannot avoid considering the want of those
advantages, *particularly* the latter, as an insurmountable barrier in the way of matrimonial alliances, or social intercourse; and the Almighty/ has wisely ordained
it that all ranks of people find their felicity made more perfect by forming con-

nections, of every kind, only amongst their *equals*; every person being best fitted for that style of life to which they were born, and to which they have constantly been accustomed. Could we take Mr. Elwood from his present situation – give him a large estate, and a title, – to support the dignity of which, both he and his wife must withdraw themselves intirely from all their present connections, and associate with none but persons of polished education and elegant manners, – should we not, think you, make them most completely miserable?'

'I have not the least doubt of it, sir,' replied I, 'if the change was productive of happiness to them it would be, I believe, as singular a circumstance as any in the annals of time: – but then, it must be allowed, their daughter stands not in the same predicament; she is calculated to fill an exalted station; having had greater advantages of education, from which she has acquired a taste far, *very* far superior to theirs.'/

'You and I disagree in that point too,' said my father, 'for I can see no superiority whatever in her. The whole difference between her parents and herself consists in this, – the former only desire to appear what they *are*, the latter wishes to appear what she is *not*, nor has any right to aspire to. – It is true, her person is finely formed, and her face sufficiently pretty to engage, at present, your attention; – but you should remember, that beauty is a trifling charm; and, when unaccompanied by any one in the mind, will, of course, soon lose its influence over the senses. Fanny Elwood's education has been very confined: a few superficial accomplishments, and those *very* superficially attained, comprize the whole of it. – Her *mind* has lain fallow from her birth; and the soil is now over-run with weeds.' Observing me about to reply, he added, 'I see, Charles, you think me too severe; but the occasion calls for it, and I must either wound your feelings or my own conscience: – the latter will not suffer me to see you precipitating yourself into a gulph of inexpressible/ misery, without endeavouring to make you sensible of your danger.'

'Believe me, sir,' cried I, 'notwithstanding my sensibility is acutely pained by your too severe reflections upon *her* who has engaged my tenderest regards, yet my heart acknowledges, with gratitude, the kindness of the motive, and has a due respect for your paternal character: - but deeply do I lament that your mistaken opinion of Miss Elwood has impressed your mind, thus strongly, with ideas at once so unjust and so injurious of the lovely girl.'

'I will not,' resumed he, 'dispute about the *justice* or *injustice* of my sentiments concerning Fanny; I shall only say, at present, she does not appear to me calculated to add to your happiness. - *You* are formed for domestic enjoyments: - *she* is not; because unqualified for them: that disqualification would render it impossible for her to heighten yours. But to drop the subject, let me only add, that I will compound the matter with you: – thus; you shall have my consent to visit her as often as you/ think proper before your departure, if you will, in return, give me your solemn promise to keep perfectly clear of entering into any engagement whatsoever with her, either written or verbal. It is my earnest desire, Charles, to have you free from every entanglement when you quit this kingdom; that, at your return, it may be in your power to follow the dictates of your heart; which will then, assisted by your ripened judgment, make such a choice as, I have no doubt, will meet my concurrence; – for, should your inclinations again return to their first object, it must be on such a thorough conviction of her real merit as your reason must approve; and, in that case, I would not oppose your wishes.'

The latter part of my father's discourse amply compensating for all the foregoing disagreeables, I thanked him very sincerely, and unhesitatingly made the requested promise, which I mean most religiously to keep. - Indeed I have no reason to apprehend being under any *temptation* to break it; for my lovely angel has, I am certain, too exalted an opinion/ of my veracity to entertain one moment's doubt of the sincerity or constancy of *my* attachment; and in *hers* I can place the most unbounded confidence. - There can be no stability in any of the sex, if my Fanny possesess it not: what need is there then of formal engagements between us? This arrangement with my father, has removed a heavy load from my spirits: – I can look forwards, now, with pleasure. - Two years will soon pass away; and, at the expiration of that time, I shall promise myself the felicity of receiving the hand of my charmer, without trespassing upon the laws of filial obedience.

I have not been over to Leeds since I wrote to you last, but intend going as soon as I have concluded this. I go thoroughly determined not to act so unguardedly as before; my watch shall be my monitor; and I will leave the house at a proper hour in the evening: for, on a re-perusal of your letter, I am not half satisfied with my conduct, in deviating so far from the rules of propriety, and the same degree of inadvertence shall not cause me to repeat the error. My sweet girl is yet/ ignorant of my intended tour, nor do I design mentioning it till we are about to depart; and, as a circumstance has arisen that will retard our departure for six weeks longer, it will save us both much pain during that time, and we may enjoy many pleasing interviews unimbittered, on her side, by the idea of parting.

Lord Lucan, my father, and Augustus, all concur with me in wishing to see you here. - Come, then, my dear Edward, as soon as possible; you shall visit Fanny with me, you shall scrutinize her *words, looks,* and *actions* over again, and I am confident they will *compel* you to retract all you have either thought or said to her disadvantage. I shall be impatient till I see you.

Yours, sincerely,

CHARLES MONTGOMERY,/

LETTER VII.

Miss Melworth, to Miss Bertills.

MELWORTH-HALL.

THINK me not unkind, my dear Rhoda, in suffering so much time to elapse without acknowledging the delight I felt, on perusing your two last welcome letters. My delay has been occasioned by that attention which the ill health and depressed spirits of my beloved brother seem to demand. – Would I could say that my attention proves successful! on the contrary, I fear his disorder increases daily, and I am, in consequence, more unhappy about him than I can possibly express. His physician says medicine is useless, and I am convinced he is in the right; – Sir Edward's disease being seated in the mind. I am, therefore, determined on persuading him to try the effect of some of the watering places. It is very possible, that change of air, and a variety of company and amusements, may prove beneficial./ But you must not apprehend, from what I have said, that my concern for my brother has annihilated in my bosom all the feelings of friendship. – Be assured, my dear, I most sincerely rejoice in the joy of our beloved Louisa, who is so truly dear to me that I cannot help considering the name of Delaporte as a part of herself, and I more than half regret the loss of that, tho' attended with circumstances so much to her advantage. I cannot express how much I long to see both her and you; it appears to me an age since we met; but you have both rendered the separation much more tolerable to me, by the punctuality of your correspondence, than it would otherwise have been; and, I trust, you will still continue to grant me the indulgence of sharing both your joys and sorrows, tho' the anxious state of my mind, while my brother remains thus indisposed, may not always admit of my making as punctual returns.

I have taken the liberty to shew your letters to Sir Edward; he admires them; and sensibly partook with me of the pleasure which the intelligence in your last afforded: on that/ account my thanks are doubly due to you. A carriage is driving up the avenue, and I must break off to receive visitors.

I embrace the earliest opportunity in my power to tell my dear Rhoda, that my visitors are no other than Mrs. Fitzallan, her son, daughter, and Mr. Ethelbert. – They came into Yorkshire to view an estate situated only eight miles distant from Melworth-hall. Mrs. Fitzallan is charmed with the situation, and all about it. – She is now in treaty for it; and, I have no doubt, will become the purchaser. This circumstance affords a pleasing prospect to Louisa and me; as we shall, then, be near neighbours. At the united request of my brother and me, Mrs. Fitzallan and her family have consented to stay a few weeks with us; but Mr. Ethelbert's presence being necessary in Oxfordshire, he departs to-morrow, which I am not sorry for, as I am not at all pleased with him, notwithstanding he appears now extravagantly fond of his long-lost children. I have the pleasure to add, that my brother's/ spirits seem rather revived since their arrival. - He tells me he sees in Miss Fitzallan, a strong resemblance of the late Lady Melworth; on which account, he takes a particular pleasure in conversing with her. I have time for no more than to add our united good wishes, and that I am

  your affectionate friend,
   HARRIET MELWORTH.

LETTER VIII.

Sir Edward Melworth, to Frederick Montgomery, Esq.
           MELWORTH-HALL.

My dear sir,

 THE unhappy and ill-judged attachment of my friend Charles, towards an unworthy woman, has been the subject of much altercation between him and me. – Could I have succeeded in my wish of disengaging him from her, it would have rejoiced me: – but, with infinite concern, I perceive/ that every degree of opposition seems rather to augment than lessen his passion for her; and, upon mature deliberation, I had determined to desist from trying my influence over him any farther; lest I should involuntarily *accelerate* the ruin I wish to avert, by stirring up in him an equal spirit of opposition, which might lead him to commit an action he would for ever have cause to lament, as it would involve him in irremediable destruction. - But I cannot see a friend, whose many valuable qualities have greatly endeared him to me, in danger of becoming a dupe to the artful machinations of a vile designing creature, without making another effort for his preservation. As the affair requires to be managed nicely, I take the liberty, my dear sir, of addressing *you* upon it rather than Charles.

 The inclosed is, as you will see, adressed to my sister, and comes from a young lady, of whose veracity I have the highest opinion, tho' I have not the honor of being personally known to her. Miss Bertills is, it seems, the only child of an eminent and wealthy merchant in/ the city of London. Her mother dying while she was very young, she was put to school at C—, where Harriet first saw her. - They were nearly of an age; their dispositions accorded; and they became soon very intimate: – that intimacy has now ripened into a solid, sincere friendship. They have not met since they left school, but have kept up a constant correspondence with each other. Harriet, – proud of every qualification her friend possesses, as it reflects a lustre on her own judgment, in selecting one so estimable, – has shewn me most of the letters she has received from Miss Birtills; and this, which came yesterday, has awakened all my fears for my friend; as it sufficiently proves Fanny Elwood a very bad character, in every respect, and a very dangerous one for an open, artless young man to be in company with, even for a single hour. – I there-fore requested my sister to give me leave to convey the letter to you; which she readily complied with. You will know best, sir, in what manner to communicate to Charles the particulars it contains. Heaven grant it may have the wished effect of shewing the infamous/ girl in her true colors before it is too late! If this does not open his eyes, I shall dread the consequence of her artifice: for, as it is not likely that the relation of Miss Bertills' should be heir to an estate equal in value to yours, we have nothing to hope for from his rivalship; Charles will, on *that* account, doubtless, have the preference over all who may address the wretched girl. - But I will detain you from her letter no longer than to add, that I am,

dear sir,

with the utmost respect and esteem,

your most humble,

and most obedient servant,

EDWARD MELWORTH./

LETTER IX.

Miss Bertills, to Miss Melworth.
(Inclosed in the preceding.)

CHATHAM-PLACE.

REAL friendship not only demands the most perfect confidence, but licences an unrestrained communication. My highest pleasures are but half enjoyed till I have made you, my dear Harriet, an equal sharer in them; and I expect you will participate equally in all my *griefs*. At present I have a subject of *that sort*, to which I claim your attention. - But I must proceed with some degree of method, to make you properly acquainted with it.

You cannot I think have forgotten Mrs. Herbert, who used to visit me frequently at school; since my return home she has been my most intimate acquaintance. My father, happy in the idea of my deriving essential advantage from the society of this excellent woman, kindly permits me to devote a large part of/ my time to the enjoyment of her company. Sometimes at our house, but more frequently at hers; as her young family claims much of her attention; and, as she is calculated for domestic pleasures, that attention which she pays to them constitutes, in a great measure, her felicity. In short, Mrs. Herbert, considered in every point of view, appears completely amiable. She is at once an engaging companion, a sincere friend, an affectionate wife, and a tender parent. Yet her happiness is not so perfect as *might* be expected, even in this state of mortality, for a character so bright as hers: but she bears her lot without repining at it. Her husband, the Major, is pleasing in his person; gay and agreeable in his manners. Notwithstanding her beauty and accomplishments have *fixed* his heart, they have not been powerful enough to engage his fidelity to her: of this she has been convinced more than once since her marriage; but her prudent conduct, upon any discovery of that sort, has ever prevented any open ruptures between them; and, I hope, her perseverence will eventually be a means of reclaiming him entirely. An affair/ of this nature occurred two days ago, when I had an opportunity of seeing her exert the best qualities of the human heart.

It happened that Mrs. Herbert was engaged to dine with us; and, the Major being gone into the country, as I knew she would prefer walking, I went to accompany her hither: - we were putting on our clogs in the hall, when a clean, healthy-looking, country woman, with a child in her arms, came to the door and asked to speak with the Major. Mrs. Herbert immediately desired to know her business with him: – the woman hesitated at first, but at length said,

'It does n't *sinnify*, madam, my business be n't much, I can come *agin* to-morrow, if so be as how the Major will be at home then; for its he as I wants, and as you are not he it does n't matter troubling o' you at all.'

'Well, but good woman,' – returned Mrs. Herbert, with a smile, – 'tho' I am not the *Major*, yet as I am his *wife*, if you think proper to acquaint me with the business you are come about, I may, very possibly, be/ able to transact it full as well, and save you the trouble of coming hither again.'

'What, madam?' – cried the woman, evidently alarmed, – 'what did you say? *you* Major Herbert's *wife*, madam?'

'Yes, indeed I am,' returned my friend, 'and have been so for several years.'

'G-d deliver me!' exclaimed she, 'then I suppose as how *I've* done a fine *job o' journey work* now.'

'No, no,' said Mrs. Herbert, 'good woman, you have done no harm in the world, – only tell me what you want, and we will soon settle the business.'

'Lord bless me, madam!' exclaimed she, 'I can't go for to do no such a thing, – being as how you are the most onproperest parson in the *wuld* for to tell my business to.'

Mrs. Herbert then turning to me, said, 'Come, my dear Miss Bertills, we have time enough upon our hands let us return again to my dressing room, and this person shall go with us; – I am certain I am no stranger to the principal part of her errand; – as she does not like to tell it to *me*, I must open/ the matter to *her*, and that will prevent her having any farther trouble about it.'

We then went up stairs, and the poor woman followed looking very foolish, – while I wondered in what manner the affair would terminate, and felt, at the same time, for my amiable friend, who I saw was much agitated, tho' she endeavoured to conceal it; at length, being all seated, she said,

'Now, nurse, – for such I suppose you to be, to the lovely boy in your arms, – let me tell you, in the first place, that the moment I looked in the face of that child I knew who was his father; for it is the Major's own face in miniature; therefore –'

'I am sure, madam,' interrupted nurse, 'you 're as good as arrow *vitch* among 'em, to know that there only by *looking* at master: – but, L - d! I'm sure as how I'm very sorry I comed here, by reason as this here affair 'll go nigh for to shock you sadly: and my master, the Major, he 'll be ready for to hang me for coming here for to make a quarrel 'tween you.'

'You may make yourself easy upon that/ head, nurse,' resumed Mrs. Herbert, 'I cannot be *more* shocked than I was at first sight of the child, nor shall I mention one word of the matter to the Major; consequently, there will be no danger of any thing you have to say causing a quarrel between him and me.'

'Lord, madam!' – cried nurse, with a face full of surprise, - 'I declares as how you' re a *was deal* more *good natureder* nor me; for, I 'm sartin, I should lug our John's ears off, if so be as how I found *him* out, in such an a thing; – but then, to be sure, there 's a *was* difference, that there is, 'twixt gentlefolks and us poor working-folks. God help us! we 've enough to do for to provide for them as God sends honestly to us; – but I axes pardon, madam,' continued she, 'I may as well tell you what I'm comed about, at once, and not keep *hendering* your walk. - All I wants with the Major is, to ax him for to be so good as to pay me for nursing little master. I loves the child, for sartin, as dearly as I loves my own eyes; for you knows, madam, its none o' his fault,/ his coming into the *wuld* the wrong way? so *that there*'s nothing: – I loves him as well as *ef* it had n't happened; but, then, I can't afford to *tend* him and purvide him with wittels and cloaths, and all out o' my own pockat, – being as how our John and me be but poor working-folks, as I said afore, – and you knows, madam, a hearty child, like master, eats a deal; and tho' they does n't *acquire* many cloaths at a time, where one washes twice a week or oftener, as a body may say, *yit* they soon outgrows 'em; and I 'a' ben fain to cut up what I could o' my own, for to keep him *dessunt*, for I ha' n't had not a penny o' money, on master's account, for above four months past.'

'Heavens!' – exclaimed Mrs. Herbert, with the deepest concern imprinted on her countenance, – 'this intelligence both shocks and astonishes me; for I have ever thought the Major a *generous* man, as well as one of the most *humane* creatures breathing; but what you have told me impeaches his character in *both* respects, and I really feel less hurt by his infidelity to me, than by his inhuman/ neglect of his own offspring: but pray, nurse,' added she, 'why did you not apply to him before?'

'Bless your heart, madam!' answered she, 'I war n't never to *ply* to *him*, not at all; being as how *he set his hand to a paper* to pay Miss Elwood, master's *mammar*, fifty pounds a year, o' purpose for *her* to purvide for master; so I was told as how I was always for to ax *her* for my money and every thing else as master wanted; and I have axed her often and often enough; but she takes the fifty pounds a year and wo' n't do nothing for him, indeed she never comes a near him now. She lodged at my house o' purpose for to lay in; and I nursed her; and, as soon as she was well, she left master with me, and *nather* he nor me ever seed her *sence* to this blessed day; its as true as you're alive, madam: to be sure she used to send me my money pretty *reglarly*, for some time, and so when she left it off, I made bold for to send her some letters, and then Miss *Marthas* comes to me in a *poshay*,[20] and tells me to come to the Major and/ ax *him*, and say as how Miss Elwood bid me for to tell him she'd spent all the last quarter's money upon herself, and cou'd n't pay me nothing. - So you sees, madam, ater all its no faut o' the Major's; he 's done the handsome thing by master, if so be as master had his right.'

'Very true, nurse,' returned Mrs. Herbert, 'and I am indeed glad to find *he* is not accountable for the inhuman neglect with which the poor little creature has been treated; – the mother must surely be a monster! However, for the future, I will provide for the child myself, and you shall be regularly paid.' She then paid her what was due to her, added a present, and, after taking her address, was going to dismiss her, when I prevented her by asking the nurse if she was at liberty to tell me *what* Miss Elwood it was she had been speaking of, and where she lived?

'It can't do no harm as I knows on, Miss, to tell you,' replied she, 'she is Miss Fanny Elwood, and she lives at Leeds, with her father, – he's a *wool-stapler* there.'

'Oh! then,' cried I, 'my fears are/ confirmed!' – and I sunk into a chair, almost ready to faint; nurse looked greatly surprised, as did Mrs. Herbert, and the former said to me,

'Why, surely, Miss, she 's not one o' *your* acquaintances, being as how she's a very unproper sort of a body for such young ladies as you to keep company with, for she'll larn you no good, as a body may say. Miss Marthas was a very pretty modest young lady, and used for to cry many a blessed hour by herself, 'cause she did not like Miss Elwood's goings on; but she was very *young*, and I pitied her very much; for I used to be sadly afeared Miss Elwood would soon make her *no better than she should be*: but I find as how I need n't ha' been afeared about it, for Miss Marthas told me as how she'd invited her for to go to Leeds to see her, but she was *atermined* she'd never go a neer her no more; and I'd advise *you*, Miss, for to cast her off too, if you be acquainted with her.'

'No! no! Nurse,' cried I, 'Fanny Elwood/ is no acquaintance of mine, I never even saw her in my life; but –'

'Then my love,' interrupted Mrs. Herbert, 'there must, I am sure, be some very extraordinary cause for your being so much interested about her; it is plain you know something concerning her; for I never in my life saw you so agitated.'

'Ah! my dear madam,' said I, 'there is indeed an extraordinary cause for the agitation you observe. Yes; I do know Fanny Elwood, but it is by report only, and the account we have now heard of her conduct alarms me exceedingly; as I fear it will be impossible to avert the impending destruction which she is preparing for a relation of mine, whom I highly esteem: but,' continued I, 'you shall hear the whole affair at another opportunity; at present, we have not time to stop longer, as the dinner will be waiting for us.'

Mrs. Herbert then dismissed the nurse, and we proceeded to Chatham-place; where finding my father alone, we related to him the occurrence of the morning; he expressed great admiration at the conduct of our amiable/ friend: but, like me, felt greatly chagrined at the idea of such an abandoned woman as Miss Elwood, becoming the wife of one whom he loves as a son. Oh, my dear Harriet, you know not what unspeakable distress this confirmation of her guilt has caused me! but you will, in some degree, judge of it, when I tell you, that a young man, a relation of mine, who is an only son, and heir to a very considerable fortune, happened, some months ago, to be accidentally in her company; when she played off her batteries so successfully, as to engage, at once, his warmest affections. – He visited her, and became more enamoured: – he then informed his father, – one of the best of men, and most indulgent of parents. – He raised no objections on account of the inequality of their situations and fortunes; but proposed to accompany his son on his next visit to her. – He did so, and dis-liked her *mind* and *manners*; upon which he grounded very strong objections; and has, since, used every argument reason could suggest, to dissuade his son from forming a connection so very unlikely to promote his happiness; but the infatuated/ young man, imagining his father's prejudices against her unjust, still perseveres in his addresses to her, and I am very apprehensive she will draw him into a marriage; as he seems determined to shut his eyes and ears to every thing that opposes his wishes. Mrs. Herbert joined me in soliciting my father to write and inform him of these instances of her depravity, we had just learned: he promised to do it, tho' without hope, he said, of working any other effect upon him than that of exciting his anger, as he was sure he would not credit the story. Alas! Harriet, if he does not, what inevitable misery will he, in all probability, be involved in, for the rest of his days! You will, perhaps, wonder that I should be so deeply concerned for the welfare of a person who is only distantly related to me; and, really, when I reflect, I am ready to wonder at it myself; for it has taken such hold upon me, that my spirits are exceedingly depressed, and I neither eat nor sleep as heretofore. I can only account for it *thus*: his father and mine have ever been upon the affectionate terms of brothers; and, – notwithstanding I have other/ relations, on my mother's side, much nearer to me, – yet, that cordial friendship which subsists here and binds the tie is *wanting* there, and prevents my being so closely united to *them*. My heart, formed by nature to enjoy all the tenderness that flows from fraternal connections, has ever regarded this relation as a *brother*. Of late years we have been but little together, but that little, with the reports I have heard of his merit, has tended to gratify my *pride* in considering him in that light. The last time I saw him is near two years back; he then spent a few weeks at our house, and I discovered in him a mind made up of every thing that is good and amiable. Oh, Harriet! you know what a *sister's* feelings are; you have a brother whom you tenderly esteem: figure, then, to yourself, what would be your unhappiness should that brother be in danger of sacrificing all his future comforts to so unworthy and disgraceful a connection, and you will know how to pity and sympathize with your distressed friend,

　　　RHODA BERTILLS.

LETTER X.

Frederick Montgomery, Esq. to Sir Edward Melworth.

FIR-GROVE.

YOUR letter, my dear Sir Edward, demands my earliest acknowledgments; - accept my sincere thanks for the friendship it demonstrates both to me and my son, whom I am far from being easy about. Never could I have supposed that such a woman as Fanny Elwood would have had attractions for the heart of Charles Montgomery, who has ever been accustomed to the politest circles. Had the girl no *vices*, yet she is by no means calculated for a domestic companion to a man of sentiment and education. I own his attachment to her has greatly deceived the expectations I had formed of him, and disappointed the *plan* I had long been forming for his happiness: – this plan I have hitherto concealed, but will now confide it to your bosom. Mr. Bertills, the father of the young lady whose/ letter you inclosed, is not only *my* nearest relation, but my dearest and *most valued friend*: – the excellent qualities of his heart, with which I have from childhood been acquainted, give him a claim to that distinction. He has ever been extremely partial to Charles, and we had determined on an union between Miss Bertills and him, if it could be effected without putting any disagreeable restraint upon the inclinations of either. This union *was* and *still is* the wish of my heart. Rhoda, tho' not strikingly beautiful, has every charm necessary to engage the lasting esteem and affections of any man who is qualified to judge of intrinsic merit, and whose own good sense prompts him to look for something *beyond* beauty, in a woman with whom he is to pass his retired hours. I yet hope, my dear sir, that my son will be convinced of his error before it is too late, and withdraw his affections from Fanny, to place them on one who will do honor to his judgment; and may that one be Rhoda Bertills! The concern she expresses gives me pain, even while it gratifies my pride and my affection.

　　　I had a letter from Mr. Bertills upon the/ same subject, yesterday; but Charles was unfortunately just set out for Leeds, accompanied by Augustus Fitzmaurice, with whom he is going this day to Doncaster races, from whence I expect they will return hither to-morrow evening. – In the mean time, I shall have leisure to consider on the best method of proceeding in this very important affair.

My best respects attend Miss Melworth. I take the liberty of detaining her friend's letter, to be perused by Charles; after which, I will return it to you: but shall be happy if you will give me an opportunity of doing it in person, by obliging us with your company here. You will find your valuable friend Augustus with us. - In compliance with my desire, he is to continue at the Grove a week or ten days.

> I am, dear sir,
>> with the utmost esteem,
>>> your obliged friend,
>>>> *FREDERICK MONTGOMERY./*

LETTER XI.

The Honorable Augustus Fitzmaurice, to Sir Edward Melworth.

HOTEL, LEEDS.

I HAVE obeyed the injunctions in your last, friend Edward, and have accompanied Montgomery in *one* visit to his Dulcinea;[21] but pardon me if I say, I should think it almost too great a sacrifice to friendship to attend him upon many more: besides, I am rather too young for the office of guardian to him; and the name of *spy* I detest; therefore, if you wish, as I know you do, to preserve him from mischief, let me advise you not to depend upon a deputy, but come over and take proper care of him yourself. Let me tell you, however, that *your* thoughts of his *dear, sweet, lovely, angelic Fanny*, exactly coincide with my own; tho' you do not speak with quite so much acrimony of her as she appear to me to merit. Heaven and earth! what a composition she is to think of for a *wife!* Did/ a man want a *mistress* indeed, why she might serve in that capacity for a little while, – but not for *me*, if I had an inclination to one, - for the jade paints, and all the world should not bribe me to put my lips to a painted face if I knew it to be so: I love pure nature; it lasts the longest. I dare swear Fanny Elwood is made up of *art*, inside and out. You may be assured, Edward, that *I* shall never pay homage to beauty; because, I shall always suspect it to be more the child of *art* than of *nature*, and even where it *is* natural, it generally engrosses so much of the attention as to leave the female, who is in possession of it, no leisure *to* attend to any thing else.

Since I saw Miss Elwood, I have asked myself, several times, whether I was not mistaken in my opinion of Charles's understanding; for this attachment loudly proclaims him a *fool*. – He certainly must be infatuated. You would have laughed, heartily, had you seen how cleverly I accommodated myself to the manners of the girl: I took care to banish all necessity for reserve, on her part, by letting her understand, at our first entrance, that I/ was no stranger to the terms my friend and she were upon with each other: this set madam perfectly at her ease, during the whole time we staid; and she behaved, as I imagine she usually does when in company with only him, and gave me thereby an opportunity of discovering that our friend's passion for her is not so formidable as we feared. – It *may* be conquered; and I have no doubt it will, if he can be kept from marrying her before his departure for the continent. *Self-love* is the basis of his attachment: Fanny is the mirror in which he sees himself in a more advantageous light than he had before done. – she is at infinitely more pains to raise *him* in his own esteem, than she is to raise *herself* in it. – She *flatters* him egregiously; and flattery, in short, is the chain by which she binds him to her. – If he once perceives that, and gains such a conquest over his vanity as to break the chain, it will not be an easy matter for any woman to hold him again in a similar one.

Charles is just returned from visiting his Fanny. - I declined going thither with him again this morning, from an idea that he would/ make his visit much longer than he has; and I thought I could spend my time far more agreeably in writing to you: but his quick return obliges me to conclude sooner than I intended. We are going to Doncaster races, and Charles is all impatience lest we should be too late for the first heat. You see by this that even his amours must give place to the amusements of the turf. Now, you know, as well as I, that he never bets; of course, his pleasure must consist solely in the company he meets on those occasions. Farewell; he is hurrying me.

I am, yours,
AUGUSTUS FITZMAURICE./

LETTER XII.

The same, to the same.

FIR-GROVE.

HERE we are again, Edward! you see we have been pretty quick in our motions; and *thereby hangs a tale*, with which you shall be entertained in due order. – But first, let me tell you, that, on our ride from Leeds to Doncaster, I rallied poor Charles so unmercifully he scarce knew whether to take it in jest or earnest. He is pretty fiery, you know, and, I believe, was more than once half tempted to treat the matter seriously, and give me a challenge: but he reserved this display of his prowess for another occasion, – a laughable one to me, as I hope it will prove to you. Here follows an account of the whole affair, which, I have the satisfaction to tell you, ended without bloodshed on either side.

The vast concourse of people usually drawn together by the pleasures of the turf, occasioned/ the Inns, at Doncaster, to be very full; and obliged us to permit two gentlemen-officers to join us at meals. - We found their company very agreeable the first day, nor indeed was *I* less pleased with them the second; but unfortunately for Charles, just after we had dined, a waiter entered with Colonel Atkin's compliments to Major Herbert and the company, and requested to be admitted to join the party; the request was complied with, and he entered: but had not sat long when the Major said to him,

'Come, Colonel, the glass stands with you, – give us your mistress; – by the way, I think you are much obliged to me for introducing you to one charming enough to hold you so long in her silken bandage.'

'You are mistaken, Major,' returned he, 'the jade's extravagance has almost ruined me; and yet I could not muster up courage to throw her off; and I have been as henpecked as any poor dog in the world ever was. - Had I been married to her she could not have tyrannized more; but now, thank my good stars, I have got my release,/ - at least I intend to make use of it in that way. Her last letter informs me, – 'that she has got an *honorable* lover whom she means to *marry*, and whose fortune is sufficient to put it in her power to testify the warmth of her affection for *me*, if I will only take care to keep at a proper distance, till after the ceremony has taken place.' - I am determined to avail myself of *this* to keep at a distance *for ever.*'

'Ha! ha! ha! – an *honorable* lover!' cried Herbert, 'and who is he Colonel? did she not tell you his name?'

'No!' resumed Atkins, 'nor do I want to know it. – So long as he does but give me a fair opportunity to be rid of her, 'tis enough for me, - tho', whoever the poor fellow is, I pity him from my soul, – for I'll answer for it, she has grossly deceived him.'

'So would I too,' rejoined the Major, 'for she has art enough to deceive the devil himself: – however, Colonel, for want of a better, we 'll e'en toast her now, and her new lover into the bargain. – So, gentlemen,'/ taking his glass, 'here 's Fanny Elwood and her *honorable lover.*'

'Fanny Elwood!' - repeated Charles, his face glowing with indignation, – 'pray, Major, is it Miss Elwood, of Leeds, of whom you have been conversing, and whose character has been thus cruelly sported with?'

'The very same, indeed, sir,' – returned the Major, with the most mortifying *sang froid.*

'Give me leave, sir,' – resumed our friend, with a furious look, 'to tell you, that the character of that lady shall not in *my* company be so very unjustly traduced with impunity. – I insist on your retracting the scandalous appellation you have bestowed upon her, or giving me instant satisfaction.'

'I presume then, Mr. Montgomery,' – said Herbert, preserving still the same degree of coolness, – 'that *you* are the honorable lover she boasts of; – therefore, for *your* sake, sir, not *mine*, I resolutely refuse to comply with your request. – I will neither retract what I have said, nor give you the satisfaction you so rashly demand. - So/ now 'to *marriage* with her with what appetite you may,' but, be *assured*, I can justify all I have said of Miss Elwood.'

'It is *false!*' – cried Charles, with additional heat, – 'Miss Elwood is *purity* itself, and if you refuse to clear away the aspersions you have thrown on her character, in this company, or to give me the satisfaction of a man of honor and a gentleman, - depend upon it, I'll post you for a coward and a scoundrel.'

'But, Montgomery,' - resumed the Major, still cool and undaunted, - 'you should first be quite certain that I merit those epithets. – I have too often signalized myself by my valor in the field of battle to fear the imputation of cowardice, and my conduct, in other respects, has been such as bids defiance to the title of *scoundrel* being justly added to my name: – and I now tell you, that I am so far satisfied with myself, that it is not in your power, by the utmost provocatives you can use, to oblige me to fight a duel by way of establishing my reputation for courage, because I know it to be unnecessary.'/

'Major,' – resumed Charles, still standing, – 'I am not to be trifled with; – I *insist* on your doing ample justice to the character of Miss Elwood, either one way or the other.'

'Now do not oblige me to *that*, in this company, Montgomery,' - said Herbert, humorously, – '*because*, doing ample justice to it will not reflect so much honor on the lady's conduct as you, doubtless, imagine it will; but, come, sit down, and be cool, and I promise, if you will give me, at some other time, an opportunity to speak with you, in private, you shall hear *ample justice* done to Fanny Elwood's character from my lips; and if you are the honorable lover she speaks of, you may, perhaps, thank me for saving you from destruction: – but if you should not then be perfectly satisfied, I know no other way of settling the difference between us than by my going up to London, and asking my wife and children to give me leave to run the risk of losing my own life, in order to try to take that of a man to whom I bear no personal enmity whatever; and, as it is impossible/ *you* can be without some friends who have a right to be consulted on an affair of so much importance, you can make use of the time of my absence in requesting them to grant you the same indulgence: for, before I enter upon a *tilting-bout*, I must positively have the consent of all parties: – but,' added he, 'as I am determined not to enter into so serious a business till the races and its attendant amusements are over, – I think the best way is to throw it entirely from our thoughts, and enjoy life while we have it, therefore let us shake hands and be friends for the present.'

This overture Charles declined, and muttering in a low voice, 'Despicable cowardice and evasion!' abruptly left the room, and I followed. In the heat of his passion he ordered the horses, which we mounted directly; and, with anger's speed, returned to Fir-grove. The worthy Mr. Montgomery was much entertained with the conduct of Major Herbert, in the contest between him and his son; and flatters himself, that Charles, when he reflects seriously, will be properly impressed by what/ Herbert said of his fair one. – I sincerely wish it may be so. Mr. Montgomery says, he had a letter from you which he wished to shew our friend; but he is desirous of trying the effects of this dose before he administers another so very powerful, as both together may be more than he can well bear.

I am yours, sincerely,
AUGUSTUS FITZMAURICE.

LETTER XIII.

The same, to the same.

FIR-GROVE.

How soon, my dear Sir Edward, are our brightest prospects clouded over, and our mirth turned into mourning! My last was written in the gaiety of my heart; – I write this under the impression of unaffected sorrow. Mr. Montgomery, - the worthy, the excellent Mr. Montgomery is no more! Yesterday afternoon, in apparent good health, and/ with his usual degree of spirits, he was walking with his son and me in the grove, when he suddenly dropped down in an apoplectic fit, and expired before he could be got into the house. Immediate assistance was obtained, but the utmost medical skill proved ineffectual; the lamp of life was totally extinct! It is impossible to paint to you the distraction and grief of poor Charles; - he was like one bereft of his senses; he caught the corps in his arms; bathed the face with his tears; called upon his father; knelt, and implored him to speak. The gentlemen of the faculty, who had been summoned, informed me of the necessity of his being let blood to prevent a fever. With some difficulty we drew him from the corps, and brought him to submit; after which, we got him to bed. I am sorry to add, that the precaution has not been perfectly success-ful: he was feverish all night; remains yet much indisposed; and has not left his chamber. They have just told me, he inquires for me. I will take up the pen again at the first leisure moment./

Charles is better! - but, alas! his thoughts again revert to his Fanny, as he calls her; he is extremely desirous that she should be informed of the afflictive event, to account for his not visiting her yet. – I have, therefore, promised to ride over to Leeds with the intelligence to-morrow, if he is sufficiently recovered to admit of my leaving him. - To keep his mind as easy as I can, I intend to *perform* this *promise*; but, be assured, I shall not fail to remind him of *that* which he made to his father, and endeavor to persuade him to persevere in his late intention of going abroad *free from any intanglement*. Heaven forbid that he should marry Fanny Elwood! for I have not a doubt of Herbert being able to justify his asser-tions. - It is not, however, a proper time, now, to touch upon that topic to him. I wish, Edward, you would come over to us; your influence might be productive of good consequences. I really cannot bear the idea of such an amiable fellow being rendered miserable for life. If you cannot come do not omit to write; you may both *console* and *advise.*/

I was this day to have returned home, but I seem now destined to make a much longer stay; as my father, whom I have acquainted with the melancholy cause of my detention, requests me not to leave Charles a prey to solitude and grief. His Lordship is sincerely afflicted at the loss of his valuable friend; but promises to come to us as soon as his spirits will permit. The post is going.

    Yours, sincerely,
    AUGUSTUS FITZMAURICE.

LETTER XIV.

Sir Edward Melworth, to the Honorable Augustus Fitzmaurice.
MELWORTH-HALL.

THE intelligence in your last has given a severe shock to my feelings; – indeed, Augustus, Mr. Montgomery was dear to me as a friend – as a father. – His character was such/ as commanded at once the veneration, esteem, and love of every person capable of those sensations: his converse, – instructive, yet entertaining; fraught with genuine piety, and untinctured with a single gloomy idea, – seemed often to raise his mind, and carry him, if I may use the expression, out of himself, into the blissful regions of immortality. He is now completely happy; and we, who mourn his departure from the world, demonstrate not so much disinterested affection for *him* as regard for *ourselves.* Alas! my friend, *self-love*[22] is too often the reigning principle within us: it is that, alone, which excites our sorrow for the loss of a pious and amiable friend. We recall to our ideas how greatly his *virtues* assisted to sweeten our own enjoyments; and, in our grief for the loss of such assistance, we renounce that consolation which the certainty of his everlasting felicity *ought* to afford us. I speak from experience: in Mr. Montgomery's death, I have lost one of the most useful and pleasing friends; tho' I desire to be submissive to the will of him who does all things *well.* Happy, thrice happy spirit! I would/ congratulate thee on thy accession to everlasting joy. Oh how do I aspire to join thee! to join my Matilda too, whose gentle spirit fancy represents as hovering over her Edward, guarding him from evil, and directing him into the paths of peace and pleasantness. Fitzmaurice, there are few things that afford more delight than the supposition that the spirits of our departed friends are permitted to become our guardian angels: it may be deemed an enthusiastic notion, but it affords a pleasure which I could not resign without infinite reluctance. – Under this idea, I can hold converse with my Matilda, and anticipate my future bliss, by a degree of participation in hers. – It even operates upon my actions and thoughts so powerfully as often to lead me to that most useful branch of study, *self-examination.* – I then see the depravity of my nature in its fallen state; am made deeply sensible of my guilt before God, and my utter inability to approach him but thro' the mediation and intercession of *Him*, whose blood has made a full atonement for sin: to that sacrifice, alone, I look, as the only/ solid foundation of hope in the mercy of God; whose counsels are immutable, and whose promises are faithfulness and truth. – On them I place the whole of my dependence, till, on the pinions of faith, I rise to heaven. If Charles experiences this sort of enthusiasm, he will draw consolation from it; he will draw spiritual improvement from it; and thus will his present affliction prove a future blessing to him. I would go over to you, but I am by no means fit for a companion to Charles just now, – I sympathize with him too deeply. In a short time I hope to be able to meet him without adding my stock of *affliction* to his. Remember me affectionately to him.

I say nothing of Fanny Elwood now, nor indeed do I know when I shall have patience to speak or think of her; our friend *must* not, he *shall* not marry her!

Yours,

EDWARD MELWORTH./

LETTER XV.

The Honorable Augustus Fitzmaurice, to Sir Edward Melworth.

FIR-GROVE.

YOU say right, Edward; – Charles *must* not, *shall* not, marry Fanny Elwood, because now he *cannot*; – she has put it effectually out of his power, by having, yesterday, married another; – 'tant mieux' – say you, and I say the same, for *that* happy event; but for another, which I have to relate, and which has been the occasion of her perfidy, you will join in saying, *tant pis:*[23] – for this circumstance I anticipate your concern, tho' it cannot exceed my own. I am, beyond measure, distressed for our Friend, under this additional affliction; as he must severely feel it: a spirit like his, was not formed to contend with the evils of poverty, or the mortifications of dependence. But I hasten to acquaint you with the particulars. – In pursuance of my promise, I rode over, yesterday, to Leeds./ On my arrival at Mr. Elwood's, I enquired for his daughter, and was, without any ceremony, immediately conducted, by the servant, to a room, where I found her engaged with a large company. On advancing towards her, I addressed her by the name of Elwood; when a fat, awkward figure of a man left his seat, and coming up to us, with a bow of affected gentility, vulgarly said,

'Excuse me, sir, I beg pardon, but you have made a trifling mistake, sir; that lady is *called* Wilkins now; she and I were *wed* this morning, sir, and I'm the happiest man in the world.'

Without making any answer, *I*, with a contemptuous look and haughty accent, desired to know of *her* whether this information was true? She replying in the affirmative, I slightly bowed, said I had no farther business, and instantly withdrew. She followed, requesting to speak with me in another room; I complied, in silence. – When we were seated, I waited to hear what she had to say, and she began as follows./

'It is possible, sir, you may think I have acted very ill by your friend; and, in consequence of that thought, may pass very severe censures upon my conduct in the affair. – As I wish to stand well in the opinion of every one, more particularly in that of Mr. Fitzmaurice, I must beg leave to justify myself, tho' it may now seem unnecessary.' She paused, as in expectation of my reply; finding I continued silent, she proceeded thus: 'While I encouraged the addresses of Mr. Charles Montgomery, it was under the mistaken idea that he was the legal heir to his father. If he was *ignorant* that he was not so, as I have been informed he was, why I have nothing to lay to his charge; but if, on the contrary, he was sensible of it, may God forgive him the deception he practiced upon *me!* which might have been of very destructive consequences to my peace. Happily, our acquaintance not having been of any very long duration, time had not strengthened my affections sufficiently to render me blind to my own interest; I was capable of reflecting seriously,/ and that convinced me I was not formed for love and a cottage, neither could I, in a single state, subsist upon my small fortune. Mr. Wilkins is wealthy, and the wishes of my parents adding strength to his intreaties, I consented to be his, and consider myself as acting perfectly right in thus securing an establishment for life. As matters now stand, I fear poor Charles will not be able to provide for himself so easily as I have done; I am sorry for his disappointment, but we have all a right to study our own advantage.'

'O, most undoubtedly *Mrs. Wilkins!*' – cried I, sneeringly, – 'but, at the same time, you must allow me to take the freedom of telling you, that if, in this instance, you have not had recourse to the meanest of all subterfuges – *falsehood*, to excuse your infidelity to my friend, you have been *grossly imposed upon*: – however, it has terminated so infinitely to his *real* advantage, that I, with all others who truly value him, will *idolize* you for the insuperable barrier which your conduct of to-day has placed between him and yourself.'/

Having said this I left her; rejoiced at heart, and full of gratitude to providence, for having, thus kindly, interposed to save Charles from a life of misery: – but revolving the matter in my mind, as I was returning to him, I found myself greatly at a loss how to reveal the affair; knowing the violence of his passions, upon most occasions, I dreaded their effect upon him, on one so trying as this;

and most heartily did I wish for you to take the business off my hands. The tale the unworthy wretch told, as her excuse for the base part she had acted, I gave not the least degree of credit to, but imagined some unknown friend had propagated it to serve the purpose it had effected; nor could I avoid triumphing in the idea of her mortification, when she should find her error. Alas! Sir Edward, her information was too true: – when I entered Charles's dressing-room, after my return, I found him and old John, the butler, together; the worthy creature was in tears, and the countenance of our friend was covered with the deepest dejection. After a short silence,/

'Augustus!' said he, 'I am fallen into the very depth of misery! Oh! I am now sunk low indeed! and –'

Imagining, directly, that some one had anticipated me, and informed him of the perfidy of Fanny, I hastily interrupted him by saying,

'Fye! Charles, fye upon you! you make me blush for your extreme weakness. – Is not such a woman unworthy of your regard? does she not merit your utmost contempt? has she not incontestably proved that your *fortune* and not *yourself* was the object of her desires?'

'I am unable to comprehend you,' returned he, 'but it strikes me, at this moment, that my amiable Fanny has heard of the change in my circumstances; and, from motives of generosity, makes a painful, tho' voluntary, resignation of her claim to my affections. Yes; it *must* be so: – noble minded creature! may *you* be happy, tho' I am miserable! Yet, alas! I fear I have undone your peace. – I have now no prospect of ever having it in my power to offer/ you my hand, without a prospect of involving you in distress; but here I vow never to offer it to another. Thy lovely image is indelibly impressed on my heart, nor can it ever be effaced. My gratitude –'

Unable to bear any longer the tortures of suspense, I interrupted his rhapsody by exclaiming,

'For heaven's sake, my dear friend, tell me at once, what is the matter? – what change is this you talk of in your circumstances?'

'Ah! Fitzmaurice,' cried he, 'it is such an one as places me almost beneath your friendship! – In short I am – oh! I am a forlorn, destitute outcast; the offspring of an illicit connection; unacknowledged by any one upon earth; and my only inheritance scorn, contempt and poverty! for, by the sudden decease of my only friend and protector, my father, I am rendered unable to procure the common necessaries of life!'

'Impossible, Charles!' – cried I, with great warmth, – 'you have been deceived; 'you *are*, you *must* be legally intitled to the/ property of the late Mr. Montgomery; he never dropped even a hint to the contrary; there must, certainly, be, at least, some great mistake in all this.'

'Would to God there was, sir!' – said old John, clasping his hands together. – 'but indeed, indeed it is *too* true; – my dear young master is an illegitimate son;[24] tho' the secret has been hitherto carefully concealed from his knowledge, and I heartily wish it had been possible to conceal it still. Mrs. Ellis and I were the only servants in the family acquainted with the affair; and, notwithstanding the death of my master made us both see the necessity of informing Mr. Charles, yet neither of us could undertake the painful task, and he would still have been a stranger to the matter but for some loose papers which, in your absence, sir, he found in my late master's cabinet.'

Charles then put the papers into my hand to peruse, and I found in them a full demonstration of the fact. They appeared to have been written by Mr. Montgomery, so long ago as within a few months subsequent to the birth/ of his son; and contained his own reflections so pathetically expressed, that the perusal excited my tears. After reading them, I could doubt no longer: – my friendship for Charles, which has gathered strength from his calamities, then led me to attempt offering some consolation, by letting him see the good it had produced, in being the means of freeing him from the snares of an artful woman, whose bad principles must have made him miserable, if he had married her. – Even poverty itself, I added, had not the power of making him so wretched as an alliance with her would inevitably have made him. It was not very speedily that he would credit my intelligence of her marriage with Wilkins; but, at length, he did; and his passion for her was vanquished at once! He viewed her in her true colors; and owned himself ready to bless the event that had unmasked her; since it was far less afflictive than the loss of domestic happiness. He is really much more composed than I could have imagined; and appears, to me, to feel little now for the loss of fortune; but confesses that he felt it, at first, very severely;/ tho' far more on Fanny's account than his own. After all, my dear Edward, I am unhappy for him. I can write no more, at present, than that

     I am yours, affectionately,
       AUGUSTUS FITZMAURICE.

LETTER XVI.

Charles Montgomery, Esq. to Sir Edward Melworth.

FIR-GROVE.

FITZMAURICE has, I find, informed you of the great alteration in my affairs and prospects; – an alteration, which, while it reduces me to the lowest ebb of fortune, gives me, at the same time, an opportunity to distinguish the difference between the *real friend* and the *flattering sycophant*. In you, my dear Sir Edward, I am secure of finding the former; nor is the friendship of Augustus rendered less conspicuous by my misfortunes: but where I had formed the fondest hopes, – there I find myself disappointed. Your judgment of Fanny/ Elwood was *just*; her conduct has proved it; tho' I weakly believed her all perfection. When I reflect on her treachery, I think, if I know any thing of my own heart, it expands with thankfulness even for the loss of all my once bright expectations; since the realizing of them would, in all probability, have been productive of endless anguish. But enough of her; – my thoughts must now take a different turn. I must devise some expedient for the means of sustaining my existence.

At present, I know not what course to take: trade I am wholly a stranger to, nor do I think I could ever bring my mind to submit to all the servile situations which the trader must necessarily be thrown into very frequently. The army seems to me the only resource I have left. How little did my late honored parent imagine that his darling son would ever be reduced to the necessity of living by his industry! yet it *must* be by the exertion of that, in some way or other, by which alone I *can* live. I can never support the idea of submitting to be a dependent upon the bounty of another. I forbear to speak thus to Fitzmaurice,/ because I perceive he derives some pleasure from the flattery of hope, which points his expectation to the generosity of Mr. Bertills, heir at law to my late father; and judging by that of his own mind, imagines he will restore to me a sufficient part of the property to enable me still to support the style of a gentleman: – vain hope! – But Mr. Bertills is totally unknown to Augustus; he is not so to me; and, therefore, I entertain no such idea: nor, indeed, could I submit to any thing so humiliating as that of a precarious dependence upon a man whose connections having been chiefly amongst the trading part, he must, of course, have inbibed opinions and sentiments despicably narrow and contracted. Mr. Bertills is a merchant in the city of London, where he has acquired a very large fortune; – he has ever professed a great partiality to me, but that has not rendered me blind to his imperfections; his love of money is not the *least* amongst them: for, notwithstanding he has only one child to inherit his wealth, he pursues business now with as much avidity as he did in the days of his youth. I think this trait is convincing/ enough to remove every such expectation, for it would be romantic indeed to build a hope upon the generosity of a man who, in the city phrase, *knows the value of money.*

From old John and Mrs. Ellis I learn that Mr. Bertills is no stranger to all the circumstances attending my unfortunate birth; he was the confidant of my father, and assisted him thro' all the difficulties he had to surmount in preserving it a secret, not only from *me* but from the *world*. – For this my grateful heart is ready to acknowledge obligation to him. – I thirst to know all the particulars; but neither old John nor Mrs. Ellis will acquaint me with them; they refer me to Mr. Bertills, whom I impatiently wish to see; but I must bridle my impatience a little longer, as I have received a letter from him, which I inclose for your perusal; – do not forget that it was written while he was ignorant of my father's having died intestate. – By this time he is informed of it, as I have written to him myself upon the subject. – His next will, without doubt, be in a different style. In *this* inclosure/ you may see something of the Citizen and trader.[25] Adieu.

    Yours,

    CHARLES MONTGOMERY.

LETTER XVII.

Mr. Philip Bertills, Merchant, to Charles Montgomery, Esq.
(Inclosed in the preceding.)

CHATHAM-PLACE.

Dear Charles,

THE intelligence of your father's death fills me with unaffected grief. – I feel too severely myself to be capable of applying the healing balm of consolation to *your* sorrows: – I can only sympathize with you. *You* mourn a tender and affectionate parent; *I*, the friend of my earliest days; the friend of my heart; whose numerous virtues endeared him to me thro' life, and will for ever endear to me his memory. You, Charles, are young, and may, of course, form other attachments/ which will heal the wound at present given to your feelings by this afflictive dispensation of providence. – Time will do much for *you*; – but for *me* it can do nothing; at least, *very* little. You and my daughter, I trust, will still continue to divide my paternal regards, as you have hitherto; but the sweet intercourse of social friendship I can no more enjoy. Your father was my *first* self: our attachment was mutual; it was cemented by congeniality of minds; the closest habits of intimacy; and the most unlimited confidence, from our boyish days. – Judge, then, my beloved youth, how painful to me must be this final separation!

Your cousin Rhoda participates in our distress; she sits weeping beside me; and, while she confesses tears are a just tribute to the memory of one so truly valuable, she laments the difficulty of demonstrating that perfect submission to the will of God, which he has a right to expect from all the creatures of his power. She desires me to present her best remembrances, and wishes you that support under your affliction which religion only can afford./

I must beg leave to decline attending the funeral; my heart is too *womanish* to brave such an encounter. – I will endeavor to blunt the poignancy of my feelings by the hurry of business, which, at present, *claims* a large share of my attention. One of my ships, – on board of which is a valuable cargo, greatest part my own property, – was yesterday stranded in the river. – I shall sustain a loss by it, at *any* rate, but my neglect at this time would make it heavier. – I will, therefore, remain upon the spot, and use my industry to avert as much of the evil as I can. When my business and my spirits permit I will be with you; till then, consider me as

your sympathizing friend,
and affectionate relation,
PHILIP BERTILLS./

LETTER XVIII.

Sir Edward Melworth, to Charles Montgomery, Esq.

MELWORTH-HALL.

To attempt a full expression of my concern for your sufferings would be in vain; I shall, therefore, my dear Charles, only say that I *feel* them; – and tho' it is *not* in my power to present you with any thing like an equivalent to the estate you expect to lose, yet it *is* to offer you independence. My heart is yours, and you shall share my fortune, unless providence bestows upon you a *better*, which, from the little knowledge I have gained of Mr. Bertills, by report, I still hope will be the case; and in this particular, I confess myself, to the full, as sanguine as Fitz-maurice, but I believe it is upon a stronger foundation. Why will you, my friend, again pretend to penetration after the recent proof you have had of your mistake in the character of Fanny Elwood? Who, with all her cunning, did not impose/ upon those of *real* experience, and discernment. I am deceived if you are not as greatly mistaken too, in the character of Mr. Bertills. – I am glad you are fallen into no worse hands; his friendship and affection for your late father, is, in my opinion, a guarantee for his kindness to *you*. I see nothing to condemn in his let-ter; he writes like what he professes himself to be – an affectionate relation. As to the mention he makes of his business, you may plainly perceive he only means to use *that* as an instrument to subdue those feelings which would be too painful to support, and two powerful to be conquered by any thing less than a subject capa-ble of engrossing his fixed attention. His knowledge of trade and attachment to it, give him greatly the advantage over such idle, useless fellows as you and me; since it offers him, at all times, a resource from the bitterness of grief; – while *we* have no other than conversation, books, music, or some such trifling things; for *trifling* they all appear, when taken up merely for the purpose of stemming a torrent of affliction with which the heart is overwhelmed. How frequently/ do we feel the inefficacy of all these in such situations! for, if conversation is suited to the tone of our minds, it rather feeds our melancholy; if it is not, it appears insipid, or impertinent; our attention cannot be engaged by it, but is perpetually reverting to the subject nearest to our hearts. Nearly the same objections may be made to every employment, merely of the *mental* kind: – but the engagements of commerce keep both body and mind in action; it engrosses the faculties; and, imperceptibly, exhilarates the spirits; nor can I, for my life, see why a man's being engaged in commerce, and living in the city, should make him *the less of a gen-tleman in his manners, contract his ideas, or harden his heart.* Prithee, prithee, Charles, never talk about these matters till you can bring more weighty reasons to support your side of the argument; but throw away directly the narrow pre-judices you have yourself imbibed entirely from books, whose authors, merely for the pleasure of sacrificing to their own splenetic dispositions, have delineated citizens and traders as the off-scouring of all things. Go amongst even the lowest mechanics,/ and you may often find those, who with few advantages of education, possess liberality of sentiment, humanity, tenderness, and benevolence of disposition, tho' in an homely, uninviting garb. I have the happiness, – I will add too, the *honor,* – to be intimate with several respectable merchants of the city of London, whose education and manners qualify them for the first company in the kingdom, and whose principles and conduct render them ornaments to society. Mr. Bertills, I doubt not, is of this class. – I have not any personal knowledge of him; but his daughter is the intimate friend of my sister, and her letters, which I consider as the transcripts of her heart, give me an high idea of her understanding and morals.

I wish much to see you; but, at present, I must say with Mr. Bertills, my spirits are unequal to the task of supporting any afflictive scenes, and some affairs of consequence require my presence here. – As soon as decency permits your leaving home, I beg you will come over to *me*: change of place and company will assist in restoring your chearfulness. – Augustus/ will accompany you. Harriet and Mrs. Horton are waiting for me to attend them on an airing; so adieu.

Yours, affectionately,
EDWARD MELWORTH.

LETTER XIX.

The Hon. Augustus Fitzmaurice, to Sir Edward Melworth.

How frequently may we observe, that the happiest events which occur to us are extracted from those we, at first view, esteem singularly unfortunate. What an astonishing escape has Charles had! but let me proceed orderly, that you may be able to comprehend the matter. The day after he wrote to you last, we were surprised by Major Herbert sending in his name, and requesting the honor of a short conference with our friend. – He was immediately admitted; and, after the customary compliments of condolence on his part, and apologies for rudeness and rashness/ on the part of Charles, we took our seats, and the Major said,

'So unexpected a visit from me, Mr. Montgomery, no doubt excites your wonder: but I come hither, sir, as your friend, on the foundation of my esteem for Mr. and Miss Bertills, with whom I have long had the honor of an intimacy; and who, I find, are not only much attached to you, but are your nearest relations. Had I known this circumstance, when at Doncaster, depend upon it we had not parted so hastily. – Accident alone informed me of it now; for, at my return home from thence, Miss Bertills was with Mrs. Herbert, who was expressing her pleasure at seeing me, when I jocularly said, as I held her in my arms,

'Why it is very well, my love, that I am come safe back to you; for I have been pretty near having a sword thro' my body, or a bullet thro' my head, only for speaking the *truth* of one of your sex, before a fiery young spark, who thought higher of her than she merited, and therefore, demanded instant satisfaction.'/

'Bless me!' – cried my dear girl, with a countenance pale as death, – 'are you sure you did not accept the challenge, Herbert?'

'No, no, no, my love,' replied I, 'set your heart at rest; you see me now perfectly safe, and I intend to keep so, unless Montgomery, who did not seem appeased, should offer me any personal insult.'

'Montgomery!' – repeated Miss Bertills, in an accent of terror, and instantly fainted. I was exceedingly alarmed at the consequence of my folly; for, I have those ridiculous feelings about me, that, I declare to heaven, I would much rather face the fire from an enemy's battery, than see a woman in a fainting fit. By proper methods she was soon brought to herself; and then succeeded a long string of enquiries about her *cousin*; which, by the way, continued he, I scarce knew how to answer, for fear I might involuntarily occasion a relapse. At length, I satisfied her; and learned, afterwards, from Mr. Bertills, the great anxiety they endured on account of your unhappy attachment to Fanny Elwood; tho' they did/ not know her character so well as I do. When I reflected on the *art* and cunning she was mistress of; the infatuation you were under; and your being now the sole director of your fortune and actions; – I expected she would leave nothing undone to bring about a speedy marriage, and I then regretted not having complied with your request at Doncaster, of doing her ample justice. – To repair my error, I gained your address, and came, with a determination to convince you how greatly you had mistaken her; tho', in so doing, I must, at the same time, take shame to myself; for –

Here Charles interrupted him, by acknowledging himself already convinced of her unworthiness, and ashamed of having so warmly defended her character. In the course of the conversation, he told the Major all the disagreeables of his present situation, and mentioned a design of going into the army. – The Major sympathized in his misfortunes, but added, that he rejoiced to find his worthy friend Mr. Bertills was the heir at law; as, from *his* knowledge of him, he could scarce believe,/ that even for the acquisition of five thousand a year, he would be tempted to deprive a young man, whom he professed to esteem, of his *natural* tho' not *lawful* right. – But, Sir Edward, I now begin to fear there is but little room to hope for any thing from him. I observed that the Major himself could not help allowing, that if a strict attention to trade, when a man was rich enough to do without it, was sufficient proof of a strong attachment to *money*, Mr. Bertills certainly must be very fond of it, as no one pursued business more attentively than himself. This confirmation of the justness of Charles's opinion of him, I own, removes my dependence upon his generosity; yet, to support his spirits, I endeavor to raise *his* hopes upon that foundation. I may, perhaps, be wrong in so doing; but he seems himself to expect so little that I have not much reason to fear it will be in the power of any thing I can say to injure him by heightening the disappointment, should *nothing* be restored to him.

The Major staid to dinner with us, and was but just departed when my father was announced. The feelings of his Lordship, at/ first entrance, were very pain-fully supported, and it was some time before he could conquer them. – Neither my friend nor myself was much less affected. My father has offered Charles his utmost assistance, should he be in need of it, and he now uses every method good-nature and humanity can suggest, to dispel his uneasiness. He remains with us till after the interment of Mr. Montgomery, which will be to-morrow.

> Yours,
> *AUGUSTUS FITZMAURICE.*

LETTER XX.

Charles Montgomery, Esq. to Sir Edward Melworth.

FIR-GROVE.

LAST night saw the remains of my much-revered and much-lamented father deposited in the tomb. Oh, my friend! what/ were my sensations when I took a last view of that countenance, on which I have so often gazed with delight! When I take a retrospect of his conduct, and reflect on his tender care – his ardent anxiety for my happiness, my heart is weighed down with sorrow; and the painful consideration, that I can no more behold him – no more hear his voice, takes place of every other idea. The loss of fortune, – the loss of her in whom I had centered all my hopes of earthly felicity, seem nothing in comparison to the loss of such a parent, who, in the tenderness of friendship, sunk parental authority. – But I must forbear dwelling upon the melancholy subject; your own sorrows are already too heavy. Augustus and I accept your invitation, and mean to be at the Hall the beginning of next week. Lord Lucan left us this morning. – He kindly insists on my accompanying him and his son on their intended tour, as was first proposed; but, in my opinion, it would be acting wrong: I should lose no time in determining what plan to pursue for a maintenance, nor in pursuing that plan as soon as formed. I shall,/ therefore, endeavor to decline the friendly offer. I would have done so at first, but his lordship would not suffer me to say a word in opposition. He defers setting out, upon my account; as he tells me it is highly necessary I should see Mr. Bertills. – I must, therefore, wait his arrival. Lord Lucan has attempted to flatter me with hopes of that gentleman providing handsomely for me; but I confess that not all which *he* or *you* can say will inspire me with any; and I fancy, Edward, you will be constrained to alter your sentiments, when you have read the letter I have just received from Mr. Bertills. You judge of him by yourself, and will be disappointed. – I feel no disappointment, because I have formed no expectation from him. I have now reconciled my mind to my situation, and am determined on the profession of a soldier. As we seem upon the eve of a war,[26] it is possible, if I discover merit, I may meet preferment; – or, I may expire on the bed of honor.

Those worthy creatures old John, and Mrs. Ellis, are visibly distressed for me, while I cannot help being more concerned for them/ than for myself; and I lament that it is not in my power to reward their affection to me, or the fidelity of their past services. It is hard upon them, in their old age, to have new situations to seek; – as will probably be the case, for I apprehend Mr. Bertills will sell this estate, as it is too far distant from London to be convenient for him to come to. I wish you had vacancies in your family for these two worthy beings; you would make them comfortable; and I should have the satisfaction of thinking, that their grey hairs would not go down in sorrow to the grave. My concern for them is really almost insupportable. – Accustomed to them from infancy, I feel an affection nearly filial; nor shall they ever be neglected by

　　　your afflicted,
　　　　　but affectionate friend,
　　　　　CHARLES MONTGOMERY./

LETTER XXI.

Mr. Philip Bertills, Merchant, to Charles Montgomery, Esq.
　　　　　　　　　　　　　　　　CHATHAM-PLACE.

Dear Charles,

HAD it been any other man but my late dear and much lamented friend, your father, who had died intestate, leaving a son born under such circumstances as yourself, and brought up with such flattering expectations as you have been, – I believe I should be tempted to inveigh most bitterly against his memory; and, perhaps, should not scruple to pronounce him either a *fool*, or a *villain*; but Frederick Montgomery was *neither*, and I confess I am utterly at a loss to account for this instance of weakness in his conduct. It must have proceeded from an idea that he was likely to live many years longer; and, according to all human probability, his expectation appeared to be well founded; but, I think, we have instances enough/ of the uncertainty of life, to convince us of the imprudence of delaying so important a concern; therefore, when I consider the benevolence and integrity of his mind, I am amazed he did not make his will twenty years ago. – I should really as soon have expected to hear that he had died *insolvent* as *intestate*. He has, however, left you reason to regret that he was not bred up to

trade; as he would then have learned that grand maxim which every man of business finds it necessary to adhere stedfastly to, viz. defer not till *to-morrow* what
should be done *to-day*. I am sorry for *you*, Charles; and I am sorry, likewise, for
myself: for I have, at all times, *business* enough upon my hands; but *more* just now
than usual, and I wanted not the *troublesome* addition to it which your father's
estates will unavoidably give me. The new arrangements I must make, will take
up no small portion of time. – But murmuring over it will not *do* it, so I shall say
no more of the matter now.

My affairs will not permit me to embrace your proposal of appearing at
Fir-grove immediataly; and, to speak the truth, I fear it/ will be some weeks
before I can conquer the weakness of my nature so far as to admit the thought
of entering that house where, in the bosom of friendship, I have passed so many
happy hours; and where I can no more experience the heart-felt delight of being
welcomed by him whose presence made the whole of that happiness. Will you
forgive me if I say, that tho' my heart yearns to meet you, yet, the sight of you, at
present, would be more than I can well bear; for which reason, alone, I decline
asking you to favor me with a visit in London: but I would by no means wish you
to confine yourself to Fir-grove, waiting my arrival; your stay there will tend to
feed your melancholy, which it is necessary you strive to dissipate by going into
society. I expect, my dear Charles, you will prove your affection to the memory
of your father, by attending to the dictates of one whom *he* honoured with his
friendship and confidence. – Remember, I shall depend upon your next being
dated from some other place; you *must* have many friends, who will be glad to
enjoy your company. – Go, then, amongst them;/ and, at those times when you
may wish to return to your home, take care to engage some agreeable associates
to enliven your hours there. That I may know always where to write to you, be
so obliging as to inform me from time to time of your rout; this will be a means
of preventing my being disappointed of seeing you when it suits me to go into
Yorkshire, as our meeting will be absolutely necessary in order to adjust every
thing to our mutual satisfaction.

Your cousin Rhoda is not quite so well in health as I could wish; but indisposition does not make her less mindful of her friends and relatives: she, of course,
desires to be remembered to you.

I wish, Charles, your natural curiosity, respecting the circumstances of your
birth, could sleep till we meet; but, if it will not, I must gratify it by letter some
other time; at *this* I have neither leisure nor inclination to enter upon the task:
the subject is indeed a painful one to me, as it never fails to revive many heart-
wounding recollections. Farewell. Rest assured of the friendship and affection of
   PHILIP BERTILLS./

LETTER XXII.

Charles Montgomery, Esq. to Mr. Philip Bertills, Merchant.

MELWORTH-HALL.

Dear sir,

AGREEABLY to your friendly injunctions, I came hither yesterday to meet, in the sympathetic kindness of my friend Sir Edward Melworth, that consolation which my recent affliction really needs; but instead of lessening my griefs, I find them augmented by my concern for this valuable man, who, in the bloom of life, and blessed with every amiable quality, is a prey to the most poignant sorrow, for the loss of a wife, to whom he had been united only six weeks, when she was torn from him by the inexorable hand of death. She was too tenderly beloved by him to leave any room to hope that the wound made by grief may be healed by another filling up the vacancy which her death has occasioned in his heart. He seems, now, as inconsolable as/ when it first happened, which was ten months back; and I often fear the life of the Baronet will fall a sacrifice to his unavailing sorrow. – This idea, when I view his altered looks, affects my spirits too powerfully to admit of my making a very long stay with him. In my adverse circumstances, a peculiar exertion of fortitude is necessary against every degree of sloth or supineness, since it is no longer in my power to indulge it. I am sensible too, that it is highly criminal. – Our great Creator formed every human being for usefulness, in some respect or other; none for idleness. Those who are not *naturally* industrious, are, often, by the wise dispensations of providence, thrown into a situation which *compels* them to be so. *I* come under this description, and cannot help considering every hour as lost while I remain thus disengaged from every useful employ. It is my wish to enter into the active scenes of life, as soon as possible; and, as I know not any thing else I am calculated for, I design going into the army. – The present appearance of war, fires my breast with martial ardor and heroic courage. – My mind presages my/ return to my native country, honored with those trophies which are the rewards of merit. I am impatient to offer my services, and am detained only by waiting your arrival at the Grove, where I will meet you, at any time you shall appoint. Permit me to beg, sir, you will hasten that period for the reason above-mentioned. – Other reasons too, contribute to render your presence necessary there. Farmer Dobson and Farmer Skellow, are in a state of anxiety about their farms. – The term their leases were granted for expired last week. – They are extremely desirous to have fresh ones; and, – as they are very industrious, worthy men, – you will not, I dare say, refuse their request. The servants at the house are likewise solicitous to know whether they may still think themselves *settled* in their stations, particularly old John and Mrs. Ellis, for whom indeed I am *most* concerned; their long and faithful services have merited to be distinguished; – but in your hands they will undoubtedly be safe, and there I must leave them.

I am very sorry to hear of the indisposition of Miss Bertills, and do sincerely wish her/ better. I accept, with gratitude, her cordial remembrance of me, both as friend and relation; and, with her permission and yours, will have the honor to thank her, in person, for such a mark of distinction.

Be not offended, my dear sir, if I add, that I was greatly disappointed by your declining in your last to give me the wished for intelligence respecting my birth. I am sorry to be the means of renewing any painful scenes to your recollection, but indeed I cannot rest satisfied till I am informed of all the particulars; which I hope you will soon be at leisure to indulge me with. – In the hope of your embracing the earliest opportunity for that purpose I remain,

     your most obedient servant,
      CHARLES MONTGOMERY./

LETTER XXIII.

Mr. Philip Bertills, Merchant, to Charles Montgomery, Esq.
                       CHATHAM-PLACE.

My dear Charles,

YOUR last has alarmed me exceedingly: surely you were not in your right senses when you wrote it, or you would never have mentioned to *me* a design of going into the army! How is it that you are yet such a stranger to me as to suppose I will ever concur in this measure? depend upon it *I will not.* I therefore insist upon your immediately laying aside all thoughts of so wild a scheme. Did I wish to exert an authority over you, I might say I have a *natural right*, derived from being the nearest relation you have in the world, to *command* your obedience in this instance. I *was*, too, the bosom friend of your father; and I now avow myself to be *your* friend likewise: as such, I again insist on your dropping all thoughts of the army. In/ the name of wonder what could put such a thing into your head, or induce you to think, for a moment, that it was in the least degree necessary for you to take such a step? Stay till you have occasion to adopt a plan for subsistence before you take the trouble of *forming* any; at present, you have not that apology to make; and if you had, I really cannot forbear saying, your choice appears to me rather a ridiculous one. Under the idea of being a *gentleman* by profession you would condescend to the very worst slavery, and let yourself out as a *mark to be shot at for so much per diem.* If a man enters into the military profession from interested motives he is generally disappointed; there being five hundred chances to one against his ever rising very high in it, merely by his *merit*, let it be ever so great. If *honor* directs his choice, still the consequence is nearly the same: for, if he loses his life in the service, his honor is consigned to the dust with his remains, and as speedily forgotten. Trust me, Charles, a man who has his living to get in the world had far better be a working *mechanic* than a *soldier./*

I hear your *adored* Fanny Elwood has played you a slippery trick; if I had not been informed by Major Herbert that you was fully convinced what a jade she was, I should be almost inclined to believe that the loss of *her* had turned your brain. But I cannot suppose you such a blockhead as to wear the willow upon her account. If that affair had not been at an end, I know not but I might have consented to your going into the army at once; for, then, it is likely a cannon ball would have afforded the speediest termination to your troubles, and I should have deemed it cruel to deprive you of the opportunity of trying so efficacious a remedy. As the case stands at present, it is unnecessary. So I beg I may hear no more of your *martial ardor, heroic courage*, or *rewards of merit*. Unfortunately, you forgot to speak of the *bed of honor*, – the most capital thing in a soldier's vocabulary. But, to be serious; remember I have assured you of my friendship; let that satisfy you till we meet; and do not forget that the *word* of a British merchant is as sacred as his *oath*; *I* dare not violate *mine:* only have patience a/ little longer, you will see how very unnecessary are all your pathetic lamentations upon those circumstances in which it has pleased the Almighty to place you, for a time; no doubt with a view to try the strength of your dependence upon his power. – Recollect that *he* has the hearts of all in his hand; let that secure your submission to his *will*, and your reliance upon his *mercy*; once again I repeat, set your mind at rest about the *future*, and be thankful to heaven for *present* enjoyments.

Mrs. Ellis, old John, and the two farmers, I suppose, imagine all of them that God never gave to any man but your father an honest and benevolent mind. I should be extremely glad to know upon what they found their right to judge, in this iniquitous manner, of the wisdom and goodness of their creator in his works? if they will please to wait patiently for conviction, perhaps their candor may compel them to allow that the successor of Frederick Montgomery discovers a noble emulation to follow such an example. Tell them I am ready to pass *my* word for him; if they/ are not satisfied with that, let them take *yours*; I' ll trouble myself no farther on the subject.

In a few days I shall prepare to gratify your curiosity; but I must dispatch this, immediately, as I am impatient to prevent the execution of your rash design. I cannot meet you at the Grove yet, or I would, upon this occasion have preferred it to writing; but the failure of two capital houses in the city,[27] in both of which I am concerned to a large amount, oblige me to remain here. As soon as I see how those matters are likely to terminate, I will prepare to see you; in the mean time, I beg you to write, and tell me you comply with my wishes; I shall be uneasy till I hear from you.

Yours, affectionately,
    PHILIP BERTILLS.

P. S. Give my best compliments to your friend Sir Edward Melworth; tell him I heartily wish I had him in my counting-house, for a few months, I would find him business sufficient to employ all his time, and leave him/ none to give to grief. I must be better acquainted with him, upon his sister's account; for I am in love with her *letters*, and that's the same thing as being in love with *her*. – I tell Rhoda so, but she mortifies my vanity by discovering no dread of the consequence of my attachment to her friend. While I am prating to you I shall be too late for my appointment at Lloyd's,[28] so adieu.

LETTER XXIV.

Charles Montgomery, Esq. to Mr. Philip Bertills, Merchant.

MELWORTH-HALL.

Dear sir,

HAVING been engaged out the whole of the day with Sir Edward Melworth, and the rest of the family, your letter has but this moment reached me; and, tho' I have scarce time to save the post, I cannot avoid writing a few lines to make your mind perfectly easy, and to assure you, at the same/ time, that I am inexpressibly concerned at having been the means of discomposing it. I beg leave to offer my grateful acknowledgments for the promise you make me of your friendship, and for the warm zeal you discover for my welfare. Be assured, sir, that I shall regard your advice as an honor, and will enter into nothing of importance that does not meet your concurrence; consequently, I shall obey the injunctions in your last. – From this time, I resign all thoughts of entering into the army. My best respects attend Miss Bertills, who I flatter myself, is now recovered, as you mentioned nothing about her health.

I am, dear sir, with esteem,
your most obliged, and
most obedient servant,
CHARLES MONTGOMERY./

LETTER XXV.

Mr. Philip Bertills, Merchant, to Charles Montgomery. Esq.

CHATHAM-PLACE.

Dear Charles,

YOUR last has dissipated all my fears for you, and now you may prepare for the long-concealed secret.

Frederick Montgomery was only nineteen when, by the decease of his father, he came into possession of the family estate. Being then pursuing his studies at Cambridge, and having a more ardent thirst after knowledge than the pleasures of gaiety and dissipation, he still continued the pursuit, and remained at the university till he had attained his twenty-third year. About that period I prevailed upon him, after repeated invitations, to spend a few months with me in London. I had then been married near two years, to one of the worthiest of her sex, and providence had blessed us with a lovely boy. My family/ was exactly suited to the taste of my friend, and he staid with us near a year. But there was an object far more pleasing than any other, that riveted him to the spot. This was a sister of Mrs. Bertill's, and the very counterpart of herself. Tho' Frederick ventured to hint that he thought Miss Musgrave had the advantage of her sister in point of beauty, we did not agree in that opinion; but, as I deemed it a very unimportant matter, I let him enjoy the flattering idea. With the consent of all parties concerned, a day was at length fixed for their union; when, alas! poor Miss Musgrave was seized with the small pox,[29] and expired two days previous to that which had been fixed on for her marriage!

The distress of your father was beyond description: – He could no longer bear the house, or the sight of any of the family; therefore left us and retired immediately to his seat in Sussex. Could he have flown from himself as well as from the town, he might have regained tranquility; but that was impossible. The bitterness of this afflictive disappointment, for a long time, overpowered every/ sweet. He was incapable of tasting any enjoyment the world afforded. – Buried in the gloom of the country, and secluded from society, he sunk into deep dejection; his letters too plainly testified the situation of his spirits; I grew miserable about him, and resolved on a journey into Sussex. – I set out; and, on my arrival, found with him his friend and fellow-collegian Lord Lucan, who was then going to France to pass the winter. Our united entreaties, at length prevailed with your father to accompany him thither. In a few months afterwards I had the satisfaction of hearing, that the diversity of scenes into which his Lordship led him, had, in a great measure, restored both his health and spirits. At the return of spring they separated; Lord Lucan being under a necessity to come home, and your father chusing to continue abroad, he spent near another year in Italy, from whence he returned again to pass a winter in France.

During the time he was at Paris, he was introduced to the acquaintance of the Comtesse de R—, at that time the most celebrated beauty in that city. This lady, tho' born in/ France, was the daughter of a Scotch nobleman, whose strong attachment to the Stuart line had led him to take so active a part in the rebellion, in the memorable year of forty-five,[30] that he was under a necessity of taking refuge in France. His lady and two young sons were the companions of his exile; the former was some months advanced in her pregnancy, when they arrived in that kingdom, and was soon after delivered of the above-mentioned daughter; but herself died in childbed. Miss Macdonald was, of course, educated in a convent, where she remained till she was seventeen; at which time, she was brought out into the world and married to the young Comte de R—, an officer of distinction, belonging to the same regiment in which her two brothers served. This being an union in which the heart of the Comtesse had no share, it is not to be supposed she felt much distress at finding herself, by the death of the Comte, in possession of a large fortune; and the uncontrolled mistress of that and her own conduct, at so early a period of her life as the age of twenty. – A love of gaiety and dissipation predominated/ in her mind; and her house soon became a receptacle for all persons of rank and fashion.

Frederick being then what the women call an elegant and accomplished young man, it is not in the least surprising that the Comtesse should distinguish him above the rest by marks of the most particular attention; but she was not calculated to attach his heart; the dissimilarity of their minds being far too apparent for him to entertain a thought of her in the matrimonial way; even if the difference in their religious opinions had not opposed the union. It is almost unnecessary to tell you *that* circumstance would appear to him an insurmountable barrier; and, as he had none of the principles of a libertine, he would have abhorred the idea of taking advantage of her tenderness towards him to enter into a criminal connection. The error in his conduct was not the effect of premeditation; his vanity slept too long, and made him blind to all her advances: and, attributing her behavior to nothing more than the freedom natural to most of her countrywomen, he continued to be engaged in her parties./

Going one day to visit her, he found her confined to her chamber by a slight indisposition; his inclination would have led him to depart without seeing her; but, in France, that was impossible, without renouncing, for ever, all *pretentions* to politeness, or even common civility. He therefore suffered himself to be conducted to her apartment. She was in bed, and alone; having dismissed her attendants at his entrance. I shall throw a veil over the rest, and only say, that it was not very long after this interview when he received a letter from the Comtesse informing him of the consequence; and soliciting his assistance in planning some method to conceal her disgraceful situation from the world. Her letter was evidently written in all the agonies of remorse and shame. She expressed the deepest contrition at having, in an unguarded hour, suffered passion to gain the ascendancy over reason. Frederick confessed to me he was horror-struck at the perusal. His high sense of honor dictated, at once, his making her an immediate reparation by marriage. He felt no affection for her; – he had an almost invincible/ repugnance to so close a connection with a woman whose religious sentiments were so materially opposite to his own; – but he determined to surmount these obstacles to her peace and reputation.

He went directly to her, and made the proposal, but how was he surprised to find his offer *totally rejected!* She acknowledged his generosity; candidly avowed her affection for him; and voluntarily exculpated him from having used any artifice to seduce her into vice: but, at the same time, declared, in the *strongest* terms that it was utterly impossible, consistently with her ideas of honor, ever to become his wife under such degrading circumstances. He pleaded powerfully in behalf of the unborn infant. She had all the pride of her ancestors and would not, even to legitimate her child, run the risk of being looked down upon by the only man in the creation whose esteem was of any real value to her.

Thus, after using many ineffectual arguments and intreaties, he was compelled to give up the point, and it was, at length, agreed between them that my friend should write me/ an account of the whole affair, requesting me to provide a suitable house for her reception, in some retired situation; and then take Mrs. Bertills over to Paris to visit the Comtesse, who would return with us to visit England, leaving him in Paris, where he was to remain till near the time of her delivery, to prevent the *cause* of the Comtesse's removal being suspected. We complied with this request; took for her a handsome house, in a retired village in the West of England; and placed the necessary servants there. Mrs. Ellis, – who then lived with Mrs. Bertills as her waiting-woman, and who, from long experience, we knew was to be depended upon, – was engaged to serve the Comtesse in the same capacity during her temporary residence. Thus, having expeditiously prepared every thing for the occasion, we set off for Paris; and, in ten days, brought the Comtesse back with us; and, having seen my charge safely disposed of, I left Mrs. Bertills with her, for a few weeks, and came to London. Every letter I received from your father demonstrated a most humane anxiety for the situation of the unhappy/ Comtesse, but it was an anxiety not proceeding from love; and I rejoiced that she had not been influenced by any regard for him, or for her own reputation, to consent to a marriage.

When she was within a month of her time, Frederick left Paris; came over, and retired to a lodging in the same village with her. He visited her frequently, but Mrs. Bertills was always present at their interviews; having, at their united request, joined the Comtesse two days before *his* arrival. As soon as business would permit, I followed her, and was there when the Comtesse was safely delivered of yourself. Ever shall I remember the affecting scene when you was first presented to your father. He wept over you; and pathetically lamented the stigma which his own misconduct had entailed upon *you* – the innocent fruits of a criminal indulgence. In the first moments of your existence, he felt the full force of parental affection. – It increased daily; and he determined not only to remain single on your account, but, if possible, to hide both from the world and from yourself the circumstance of your illegitimacy, as the most/ effectual way of securing *you* from scorn and contempt, and *himself* from the dread of your future reproaches for having subjected you to it. He consulted me upon the management of it; but after much conversation on the subject, we were at length obliged to refer the matter to Mrs. Bertills, whose good sense, assisted by her benevolence, presently struck out a plan which, with the concurrence of your mother, was adopted. You were to bear the name of Montgomery, and to pass for the child of a lady whom your father had *married* and *buried* abroad; and Mrs. Ellis was to have the care of you, as the person who had been sent to fetch you over. This agreed to, it was necessary, under the seal of secrecy, to inform her of the whole truth: for she, as well as the other servants, had imagined that the Comtesse was pregnant with you at the time of the Comte's decease; old John, who was then your father's valet, having, agreeably to the promise he had made on their arrival, never contradicted that idea. Mrs. Ellis appeared surprised at so unexpected an explanation; but readily promised, as did old John,/ to preserve the secret inviolably, and they have faithfully adhered to their word.

The most material point thus adjusted, your father went off to Dover; after which, you were christened; and your mother, having a predeliction for the name of Charles, gave it to *you*. In a week you, with Mrs. Ellis, followed my friend to Dover; from whence he took you both to his seat in Sussex; where you were thought, by every one, to be his legal heir. Mrs. Bertills and I staid only a few days after your departure; but the Comtesse continued in her house another month; at the expiration of which she discharged her servants, and came to London; – where we had taken her suitable apartments, and engaged a carriage for her, with the neccessary attendants. Having many acquaintance amongst the *great* and *gay*, she remained in the metropolis long enough to partake of all the various amusements it affords, and then set out for Scotland to visit some relations there whom she had never seen. After continuing amongst them three months, she determined on returning again to France; tho'/ not without making your father's seat in her way. There, in compliance with her wishes, Mrs. Bertills and I again met her. The maternal fondness she could not conceal, was disguised by her professing to have had a tender friendship for your mother, from her earliest remembrance. After a few days stay in Sussex, she took an affecting farewell of you and Mrs. Bertills; and, attended by your father and me, went to Dover, where it was not without some degree of pain that we saw her embark for Calais. Both of us had a *presentiment* that we should never see her more; and the event proved it *just*: – for, finding herself unable to conquer her attachment to my friend, and growing disgusted with the world, she soon quitted it, and retired into a convent, where she was presently carried off by an epidemic fever, of the malignant kind that raged with violence in the house and swept off numbers of its inhabitants. She was, in person, a very fine young woman; possessed of an agreeable temper, and solid understanding; but, with these advantages, she was not formed to make Frederick happy/ in a marriage state. A French Education had given her too much levity in her manners to please an English husband; and her ancestors had left her the inheritance of a high, haughty spirit, which gave her an air of insolence. She expressed a wish to settle part of her fortune upon you; but my friend would by no means suffer it, vowing to her, at the time, his firm determination to provide handsomely for you, and I have not a doubt he *intended* it.

And now, Charles, as some account of my own life has unavoidably been connected with the foregoing, I will add, that in a few weeks after the departure of the Comtesse, my family was increased by the birth of another son, and in something less than two years more of a daughter. Both my sons were carried off by consumptive disorders, in consequence of the meazles, and my beloved – my amiable wife, was so far overcome by this afflictive stroke, that she survived them only a few months. My distress for these repeated losses, was great indeed! – but every look given me by my infant Rhoda, seemed to say, *live for me./* I determined to attempt it, that she might not be left without a protector; Yet I believe that even my wish to preserve life, upon her account, would not have enabled me to conquer my sorrows, if I had not been engaged in commerce. I formed a resolution to devote my principal attention to it; and I soon found trade was the best restorative to health and spirits, as the employment it produced left me but little leisure to reflect upon my troubles. And to avoid devoting *that little* to so useless a purpose, I spent it with your father, in Sussex, till he purchased the estate in Yorkshire; and, in consequence, removed to Fir-grove; the distance of which prevented my enjoying the pleasure of seeing him so often as formerly, and conversation was changed into correspondence by letters.

Having now, my dear Charles, complied with your wishes, I shall only tell you farther, that this day three weeks, – by way of fulfilling a foolish promise made to Rhoda, in a moment of parental fondness, – I shall set out with her to enjoy the pleasures of Scarborough; where I intend to give her the slip, and join/ you at the Grove in a fortnight after. It must be allowed, this said jaunt is a very wise scheme of mine, at *this time*, when *Prudence* would direct me to stay at home and live *savingly*: but her dictates are often disregarded, as is the case now; for *Pleasure* disguising herself under the mantle of *Truth*, says, a promise ought to be held sacred. This argument cannot be controverted; therefore, her mandate is to be obeyed; and to Scarborough we go, notwithstanding I am likely to sit down with a loss of seventeen hundred pounds, by *one* of the failures I mentioned to you in my last, and two thousand by the *other*. Heigh-ho! these are dismal subjects, and must not be dwelt upon.

I intreat you will endeavor to regain your spirits against our meeting; therefore let me advise you, Charles, to go and visit some other friend, who is not oppressed with sorrow. Sir Edward Melworth and you are by no means proper company for each other, at present. Apropos, tell your friend that I am forming a design upon him: it is nothing less than bringing him up to town with me, either/ by force or stratagem; annihilating his title, for a while; and making him my head clerk till the drudgery of business releases him from the slavery of grief and melancholy.

Yours, sincerely,
PHILIP BERTILLS.

LETTER XXVI.

Charles Montgomery, Esq. to Mr. Philip Bertills, Merchant.

HARROWGATE.

Dear sir,

My warmest acknowledgments are justly due to you, for the trouble you have taken to gratify my curiosity: but how shall I sufficiently express the gratitude which warms my heart, when I reflect, how greatly I am your debtor, for the kind assistance you afforded in securing me from the scorn of the world; which, in such cases, is often too apt to confound the innocent with/ the guilty: – for this, my dear sir, accept my best thanks. – I would say more, but no words whatever could fully convey to you a just idea of my feelings. I should be equally at a loss to give you a conception of my sensations upon perusing the whole of the account, nor will I pain your sensibility by the attempt; I will only add, that I bedewed the memory of both my parents with tears.

I hope, my dear sir, I shall not incur, in your opinion, the imputation of treating your advice with disrespect, when I add, that tho' I am removed to this place, I am not separated from my friend Sir Edward; on the contrary, I persuaded him to accompany me in the excursion, with the hope of his deriving some advantage from the change of scene and variety of company; as the latter are numerous, of course, gaiety and chearfulness predominate. – I find it already takes a good effect upon me, and I hope it will have the same upon my friend. We intend continuing here till within a few days of the time you have fixed on for being at the Grove; we shall then part; Sir Edward having agreed to attend/ Mrs. Horton and his sister to Scarborough, to give the latter lady an opportunity of joining the beloved companion of her childhood, Miss Bertills; in whose praise Miss Melworth speaks warmly.

I am very sorry to hear you are likely to sustain so heavy a loss by the failures you mention; your strict attention to trade merits a better return. – Happily, however, you are able to support it without inconveniency. I beg my best respects to Miss Bertills, and am,

dear sir,

with the utmost esteem,

your obedient servant,

CHARLES MONTGOMERY./

LETTER XXVII.

The Hon. Augustus Fitzmaurice, to Charles Montgomery, Esq.

WESTBROOK-LODGE.

PREPARE yourself, Charles, for a piece of *excellent* news. If you are as much my friend as I believe you to be, you *must* think it so. Lady Lucan is quite well! That foolish fellow, Humphrey, when he came to the Hall with an account of her illness, alarmed me causelessly: but I should not blame the poor fellow; since it was only his value for his lady that magnified his fears, and represented her indisposition as a *dangerous* one. It was happy for me that I heard the intelligence in no other company than that of yourself, and the Melworth family; as I might, possibly, have had the severest shafts of ridicule levelled at me for discovering so much weakness upon a mother's account.

Her ladyship had, it seems, eaten something that had disagreed with her stomach;/ and my father, ever tenderly solicitous about her, after persuading her to lie down upon the bed, dispatched honest Humphrey for the physician. The good creature set spurs to his horse; sent away the doctor; and then, concluding *my* presence to be equally necessary, went forwards to me; and, by this simple mistake of his, was I prevented from partaking with you of the pleasures of Harrowgate. But let me not speak of that as a pleasure which would, in reality, have afforded me none. I am ten times happier where I am; therefore do not expect me to join you there; I should then be at least ten miles *farther* distant from Melworth-hall. In my last visit to that place, I found myself in the oddest way I ever was in, in my life; – I could not conceive what was the matter with me. – At first, I began to be frightened; thinking I certainly was going to be very ill. – I examined my pulse; *that* was as well as usual. Then I concluded that my disorder lay in the *brain*, and that my senses were likely to be disagreeably affected; but, on a thorough investigation of the matter, I was convinced of my mistake;/ nothing very uncommon was amiss there. At length, on recollecting all the symptoms, I discovered that my disorder was seated in the *heart*, and was the effect of witchcraft! It is very true, Charles, I am bewitched; absolutely bewitched! but the *spells* and *charms* operate upon me in so pleasing a manner, that I have never yet entertained a single wish to exorcise the spirit that has taken entire possession of all my faculties, mental and corporeal. Now would I give something to know whether your sagacious worship is able to penetrate into this great and grand mystery; if not, take my word for it, my boy, you were never *really* in love. – The passion you felt for Fanny Elwood, proceeded merely from the strength of your imagination, not your affection; therefore, to prevent your stumbling into such another mistake, I'll e'en take the trouble to give you a slight sketch of the true symptoms, as I have experienced them.

In company with Miss Melworth, I feel a serene, tranquil delight, unknown to me before. The awe her presence creates, deprives me, in a great measure, of the use of my tongue;/ but to atone for that, the two senses of hearing and seeing are amply gratified; her conversation, dictated by good sense and enlivened by innocent chearfulness, sinks deep into my heart. Her voice is harmony itself, and vibrates on my ear more pleasingly than the most delicate touches of the finest toned instrument. The elegant symmetry of her person, and the animated beauty of her countenance, strikes me with pleasing wonder; and I forget the use of all my other senses in the satisfaction of gazing.

Absent from her, I am thoughtful and inattentive to surrounding objects; her dear idea pervades my whole soul; and, in the hours of rest, chases sleep from my eyes, till exhausted nature reluctantly yields: then busy fancy again presents in dreams the angelic Harriet to my view, arrayed in all the charms of native elegance and simplicity; and, on awaking, I sigh to find it all a *dream*. I have here given you but a very indifferent sketch of the symptoms; and, indeed, a man, who is so thoroughly in love as I am, is as little qualified to describe it coherently, as a person in a/ fever and delirious is to give his physician a regular account of the symptoms attending his disease. Love itself may justly be compared to a delirium; as it takes an entire possession of the senses: for instance, I can neither think nor converse on any other subject but the charming Harriet Melworth; and, when addressed to in conversation, if I answer at all, it is generally foreign to the point. Yesterday we had a drawing-room full of visitors, amongst whom was that tiresome, little coquette, Lady Bab Stanfield. – She, I suppose, had an inclination to torment some of her fancied admirers by flirting a little with me; in consequence of which, it so fell out, that we two got seated together upon a sopha: but as I was not in the least inclined to talk, her ladyship was forced to begin; – a five minutes' silence being, in her ideas, I believe, a five minutes' purgatory.

'Lord! Mr. Fitzmaurice!' cried she, 'you have surprised me so, you can't think! for, I declare to heaven, I had not the least idea in the world of seeing you here; and, at first, I really took you for an apparition!/ Lady Lucan told me, a few days ago, that you was going with a party to Harrowgate; but I suppose you altered your mind, and did not go, for you have hardly been there and back in this time?'

'In about three weeks,' returned I, 'she goes to Scarborough, Lady Bab, she gives that the preference.'

'Ha! ha! ha! well, I vow, Fitzmaurice,' – exclaimed she, still laughing, – this is a good jest indeed! why what's the matter with your intellects? for I am sure they are not in a state of comprehension. I do not think you know one word I said; I was not speaking about Lady Lucan's going to Scarborough – I know very well what time she goes there. But, G-d forgive me, how forgetful I am! I had like to have forgot asking you, if Lord M— has sent you a ticket for the concert at his house next week? – they tell me he has engaged that inchanting Signora – *some-*

thing – I forget what – to sing there. What a heavenly voice she has! I would not miss hearing her for all the world; would you?'/

'She sings very agreeably, Lady Bab,' replied I, 'but that is her least accomplishment; – her mental endowments are far superior; – and even beautiful as she is –'

'Lord bless me! *beautiful!* – interrupted Lady Bab, in the utmost surprise, – 'why, Fitzmaurice, you certainly must be mad and not know what you are talking of! *She beautiful?* I think she is the ugliest creature I ever set my eyes on in my life! and, as to her mental endowments, I care nothing about them. – But,' continued she, 'I never knew before you was so well acquainted with her.'

Some of the rest of the company taking up the subject, and pronouncing the said Signora to be a very ordinary woman, I was roused from my reverie, and forced to confess I had never seen her. This raised the laugh against me, and Lady Bab repeating the whole of our conversation, it was declared by every one, that I was absolutely in love: upon which discovery, I, of course, passed the ordeal of common-place raillery, and had no other resource from a tedious indurance of it, but/ by flirting away the rest of the afternoon with Lady Bab. Remember me to Edward, I hope he, and you too will find benefit from the air of Harrowgate.

I am yours,
AUGUSTUS FITZMAURICE.

LETTER XXVIII.

Charles Montgomery Esq. to the Hon. Augustus Fitzmaurice.

HARROWGATE.

YOUR letter gave me great pleasure; – I rejoice to hear Lady Lucan is well, and sincerely congratulate you upon it. – The filial affection you demonstrated at the news of her illness, and the joy you express on her recovery, do the highest honor to your heart; while the judicious choice you have made in the object of a still more tender attachment, reflects equal lustre upon your judgment. May Miss Melworth be as propitious to your wishes as/ her brother is! He tells me, that he thinks he discovered your love for her before you were sensible of it yourself: after saying this, he added a few encouraging things, which it is not so proper you should be acquainted with yet, lest you grow too vain.

I wish I could give you a better account of the health of our friend Sir Edward; some very *wise ones* here think him in a consumption, and give many significant glances and expressive shrugs; but, notwithstanding this, he has still very powerful attractions for the fair sex. Lady Gertrude Carruther, a fine *blooming virgin* of forty-four, is laying strong siege to his heart; and, tho' she meets with many repulses, remains undaunted, and continues her attacks daily with renewed vigor. The little blind urchin is engaged in her service; and, at every glance of her eye, sends forth his arrows in abundance: but, unfortunately for her, not one of them has succeeded; and, I fancy, she will find Edward's heart as impregnable as the rock of Gibraltar. Heaven forbid it should ever be otherwise to *her*, for I am certain she would soon torment him to death with her tongue;/ it never ceases; and there is an utter impossibility of enjoying one's own thoughts, for a moment, where she is present. Added to this, her consummate quackery[31] renders her almost an insupportable companion: – She has got all the physical jargon by rote; and, I verily believe, thinks herself as well skilled in theory and practice, as the first physician in the kingdom. You would laugh heartily, Augustus, to hear her holding forth to Edward upon his complaints, and prescribing for him with the utmost self-consequence, mingled with an affectation of all imaginable tenderness. When we met at breakfast, this morning, she began thus:

'Good morning to you, Sir Edward; I hope you rested well; I have been extremely unhappy indeed about you, all night; I could not sleep for thinking of you.'

'You do me too much honor, madam,' – returned he, bowing gracefully, – 'I am very sorry that so insignificant an object as I am should be the means of breaking your ladyship's repose.'

'Really, sir,' – resumed she, concealing/ part of her face with her handkerchief, as if to hide her blushes, – 'you entertain *too* mean an opinion of yourself; it is impossible that any of your friends should not be interested in your complaints. I am really grieved to see you look so poorly to-day; these nasty nervous disorders[32] are very hard to be conquered; and, I am greatly afraid, the air of Harrowgate does not agree with you.' Then turning to me, added, – 'What do *you* think, Mr. Montgomery? can *you* perceive any alteration, for the better, in your friend?'

'Our time here has been so short, my lady,' replied I, 'that it is scarce sufficient to form a judgment upon; but the air has certainly made no alteration for the *worse* in Sir Edward yet.'

'My dear sir,' cried she, 'you do not understand these matters so well as I do; a single day is quite sufficient to form a judgement of the effects of the air; if in that time it does not appear to do good, it will infallibly prove injurious; and such kind of complaints as your friend's are not to be trifled with.' Then addressing him, she/ said, 'I am sorry, Sir Edward, I have not influence enough to prevail with you to try that medicine I recommended to you yesterday; I am certain it would do you infinite service.'

'Possibly it might, Lady Gertrude,' – replied he, with a half-smile, – 'but the nauseous ingredients you compose it of, make the remedy appear to me, if not *worse*, yet, at least, *equal* to the disease.'

'Ah! I know well,' – resumed her ladyship, laughing, – 'what cowards you all are at encountering an unpalatable medicine: but, as I cannot persuade you to take that, suffer me to intreat you will try the effect of the Bristol waters,[33] this season; there is nothing disagreeable in them, and my recommendation is warranted by my own experience of their efficacy. I was once far gone indeed, in a nervous disorder, much in the same way you are in, sir, and they raised me from the very borders of the grave!'

'I do not think myself,' returned Edward, 'quite in so bad a state as that, madam;/ yet, I assure you, I will not object to try that part of your recommendation.'

'You rejoice me to hear you say so, sir,' cried she, 'for I have not a doubt of its proving sufficiently efficacious to remove your disease. – Those waters will take an amazing effect upon your spirits; the second glass will enable you to breathe abundantly more freely; and then, of course, your cough will diminish, as will those pleuretic pains, the constant attendant of these disorders, and the hectic heat will be presently carried off by perspiration.' As I had never heard him complain of any one of these symptoms, except dejection of spirits, I sat in silent astonishment, while Lady Gertrude proceeded thus: 'but indeed, Sir Edward, you require the tender attention of one of my sex; for you stand in need of a little *good nursing*; therefore, as I always go to Bristol, every season, I'll suit my time to yours, that you may have a tender female friend on the spot, to take a little care of you. – Tho', undoubtedly, the attentions of a wife would be far superior to any that it/ would be in my power, as a friend, to pay to you; and, seriously, I would advise you, for your own sake, to *marry* directly.'

'Good heavens, madam!' – exclaimed he, with a smile, – '*marry?* what with such a long catalogue of disorders upon me, as you have pointed out? It is true I am not sensible of them myself; but *you* certainly must know best; and I will not pretend to dispute the superiority of your judgment. I will only observe, that since you have taken the trouble to point out to me my dangerous situation, matrimony appears, to me, a thing quite out of the question; it is more necessary to turn my thoughts entirely to the grave.'

'Oh, sir,' resumed she, 'you mistake me quite; I do not look upon you to be so far gone as that neither: I have not a fear of your being yet irrecoverable; with proper care, I dare say you will do very well again; and I think that the tender attention of an affectionate wife, would greatly facilitate your restoration to health; – a little good nursing does a great deal.'/

'I readily admit *that*, Lady Gertrude,' said Edward, 'but pardon me if I add, that I positively cannot *now* follow your kind advice, even if I had an opportunity. Possibly such a thing as matrimony might have entered my head sometime or other, if your ladyship had not made me fully acquainted with the nature of my disorder, and opened my eyes to a thorough knowledge of the natural consequence of it. No; I could never think of involving an amiable woman in all the

horrors of a sick-bed attendance, from the narrow motive of being myself better
attended than by an hireling nurse.'

'You think *too* nicely, Sir Edward,' returned this kind hearted *fair-one*, 'self-
preservation is, you know, the first law of nature; therefore, it is a duty incumbent
upon you to think seriously of adopting the plan I advise. Remember, sir, every
amiable woman who loves her husband, with the tenderness she ought, will feel
all her trouble fully compensated by reflecting, that she is contributing to his
ease and comfort. I am/ very certain,' – she added, with a languishing look and a
deep sigh, – 'I should think so.'

'The humanity and tenderness of your amiable and lovely sex, my Lady,'
– said our friend, with great gravity, – 'is not, for a moment, to be doubted:
those heaven-born virtues are its most distinguishing ornament, and give you an
irresistible claim to our profoundest respect. – But permit me to ask, madam,
what man in the world, possessed of a spark of goodness, could, in my unhappy
situation, offer his hand to any lady whatever? Consider, accurately, the circumstances of the case, and you will see the impropriety as clearly as I do. Thus visibly
sinking to the earth, under the complicated weight of such dreadful disorders as
a *dejection of spirits*, an *asthmatic oppression of breath*, a *nervous cough, pleuretic
pains*, and a *hectic fever!* – with what degree of assurance could such a being offer
himself to the acceptance of one who, if she had good sense, must see the motive
of his conduct; and if she did not reject, with disdain, him of whom she *must*
entertain the/ most contemptible opinion, she would deserve to be despised herself; and no one would be more likely to despise such a woman than *I* should.'

'Oh fye, Sir Edward!' resumed she, 'I did not think you could have been so
severe; you seem to condemn, as a *crime*, what most others would esteem as a *virtue*. A woman of *tenderness* and *sensibility*, may oft-times be made very unhappy,
by being obliged, thro' the necessary attention to decorum and character, to
neglect the performance of those kind offices to a sick *friend*, which she might
perform without a dread of censure under the honorable title of wife.'

'That may perhaps be the case sometimes, Lady Gertrude,' returned he, 'but
then the attachment must have commenced previous to the sickness.'

'Perhaps not, sir,' replied she; he shook his head, doubtingly, and she added,
but I see you are not likely to become a proselyte to my sentiments; you are really
the most incorrigible creature I ever met with; so good morning to you, it is time
for me to dress.'/

Her ladyship then tripped away with the affected air of a girl of sixteen; after
which we ordered our horses and rode out; enjoying, on our way, much laughter
at her expence. Upon the whole, I believe this conversation has been of some
service to Sir Edward, in having afforded him diversion; he has been in better
spirits since, than I have seen him for many months past. – Upon my making the
observation to him, just now, he replied,

'Why, really, Charles, Lady Gertrude's attacks begin to grow so very formidable, that I must either quit the field, coward like, or rally the whole force of my spirits to repel her advances; and I think I shall prefer the *latter* a little longer.' So you see, Augustus, we have a fine fund of amusement before us! I have only room to say,

I am your friend,
CHARLES MONTGOMERY./

LETTER XXIX.

The Hon. Augustus Fitzmaurice, to Charles Montgomery, Esq.

WESTBROOK-LODGE.

You have, I'll allow, thrown a strong temptation in my way, but it will not do. No, Charles, notwithstanding all the entertainment I should derive from developing the character of your sentimental Lady Gertrude Carruther, yet, such a foolish love-sick puppy am I, that I cannot reconcile my mind to the idea of removing so much *farther* from the lovely, the captivating Harriet Melworth; tho' I might as well be an hundred leagues off at once, for no pretence can I form that appears plausible enough for visiting her in the absence of her brother, and I dare not shew my face at the Hall without a proper apology for it. – Yet, I do believe, from my conscience, that the sweet girl would not be displeased at seeing me. '*Vanity! vanity!*' –/ I know you will say; well, say so, if you will, I care not; 'tis a part of the foundation on which a lover's hopes are built, consequently, there is no such thing as doing without it; therefore, I tell you plainly, that I *have* the vanity to think her sparkling eye, when directed towards me, expressed a 'sympathy of soul.' And *this* is one of the '*encouraging things*' Sir Edward told you, and which you chuse to make such a mighty secret of; but remember, my boy, a time may come when I may have it in my power to be even with you, and then beware of my revenge.

But really, Charles, I cannot help regretting too, that such a charming laughter-moving subject as Lady Gertrude would prove, if properly treated, should be reserved for an exhibition to two such dull mortals as Edward and you. Why, neither of you possess half spirit enough to make the most of it. If I was with you, I would play her off to the utmost advantage, for the benefit of the spectators; and, for that purpose, I struggled hard every day last week to conquer myself, and set out to join you at Harrowgate, but in vain;/ for, mount my horse when I will, I can turn his head no other way than towards Melworthhall. So you must e'en do the best you can with your languishing *virgin-tabby*,[34] without any assistance from me. I know I should greatly contribute to heighten the mirth she affords you, but I cannot put so great a restraint upon my inclinations, for your amuse-

ment. – However, tho' tis against myself, friendship compels me to say, I hope Edward will remain at Harrowgate as long as he can. I venture to pronounce, that her ladyship will prove an excellent physician to him. The oppression upon his breath, which her deep penetration has discovered, she will remove presently by obliging him to exercise his lungs in answering her; his dejection of spirits will be carried off by laughter; and his hectic fever, by the perspiration excited by both. Thus, you see, the most formidable of his numerous complaints will soon vanish, and all the rest will follow their companions of course. But let her not pour any of her confounded nostrums down his throat, I beseech you; tell/ her she has skill enough to cure him without; she'll easily digest the compliment. I am going to attend Lord and Lady Lucan on a visit; the carriage waits only for
　　your friend,
　　　AUGUSTUS FITZMAURICE.

LETTER XXX.

The same, to the same.

WESTBROOK-LODGE.

ONE letter is no sooner sent off, than I prepare to dispatch *another* to you. I hope, Charles, you will acknowledge, as you ought, the mighty obligation, – for mighty it is, when you consider how very precious my time is, – every hour devoted to any other purpose than talking or thinking of the engaging Harriet Melworth, is set down, in my calendar, as totally *lost*; at present, however, I mean to/ write upon subjects with which she is so closely connected, that my own inclination will not be wholly ungratified. I concluded my last to go with Lord and Lady Lucan, to pay our respects to the Earl and Countess of Castleton, who had arrived at their seat the day before. I believe, Charles, they are not amongst the number of your acquaintance. – I have known them long. They are, now, past the meridian of life; yet, still, there is something in the manners of both, so extremely pleasing, that while they create your respect, they command your affection and confidence. The Duke of —, married their second daughter, two years ago; the match was not highly agreeable to them, as it was extremely disproportionate in point of age; his Grace being full eight years older than Lord Castleton: but a ducal coronet was not to be resisted; and the remonstrances of her parents, who did not fail to delineate to her, in striking colors, the imprudence and folly of such an union, were all ineffectual; she was determined to be a duchess; and a duchess she is: but, I think, her high rank cannot be a compensation for the misery/ she must endure with such a companion. – His tongue is as glib as glass; and he makes it a difficulty for any one else to put in a word when he is present. He and his Duchess are come down now, with the Castleton family. I had, upon this visit, the honor of being in his Grace's company, for the first time. We had not been in the house five minutes, – nay, I believe, we were scarce seated, – when the Duke, as he sat looking thro' the window, began with saying,

'Yours is a charming park, my Lord; a charming park indeed! well stocked with deer, too; plenty of game, ha, my Lord? plenty of game I suppose? and then those rows of fine, tall elms up the avenue, have a very pretty effect indeed! Ay, ay, your uncle knew what he was about, when he bought this estate. – I say, my Lord, he knew what he was about; its a fine place – a fine situation indeed! But, I say, he lived to a good old age, ha, ha, ha!'

'Not a day *too* long, my Lord Duke,' returned the Earl, 'he was a very worthy character, and has left few that equal him.'

'Very true, very true, my Lord,' interrupted/ the Duke, 'you say quite right; he was a worthy man; many a pleasant hour have I spent in his company. He had but one fault, my Lord, only *one*; he was a little too fond of the measures of government. He did not sit in our house, you know; but my friend W—, who sat in the House of Commons, and was, at that time, member for —, used to tell me so. – He had a sad piece of work to get returned as the sitting member. Your uncle's interest was against him; arid yet Jack W— was a clever fellow, too. – He was a little bandy-legged, or so, but that was nothing; he always said it was the fault of his *nurse*. She ought to have taken more care, if it had been only from gratitude; for I remember he told me she was the wife of a soldier in his father's regiment; his father made the man a serjeant for bearing away the enemy's colors, at the time we obtained that compleat victory there over the French. You, doubtless, remember the time, my Lord? that was a glorious day, a very glorious day indeed for old England! Ah! poor General/ Wolfe![35] he was a brave fellow, we have no such Generals now-a-days, my Lord? No, no, those times are over; – Britons are degenerating.'

'Your Grace and I differ in opinion, in that respect;' cried the Earl, 'I am certain we have as brave men now, both in army and navy, as ever we had: witness the gallant feats of Rodney; and the noble resistance made by the brave Elliot, in the siege of Gibraltar.[36] – Where will you find, in the annals of history, –'

'Right, right!' interrupted his Grace, 'Elliot is, I confess, a fine old veteran, my Lord; a little past the prime of life, to be sure; but what's that? just nothing at all; he can fight as well as ever; he always loved it. I remember him a young man, and then he would stand an hour to hear an old soldier give an account of a battle he had been engaged in; and, all the time he was attending to it, you might see he was fired with emulation. The first time I visited at Lord M—'s, after I came from college, I met Elliot there; it was just as/ M— was come to his title and estate. – He had then been married about a month, to the daughter of Sir Archibald Lockwood; and he got devorced in less than three years after: for Lady M— took a fancy to Colonel S—, of the Guards, and they went off together. The affair made a great noise for about eight or nine days, but nobody minded it after. S— soon came back again, and left her: or his father paid all his debts, in his absence, in hopes that would be a means of bringing him; and it proved the best method he could have devised. I dare say you remember the Colonel's father, my Lord, do n't you? Poor old S—! he was remarkably fond of pictures. Mrs. S— and he used often to disagree about it; ha, ha, ha! The old lady had not much taste that way, and did not like he should part with his money for them. I once met him, accidentally, in Italy, when he was over there, purchasing some very fine pieces. Sir Simeon Clarkson was with him, then. Sir Simeon was a city alderman; and was knighted, you know, on/ carrying up an address. He had a second cousin, I forget his name – but he was a lieutenant in the — regiment; he was a fine fighter, and ought to have been preferred; but, having no interest among the people in power, he soon found his services slighted; and, in a fit of resentment, sold out, and entered into a foreign service, married a foreign lady of large fortune, and, –'

Lady Castleton, wearied with the Duke's nonsense, I suppose, and imagining that we were also, proposed a walk in the gardens, and we left him and the Earl to themselves. The former, I would venture almost to swear, never missed us, so intent was he upon talking. The weather being very hot, we seated ourselves in a beautiful temple, at the end of the terrace, and entered into social converse: in the course of it, her ladyship told us she was going to Scarborough earlier this season than usual, having engaged to meet there a young lady from London, a Miss Bertills; whose father, she added, had occasion to go to some other part of the county for a short time, and, during his absence, was to leave his daughter/ under the protection of her ladyship. She then spoke in very high terms of Miss Bertills; nor did she speak less favorably of her father, whom she had known, she said, many years; having been intimate with him and Mrs. Bertills long before the latter had a right to that appellation.

'I think, Mr. Fitzmaurice,' – said Lady Castleton, to me, – 'I have heard you speak of Sir Edward Melworth, have not I?'

'Yes, you have, often, my lady,' I replied, 'he is a very particular friend of mine.'

'It must, I think, then,' resumed she, 'be a sister of his who is to join our party at Scarborough; Sir Edward has a sister, who is likewise his ward, and reckoned a very pleasing young woman, has he not, sir?'

Would you believe it, Charles, I was such an idiot as to redden like scarlet, and tremble from head to foot, at the bare mention of her; and it was with the utmost difficulty that I could conquer my confusion so far as to articulate an affirmative in reply to Lady Castleton's question. My father sitting opposite/ to me observed the change, and, not knowing from what cause it proceeded, became immediately alarmed, and eagerly exclaimed,

'God bless me! I am sure you are not well, Augustus, for heaven's sake speak, and tell me what's the matter with you?'

My mother too was terrified, and, rising hastily from her seat, came towards me.

'My dear son,' cried she, 'I fear you are very ill. I have seen an alteration in you for some time past: you must have advice immediately.'

I took my mother's hand, as she stood leaning over me, and, kissing it, said,

'My dearest madam, pray make yourself easy; indeed, I am well now; perhaps the heat of the weather was a little too much for me; but my indisposition was nothing more than a slight palpitation of heart, which has quite left me. Believe me, my lord,' to my father, 'I am *perfectly* recovered.'

And I really told him the truth, Charles, but my veracity, in this instance, I found was not to be depended upon. Lady Castleton/ had ordered drops and water, and I was absolutely obliged to swallow them. However, this said frightful, alarming indisposition of mine, not only put an end to the conversation, but likewise to our visit; for Lady Lucan, tenderly anxious that her son should have advice, and every proper care taken, in time, requested the carriage to be ordered directly, and we came away. This, alas! is one of the misfortunes of being an only child! When we drove off,

'Augustus,' said my mother, 'you have done very wrong to conceal from us your indisposition till you could do it no longer; you know, my dear son, that your father's happiness and mine, are, in a great measure, dependent upon your life and health; indeed you ought to have had advice before. You may recollect I have asked you several times, lately, if you were perfectly well, and you have evaded answering to the purpose; but I have perceived a great alteration in you ever since you returned from Melworth Hall.'

I replied, with a smile, 'I am very sensible,/ madam, of the alteration in myself, and I believe, indeed, I caught the *infection* there.'

My father started, and said, 'What! Augustus! have you been so indiscreet as to reside a fortnight in an house where there was some one afflicted with an epidemic disease, and be sensible of having yourself caught the infection, yet attempt no means of recovery?'

'I believe, my dear lord,' returned I, the disorder was not *very* epidemical; for I do not think any one in the house caught it but myself; and I am certain there is nothing malignant in it, so that I cannot apprehend any danger in the case, and I hope my mother and you will be perfectly at ease about me: I flatter myself I shall do very well.'

'At ease!' repeated her ladyship, '*that*, Augustus, is an impossibility, till we see you perfectly recovered; I am therefore determined to send for the physician directly, and must insist upon your adhering strictly to his directions.'/

'Certainly,' rejoined my father, 'proper means must be used before we can have any reason to expect a perfect recovery. Indeed, I am amazed at myself, that I suffered you to neglect it so long; for *I* have observed a change in you too in every respect, but particularly the loss of your spirits.'

I now found it impossible to contain my *laughter*, or my *secret*, any longer, and, after yielding to the former propensity, I said,

'I find, my Lord, that you and her ladyship are determined to dive into the inmost recesses of my *heart*; where, alone, my complaint is seated. Perhaps Lady Lucan can bear witness, from what she once saw in you, to the possibility of an amiable young woman causing just such an alteration as is perceptible in me.'

'I understand you, now, Augustus,' – said her ladyship, with a more chearful countenance, – 'all this circumlocution tends to inform us that you are in love.'

'Oh, ho!' rejoined his lordship, 'is that the case? – Well, I trust you have/ not made an improper choice; but pray, sir,' – smiling, good humoredly, – 'if it is not *very* impertinent, let me be favored with some little knowledge of the object. Pray who is the lady?'

'It is one, my Lord,' I replied, 'who will meet your entire approbation; I only wish I was equally certain of obtaining hers. It is Miss Melworth, the sister of my friend, and the most amiable and engaging creature in the universe, I saw her, for the first time, on my late visit at the Hall, where she now resides with her brother.'

'You should have told me that before,' cried my mother, 'I would certainly have paid my respects to Miss Melworth ere this. – It is due to her, both on her own account and her brother's; but more particularly on account of my regard to the memory of her mother, whom I highly esteemed. What *must* Sir Edward think of us, for being guilty of such a piece of neglect! You have, certainly, been very remiss, Augustus, in not informing me; but I insist upon your clearing me from the imputation/ of rudeness and slight, by taking the whole blame upon yourself; for, I declare, I had not the least conception, till this minute, that Miss Melworth was come into Yorkshire.'

'Well, my love,' said my father, 'your son has undoubtedly acted very wrong, but it is not too late to repair his error. I suppose, Augustus, you will have no very weighty objection to introducing your mother and me at the Hall to-morrow? especially when I tell you, that I feel a strong desire to see Miss Melworth, after what has just now passed; and, I firmly believe, I shall have every reason not merely to *approve* but to *congratulate* your judgment in the choice of so unexceptionable an object. I think too, you have no reason to doubt the concurrence of your friend, Sir Edward, with your wishes.'

'And I am sure,' resumed my mother, there can be no reason to fear any opposition to them from *Miss* Melworth; as I really think, there are few young women, of sensibility and understanding, to whom Augustus Fitzmaurice would not appear an irresistible object.'/

'There,' cried I, 'spoke maternal partiality, madam; but *I* am not intirely without fears on that head, tho' I know of no *particular* reason for them,'

After having made the proper acknowledgements for their kind indulgence, it was agreed amongst us, to set out to-morrow for Melworth-hall, directly after breakfast. When I was quitting them to write you this, Lord Lucan called me back, and archly said,

'Augustus, besure you do not make your mother and me *wait* for you in the morning.' –

I promised I would not; and, I dare say, I shall keep my word.

    Your friend,
      AUGUSTUS FITZMAURICE.

P. S. I finished my last in such haste, that I omitted to express a proper resentment for your exposing my former letter; you are, really, a very pretty fellow for a lover's confidant!/

LETTER XXXI.

Charles Montgomery, Esq. to the Hon. Augustus Fitzmaurice.

HARROWGATE.

WHEN I read your last, I could not avoid exclaiming, 'would to heaven Lady Gertrude Carruther and the Duke of — were shut up together for life, that the rest of the world might not be tortured with their folly!' There is nothing upon earth, Augustus, more provoking, than that it should be in the power of one or two such frivolous mortals, to banish good sense from the conversation of every social party they join. Our friend Edward begins to be almost weary of Lady Gertrude; she still persecutes him with assiduities, in hopes, I suppose, of conquering his stubborn heart, at last; he seems, now, to have no other resource but flight; and we are preparing for it; as I have, this day, had a letter from Mr. Bertills, signifying his intention/ to be at the Grove on Thursday next. – I shall, therefore, be with you at Westbrook-lodge, on Tuesday; when I hope to have the pleasure of finding Lord and Lady Lucan and yourself in perfect health.

Ah! my friend, my spirits now begin to sink at the near approach of that period when I must totally renounce all that I have ever, till lately, been taught to look upon as my paternal inheritance. I have endeavoured to reconcile my mind to this adverse stroke of fortune, and to support it with calm composure, humiliating as it is; and, I hope, I shall be able to submit with resignation, tho' I cannot avoid *feeling* it and that severely. It is true Mr. Bertills has, in some measure, *obliged* himself to make a provision for me, by having insisted on my declining all thoughts of the army; but the strongest doubts still arise in my mind respecting the *nature* of his intention towards me. – My spirit revolts against a state of servile dependence; and trade, which seems to be so much *his* hobby-horse; I am not fitted for either, by nature or education; nor indeed could I bear the idea of entering/ into it. – Tho', from his saying so much in favor of it, in all his letters to me, I am greatly inclined to think he has some view of fixing me in that sphere: if so, his intercourse and mine will soon be at an end; for I will not commence trader. – I would rather turn author, and write any nonsense in a garret for a shilling a sheet.[37] You may laugh, Augustus, but I speak the truth. – I always entertained a detestation to trade; I mean to engaging in it myself. I have no expectation that Mr. Bertills, who takes so much pains to get money, will sink any part of his property by settling a sufficiency to support me in a style of tolerable gentility. – But I will tire you no longer with the painful subject; my doubts will soon terminate in a certainty.

I hope you had the satisfaction to find Miss Melworth well. Lady Lucan's proposal of visiting her, was a very fortunate circumstance for you, and no less pleasing to Sir Edward, who is truly happy in the acquisition of so valuable a friend for his sister as her ladyship. – But he writes to you himself, which renders it unnecessary for me to say/ any more upon the subject; and, really, my ideas are all, at present, wholly engrossed by my own concerns; therefore, adieu till Tuesday. – On the day following, I expect that you fulfil your promise, and accompany to Fir-grove, your friend

CHARLES MONTGOMERY.

END OF THE FIRST VOLUME./

THE CITIZEN,

PRICE SIX SHILLINGS./

THE

CITIZEN,

A Novel,

IN TWO VOLUMES,

BY MRS. GOMERSALL,

OF LEEDS,

Author of Eleonora.

VOLUME SECOND.

LONDON,
PRINTED FOR SCATCHERD & WHITAKER,
Ave-Maria-lane;
and sold by
Binns, Leeds, and Edwards and Son, Halifax

1790./

THE CITIZEN.

LETTER XXXII.

Miss Melworth, to Miss Bertills.

NOTWITHSTANDING I am likely to see you so soon at Scarborough, yet I cannot forego the pleasure of informing you, that our party there will be enlarged by the pleasing addition of the Fitzallan family. They have been passing a few weeks at Matlock; their house being now ready for their reception, they came to it three days ago; and, yesterday morning, Louisa surprised me with her presence/ here. – She came to request our company home with her, to spend the day; a request which Mrs. Horton and I readily complied with. In our way thither, I remarked, to Louisa, that she appeared more grave than usual; in return to which, she said, that her happiness was but half complete till the arrival of her father. This, I think very natural; but, *entre nous*, my dear Rhoda, I thought she appeared exceedingly disappointed at the absence of Sir Edward: nay, I may say, I am *certain* she was so; for Mrs. Horton made the same observation, and spoke of it to me afterwards. – This is a circumstance which does not, in the least, excite my wonder; since my partiality to my brother leads me to think it next to an impossibility, that an amiable young woman like our friend, whose affections are perfectly disengaged, should be, for the space of a fortnight, constantly in his company, and yet remain insensible to his merits – to his numerous attractions, both personal and mental. To you he is a stranger; but I flatter myself, that when you are acquainted with him, your opinion will coincide with/ mine. At present, I am half tempted to wish he were less amiable – less agreeable; or, rather, that he had been absent from home when Louisa was here before; as the idea of her being attached to him fills me with much concern: not because such an alliance would not be highly pleasing to me, but because I fear that my brother's affections are too firmly fixed on the memory of his adored Matilda ever to admit of his making a second choice; and, therefore, I fear for the happiness of my friend. – But I will not *meet* trouble, it is always swift enough in its approach.

I had the pleasure of being a few hours in the company of Lady Castleton, for the first time; who, together with her two daughters, the Duchess and Lady Jane, called to pay their respects to Mrs. Fitzallan. The acquaintance of the two families had, I found, commenced at Matlock, and bids fair to be lasting; as they all seem equally pleased with each other. Her ladyship did me the honor to express much satisfaction at meeting me; for which mark of her politeness, I find, I stand indebted to you; as she informed me, that she had/ often heard me mentioned, with much esteem, by Miss Bertills; who, she added, had promised to introduce us to each other at Scarborough. Mrs. Fitzallan then said, that she must beg to be admitted of the party, for that neither herself nor Louisa could be happy if they did not embrace that opportunity of enjoying the company of Miss Bertills, who, she hoped, they should prevail upon to return and spend a few weeks with them, in her way to London. But upon this subject they intend writing to you. My brother is this moment returned from Harrowgate; you will, therefore, excuse this abrupt conclusion, from

> your ever affectionate
> *HARRIET MELWORTH./*

LETTER XXXIII.

The Hon. Augustus Fitzmaurice, to Sir Edward Melworth.

FIR-GROVE.

I'll take *your* word for a city merchant another time, Edward: you perfectly know them I find, if I may take Mr. Bertills as a specimen of the whole body; but no doubt there are some exceptions. – That gentleman arrived here yesterday, and I think he exactly answers your description. I am infinitely pleased with him already. He has not, yet, developed his designs, with respect to Charles; but, I verily believe, he means to act in a friendly, generous manner. – Were you an eye witness of his behaviour, I am certain you would coincide with me in that opinion. I only wish our friend possessed a larger share of patience; his uneasy doubts appear to me wholly unnecessary; and, I hope, he will yet have reason to blush for his rash judgment of/ Mr. Bertills. He yielded to its dictates more yesterday than ever he had done before; so you may suppose we were neither of us in an enviable situation when the carriage stopped at the door. Charles, however, mustered up some small degree of fortitude; and, with me, went into the hall, just as Mr. Bertills was alighting. He bowed to me, took Charles affectionately by the hand, but *could not* speak. The door of the dining-parlour stood open; he rushed hastily into it; and, the moment he entered, leaned his arm against the wainscot for support, and burst into tears; nor could either of us avoid being affected. It was some time before Mr. Bertills recovered so far as to be able to articulate a word; at length,

'Would to heaven, my dear Charles,' said he, 'that we had met under happier auspices; I should then have said I rejoice to see you: but the will of God be done!'

A solemn pause ensued. – Mr. Bertills wept again, accompanied by our friend. – After some minutes, the former resumed,

'It is little more than two years since I saw you, and I perceive an amazing alteration./ – Your person is the exact representative of your father's. – May you, likewise, my dear boy, inherit all his good qualities!'

Being now all of us brought into a tolerable degree of composure, Charles took the opportunity of introducing me to him as the son of Lord Lucan. – I find he formerly knew my father, and he inquired after him and Lady Lucan, of both of whom he spoke in terms of politeness and respect. The conversation became general, when poor Charles *affected* ease. – I could plainly see he did not *feel* it. After some time, Miss Bertills was mentioned, and Mr. Bertills talked of her with the partiality natural to a fond parent.

'My daughter is the delight of my life,' cried he; 'Mr. Fitzmaurice, I am *proud* of my Rhoda: but I must not say too much, lest you should be doubly disappointed when you see her; – for she has not the advantage of personal attractions. – She requires to be known e'er she can excite admiration and then, she seldom fails of engaging esteem. She is much altered, Charles,' added he, 'since you saw her,/ and is not near so handsome *now* as *then*; so you may suppose she stands no chance of being toasted as a celebrated beauty.'

I rather doubt his veracity in that point, Edward: I own to you, when I look at *him, he* is really *very* handsome for his years; he is a tall, portly, elegant figure, and his face pleases me extremely; there is in it an expression of every thing that is good, amiable, and engaging; and he looks, at least, twelve years younger than he says he is.[1] All these circumstances considered, you will not wonder that I should be a little alarmed by some part of the conversation that ensued as we were sitting over our glass after dinner yesterday.

'Well, Charles,' – said he, with a smile, – how stands your heart affected now? did you see no fair-one at Harrowgate worthy the honor of filling up that vacancy Fanny Elwood has left in it?'

'No, really, sir,' – replied he, laughing, – 'I did not: without doubt, had I sought for one there I might have found many much more worthy than her; but she has taught me caution. – I shall not fall in/ love again very quickly; I am pretty well cured of that passion for some years to come, if not for life.'

'What will you say,' – resumed Mr. Bertills, gravely, – 'If I should be married first then? – I intend, before I return home, to pay my respects to Miss Melworth, and try what interest I can make for myself in her affections.'

While he was speaking, my whole countenance was of a glow; I absolutely felt myself tremble.

'Heaven forbid, sir,' I exclaimed, 'that you should be serious!'

He laughed out. –

'Oh, ho!' cried he, 'serious or not serious, I find I must relinquish all pretensions to the prize at once; for, I perceive, I have a rival in you, and it is rather too late in the day for me to put myself in competition with a fine young man, in an affair of love; so you have no interruption to fear from me.'

'Thank you, sir,' returned I, 'you have relieved me; for had you been really serious/ I should have thought you a very formidable rival.'

'Pho! prithee, Fitzmaurice,' replied he, 'do not let your politeness transgress the boundaries of *truth*; you could not think any such thing; nor am I so vain an old fellow as to imagine Miss Melworth would ever have bestowed a serious thought upon me, if you had *not* stood between. No, no; I was merely exercising the privilege of *age*, in jesting on a subject which I believed no one could have thought me in *earnest* about.'

Here the discourse dropped, and the rest of the day passed over agreeably enough. *I* should have thought it perfectly so, could I have divested my mind of concern for Charles, who, I was sensible, suffered a great deal of anxious fear, which was not lessened by his suspense. This morning, when we met at breakfast, Mr. Bertills drew his chair to the table, and, taking out his pocket-book, examined several papers, when having, I suppose, found the one he wanted he said to my friend,

'You see, Charles, I have not left my business entirely behind me; and, I think,/ I never do; for, when I leave my home and retire into the country for a little relaxation from the cares of life, something always arises that lays me under a necessity of mixing affairs of commerce with my pleasures. – It is just so now; I have business to do at Leeds, and it is of that nature, that I shall, probably, be a considerable loser, if I neglect going about it this forenoon. If you will order a carriage to be got ready, and oblige me with your company thither, I'll thank you.'

Charles complied; but, as I wished to write to you, I declined attending them upon that plea, which was not admitted as the *reality* by Mr. Bertills.

'The true state of the case,' said he, 'I suppose is this; you think, Fitzmaurice, you shall be happy in having a leisure opportunity to contemplate the virtues of your lovely Harriet; so I'll use no farther persuasion with you.'

I have now, my dear Edward, the pleasure to add, that I shall, this evening, return to the Lodge, where I shall continue two days,/ and then go over to Melworth-hall, to enjoy, in the converse of your lovely sister, a pleasure far superior to any which contemplation can afford me. Say something handsome for me to the ladies.

　　Yours,
　　AUGUSTUS FITZMAURICE.

LETTER XXXIV.

Miss Melworth, to Miss Bertills.

MELWORTH-HALL.

WITH inexpressible concern, I take up the pen to inform you, my dear Rhoda, that an event has occurred which puts it out of my power to gratify your wishes and my own by meeting you at Scarborough this season. It would be superfluous to add, how severely I feel the disappointment, after having so long flattered myself with the pleasing idea. – But daily experience convinces us of the uncertainty/ of every human enjoyment; and we ought to learn not to depend very strongly upon the completion of any of them. It is the fate of every mortal, while in existence, to be perpetually *learning*; but few are thoroughly *taught*. The various dispensations of providence towards us, afford innumerable lessons for our advantage; but, like thoughtless children at school, we are apt to turn over the leaf, when we find a difficulty or dislike in our hearts to read it. – *This* is a lesson to me of submission and patience on *one* account, and on *another*, of pious gratitude to the most high for having mercifully preserved the life of a valuable relation in a time of great danger.

You have often, my dear, heard me speak of my uncle Watson, my mother's brother. He has been in the East Indies during the last ten years and was returning hither, with an intention to spend the remnant of his days in his native country, when the ship he was on board of was wrecked, and many lives were lost in consequence. Providentially, Mr. Watson was amongst the few who were preserved, by clinging to pieces of the wreck; in which dismal/ situation, hopeless of relief they continued a night and a day – destitute of food – nearly so of covering; and their strength so nearly exhausted, that they would inevitably have perished, if a French vessel, bound for Havre-de-Grace, had not appeared in sight; and, as soon as they came near enough to behold the poor sufferers, immediately sent out their boat and took them all on board, where the utmost humanity and tenderness was extended towards them. Mr. Watson, who was before in a very precarious state of health, was rendered so much worse by the bruises and terrors he had undergone, that he was confined to his bed till the ship arrived at her port. The Marquess de Rivieres, who was a passenger, had him taken, with caution and tenderness, on shore, and immediately conveyed to his seat near Versailles, where he has ever since been entertained by the Marquess and Marchioness with the utmost hospitality and friendship. He is now almost well, but they will not consent to part with him till he is *perfectly* so. They have, therefore, written a very pressing invitation to my brother and me to go over to/ him; their letter is dictated in polite and friendly terms, and was accompanied by one from Mr. Watson, enforcing their request. We are now preparing for our departure, which takes place in three days; my tender and estimable friend, Mrs. Horton, goes with us. I hope we shall return before the beginning of winter; when, if nothing happens to prevent, I promise myself the satisfaction of passing a few weeks with you in London. Heaven grant my dear uncle may be as well as he is represented to be! but forgive my superstition, Rhoda, if I say, I have strange disagreeable forebodings. I like not the prospect of the voyage, tho' short; I like still *less* the leaving of my friends. A tremendous tract of ocean separating me from the greatest part of those whom I most highly love, esteem, and venerate; amongst the number of them, I feel particularly distressed at quitting Lord and Lady Lucan, who have done me the honor to distinguish me by many marks of the kindest partiality. We have lately spent a great deal of time together, and their company and conversation has constituted much of my happiness./

I have been interrupted, my dear Rhoda, by a friend of Sir Edward's; it was Mr. Fitzmaurice, the only son of Lord Lucan. In this amiable young man, you see expanding into blossom all those virtues which time has, long since, matured, ripened, and brought to perfection in his parents. Added to this, he has, in his manners, an agreeable vivacity that makes him extremely engaging. He left Firgrove a few days ago; your father and your cousin Charles were both well. Mr. Fitzmaurice speaks of the *former* with delight. – When he comes into *your* company, Rhoda, he will think of you with rapture. He has agreed to join our party to France, and is now writing to Lord and Lady Lucan to request their concurrence with his wishes. I am well pleased at it, as I know his company will make my brother additionally happy. The latter has received great benefit to his health and spirits by his short excursion to Harrowgate; this, to the Continent, will, I hope, be a means of perfectly restoring both.

I am glad to find, my dear, that you enjoy the happiness of Lady Castleton's company;/ may it prove an ample compensation to you for being obliged to bear with so much of the Duke's! Mr. Fitzmaurice knows him, and has diverted me highly by an account of *his* method of supporting a conversation. It is such an one as leaves no room to complain of his incapacity of affording *entertainment*, at least; and the greatest part of the world seek for nothing farther.

Accept sincerest wishes for your health and happiness, from
> your affectionate friend.
>> *HARRIET MELWORTH./*

LETTER XXXV.

Charles Montgomery, Esq. to Sir Edward Melworth.

FIR-GROVE.

TRUTH compels me to declare, that the idea I had so very rashly formed of Mr. Bertills was not only *injurious* but *unjust*; and you, my dear friend, cannot more severely condemn me for judging so harshly of him, than I condemn myself. In the course of my life, I have been much in his company, but never, till now, knew his true character. I never, before, had occasion to study it. From his intense application to trade, I drew the very ridiculous inferrence, that he must, necessarily, be of a mercenary disposition; foolishly supposing, none but a miser would devote the principal part of his time to that pursuit, if he were able to live without. I am now thoroughly convinced my opinion was founded in error. I am, yet, in ignorance of Mr. Bertills' designs/ respecting me; but my heart is at ease, from a certainty that he has too elevated a turn of mind to entertain a thought of reducing me to indigence by taking the utmost advantage that the law allows him; or, of placing me in a state of precarious and degrading dependence. I have, therefore, dismissed all my fears, and in his hands I think myself safe. Let me now inform you of the event that has caused this change in my opinion; your benevolent heart will be gratified by the relation.

When I accompanied Mr. Bertills to Leeds, it was, I confess, not without some little degree of reluctance; concluding, from what he said previous to our setting out, that he was going upon some buying and selling business: – however, I covered my chagrin as well as I could, by an assumed chearfulness, and asked no questions. On the way, he conversed in a very agreeable manner upon other topics. On our arrival, by his order, we drove to an inn; where, leaving the carriage, he enquired for the house of a Mr. Clements; and, having obtained information, we walked thither. A servant presently appeared/ at the door, and conducted us into a room where a lady was sitting, alone, at work, At our entrance, she rose up, and, seeing Mr. Bertills, she turned pale and trembled; but his polite friendly manner soon dispersed her fears. He took her hand, and with a smile, said,

'You see, my dear madam, old friends are not so easily thrown off as you, perhaps, imagined. – I have found you out, at last. Rhoda will be rejoiced at the intelligence, for she has not yet ceased regretting your loss.'

'I am greatly obliged to Miss Bertills, sir,' returned she, 'I hope you left her well?'

'Perfectly so, madam,' he replied, 'she is now at Scarborough, where she purposes staying a few weeks, and, I am certain, her inclination to see you will be too strong to suffer her to return to London without making Leeds in her way. But where,' added he, is 'Mr. Clements? I should be glad to see him upon a little affair of business,'/

Mrs. Clements turned pale again at this, and visibly experienced some painful emotions she wished to hide; rising from her seat, she rang the bell, and ordered a servant to fetch his master.

'I should be sorry, my dear madam, to be guilty of any impertinence,' resumed Mr. Bertills, 'but I cannot help expressing the concern I feel at seeing your countenance overspread with dejection. – You were, formerly, happy in an excellent flow of spirits, and I fear the loss of them is occasioned by some unfortunate occurrence.'

'You judge right, sir,' returned she, it is really owing to a very unfortunate occurrence, which I fear will terminate greatly to our injury, if not cause our ruin. But, to deal ingenuously with you, sir, I will add, that I am no stranger to the business you have at present with Mr. Clements, as he heard, some time ago, that a bill for a large sum, drawn payable to him, (the drawer and acceptor of which are both bankrupts) lay in your hands. – The moment I saw you I conjectured what you came upon;/ and knowing the utter impossibility of Mr. Clements taking it up, at this time, I felt a great deal of pain and confusion.'

'And *I*,' cried Mr. Bertills, 'feel equal pain at finding you know so little of me as to suffer my presence, upon *any* occasion, to give you alarm; but, I trust, we shall be better acquainted shortly; for I really am not come to *demand* payment of it: therefore, my good lady, in *me* view only a friend ready to serve you. – I am happy the bill fell into my hands. – The name of Clements upon it struck me, the moment I saw it; and, on enquiry I was convinced it was no other than my worthy friend, your husband; finding it was not paid, when due, I feared something was wrong, and determined to keep it till I came hither; tho' Mr. —, of the Old Jewry,[2] of whom I had it, offered to take it up, but I was too well acquainted with his principles to run the risk of putting in his power the man I esteemed, tho' I am much displeased with him.'

'I am very sorry, sir,' – said Mrs. Clements, with a serious look, – 'to hear that; I/ am certain he never intended giving you any offence; but I think if you will explain your meaning, it is in my power to exculpate.'

'You had better not undertake so arduous a task,' interrupted Mr. Bertills, 'it will be sufficient for you to justify your own conduct in another affair, I mean your quitting London, without letting Rhoda or me know of your design, and not leaving us even a clue whereby we might trace your wanderings.'

'I confess,' replied Mrs. Clements, 'it had the appearance of rudeness, but it was wholly undesigned; my ill health caused our removal, and it was done in such a hurry that we had no time to think of taking a proper leave of our friends; nor would the weakness of my spirits, then, have been able to support such a scene. I have never been in London since; but it has been always my intention to repair the error, as far as possible, by paying my respects the first time I went, particularly to Miss Bertills; who, I had no doubt, would vouchsafe her pardon to me.'/

She had scarce done speaking when Mr. Clements entered the room. The first look interested my heart in his favor; he is young, tall, and well formed; his countenance remarkably expressive of good sense and good nature. There is something strikingly pleasing in his manners, and the affectionate attention he pays to his wife, – to whom, I find, he has been married several years, – does him infinite honor. When we were again seated, Mr. Clements mentioned the bill. By this time I was heartily sick of that subject, and so, I suppose, was Mr. Bertills, for he stopped him short by saying,

'Mrs. Clements and I have finally settled all that business; and now, as I have not a vast deal of time to spare, be so good to come to the main point, at once, by candidly opening your affairs to me, that I may know *what* I can do to serve you; for that in fact was what brought me hither. The trifling sum of two hundred pounds would not have caused me to come so many miles to-day merely to demand it.'/

With a look of astonishment, Mr. Clements answered, 'I am very ready, sir, to make you acquainted with my affairs in return for your generous kindness, tho' I am really ashamed of the imprudence of my conduct, which has thrown me into embarrassments too great to hope for deliverance. The cause is this; I have been long very intimate with a person who is a partner in a commercial house in this town; the trade of it was very extensive, and they were often in great want of cash; I thought the house perfectly safe, and to serve that person I frequently assisted them with loans. A few months back, I very imprudently advanced for them a large sum, the security they gave me for it was in bills drawn by them upon their agent in London, who accepted them; and, in a few days after, stopped payment. This immediately caused *their* house to do the same; and, as I had previously negotiated those bills, in the course of trade, the different holders of them must, consequently, look solely to me to take them up, which I am now unable to do; for, in addition to/ this severe stroke, my own agent, in London, has just stopped with a considerable sum of mine in his hand, and all the bills I have drawn upon him are, unexpectedly, returning to me. I have, therefore,' continued he, 'no other resource now but calling my creditors together, and delivering up my all to them; and, as the principal part of them are in London, I intend going up tomorrow for that purpose.'

'But, my dear sir,' said Mr. Bertills, 'before you take such a step, let us first examine farther into the necessity for it; for the consequence of that would be not only throwing yourself out of trade, but so effectually deranging your concerns, that when you enter upon it again, you will have new connections to seek, and that want of confidence which would naturally for a long time influence the minds of the manufacturers in this part of the world, would subject you to infinite inconvenience; whereas, on the other hand, should a friend advance you immediately a sum sufficient to take up all the bills in question, and likewise

enable you to/ pay ready money for your goods, till your credit is perfectly rees-
tablished, you would be completely easy and upon firmer ground than before.'

'Ah, my good sir!' cried Clements, 'I feel the full force of all you have been
saying; but the sum necessary would be far too large for me to ask the loan of
it from any person, particularly after what happened to me yesterday, which has
sunk my spirits, and determined me to struggle no longer.'

'What was that?' asked Mr. Bertills, 'I beg you will let me know all without
reserve.'

'You shall, sir,' replied Clements, 'I have no wish to conceal it. Mr. — of the
old Jewry, holds another bill for the same sum as *that* you have; he has written
twice, threatening to strike a docket, if the money was not paid directly. As I
was not in the way when one of the letters came, Mrs. Clements opened and
answered it; she pleaded for an allowance of time, and stated to him clearly my
situation. In reply to her, I was arrested yesterday, at his suit./ Fortunately, I had
a friend who bailed the action; but, as the money must either be paid in three
days, or special bail given till November, I took the resolution of going to town
to procure the latter, and adopt the measure I before mentioned.'

'What do you deserve,' cried Mr. Bertills, 'for all your imprudent conduct?
particularly in not taking care to get out of the power of such a wretch as Mr. —?
I know him well; he minds neither *law* nor *equity*. However, these troubles have,
I hope, cured you of taking *more* care for others than for yourself; and, if so, the
experience will, in the end, prove *worth* the purchase, tho', it must be allowed, you
have paid a high price for it. But, now, Clements,' continued he, 'tell me at once,
what sum will be fully sufficient to answer all the purposes I mentioned, and I am
ready to advance it before I leave you. But take this caution; do not, from false
delicacy, deceive me by mentioning too *small* an one, for that would only be a
means of plunging you into greater difficulties. – I *expect* it is not a trifle will do.'/

Mrs. Clements walked to the window, and applied her handkerchief to her
eyes; I could scarce forbear doing the same; while Clements, in a rapture of joy,
exclaimed,

'Gracious heaven! what an offer! Mr. Bertills! my friend! my benefactor! my
deliverer! Oh! teach me how to express my sense of your kindness! You are saving
me from the torture of seeing my Theresa, my wife, reduced almost to poverty. –
In this time of our extremity, you generously hold up a prospect of relief, and –'

'Psha, psha! man,' – interrupted Mr. Bertills, peevishly, – 'this is saying just as
much as amounts to nothing, in the settlement of the matter before us; therefore
speak to the purpose, and tell me how much money you want.'

'Oh, sir! cried Mrs. Clements, 'you must, indeed, you must suffer us to pour
forth the grateful effusions of our –'

'I tell you, madam,' interrupted he, 'I will not suffer any such doings; it is
really a very strange thing, that you ladies will never permit two men to adjust a

little affair/ of business together, when any of you are present, without teazing them with your interruptions. Come, Clements,' added he, 'speak your wants; I am all attention to *that* subject, but I'll not hear a word upon any other.'

'I am really ashamed to tell you, Mr. Bertills,' returned he, 'that not less than *two thousand pounds* will be sufficient to answer your design completely.'

'And *will* that sum do completely?' said he, 'for, I confess, it is less than I expected.'

'I assure you, upon my honor, sir,' replied Clements, 'it is amply sufficient.'

Mr. Bertills then requested pen and ink, and, taking some banker's checks from his pocket-book, said,

'I'll write a draft for the money, and then we'll go together to a banker here to get it discounted; mean time, do me the favor to send for that friend who bailed you yesterday, I wish to speak with him.'

In a few minutes, Mr. Bertills presented Mr. Clements with a draft for the money,/ which was received in a manner better imagined than described. He had just finished drawing another, when the gentleman who had been sent for entered to us, and Mr. Bertills, with all the dignity of conscious goodness, rose and took him by the hand, saying,

'You and I, my dear sir, meet as old acquaintances. You have, I find, rendered an essential service to the friend I esteem, for which accept my thanks. I took the liberty of sending for you now, sir, to request your farther assistance; but in the first place, I must insist upon your taking this,' presenting him with a draft for two hundred pounds, 'which we will get discounted immediately, and you shall retain the sum as your indemnification till the bill in the hands of Mr. – is paid, if you will, *for form's sake*, join me in special bail; as I am determined he shall now wait till November for the money.'

This proposal was readily agreed to, and we went out together to the bankers; where, from the cordial reception Mr. Bertills met, we found he was well known to them. The/ drafts were discounted directly, and we proceeded to the attorney's, who looked at the plain dress Mr. Bertills wore,[3] and, I imagine, conceived from *that* no very favorable idea of his fortune. He hesitated about accepting him, prefacing his doubts by a speech upon his duty to his client, and then told Mr. Bertills that he would not do unless he could swear himself an housekeeper, and worth four hundred pounds. Neither Clements, his friend, nor myself, could forbear laughing; but Mr. Bertills kept his countenance, and desired he would do him the favor to send, in his name, for Mr. —, the banker, gravely adding, 'I believe he will satisfy you that I may safely swear to being worth *four thousand*.' The banker came, and, after laughing at the circumstance, convinced the attorney he was safe in accepting him, at the same time offering himself in stead if he had any doubts remaining; the attorney said he had not, and the affair was soon settled. When we were coming away Mr. Bertills said to him,

'Tell your client, when you write, to send the bill to *my* counting-house next November;/ it will be paid there *then*, and not before. He'll think himself very safe, for he knows Philip Bertills perfectly well.'

When we got back to Mr. Clements's, he expressed a desire to give his bond for the money Mr. Bertills had advanced to him, who only replied,

'Nonsense! an honest man's *word* is as good as his *bond*, at any time, and I cannot now stay for one to be prepared.'

He then *insisted* on giving his note of hand, as some small security for the repayment of it.

'Well, well,' cried Mr. Bertills, '*satisfy* yourself then.'

On receiving the note, he presented it to *me*, saying, 'There, Charles, I make *you* a present of this.' I immediately tore it in two and threw the pieces into the fire, upon which, he, with a look of pleasure and satisfaction, exclaimed,

'Well done, young man! I thought I was right in supposing you had not worldly wisdom enough for a man of business; you will not do for a partner for me. – I see you/ would be just such another imprudent fellow as Clements has been. But here, take this bill, which caused Mrs. Clements so much pain, and see if you can dispose of that *better.*'

A work-bag lay upon the table, and I put the bill carefully into that. Mrs. Clements was beginning to speak, but was interrupted by Mr. Bertills.

'I wish, my dear madam, you would be so obliging to keep silence just now; – I have a pleasure in hearing you talk when business is not interrupted by it, but, at present, I have something more to say to your good man.'

He then gave Mr. Clements some friendly advice respecting the immediate arrangement of his affairs, promised to see them again very soon, and we came away. As soon as we were seated in the carriage,

'Well, Charles,' said Mr. Bertills, 'how do you like my two young friends, whom we have just quitted?'

'Extremely well, sir,' returned I, 'I look upon Mr. Clements to be a noble, generous fellow.'/

'Ay, I thought,' resumed he, laughing, – 'that such a man as Clements, who has, hitherto, regarded all mankind as his brethren, was just calculated to please *you* who know nothing of the world but by theory. – I dare say now, you like him the *better* for this egregious folly he has been guilty of.'

'And really, sir,' returned I, 'you will not easily make me believe that *you* like him at all the *less* for it.'

'Your penetration is not deceived in that particular,' he replied, 'but I hope he will now learn a little more wisdom; tho' not so much as to make him covetous, for I hate to see a *young* man of a sordid disposition. – It is a despicable vice at *any* age, but in youth it is invariably a mark of a very *bad, depraved mind*; and how should it be otherwise? for when avarice has once entered the citadel, he keeps quiet possession for life, and bars the doors against every virtue – every amiable principle. – The tear of sympathy is no more seen to fall for others' woes. – The sound of distress enters not thro' the ear into the heart. – Nor, is/ the hand any more extended to afford a voluntary relief to the wretched. I declare to you, if I had a son, I would far rather see him a spendthrift than a miser.'

'I entirely agree with you, sir,' said I, and I most sincerely hope avarice will never enter my breast; but allow me to say, I did not think, when we left the Grove, that you were coming about such business as this. – I rather expected you were going to *take* money than *give* it, as you told me, I remember, that if you deferred it longer you might probably be a *loser*.'

'And did I not tell you the truth?' resumed he, 'should I not have *lost* the delight of reflecting on that happiness which the goodness of God put it in my power to bestow?'

We had more conversation to the same purpose, in which he displayed sentiments that did him the highest honor; and I am certain, my friend, I can have nothing to fear for myself after having been witness to such a noble act of generosity, nor can a single idea to the prejudice of Mr. Bertills ever again enter my/ mind. I now feel a veneration and affection for him equal to that which I felt for my late revered father, and I only regret that my relationship to the former is attended with a circumstance so dishonorable to the pride and respectability of his family; this, whenever the thought enters, sensibly wounds the feelings of

Your friend,

CHARLES MONTGOMERY.

LETTER XXXVI.

Miss Bertills To Miss Melworth.

SCARBOROUGH.

ALAS! my dear Harriet, what a mortifying disappointment is this! after entertaining for some weeks the most delightful expectations of seeing you here, to be informed that/ you are going farther distant from me than ever! Lady Castleton and her daughter, the Duchess of —, are likewise greatly disappointed; – they had promised themselves much pleasure in the addition of my Harriet's charming society; but, as *your* friends, we ought not to murmur, since you are going to be again united to an amiable and beloved relation, from whom you have been long severed. May you enjoy a happy meeting with each other! and may Mr. Watson's life be long spared to heighten the felicity of his nephew and niece! I shall expect the pleasure of seeing him and Sir Edward with you in Chatham-place, early the ensuing winter; but forgive me, Harriet, if I say, I am rather in fear of your attracting the heart of some one amongst the young noblesse who may visit at the Marquess de Rivieres', and may have power to prevail upon you to fix your future residence in France. Heaven forbid *that* should be the case! and may your brother's friend, Mr. Fitzmaurice, forbid it too! I flatter myself *you* are the magnet that attracts him from this kingdom. I find he has been/ often enough in your company to enable you to discover *his* merit, and I shall have but a poor opinion of his discernment if he has not yet discovered *yours*. I thank you for your intelligence of my father and cousin; I hope it will not be long before *the former* returns to me, for I am almost weary of being so much in the company of the Duke of —. I wonder how Lady Castleton does to bear it; – to me his tongue is exceedingly tiresome: nor do I believe *you* would find so much entertainment from it as you imagine. Yesterday, when we assembled, at dinner, Lord Castleton happened to remark, that I looked unusually grave; and added, that he hoped it was not occasioned by any ill news I had received.

'Indeed, my Lord,' said the Duchess of —, 'Miss Bertills has just now had a piece of intelligence sufficient to make us all look grave; a letter from Miss Melworth informs her, that –'

'Melworth – Melworth –' interrupted the Duke of –, 'I have heard you often mention *her*, Miss Bertills; I think you told me she was the daughter of the late Sir/ Thomas Melworth. – I remember him very well; tho' our intimacy dropped before he was married. His lady was the daughter of Colonel Watson. Sir William Rivers paid his addresses to her first, but she did not very well like him; and then finding out that he kept a mistress, by whom he had nine children, she broke off the match. Poor lady! she knew but little of the world to make such a trifle a serious objection to a man of his fortune.'

'Upon my word, cried the Duchess, 'I think it was a very reasonable aud solid objection, and I –'

'True, Charlotte, true,' interrupted he again, 'it was reasonable enough there I'll allow, because the mistress Sir William had then was seduced by him when a mere child. He persuaded her to elope with him; and he kept her so snug, that her poor father never heard what became of her; and, at length, died of grief for her loss. Not but Sir William was very kind to him, and offered him a living of two hundred a year, for he was only a poor curate, but he declined accepting/ it, saying, it would be of no use to him, now; he had lost all that was worth living for – his only child.'

'Pray,' said Lady Castleton, 'is your Grace aware of the diabolical character you are giving your quondam[4] acquaintance, by relating this anecdote of him?'

'Lord bless you! my lady,' resumed he, 'it was a bad affair, I confess; but what then? he was but a *young* man, and she was a lovely girl, so it was natural enough. I have visited her often with him. He took care of her, too; he did not throw her off to go upon the town, as Harry Lisson did. – *His* amours are *too* bad to be talked of; but Harry was a sad rake, while his father lived; now, indeed, he has thrown aside his gallantries with his red coat; tho', perhaps, he had better have retained them both; for the mischief he did amongst the girls was amply compensated by his generosity to the whole world. He did not think much about paying his debts; yet, as long as his money lasted, he *would* give to the poor. – But, now, his fortune is increased, he says,/ he cannot afford it. Gad, I'll tell you a droll story about that, my lady: when Lisson was a young man, he had a favorite servant who attended him upon all his exploits. In one of Harry's mad pranks, when they went out together, the servant was mounted on a very spirited beast, which ran away with him, threw him into a ditch, broke one of his arms, two of his ribs, and almost tore an eye out. In this condition, he was conveyed home; where, with proper care, his health was restored; but he totally lost the sight of his eye, and the use of his arm; and, as some recompense, his master gave him a little neat cottage upon his estate, and allowed him thirty pounds a year, which was regularly paid till the death of Lisson's father, when Harry ordered it to be withdrawn. The poor fellow took courage and went to his master to know if it was true. Lisson very gravely told him, he had given the orders because he could not *afford* the payment any longer. 'I am very sorry for that, sir,' said the man, 'I thought you could do it *easier* now, you are come to/ such a fine estate? That, said his master, 'is the very reason I cannot afford it. – I have *now something worth saving* – and I never had before.'

'I wish,' – cried the Duchess, pettishly, – 'your Grace would take my advice, and never give any more anecdotes of your friends; for, I think, they reflect no lustre upon your judgment, in having made choice of them. – I protest, I shall never like Lisson again.'

'Ha! ha! ha!' resumed he, 'why they are all very well in their way, and men of honor too; no man fought more bravely for his country in the last war than Lisson did. He was standing very near Lord Howe[5] when a shot came and took his Lordship off so hastily. Ah! he was a great loss to us; but he died with honor, as he had lived. The Howes were truly valiant. The General, Sir William Howe,[6] where will you find such another noble, intrepid commander? I met him t' other day, he is grown very fat since he came from America; very fat, indeed. After all,/ the air of Old England agrees best with him. Give me Old England, there's no place like it; what say you, my Lord, don't you think so?'

'Your Grace cannot be more partial to it than I am,' replied Lord Castleton, 'on every account, but particularly on that of its constitutional government. Our laws are founded in equity; and the liberty which the legislative power secures to the people, prevents any infringement upon them. Thus every subject may live at ease; enjoying, without molestation, the gatherings of his vintage, and the profits of his industry. – And, while the British sceptre is swayed by a monarch like the present,[7] with wisdom to govern, and virtues to endear him to his people, this island may boast the superiority of its blessings; and it is with delight I behold, in the numerous progeny of our good and gracious Sovereign, a long, succession of the Brunswick line,[8] to fill the throne of Britain, and convey to *succeeding* ages the blessings of *this*. But, Miss Bertills,' continued his Lordship,/ 'the Duke has somehow or other caused our discourse to wander widely distant from its origin. Give me leave to ask, what has happened to Miss Melworth, to cause the concern which is so visible in your countenance?'

'An unexpected event, my Lord,' returned I, 'obliges her and Sir Edward to go over to France; and, consequently, disappoints me of the pleasure of seeing her till the commencement of winter.'

'That *is* vexatious indeed,' cried the Duke, 'very vexatious; I wanted to see her myself. I suppose she is much like her mother; and, if so, I think Sir Edward does wrong to take her to France. She'll marry there, very likely, for Frenchmen know how to distinguish between *natural* and *artificial* beauty. They like our English ladies, better by half than they do their own painted ones. Lord Ackworth's daughter, you know, married a French Marquess. She had but a small fortune; which made his Lordship give consent to the match; for he could not help himself, having gamed/ away the greatest part of his estate, and the rest was at *nurse*, while he and his family resided upon the continent; of course, he could add nothing to her fortune, and doubtless might be glad to save expences by getting her off his hands. His beautiful seat at R— is now inhabited by Sir Thomas Brown, the well-known usurer. Sir Thomas knows the value of money; he lent Lord Osborn a large sum once, in my presence, and he made him pay a confounded premium for it. However, my Lord was his very humble servant, and waited on him half-way down stairs. I suppose he thought he might want him again in a day or two, for *he* made no more of guineas than I make of half-crowns.'

The Duke would most likely have run on much longer, but he was interrupted by the entrance of Lady Ann Lenox, who ran in without waiting to be announced.

'I intrude, very abruptly,' cried she, 'but I have been looking every where in the world for you, all this morning; where, in the name of wonder, did you hide yourselves?/ there's the sweetest gown-piece to be raffled for, that ever you saw in your life, and if you do not set down your names before night the raffle will be filled, and you cannot think what a lovely thing it is.'

'Pray Lady Ann', said the Duchess, 'what is it? silk, chintz, muslin, or what?'

'Oh, Lord bless you, my dear,' resumed she, 'you cannot form any idea of the beauty of it, you must see it, 't is superlatively elegant, and quite undescribable. – A white Italian crape, wrought with silver, and all done in –'

'Lady Ann,' interrupted the Duke, 'have you seen the sword knot at —? I was raffling for it this morning; his Grace of L— came into the shop, mean time, and told me, that the beautiful Miss Gray, who was so much admired at the last ball, eloped last night with the Honorable George Ashburn. – It is supposed they are gone to Scotland; but the finest part of the jest is, they managed the matter so very cleverly that neither of them were missed till near breakfast time this morning; when it was too/ late to pursue them with any hopes of success. So she stands fair to be *my Lady*, in time; for the title *must* descend to Ashburn; and as to the estate, what need he care about that; – *one* room-full of old Gray's pledges will purchase a better than his father is in possession of; for a pawnbroker is certainly the best business in the world.'

'Well, I declare,' cried Lady Ann, 'I never, in my life, met with any person so intelligent as your Grace! I wonder how you gain all your information; for you know *every thing*, and *every body* in the universe I believe!'

'There's nothing easier, Lady Ann,' returned he, 'people may gain information upon every thing, if they will but take pains to attempt it. I once had a valet that was a pawnbroker's son, and I used to ask him so many questions about that business, I soon gained from him knowledge enough to qualify me for the management of it myself. You would not believe what immense gains they make. I wanted to persuade *him/* to go into the same way, when he married, but the fool despised it, and he now keeps the Talbot-Inn at –; I think, however, he will not die so rich as his father did, tho' his wife is a pretty woman too, and in the hunting and shooting season their house is always full of company. – They are often obliged to turn away travellers. The Duchess and I stopped there, one night, in our way to town; they would not turn *us* away, but they sat up themselves all night to make room for us.'

'That was the least they could do,' said Lady Ann, 'it would have been odd indeed if they had sent *you* away.'

'Not at all, my lady, not at all;' resumed the Duke, 'for Lord Dunmow put up once at an inn, upon one of his own estates, and they could not make room for him, but obliged him to go five miles farther for accomodation, and yet he had been very kind to the landlord too; the fellow had been a private in his own regiment. His Lordship, for some trifling affair, raised him to the rank of quarter-master, and he/ enjoys half pay now. They tell me, my Lord,' continued he, 'that a vast number of subaltern officers have been lucky enough to get appointed for guards to the mail-coaches; it's a charming thing for them, a very charming thing indeed. Government, I believe, pays them half a guinea per week, and they have what they can get of the passengers besides, which is, I suppose, pretty considerable.'

'I vow and protest' exclaimed Lady Ann, 'your Grace should be called the repository of universal knowledge; for all subjects come alike to you: but I have not time now to stay to hear the discussion of any more. I want to know how the raffle fills; so, ladies,' added she, 'if you are ready we'll go; but I declare if either of you get the *sweet, dear gown*, I shall almost expire with envy.'

Her ladyship then hurried away, and the Duchess and I with her. But oh! dire to tell! the raffle had been filled, and the *dear, sweet* gown won, and carried off in triumph by the Honorable Miss Poulteney./

I have covered a deal of paper, Harriet, and yet I seem to have said nothing. Indeed, I felt an irresistible propensity to give you one of *my* specimens of the Duke's conversation. – I suppose it will accord with that before given you by Mr. Fitzmaurice; tho' it cannot afford you so much diversion, because there wants the peculiar air and manner attending the delivery. An attention to his Grace's discourse is something similar to following a long fatiguing fox-chase; you may probably arrive at the honor of being *in* at the death, but you can bring away nothing to repay the toils you have endured in the pursuit. Adieu my valuable friend,

      I am ever yours,

    RHODA BERTILLS.

P. S. Disappointments, they say, never come singly; and I now painfully experience the truth of this assertion. – The post has just brought me a short letter from Louisa Fitzallan; which informs me, that she and her/ mother were in hourly expectation of the return of her brother, who was gone to London to transact some business of importance at the India House,[9] when an express arrived, with intelligence of his having been unfortunately overturned in an hackney coach, by which accident his shoulder was dislocated. She adds, that her mother and herself were inexpressibly wretched on the occasion, and were preparing to set out for the metropolis with all possible expedition; where, she thinks, they shall wait the arrival of her father, and, of course, not return before the next spring. Heaven grant they may find their beloved Henry better than they expect!/

LETTER XXXVII.

Charles Montgomery, Esq. to Sir Edward Melworth.

FIR-GROVE.

AND so, my good friend, I am not likely to see you again during the summer? a circumstance, this, which chagrined me greatly, when I perused your last letter:* yet, even then, I could participate in your joy at the safety of Mr. Watson: but, as I have a heart capable of feeling for the *woes* of others, the fervor of my rejoicing is somewhat allayed by the recollection of poor Lady Gertrude Carruther's distress. How great, how severe will be her disappointment, at finding you do not meet her at Bristol hot-wells! Alas! what will become of her! she must lay by the *primrose* and substitute the *willow*. I fear she will sink under the mortification. I

---

*   Omitted as unnecessary./

hope you/ have written to *console* her under so heavy a calamity. Yes; you must have done it; your feelings are abundantly too tender to suffer you to leave England without attempting to *alleviate* her misery; which would be too powerful for any thing less than your presence to *remove* totally. Methinks I see her now; – she has just received your letter. – Imagination carries me upon its wing. – I, at this moment, ascend Clifton's delightful hill; I seek the forlorn, desolate Lady Gertrude. At length, I find her, in some solitary spot; seated on a verdant hillock; under the spreading branches of a venerable old oak. Her looks wear the traces of heart-felt distress; she is soothing her sorrows with the sound of her lute, accompanied by her voice, interrupted by sighs and tears; and, as love, they say, like all other troubles, makes people poetic, she is warbling forth some *dismal ditty* she has composed for the melancholy occasion, in the true pastoral style; something like the following; which you may, if you please, *entitle, and call/*

THE ANCIENT VIRGIN'S LAMENTATION,[10]
for the loss of her
BEAUTY AND HER LOVERS.

YE tender – ye delicate fair,
 To whom woes, such as mine, are unknown;
May ye ne'er feel the pangs of despair,
 Nor by love be your reason o'erthrown!

Ah! attend, I beseech you, a while,
 And hear me, my sad tale relate;
From your face should it banish a smile,
 Such pity would soften my fate.

Like *you*, I was *once* young and gay;
 Like *you, too*, had charms to engage;
Each shepherd to *me* tun'd his lay,
 And urg'd me his grief to assuage.

Elated with pride, I disdain'd
 To be captive to those I'd subdu'd;
O'er the plain I with tyranny reign'd,
 Nor was mov'd when for pity they sued.

But, ah! their revenge is complete;
 My *beauty*, alas! is decay'd;
No shepherd *now* sighs at my feet,
 And I fear – I shall *die* an old maid./

This heart, too, once hard as a stone,
 Love's arrow has pierc'd to the core;
The dear object I doat on is gone,
 Nor knows how his loss I deplore.

Oh! would I my Edward had known,
    Ere *wrinkles* had furrow'd my face!
Ah! his heart, it had then been mine own,
    And in mine it had left no void space. –

But, now, I may sigh thro' the day,
    And, at night, wash my couch with my tears;
For my Edward is gone far away,
    All unheeding my hopes or my fears.

How strenuous my efforts to please!
    With what care did I deck *my few* charms!
Nay, I 'd e'en have gone *down on my knees*
    To allure the lov'd swain to my arms.

Alas! my advances were vain;
    He quickly withdrew from my sight;
Since when, I 've no joy on the plain,
    In which, once, I was wont to delight.

What say you to my poetic talent? I believe you will think I am not much indebted to the *muses* for their assistance in the foregoing; however, be that as it may, it will suit/ the occasion: if ever Cupid send an arrow to my heart, the tuneful nine will then, undoubtedly, pay me a consolatory visit in form; and by their inspiration, I shall, of course, be more successful. – Till that period arrives, Edward, you must wait with patience for the full perfection of my genius; at present, as you may perceive, it is but in the bud; so I'll leave it there, and turn to something else.

I have the satisfaction to tell you, that every hour I spend in the company of Mr. Bertills increases my esteem for him. I often wonder, that, after having intimately known him so *long*, I should, till now, know him so *little*. I declare, to you, he appears perfectly *new* to me; and, far from *un*entertaining, he possesses a great degree of chearfulness which enlivens his conversation very much. Yesterday morning, we were strolling about the grounds together, when a sudden storm of thunder, lightening, and rain overtook and wetted us to the skin, before we reached the house. The door leading into the housekeeper's apartment being nearest, we entered by that, and went immediately into the parlour, where old/ John and Mrs. Ellis were sitting; the former went in quest of dry apparel for us, while the latter prepared some mulled wine. We had changed our raiment and were regaling ourselves by the fire when Mr. Bertills said,

'This is a sweet situation; you live very pleasantly here, Mrs. Ellis.'

'Yes, sir,' returned she, 'it is impossible to find a more delightful spot; I am sure I should be very sorry to leave it.' – Sighing, she added, – 'But John was saying, just now, that he supposed you would *sell* this estate; and to be sure, sir, it is natural to expect you will, because it is too far from London for you to come here often enough to make it worth while to keep it.'

'I imagine then, Mrs. Ellis,' resumed Mr. Bertills, 'John is *your* oracle; but in this instance, he does not prove a very true one: neither he nor you know any thing of the matter, for I have not the smallest intention to *sell this estate.*'

'I am very glad of it, sir,' – cried she, much pleased, – 'and I hope you find every thing to your satisfaction that is under *my* management here?'/

'O, perfectly so;' replied he, 'but pray, Mrs. Ellis, what does this question lead to?'

'I hope you will excuse me, sir,' resumed she, 'for making so free, but, indeed it would make me very happy to be informed by you that I am to have the honor of continuing *here* in *your* service.'

Mr. Bertills, with some degree of sternness, replied, 'The *happiness* you would derive from such a piece of information as *that*, Mrs. Ellis, depends upon circumstances you are not in the least aware of; I shall, therefore, leave your petition unanswered. But,' added he, 'let me ask you one question, Mrs. Ellis: pray how many years have you known *me?*'

'Sir?' – said she, with such apparent confusion and surprise as made me feel heartily for her.

'I ask you,' repeated he, 'how many years you have known me?'

'I really – sir,' – cried she hesitating, and I believe, scarce knowing what answer to make, – 'upon my word, I can't tell exactly,/ sir; – but I think it is somewhere about thirty years.'

'Yes,' said he, 'I think it is; and in that time you have had opportunities of seeing and knowing a great deal of my conduct: and now, Mrs. Ellis, I should be glad to know if you ever yet found me guilty of one premeditated act of injustice?'

'Oh, dear! no, sir!' cried she, 'never in my life.'

'Very well, then,' said Mr. Bertills, 'I am satisfied; and, in return, will satisfy *you*, by an assurance, that five thousand a year is not temptation strong enough to cause me to be guilty of one now; so you have only to make yourself easy, and depend upon it *you'll* be no sufferer. – You reign here, *sole* mistress; you have every thing your own way; no one presumes to interrupt or control you; and, if you are not happy and comfortable, why it *must* be your own fault, I think.'

'Indeed, sir,' replied she, 'I beg your pardon, I did not mean to offend – I am –'/

'Nor am I offended,' interrupted he, but I cannot help being provoked when I see people taking an infinite deal of pains to search for troubles which seem unwilling to approach them.'

Just at this moment old John came into the room. Mr. Bertills started from his seat; and, between jest and earnest, said to him,

'You are come, I suppose, sir, to give me the *second part* of the tune; but the music is *discordant* – I had rather not hear it.'

John looked queerly, and hardly knew whether to speak or remain silent; at length, he ventured to say,

'I only came to tell you, sir, that farmer Dobson is here, and desires me to present his *humble duty* to you, and hopes you'll be so good as to give the steward directions to grant him a new lease of his farm.'

'Pray, John,' – said Mr. Bertills, resuming his good humor, – 'do me the favor to present, in return, my best respects to farmer Dobson, and desire him to carry *his humble duty* back again, or else to a *better* market; for it is one of those commodities/ I never deal in; and, consequently, do not understand: nor do I recollect having ever heard it mentioned in my counting-house, so I suppose it is not a very saleable article.'

'But pray, sir,' – cried John, who could scarce forbear laughing, – 'what must I say to him about the lease?'

'Tell him,' replied he, 'to give himself no farther concern about the matter, but contentedly leave that affair in the hands of providence; all *he* has to do is to endeavour to perform his duty to God and man. – In the day time, to culti-vate his lands; and, when he has done work, at night, go home to his family in good-humor; kiss his wife; play with his children; eat his supper; return thanks to his maker; and lie down to sleep with a quiet conscience. – Let no worldly cares disturb him, and he will do very well lease or no lease. You need not stop, John,' added he, 'that is all I shall say about it; and if the other farmer should come upon a similar errand, the *same* answer must do for him too – I shall give no other; for I do not like to be teazed about business,/ when I come into the country for pleasure only.'

Then addressing me, he said,

'What a strange perverseness there is in our nature, Charles! for, even when we have all we can possibly want or wish, yet if it is not obtained or secured exactly in our own way, a train of dissatisfactory ideas enter our minds; – rob our *great Creator* of that gratitude he has a just claim to, and *ourselves* of all the happiness we might otherwise enjoy from his beneficence. But come, let us quit this apartment, or I may have more petitions; and I am not in the disposition to attend to any.'

We then went to the library; and after a short silence, Mr. Bertills exclaimed,

'What an unbounded curiosity there is amongst these servants, and people of their class in life! Mrs. Ellis may, perhaps, have some concern for *your* welfare at heart; but still I believe her curiosity is the strongest of the two. The anxiety she affected about her own station was *merely affected*; for it/ is impossible *she* can have any fear of not being provided for comfortably, nor can the farmers fear being turned out of their farms. – The sum and substance of all is, that they every one want to know *how* this estate is to be disposed of. – I saw *that*, clearly, and therefore chose to answer equivocally, to leave them as much in the dark as ever; and I really should like to keep them so; but that is not possible, a very short time

will explain every thing. I expect Mr. Dalton, one of my clerks, to come down
with the necessary papers for that purpose; which, I suppose, are not yet ready,
or he would have been here before now, as all his family connections live in Yorkshire; and I have given him liberty to spend a month amongst them; so there is
no doubt of his coming the moment the papers are ready for him.'

I have only room to add,

yours, sincerely,
    CHARLES MONTGOMERY./

LETTER XXXVIII.

The same, to the same.

FIR-GROVE.

YOU must not expect coherency from me, Edward; the nature of my present
subject forbids; – it has absorbed every faculty I possess in admiration and grateful joy. What a man is Mr. Bertills! how noble, how generous, how exalted is his
conduct! In the amiable qualities of the heart *no one* ever surpassed him, and *few*
ever equalled him. Every day displays to my view some excellency in his character
unseen before, but which, perhaps, had not been so long concealed had I studied the character of his mind, as accurately as I have of late done. Methinks, my
friend, the study of mankind must be more pleasing than I have hitherto thought
it; henceforth I will accustom myself to it. The brightest *jewel* may, in a cursory
view, pass unobserved, undistinguished. It is just so/ with respect to characters.
– The outward graces are attractive; but the nobler virtues, being generally hid
behind a veil of modesty, pass unperceived, till some discerning eye penetrates
thro' the veil, and discovers the valuable gem. We do not, often, see an instance
of the *virtues* accompanying the *graces*; but they meet in Mr. Bertills. Every favor
he confers is enhanced by his manner of conferring it. Early this morning, Mr.
Dalton arrived from London, and was immediately introduced to us, when I felt
particular pleasure in observing the polite and friendly manner in which he was
received by Mr. Bertills, who inquired after all his servants as affectionately as if
they had been his children; after which he said,

'Well, Dalton, I imagine you began to despair of the lawyers finishing the
deeds before the summer was over; I acknowledge *my* patience was nearly
exhausted. I want to get back to Scarborough, as much as you wish to be amongst
your relations.'

'Really, sir,' replied he, 'my patience has been pretty severely tried; but the
lawyers are a tedious set of beings; all one can/ urge to induce them to expedite
business is ineffectual: for instance, I never failed calling once a day upon Mr. L
–, but all to no purpose; he would take his own time. However, he has, at length,

completed the affair, and, I suppose, that the *substance* of those writings might be comprised in a fourth part of the compass.'

'Without doubt it might;' said Mr. Bertills, 'but lawyers must *live* as well as others; and when they happen to be men of superior abilities, who will act for the interest of their client, nor ever undertake any business of a dishonorable kind, then the consideration that a fortune must necessarily have been expended in *qualifying* them for their profession, should teach us to submit, without murmuring, to that prolixity which apparently entitles them to make an heavy charge. But,' continued he, 'did you get my good friend M—, the counsellor, to examine the deeds?'

'I did, sir,' replied Dalton, 'and he says they are as you would wish – without a flaw: but you will find a letter from him, in the parcel, sir.'/

Mr. Bertills read it with perfect satisfaction; after which he perused the deeds; and then, the steward being called in, he requested him and Mr. Dalton to witness his executing them. *I* was ignorant of the nature of the deeds; but, as I was, apparently, deemed an incompetent witness, of course, could not help thinking they concerned me very nearly, and some degree of impatience mixed with my curiosity to be satisfied in that particular. When the business was over, Mr. Dalton took his leave, and we were left to our selves. – A silence of some minutes succeeded. – At length,

'My dear Charles,' said Mr. Bertills, 'my thoughts have just now reverted to the contents of some letters I received from you, soon after the decease of your father; they made an impression upon my memory, because I read them with much pain, proceeding from my concern at finding that the care which had been bestowed upon your mind, by the most arduous endeavours to inculcate the purest principles of genuine piety, had been bestowed in vain. The long series/ of blessings you had enjoyed, appeared to be all obliterated from your remembrance by the destructive hand of ingratitude, which had planted in your breast the seeds of doubt and despair; you forgot to trust in the mercy and goodness of the Most High, and you felt no dependence upon his omnipotence.'

'Oh, my dear sir,' cried I, 'I stand corrected; and with anguish have I lamented the weakness of my faith: but it is, I believe, not only a common but a *just* observation, that, in this state of frail humanity, the most experienced christians too often find it difficult to penetrate thro' the dark clouds of temporal afflictions, and view a supporting God with that degree of resignation to his will and dependence on his power, which is due to *his* glory, and necessary for our *own* comfort.'

'Ah, Charles,' resumed he, 'I perceive you are making the practice of others a rule for the government of your own conduct; and attributing to the weakness of human nature those errors which result solely from/ the depravity of the heart. You rest satisfied under the idea of an incapacity to resist; and, forgetting that the life of a christian is a state of continual warfare, you neglect, when temptations assail, to *put on the whole armour of God*. Believe me, my *dear* Charles, I have your eternal happiness at heart, and I cannot evince it more strongly than by beseeching you henceforth to make the sacred writings the *only* standard of your faith and practice; it is the only one that will not lead you into error. It has been the will of God to try your patience, for a short time, by divesting you apparently of every *human* support; that you might thereby be compelled to place your dependence upon him alone, and to pour out your soul before him. I trust this short trial has been productive of these happy effects. It was my wish to assist in the means of promoting them; and, therefore, I refrained from informing you of my designs long ago. The ambiguity of my letters and behaviour has doubt-less excited your wonder. I have now explained my motive; and will, therefore,/ release you from suspense, by telling you, that, as I never had any expectation of inheriting the estates of your late father, I can feel no loss in relinquishing an apparent right to them. It never was my intention to exert the power the law gives me of appropriating them to my own use; for, from the first moment I was made sensible of the situation you were left in, I considered all the property both *real* and *personal* as your *natural and equitable right*, and myself as a guardian to *secure* that right to you firmly. Thro' the goodness of the Almighty, my own for-tune is such as leaves me without even the shadow of an apology, satisfactory to my conscience, for unjustly infringing on the property of any person upon earth. These,' continued he, 'are the deeds which now invest you and your heirs for ever with a *legal* title to the estates. The writings have taken more time in preparing than I expected they would, because the estate in Sussex, being entailed upon the male heirs of my family[11] (who, by the way, have no more occasion for it than I have),/ required me to pass *a fine* and *suffer a recovery* to enable me to *dock* the *entail*. I know not whether I have given you the right law terms, but that is of little consequence, Charles. – I have done that which was necessary to make it yours entirely; for, without this process, Counsellor M— told me I could give you no more than a life interest in it.'

Mr. Bertills then put the parchments into my hands, and precipitately quit-ted the room. I remained some time lost in astonishment; at length, having wiped away the tear of gratitude, I went in search of him. When we met, I was beginning to make some acknowledgments of his generosity and goodness, but he prevented me by saying,

'*I* have no claim upon your gratitude, Charles, I arrogate to myself no merit in the action – could not have done differently. – If you think thanks are due, pay them to the supreme being; and testify your sincerity by emulating the conduct of my friend, your late father, in the *use* of what is committed to your charge: – ever bearing/ upon your mind that *to whom much is given of him will much be required*.[12] You are now, my dear youth, convinced that the *heart* of every creature is in the hand of the *great Creator*; consequently, your late fears were not only unnecessary but injurious to his honor. Let the remembrance of this event prove an important lesson to you thro' life: but,' added he, 'as we have adjusted the business, we will now drop the subject. I imagine you will have no objection to give me your company to Leeds? I have an inclination to go over thither in the afternoon.'

'I will attend you, with pleasure, sir,' I replied, 'for I wish to cultivate an intimacy with Mr. Clements.'

'And I will venture to pronounce,' cried Mr. Bertills, 'that you will have real satisfaction in it. – The more both he and Mrs. Clements are known to you, the more highly will you esteem them. I wish, at present, to pay them particular respect and attention; their late unfortunate situation gives them that claim to it which feeling/ minds cannot resist. The humiliating circumstance of having been obliged to submit to receive pecuniary assistance from me, renders it doubly incumbent upon me to convince them, by my conduct, that they are not lessened in my estimation.'

The carriage is ready, and Mr. Bertills is waiting; I must, therefore, conclude.
Yours,
CHARLES MONTGOMERY.

LETTER XXXIX.

From the same, to the same.

FIR-GROVE.

MR. Bertills is retired to rest. – May his slumbers be sweet and undisturbed! But from me every invocation to Morpheus would be in vain till I have disburdened my mind by communicating to you the intelligence I heard at Leeds./

Poor Wilkins, who married Fanny Elwood, and who was generally supposed rich, is now in a situation which has stripped off the mask and convinced the world that he married her with a view to make his affairs easy, by means of the thousand pounds it was thought she possessed; but which, on his enquiring for it a few days after their marriage, she, with all the rage of a disappointed woman, and all the effrontery of hardened impudence, avowed having lost the *whole* of one night at a gaming table in London. Thus, disappointed of his *dernier* resource, he was, in a very few days afterwards, obliged to become a bankrupt, and his wife has, it seems, decamped no one knows whither. The sale of his effects commenced yesterday. Mrs. Clements had accompanied some ladies to it; where being tempted by the sight of a very curious little India cabinet, she became the purchaser, and it was brought home while Mr. Bertills and I were there. It was immediately opened; and, in examining it closely, we found one of the drawers obstructed in its passage by something. I presently discovered that the obstruction proceeded/ from some papers that had been left in the inside; and, on taking them out, they proved to be two letters addressed to Mrs. Wilkins. The signatures struck me. I had often heard her mention the names of the writers as her intimate friends, and was therefore curious to know what was the subject of their correspondence. I was looking over them when Mr. Bertills cried out,

'Charles, you have got something that seems to engage your attention closely; of course, it must be very pleasing. – Be so obliging as to read aloud, that we may be all equally entertained.'

I did as desired, and then put the letters in my pocket for the purpose of enclosing them to you. – The perusal rather surprised me, as I really did not expect such letters would be the production of any of her acquaintance. Good night.

CHARLES MONTGOMERY./

LETTER XL.

Mrs. Fleetwood to Mrs. Wilkins.
(Inclosed in the preceding.)

Madam,

ACCIDENT threw in my way your last letter to Miss Matthews, my niece. The perusal of it shocked me beyond expression. I was really horror-struck at the reflection of having permitted, nay, even *encouraged* an intimacy and correspondence between you. My beloved Arabella has ever been infinitely dear to my heart, and is the chief solace of my declining years. Her whole conduct, hitherto, has been such as made her appear, to my partial eyes, equal to my most sanguine wishes, and I was happy in the conviction that the pains I had bestowed on the beauteous blossom were not in vain. While ignorant of the duplicity of your character, and the large sacrifices you were making to vicious gratifications, her attachment to you met my warmest/ approbation. I applauded her choice of a friend, and readily indulged her with the privilege of enjoying, unrestrained, all those delights which flow from the social intercourse of virtuous friendship. You *appeared* amiable; I believed you to *be* so; and considered, that your being a few years her superior in age gave you a degree of influence over her, sufficient to add weight to your sentiments, and the example afforded by your conduct. Thus, I was led to imagine she might be essentially benefited by her intimacy with you. Alas! how have I been deceived in my ideas!

You, Mrs. Wilkins, have endeavoured to counteract all my views for my Arabella, by setting a *vicious* example before her, and artfully striving to seduce her into the paths of infamy and destruction. But, I thank heaven, my eyes are opened, before it is too late, to shew her the danger and disgrace of continuing to hold any farther intercourse with you. I humbly trust the dear girl's mind is yet uncontaminated; her principles yet unperverted. – Her candor/ assures me of it; she deeply regrets her former acquaintance with you. – She *blushes* for it; and promises to detach herself from you entirely. I am persuaded she will stedfastly adhere to this resolution, and I shall yet behold my Arabella as the darling of my fond heart, and the ornament of her sex.

She has informed me of all she knows relative to your past conduct, and confirmed her account by the undeniable testimony of your own letters. The whole is too bad for me to descant upon. – What is past cannot be recalled; but it may be in a great measure atoned for and expiated by the course you have it henceforth in your power to pursue. Let me, therefore, as a friend, who would rejoice to hear of your being restored to the paths of peace and happiness, advise you to consider well what you are about, and the extent of the *sacrifice* you are making to vicious splendor. It is no less than innate comfort and felicity in *this* world, and all solid expectation of eternal bliss in *the world to come*./ You allow that heaven itself is against you; depend upon it *it is*, and ever will be, while you continue in your guilty career. – Stop, then, in time; you are yet a very young woman, and may be spared many years.

Your happiness, during the rest of your life, depends, in a great measure, upon yourself; do not throw away all prospect of attaining to it. The fertility of your invention has, hitherto, been employed in planning schemes prejudicial to others, and dishonorable and destructive to yourself: the Almighty has seen fit, in his wisdom, to frustrate those which appeared, to you, to be most advantageous; look upon these disappointments as so many warnings to you to avert, by penitence and prayer, that wrath you have so justly incurred. Reflect a little on your present situation; – you have voluntarily entered into the most sacred of all earthly connections, and taken upon you the honorable character of a *wife*: endeavour to discharge the duties of that state; be a *virtuous wife*; try to conciliate the affections of your husband by every attempt to alleviate his distress. You would/ have expected to share his prosperity; submit, then, with patience, to share with him in his adversity. – But, you say, he has *deceived* you: – is *deception* an unpardonable crime in *your* eyes? if so, how can you acquit yourself? Does not conscience remind you how very grossly you have deceived Mr. Wilkins in *every* respect, but particularly in *one*, – one, too, which touches a man of delicacy and sentiment more nearly than any thing else could do? Happily, however, he is, I suppose, still ignorant of this circumstance; let him, if possible, remain so. But *you* would do well to remember, that it takes from you all just right to resent, or even to utter a single complaint, on the score of *deception*.

If the *foregoing advice* is not thought worthy your attention, let me beg you will not withold it from that which I am now going to give, upon another subject. You have already injured Mr. Wilkins; do not then suffer your care for yourself to lead you into an action that may injure him still more at this critical period, by fixing marks of dishonesty on his character, and, thereby, depriving him/ of all hopes of future kindness from his creditors. It is he who must be accountable to them, and if you act unjustly the disgrace will reflect upon him alone, however innocently, because they will suppose you have acted with his concurrence, if not by his direction. If you will not remain with him, do not resolve to be the *total ruin* of him; for this must inevitably be the consequence if it is hereafter discovered that any *part* of his property has been secreted from those who have both a *legal* and an *equitable* claim upon the *whole*. *You* cannot have *any* claim; you brought him nothing; and, admitting you had given him a fortune, still it would have been the just right of his creditors. These were the dictates of *my* conscience, Mrs. Wilkins, in *similar* circumstances; and one of the highest pleasures I have since known, has arisen from the reflection of having implicitly obeyed those dictates.

I had been but a few years married, when a train of unavoidable misfortunes necessitated Mr. Fleetwood to submit to a bankruptcy; and, tho' I brought him a large fortune, yet,/ as no part of it had been settled upon myself,[13] it became, of course, the property of his creditors. I expressed no regrets; no reproaches of my husband mingled with my grief. I submitted patiently; and, with readiness, resigned all my jewels, with every thing of value I possessed, – contrary to the persuasions of several persons, who *too* zealous for my interest, urged me to measures they would not, I am convinced, have adopted themselves. I allowed the kindness of their motives, but still persevered in the path of rectitude; nor had I ever the least reason to repent. *I* became the object of general concern; my jewels and trinkets were restored to me; and a sum of money immediately raised to put Mr. Fleetwood again in business. Success attended every step we took; and, in a few years, he made up the deficiency to all his creditors, and, at his decease, left me an ample fortune, acquired by his industry. Let this encourage you to merit the applause of your own heart, and the hearts of others, by acting uprightly. I sincerely wish you well, and shall think my trouble well compensated, if any thing I have written/ should be sufficiently effectual to conduce to the promoting of your best interests.

Suffer me once more to remind you, that you stand on a dangerous precipice – on the very brink of perdition; – you cannot draw back too soon. – Shun, I conjure you, shun the paths of vice; they will only lead you to misery and everlasting destruction. Arabella and you must meet no more upon earth; but, that you may meet each other in heaven is the fervent wish of,

madam,
   your humble servant,
      SUSANNA FLEETWOOD./

LETTER XLI.

Miss Matthews, to Mrs. Wilkins.

Madam,

My aunt has just brought me her letter to enclose to you. – I have perused it, and find she has rendered it almost unnecessary for me to make any addition to it: but, lest you should do me the injustice to suppose I am acting only by compulsion, I cannot omit telling you, that every sentence she has written, meets my warmest approbation. Our friendship, if it can be called so, where there is no congeniality of mind to cement the union, has, for a long time past, been a source of disquiet to me. Tho' I wanted *strength of mind* to break the attachment, and *courage* to avow my abhorrence of your principles and conduct, *hints* have been passed over with ridicule or inattention, and a false delicacy prevented my going farther./

The *resolution* I have formed of relinquishing all intercourse with you, relieves my spirits from the painful weight which has long oppressed them. I intend, firmly to adhere to it. Henceforth, I will endeavour to copy the bright example my aunt's conduct sets before me. I will form no friendships, no connections of any kind, that are not founded on the basis of virtue. – I can then have no reason to blush in secret, for the sentiments of a correspondent. I had hoped, alas! how vainly! that the conjugal tie would have been a means of reforming both your principles and manners; I am concerned at finding myself mistaken, since only *that* reformation could have restored you to my *esteem*, which has long ceased.

To assure you, however, that the apparent alteration in *me* does not, in the least degree, proceed from the alteration in your circumstances, I add, with the permission of my aunt, that we will either of us be ready, at any time, to render you pecuniary assistances, if you will apply them to *virtuous* purposes. – But upon this subject you must address *her*;/ for *I* will not open any more letters with your hand writing on the superscription. Yet, believe me, I feel for you inexpressibly. God grant that this last afflictive stroke may be the means of bringing you to repentance! and then it will eventually be productive of your happiness. Farewell.

   ARABELLA MATTHEWS.

P. S. I have opened the packet again to inform you that Nurse has been here, overwhelmed with sorrow for the loss of your child. She desired me to tell you, the poor thing was this morning in perfect health, playing upon the floor with *her* little ones, and laughing very heartily; when he was suddenly attacked by a convulsive fit, in which he expired before any assistance could be obtained. She had dispatched a messenger to the Major with the intelligence./

LETTER XLII.

Charles Montgomery, Esq. to the Hon. Augustus Fitzmaurice.

SCARBOROUGH.

IN writing to you, Augustus, I seem to be perfoming a work of supererogation; you have not desired it, and possibly may not attend to it. Engaged, thus happily, in the company of your beloved Harriet, *inferior* pleasures are only interruptions; yet, I claim the privilege of friendship; and, while I communicate my pleasures and my pains, let them both meet your participation.

At the request of Mr. Bertills, I accompanied him hither, a few days after I wrote last to Sir Edward. Mr. and Mrs. Clements came with us, and prove an agreeable addition to our society. The sight of them afforded a most agreeable surprise to Miss Bertills, who thinks the company of the latter some compensation for the disappointment which Miss/ Melworth's departure from England occasioned her to feel.

Your old favorite, the Duke of —, is much with us; and, sometimes, affords a fund of entertainment; because, when we cannot laugh *with* him, we can laugh *at* him. Mr. Bertills indeed does not often do either; for the Duke's folly disgusts and makes him rather pettish. His Grace no sooner hears a name mentioned, than he gives you the family pedigree, and lengthens it by relating the history of every branch that has sprouted from the trunk. The first evening he was with us, he traced the ancestors of Clements so far back that he was struck dumb with amazement at finding he was descended from such an *ancient* family. He was beginning with *Mrs.* Clements, but was happily interrupted in the middle by her great great uncle, Owen Fitzowen, who fell in the service of his country, and the account of his last battle, which the Duke interspersed with the history of several other officers engaged in it, carried him so far away from the original intention of his discourse, that he left us in ignorance of the *age* of her/ house, in which we are likely to remain, as the Duke and Duchess leave this place to-day.

Scarborough is full of fine women, but I am proof against all their charms. Instead of being fascinated by their fine eyes, &c. I look at them, not with indifference but displeasure, at observing how very much they are wrapped up in themselves, and how secure of conquest at every glance; while Rhoda Bertills, conscious of her deficiency in point of beauty, has taken pains by her intellectual attainments to render herself lovely without it; and, tho' almost irresistibly attractive, shrinks back from the general admiration she involuntarily excites by her elegant accomplishments, and the amiable qualities of her heart. She is most amazingly improved within the last two years, nor do *I* think her *less* handsome, notwithstanding what her father says; but her charms will be infinitely more *durable* than beauty. *Entre nous*, Augustus, I am in some fear for my heart;

it seems much inclined to take up its residence in the bosom of Rhoda; but I must call the wanderer back before it is too late. – I now see I have done wrong. Unsuspecting/ of *danger* from any source but *personal* attractions, I have been wholly unguarded against its approach. Finding the dear girl's manners and conversation inexpressibly delightful, under the privilege of being related I have indulged in the frequent enjoyment of her company, till I feel myself, when *out* of it, truly uncomfortable, *restless, absent,* and *dejected.* As a convincing proof of this, Mr. Bertills has more than once enquired what was the matter with me, and expressed his concern for the loss of my spirits. I believe, Fitzmaurice, I must, tho' it will be attended with infinite reluctance, tear myself from this darling object, or my wound will shortly be incurable.

Oh! how deeply do I now feel the reproachful sting of illegitimacy! since, but for that circumstance, I might enjoy the flattering hope of being accepted. The behavior of Miss Bertills would not *discourage* it; she converses with me with an easy, polite freedom, and appears happy in my company; but this may, perhaps, proceed only from her having ever considered me as her *cousin*, which/ is the appellation she generally gives me. I dare not allow myself to suppose it proceeds from any other cause. Her father behaves to me in the same manner; yet it would be unreasonable to imagine he would permit his daughter, whose birth, fortune, and accomplishments entitle her to an alliance with families of rank, to marry a man who can claim an alliance to no family upon earth! No; it cannot, it will not be! nor will I endure the mortification of a refusal. I shall, therefore, in a short time, feign some excuse, and depart suddenly to Fir-grove; there reflection, aided by philosophy, must assist my efforts to gain a conquest over my passions. Should these prove ineffectual I think I shall make the tour of France and Italy; and, of course, see you in my way; mean time,

I am yours,
CHARLES MONTGOMERY./

LETTER XLIII.

Sir Edward Melworth, to Charles Montgomery, Esq.

CHATEAU DE RIVIERES.

THE account Augustus Fitzmaurice gave me of Mr. Bertills was such as confirmed my own ideas of him, and made me quit England, and leave you in his power, with perfect satisfaction; or be assured, I had not departed without giving you some substantial proof of my esteem and friendship. I rejoice to find, by your letters, that I was not mistaken in my opinion, and that I may now congratulate you on an accession to your *natural* right. May you, my dear Charles, use your fortune as your father did! He displayed a benevolence of disposition which made all around him happy; and I can have no doubt of your doing the same, as I know nothing in which your disposition and sentiments differ from his, except a certain degree of rashness in forming/ your judgment of men and things: but time and experience will correct that, and their efforts will be aided by your readiness to yield to conviction. You have already seen your error in many instances, and with candor condemn yourself. I imagine you have now discarded all narrow prejudices against citizens and traders; and, in future, will judge of persons only by their sentiments and conduct.

I have reason to apologize for not writing to you sooner, but I have really had no leisure; and indeed *you* forbad my doing it often, by extorting from me a promise not to habituate myself frequently, or for any length of time, to sedentary amusements, till my health was restored. I remind you of this, Charles, lest you should think me unkind; however, I have the pleasure to tell you, I am much better; and, perhaps, I owe it in a great measure to your advice in this respect, as I have kept my word with you tho' it has often been a great piece of self-denial to me: but it is a maxim of mine that every man should hold a promise sacred even in the most trivial concerns of life./

We had very stormy weather from Dover to Calais. The packet had just sailed out of the harbour when the wind shifted against us; which made the voyage both unpleasant and tedious. Mrs. Horton and Harriet were extremely sick. I paid all *my* attention to the *former*, which gave Fitzmaurice an opportunity to display his gallantry by assiduities about the *latter*. As I was not troubled with sickness, I was at leisure to make my observations upon him, and was not a little diverted at seeing the difficult situation he was thrown into. Not all his love, combined with his solicitude for the object of it, could chase away his own sickness. He struggled against it a long time; nor did his assiduities slacken, till, unable to speak or move, he was obliged to submit to relinquish his post to me, and suffer himself to be put to bed, from whence he was incapable of rising till we made Calais. He then dressed, with alacrity, and as soon as we were safe on shore his usual vivacity returned, and has not forsaken him since. Augustus, without the least duplicity of character, possesses the happy art of accomodating himself/ to the company he is with; and, by his engaging qualities, renders himself the very life of the whole set. I know not how he manages, but he makes every person satisfied with themselves; and this you must allow is a never failing recipe to win all hearts. After saying thus much, you will not be at all surprised to hear that poor Harriet is in danger of a rival, and a very formidable one too, for she has *birth, beauty,* and *fortune.* The lady I mean is Mademoiselle de Cherville, niece to the Marchionesse de Rivieres, and a ward of the Marquess, to whose eldest son she is, by mutual consent, contracted. At present, he is in the imperial army engaged in the war with the Turks;[14] which rendering his life precarious, it is likely Mademoiselle may think it necessary to provide against such a contingency, by securing one of equal rank and fortune, to supply his place in her heart. She certainly takes infinite pains to engage the attention of Augustus; but he has too much honor to amuse himself by trifling with her; therefore, as *she* advances *he* retires, and I sometimes fear that his politeness to her will retire too. I/ should feel concern for her, if I had not sufficient penetration to perceive she is not of a constitution to *suffer* much from the tender passion.

The Marquess and Marchioness are a most amiable pair; happy in each other, and diffusing general joy thro' the hearts of all connected with them. Mr. Watson is quite at home here; he is indeed under infinite obligation for their kindness towards him: they express no *less* to him for *his* company and *ours*. – They propose to us to winter at Nice,[15] for the benefit of my uncle's health, whither they will accompany us; and, in the ensuing spring, return with us to Melworth-hall. – No objection having yet been made to this plan, I suppose it will be adopted.

Augustus has just entered my apartment, with a letter from you in his hand, triumphing in the idea of your being again caught in the soft toils of Cupid. He is too much engaged to write, but desires me to add, that you have described the *right* symptoms, and you may now struggle for ever, you will not be able to disentangle yourself; in which opinion I concur,/ and, therefore, it is my advice to you, Charles, to lay aside all apprehensions of a refusal on account of your birth; Mr. Bertills is convincing you, by every action of his life, that his sentiments deviate from those of common minds. In this instance, I will venture, without any supernatural assistance, to predict, you will meet no repulse from either him or Miss Bertills. Remember, my predictions in your affairs have proved right hitherto; let that encourage you to make a declaration instead of withdrawing from their society. *This* attachment is founded on the basis of esteem; and, depend upon it, it will be crowned with success. – That it *may*, is the warm wish of

yours, sincerely,
EDWARD MELWORTH.

P. S. Harriet requests you will deliver the enclosed* to Miss Bertills./

LETTER XLIV.

Miss Bertills to Miss Melworth.

SCARBOROUGH.

YOUR description of your voyage, my dear Harriet, made me shudder. Possibly, as you observe, your fears, and your inexperience of the sea, might magnify the

---

*   The insertion omitted as unnecessary./

danger; but, if you have painted from nature, the scene must, I think, appear very tremenduous to any person. Heaven be thanked, you escaped in safety! I shall be glad when you are returned to England, for my mind will not be thoroughly at ease till then. – The period of our meeting seems now fixed at a painful distance, and I am, consequently, again much disappointed at being obliged to renounce all expectation of seeing you the ensuing winter in Chatham-place.

I have heard and read much of the salubrity of the air of Nice, which I hope will be/ proved by the restoration of the health of those so justly dear to you as Sir Edward and Mr. Watson; the satisfaction you will derive from that circumstance will enter into my heart, since my affection leads me to divide with you equally your *joys* and *sorrows*: may it be long ere you experience the latter!

Our party here is quite broken up; the most pleasing part of our society have left us – my father and my cousin Charles. The former left us yesterday morning; an occurrence in business obliged his head clerk to dispatch an express for him. Before his departure, it was agreed that I should spend a month with Mr. and Mrs. Clements, at their house at Leeds, for which place we set off tomorrow. They, in return, are to accompany me to London, and stay a few weeks. Lord and Lady Castleton are still here, and purpose staying another month, after which they intend going over to the Continent for the winter.

It is peculiarly unfortunate to me, Harriet, that you are at such a distance; I want you to aid me in developing the motives of Charles Montgomery's behavior towards me./ I know not what construction to put upon it. He is, undoubtedly, a most pleasing, sensible, well-bred young man; but he has certainly some very odd unaccountable humors, which I am wholly at a loss to understand. He came hither with my father in great spirits, and remained upwards of three weeks in a disposition perfectly agreeable. He assiduously sought my company; took pains, by every method he could devise, to appear to me in the most pleasing point of view; evidently gave me the preference to all the rest of my sex in this part; and, in short, appeared so desirous of engaging *my* affections, that I made little doubt of being myself in possession of *his*. Having no reason to apprehend any objection being made by my father, and at the same time feeling a strong attachment to Charles, I scrupled not to conduct myself so as to convince him I was not displeased with his attentions; on the contrary, I gave him every mark of preference, consistent with female delicacy, and this distinction he seemed delighted with. Judge, then, my dear friend, what must be my surprise to find his behavior,/ without any visible cause, suddenly changed; he shunned my presence; and when *obliged* to be in it, was grave and reserved. After passing a few days in this way, he pretended some pressing occasion to return to Fir-grove, and in that humor departed. – My father, who makes it a rule never to lay any person under a restraint, made no effort to detain him longer; but as soon as Charles was gone, burst into a laugh, exclaiming,

'Bravo! bravo! Montgomery, this is carrying it off finely! but, trust me, my boy, it won't do: you are fairly caught; and, like a bird in a cage, may flutter your wings till you are weary, without being able to set yourself free.'

'My dear sir,' cried I, 'I am really as much at a loss to comprehend *your* meaning, as I am to comprehend the behavior of my cousin Charles. – He seems greatly altered, and I am wholly unable to account for the *cause* of the alteration.'

'*That* will not do neither, Rhoda;' – returned my father, with an arch smile, – you cannot make me believe you so very/ ignorant as not to perceive that the young man is, at present, troubled with a fit of *jealousy*.'

'It is utterly impossible, sir,' replied I, 'that he should be *jealous*, since he has not had the slightest foundation to ground it upon.'

'An honest confession, however, Rhoda,' said my father, 'and I readily give you credit for it. I well know you are superior to the little paltry airs of a coquet, but such impetuous sparks as Charles Montgomery are often jealous *without* cause. But he will come about again shortly; now he is left to himself, the fit will work off in a few days. Take my advice, my dear, and be under no concern at it.'

This advice, Harriet, I have in vain endeavoured to observe, for I find it impossible to throw the affair from my thoughts. In a little time, I suppose, I shall have an explanation, as Montgomery is beginning to come round. – Your letter came to me to day, enclosed in one from *him*, dictated in polite and rather affectionate terms. He requests to be/ informed what stay we intend making here; adding, that if we do not depart in a few days, he will come over and join us, as he cannot bear the idea of passing another week without seeing us. – Strange being! is he not, Harriet? As the laws of good breeding render a reply necessary, I must write to him to-night; for which purpose, I will now take my leave of you, after assuring you that I am your very

    affectionate friend,
      RHODA BERTILLS.

LETTER XLV.

Charles Montgomery, Esq. to Sir Edward Melworth.

CHATHAM-PLACE.

MY past engagements, my friend, will, I know, successfully plead my apology in your breast for this long, *very* long silence; I will therefore lay them before you. In pursuance of the measures I had planned, to effect a conquest/ over my tender attachment to Miss Bertills, I returned to Fir-grove a few days after I had written to Augustus. When there, I revolved my conduct again and again, and was much dissatisfied with myself for leaving Scarborough so abruptly. Every plea suggested by *prudence* was ineffectual to restore me to peace. I was conscious of having, in appearance, been guilty of ingratitude, where I owed the highest obligation. The thought distressed me beyond expression, and added considerably to the misery I felt, in contrasting my solitary situation with the happiness I had so lately enjoyed in the converse of my beloved Rhoda. In vain did I strive to combat my *feelings* with philosophy; they were too powerful; and the result of every effort was an increase of wretchedness. Thus perplexed, I knew not what course to take, till the arrival of your friendly letter once more raised my hopes; and, tho' in direct opposition to the opinion my fears had formed, I determined to adopt your advice. It concurred, indeed, too strongly with my wishes to leave me the power of resisting, for a moment, my propensity to/ follow it. Shame for the folly I had discovered, now rose, and opposed my inclination for going again to Scarborough without first announcing my intention by a letter. I therefore enclosed that from Miss Melworth in one from myself to Miss Bertills. She favored me with an early reply, informing me, that Mr. Bertills was gone home; and that she was going the next day with Mr. and Mrs. Clements to spend a month at Leeds. You will not doubt but I flew thither on the wings of love to meet her; she received me with her accustomed cordiality, and I experienced a return of happiness. Availing myself of a polite and friendly invitation from Mr. Clements to visit them frequently, I let not a day pass without seeing them; yet still I wanted courage to avow my sentiments to the lovely girl: for every time I attempted to speak upon the subject, the idea of my unfortunate birth suggested itself immediately, and locked up all the powers of articulation. In this way I went on, hoping and despairing, till the last week of her stay at Leeds, when I received from Mr. Bertills the following letter./

'Dear Charles,

   I learn, by letters from Rhoda, the pleasing intelligence that you are perfectly recovered from that *alarming* disorder which occasioned your hasty departure from Scarborough. It gives me great satisfaction; as I really could not avoid feeling much concern for you, and particularly as I was apprehensive you were not sufficiently acquainted with the nature of your disease to apply the proper remedy, or even to think it necessary to solicit the advice of any amongst the skilful in those cases. Upon the *first* approach of a dangerous disorder, the best assistance should be called in; as yours is rather of a dangerous kind, I would advise you not to neglect it lest it becomes habitual, and, in time, tends to make your existence almost insupportable. I know nothing of the complaint from experience, having never yet been troubled with it, and am now I think past the time of life to dread such a kind of an attack; but I have known many who have labored under it for a series of years, and been worn to a/ shadow, without using any proper means of recovery, because ignorant of the *source* from whence their malady sprang; while the symptoms discovered it to every discerning eye. I know not by what name the faculty would distinguish this disease, but, for my own part, I think it may be justly termed a species of the *bile*, since it is apt to make the patient very choleric, and generally, at each attack, produces the jaundice in a greater or less degree, as is easily perceived from the sallow hue in which every thing appears to the patient: as the reflection of his eye discolors, to his imagination, every object it fixes on. Sometimes the complaint gets to such a height as to imbitter all his comforts, by throwing a shade of black over his brightest prospects. When it arrives at this stage the consequence is to be dreaded, as it then wears the *appearance* of insanity, and is not many degrees removed from the *reality*. I would, therefore, my dear Charles, caution you to take care in time that you may not fall a sacrifice to so cruel a distemper./

I expect our good friends Mr. and Mrs. Clements will bring my beloved daughter home next week. If you should not be unfortunately attacked with a return of your late complaint previous to their setting out on the journey, I shall hope for the pleasure of seeing you with them. The air of the metropolis will be useful to you; and if your *mental* faculties should be again a little *deranged, I* will undertake your cure. I have another motive too for desiring your company. I shall have employment for you; not in my counting-house, for *that* would not suit your taste, and you would only do mischief there: I mean to place you in your proper sphere, in which every person appears to most advantage. Therefore, you shall attend the ladies in the *forenoons* to the various shops; mercers, mantuamakers, milliners, trimming-makers, perfumers, jewellers, &c. &c. &c. They *must* have a male attendant, and you are much better qualified for the *office* than either Clements or myself; it would not suit *us*, neither should we be any judges of the articles to be *viewed*;/ I omit saying *purchased*, because that is not always the motive for shopping. In the evenings, you shall attend them to the places of public amusement; and if, by chance, you fix upon one that may with propriety be termed *rational*, we will give you our company, if we have nothing more material to do. But while I continue in business I shall always make amusement give place to that.

Tell Rhoda that the ship I feared was lost is arrived safe, and Captain Gillam's wife, to whom I bore the welcome intelligence, almost overcame me with her demonstations of unaffected joy, and pious gratitude to heaven. Gillam is an excellent captain, and has studied my interest as much as his own ever since he has been in my employ; but I am determined he shall not go out again for *me*. His good woman, I am certain, suffers extreme tortures in his absence, from her ideas of the dangers he is exposed to; therefore something else must be thought of to enable him to live upon terra firma; I have no notion of filling my coffers at the heavy expence of another's peace./

I shall expect to see you all to dinner, on Saturday, till when,

 I am

  dear Charles,

   yours, affectionately,

    PHILIP BERTILLS.

P. S. If you think the first part of my letter needs explanation, ask your cousin for it; she can give you one if she pleases.'

After reading the foregoing several times, without being able to comprehend its meaning clearly, the hint in the postscript struck me; and, ordering the horses, I went immediately over to Leeds, where I was so fortunate as to find Miss Bertills alone in the parlour. The usual compliments having passed, I put the letter from her father into her hand; and, while she was perusiug it, I went towards a window, where I stood examining her countenance attentively, to see if I could gather any thing like explanation from thence. I observed that the color rose into her face and/ neck, tho' she could not avoid laughing to herself, which I would not appear to notice. When reading the postscript, I perceived a visible confusion overspread her countenance. – This she in vain strove to hide; returning the letter to me, she said,

'It gives me infinite pleasure to learn that Captain Gillam is arrived in safety; he is a worthy man, and his lady, Mrs. Gillam, has long possessed my esteem; she is really an amiable –'

'Pardon me, my dear Miss Bertills,' cried I, 'for presuming to interrupt you; any other time I shall be ready to participate with you in the happiness of your friends, but permit me now to indulge in the gratification of my own curiosity. Did you, madam, observe the postscript of Mr. Bertills's letter?'

'Yes, sir, I believe,' – returned she, hesitatingly, – 'I think I did read it – but – but I saw nothing – I mean – nothing *very particular* in it.'

'Do give me leave,' resumed I, 'to read it over to you.'/

'Oh, no! by no means;' – cried she, eagerly, – 'it is quite unnecessary indeed.'

'Your *manner* of answering, madam,' said I, 'convinces me of that; I will, therefore, only intreat you will favor me with the explanation, which I understand you are so well qualified to give.'

'My father was mistaken, indeed, sir,' she replied, 'I really am not *properly* qualified for it; not at present however: besides, it is time for me to dress. I wonder where Mrs. Clements is? – I do not like to leave you alone.' Then rising from her seat, she added, 'I'll ring for a servant to inform her you are here, for if I do not go up to dress I shall not be fit to appear at the dinner table.'

Before she could get to the bell, I arose, and, taking her hand, led her back to her seat saying,

'Permit me, Miss Bertills, to take the liberty of turning you from your purpose a little; your dress *needs* no alteration; you are, at this moment, fit to grace the most splendid circle; therefore, let not so trivial a circumstance/ separate us before you have granted my request: I am very sensible it is in your *power* to do it.'

After a short silence, she collected her scattered spirits, and replied, with an air of dignity,

'To be ingenuous with you, Mr. Montgomery, I will allow that it *is* in my power, but *you* must *first* account for the real cause of your sudden departure from Scarborough, and for the very visible alteration in your behaviour preceding it; for the *propriety* of my granting your request depends upon the *reason* you allege. – My father put his own construction upon that part of your conduct; *possibly*, it might not be a *just* one.'

You now see, Edward, that the moment I had so long and so ardently desired was come; and yet, fool that I was! I felt inexpressibly afraid of seizing the opportunity, favorable as it appeared. – Conscious of having gone too far to recede, I at length said,

'If I dared, I would tell you, Miss Bertills, that the terms you exact are extremely/ hard. – I am necessitated to comply with them, and in doing so you know not how great is my risk.'

'Of being thought capricious I suppose,' – resumed she, with quickness, – 'but, perhaps, a candid confession may be deemed a sufficient attonement. – Yet, do not mistake me, Mr. Montgomery, I by no means wish to persuade you to any thing that may be in the least degree disagreeable to you; allow *me* only the privilege *you* claim of mental reservation, and the subject drops.'

'I *renounce* the claim, my dear madam;' cried I, 'I will have no reserves with you; nor do I dread being thought *capricious*; for I can assure you, upon my honor, that caprice has had no share in my conduct; I only fear your displeasure. – Promise me not to be offended with my presumption – not to banish me from your sight – but to grant me the continuance of your friendship, and the happiness of sometimes conversing with you as a relation, and I will readily account for the cause which produced an effect more/ painful to me than I can express. Oh! my father!' I added, 'it would be impious in me to reflect upon your much-loved memory; but I cannot help regretting *that* error in your conduct which –'

She hastily interrupted me. – 'Mr. Montgomery, I must hear no more upon this subject; your father's sufferings for an involuntary deviation from virtue, should obliterate, for ever the only instance which the record of his life could, I believe, produce of a crime. You are not in any respect injured by it; consequently, you have no right to speak of it with reproach to his memory.'

'You know not,' cried I, 'the agonizing pang which I endured at the moment I uttered that apostrophe. – I confess my fault, and the justice of your remark. I have not apparently been injured by it. To the amiable benevolence of your excellent parent I owe all that even a legitimate heir would have had a right to claim; but there is yet a gift in his power to bestow, without which I must be completely wretched; a gift too of such inestimable value; I hardly dare indulge/ a hope, considering that disgraceful circumstance I before mentioned.'

I paused a few minutes; she made no reply; and, as I perceived nothing repelling in her countenance, I at length ventured to proceed, till I had clearly acquainted her with the true situation of my heart. I saw encouraging tokens in her eyes, which her tongue modestly confirmed. O how unlike Fanny Elwood! Before we separated, I gained an explanation of the letter from Mr. Bertills. He had painted *jealousy*, tho' I knew not the portrait. This, however, was fresh encouragement, and I went home to answer his letter, in a state of felicity beyond any I had ever before experienced. We set off for London in a few days after, and Mr. Bertills and I soon came to a right understanding. I am now, Edward, looking forward to a most delightful prospect. – I hope I shall not experience such a dreadful disappointment as my dear father met with in similar circumstances, when he had almost arrived at the summit of his hopes. But I will not dwell upon so melancholy a theme. – Indeed such a thought never intrudes when I am/ in company with my Rhoda, and I am very seldom out of it. Mr. Bertills adheres to the plan he laid down for me; I am the ladies' attendant upon all their excursions both of pleasure and business. He and Mr. Clements devote themselves chiefly to their commercial affairs.

Since I came to town, I have been frequently in company with Major Herbert, who, this morning, told me, that, a few nights ago, he saw Mrs. Wilkins, once Fanny Elwood, sparkling in a side-box at the Theatre, and had the curiosity to make some enquiry about her; from which he learned that she was the mistress of Lord Hanville, but much dissatisfied with her situation, and in search of a better; nor is that to be wondered at, when we consider his Lordship is neither rich nor generous, and her extravagance requires he should be both. Poor, unhappy, unthinking woman! I cannot help feeling concern at the idea that she will ere long, perhaps, fall a victim to infamy and disease. Adieu.

Yours, sincerely,
CHARLES MONTGOMERY./

LETTER XLVI.

Miss Melworth, to Miss Bertills.

NICE.

THERE is always something wanting to make our happiness perfect. I think mine would be so now, could I enjoy your company, Rhoda: yet, perhaps, even then, some other wish ungratified would, as some poetic writer observes, 'corrode and leaven all the rest.'[16] Be that as it may, I do most ardently long to see and converse with you upon many subjects on which I have not leisure to excercise my pen. The Marchioness almost perpetually engrosses me; yet, when I say this, I do not mean it as a complaint; on the contrary, I consider it as a circumstance that does me infinite honor, while her company gives me delight. She is, in reality, a charming woman. She has all the vivacity natural to the climate she was born in, but none of the insincerity./ She possesses the soul of friendship, blended with all the fine feelings of humanity. An extensive knowledge of books, with an elegant taste for the fine arts, renders her both a very pleasing and a very instructive companion. Her esteem is worth all the pains I can take to cultivate it; for the mind and manners which she condescends to assist in forming, must be extremely defective by nature, if she fails to make them appear amiable by exciting the strongest emulation to reduce to practice every virtue. I think myself peculiarly fortunate in having been introduced to such a woman. I am well convinced it must be my own fault if I do not gain considerable improvement from her conversation.

Never, my dear Rhoda, shall I regret the sufferings I endured on the voyage; since they were only the forerunners of many pleasing events; one of which is the satisfaction of perceiving that my valuable brother is regaining his health and spirits very rapidly, and I now entertain the most sanguine hopes of his perfectly recovering both. The company of his agreeable friend, Mr. Fitzmaurice, contributes/ much to his felicity by readily accomodating himself to all his humors: for whether Sir Edward is disposed to be grave or gay, Mr. Fitzmaurice can render his converse equally pleasing to him. – But the young man had some difficulty to support his usual equanimity of temper, while we were at the Chateau de Rivieres. Mademoiselle de Cherville, niece to the Marchioness, having a very susceptible heart, soon discovered a violent penchant for him, and took much pains to make him sensible of it. – At length she succeeded in that attempt; but he, instead of testifying gratitude for so flattering a distinction, became immediately disgusted; and took every opportunity to avoid her presence, hoping to disgust her equally by his neglect of her advances. It happily had the wished effect. She declined accompanying us hither. The Marchioness, who suffers nothing to escape her observation, approved her conduct in silence, and viewed it as a proof that Mademoiselle's attachment was merely an imaginary one. In this opinion I concur; as I think a solid and lasting affection cannot exist unless founded on virtuous principles:/ and *virtue* and *delicacy* are twin sisters; too happy in the company of each other to dwell *separately*. When these inhabit the female mind, they infallibly produce that engaging modesty of deportment, which studiously endeavors to hide, from *every* eye, a tender attachment; but particularly from the object who excites it.

By a letter from Mr. Montgomery, to my brother, I find the former has cleared away the ambiguity of his conduct, at Scarborough, perfectly to your satisfaction. The very wisest amongst us may sometimes be guilty of an error in judgment; I am glad to be assured that Mr. Bertills, in this instance, erred in his. It was easy, to me, to see that your future happiness was, in a great measure, dependant upon your cousin Charles; and, in my opinion, his utmost affection could not have counter-balanced the misery which a variableness of temper, proceeding from a jealous habit, would have caused you. But there is no reason to entertain a fear of that sort. The little I have seen of him convinces me he is amiable; and providence seems to have formed you for each other./ May you, my beloved friend, find lasting happiness succeed to your union! which I expect will take place before we meet. I must now reluctantly take my leave, that I may have time to write to Lady Lucan, who has honored me with several marks of her attention since I left England.

Mrs. Horton esteems herself obliged by your kind remembrance; she desires you will accept her warmest wishes for your happiness.

> I am,
>> dear Rhoda,
>>> yours, most affectionately.
>>> *HARRIET MELWORTH.*/

LETTER XLVII.

The Hon. Augustus Fitzmaurice, to Charles Montgomery, Esq.

NICE.

WELL done, my friend! I congratulate you on the fair prospect of happiness now before you. I am glad to find you gained courage at last to avow your sentiments to Miss Bertills. Upon the whole, you have done much better than I expected, considering the great disadvantage you laboured under in not having me at your elbow to inspire you with heroism sufficient for so capital an undertaking; tho' it must be allowed you threw away a vast deal of precious time in conjuring up dangers and difficulties where they had no existence in reality. Edward says, he could have told you a *secret* which would have removed them all in a moment, but from motives of kindness he chose to withhold it; because a lover's greatest pleasures spring out of/ his pains. When you are married, he will devulge the said secret to you, and not before; when that time arrives, may you and Miss Bertills experience for a long succession of years, the utmost felicity that state affords!

You see, Charles, I have disdained to copy the selfish example you set me, by writing only upon my own affairs, and neglecting to say one word upon yours. – On the contrary, *I begin* with the subject nearest *your* heart, and, afterwards, proceed to that in which my own is interested; tho' I am to tell you, that I am not wholly without doubts and fears, which sometimes take possesion of my bosom, and make me as miserable a dog as ever was created. This tender passion, when it is sincere, makes shocking work with a man. I declare to you, if I were not happily stocked with a tolerable portion of *vanity*, I could never go thro' the *probation* time; that alone enables me to support it. If vanity did not always take care to step in, and, like a good housewife, clear away the trumpery which is scattered up and down over the wide expanse of my mind, and set things perfectly to rights there, I know/ not what would become of me; for the moment I am alone the powers of imagination go to work, and present my loved Harriet to my view, decorated with all the numberless beauties of her face, and graces of her person.

Whenever this causes any very uneasy apprehensions, I attend to the whispers of my kind monitor, vanity; and take the readiest method to remove them directly, by an accurate survey in a mirror of the various charms centered in my own person. This does the business effectually; how indeed should it fail? But when all the amiable qualities that adorn Miss Melworth's mind and heart appear before me, united in one beautiful mass of perfection, and I am wholly at a loss to find its counter-part in myself; then hope forsakes me, and I remain in a desponding way for the tedious space of five minutes; at length, my ingenuity aids me to *disunite* those amiable qualities, and view each of them separately; they are not then quite so formidable, because I can *here* and *there* find a good quality in myself to match *some* of hers; and as to the *rest*, she is so utterly unconscious of possessing them, that I/ very rationally conclude *they* will be no barriers in the way of my preferment. I now take another survey of my person; my features enlivened by the bright powers of hope, appear additionally pleasing. I omit not to set down the *few* good and agreeable properties I possess, and am, in a short time, fully convinced that the *tout ensemble* must inevitably prove irresistible to a female who has not vanity enough to perceive in herself half the engaging qualities she *must* see in *me*. Thus you see, Charles, the settling of the whole matter in a satisfactory way depends entirely upon the proper assistance of *my* monitor. Who would wish to be without such an attendant that has but common sense to manage it properly? *I* would not I assure you.

Surely your old acquaintance, Lady Gertrude Carruther, employs some *familiar* in her service to inform her of all the motions of our friend Edward; for her ladyship is, positively, at Nice at this moment. We met her yesterday morning, accidently, at the apartments of Sir James Craven; she took the visit as a mark of respect to herself, and addressed Edward as/ a friend with whom she had been long intimate, while he looked more than half ashamed of the recognition; and well he might. When we were seated, her ladyship informed us of what it was undoubtedly very important for us to know; namely, that she had not the least idea of visiting Nice till a week before she set out; when meeting her long esteemed friend, Lady Dunbarty, at Bath, who she found was coming over hither to her brother, Sir James, she agreed to accompany her. 'And I am very happy,' added she, 'that I did, as it has been a means of gratifying my wishes by bringing me again into *your* company, Sir Edward; I was inexpressibly disappointed in not seeing you at Bristol Hot-well; but the view of your countenance, altered so greatly for the better, makes me ample compensation.'

Edward bowed, and thanked her, and she resumed the discourse by saying,

'I think myself singularly fortunate in this excursion, as I make no doubt of being happy enough to add to the pleasure both of your party and my own, by introducing each to the other.'/

'We are all, without doubt, much obliged by your kind intentions, my lady,' – cried Sir James, hastily, – 'but, in that respect, your efforts are not necessary. Sir Edward Melworth's father and I were school-fellows, at Westminster, where we commenced an intimacy that has been kept up between the families ever since.'

Lady Gertrude looked rather chagrined at this intelligence, as it at once let her see that Sir Edward's visit was not to her. – However, she recovered presently, and some farther conversation passed, in the course of which she learned that *Miss* Melworth was at Nice; her ladyship took advantage of this to improve the acquaintance; and, as we were coming away, she requested my friend to present her *baisemains*[17] to his sister, and let her know that she would take the earliest opportunity of paying her personal respects to her. As it is not likely that Lady Gertrude will delay the visit, Miss Melworth is every moment in expectation of her, but does not seem at all elevated by the approaching honor. I, however, am likely to be disappointed of the pleasure of playing her off/ to advantage, as I had intended, Edward being gone out with the Marquess and Mr. Watson. I believe I have scarce mentioned the latter to you before, but that is of little consequence. I like him prodigiously; he is one of those elderly men, with whom it is impossible to avoid being pleased; he has made us all shudder by his account of the narrow escape he had; it has taken an effect so violent upon his spirits as I fear will hardly ever be conquered. His nephew and niece are tenderly attentive to him, as are the Marquess and Marchioness, to whose humanity he thinks himself a considerable debtor. But I have only room to add,

I am,

yours, sincerely,

AUGUSTUS FITZMAURICE./

LETTER XLVIII.

Miss Bertills to Miss Melworth.

CHATHAM-PLACE.

I MAKE no apologies for not writing before, as I am well persuaded you will attribute the omission to its true cause, – want of leisure and not want of friendship. You, my dear Harriet, both know and feel the full force of that attachment; consequently, will not think the proofs consist merely in those little punctilious observances, which may with most propriety be deemed the *fetters of friendship.*

Yesterday I parted with Mr. and Mrs. Clements, who are gone back to Leeds with Mr. Montgomery. You will naturally suppose the separation was rather painful to all parties: indeed it was extremely so to *me*, and I have not been able to raise my spirits since. I am ingenious at tormenting myself with ideal dangers upon the journey. – I say to myself,/ Two hundred miles – what a tremendous distance! Roads bad; the waters out, in many places; days, very short; air, piercing cold; damp beds, perhaps; and my poor Charles may get a cold, to which may succeed a fever, or a consumption; or he may be – but I will enumerate no more of the disasters I dread, lest you should be shocked at my evident want of dependance upon him by whose power alone every human being is protected. I feel distressed, when I consider my own ingratitude and weakness in this instance; but I will henceforth commit my beloved Charles to the care of him who cares for all his creatures, and on his protection of him will I rely. Had I seen a *necessity* for his undertaking the journey, at this time, I think I should have submitted to it with more fortitude, from conceiving him to be engaged in an act of duty; but now I consider him as only engaged in the service of *pride*. He is really gone for no other purpose but to set the workmen about repairing and beautifying the good old mansion at the Grove, to make it what he terms a fit habitation to receive its mistress. My father said he saw no alteration/ no repairs it wanted, unless I had more ambition than a woman ought to have; but Charles insisted that in its present state it was not worthy to receive me, therefore, he was not to be turned from his purpose. In all probability he will shortly see how very unnecessary is all his trouble about it, for I am convinced I shall never become the slave of appearances; consequently, the alterations will not add the least to my happiness.

It is really very strange, Harriet, but it is nevertheless true, for I have made frequent observation of it, that the young men of the present age no sooner settle all the preliminaries previous to their marriage, than they immediately set about modernizing the noble gothic structures reared by their forefathers; and, in general, strip them of all their ancient grandeur – of every thing that made them venerable; and, in conforming with fashion and false taste; when, after an enormous expence, they appear at once despoiled of every beauty. But I hope this will not be the case at Fir-grove: I have petitioned in its behalf. – It would grieve me to lose the beautiful paintings upon/ the ceilings of some of the apartments, or the elegant stucco-work on others, together with the carved work on most of the wainscots, and on the balustrades of the great staircase. I know these things are quite out of date, but I am an admirer of them, as well as of the sculptured stone which adorns the outside of the building; and I should be sorry there should be any of it displaced. You will, perhaps, wonder at me for adding, that I like the furniture better than any more modern. The world is at liberty to laugh at my taste; I am not ashamed to confess, that I have a strong predilection in favor of *old* furniture, and *old* servants; if they *are*, or ever *have been* good. – The *former* I hate to part with, till age makes it totally useless; and the *latter*, I would, if possible, keep till they are called from earth to heaven; and, by my attention to their various infirmities, testify that gratitude which is due to their former faithful services. How often, my Harriet, do we see that making a great figure in life, with respect to *dress, house, furniture, equipage, and a suitable number of servants*, by taking away the ability deprives the really/ benevolent mind of the pleasing satisfaction of performing the necessary duties of humanity, and not seldom reduces persons who are slaves to such an appearance of splendor, so low as to stand in need of that benevolence themselves which a proper degree of caution would have enabled them to extend to others. This reflection brings to my mind a circumstance, which, tho' in very humble life, is in some degree similar.

About three summers ago, I went with Mrs. Herbert to spend a few days at a little villa of the Major's, situated about twenty miles from town. We were one morning walking out together, and passing by a small public-house, neatly fitted up, we saw a poor woman, the mistress of it, sitting near the window of a little room, evidently much distressed. Without stopping to consider of the matter, we went in, and asked the cause. The poor creature soon informed us that the landlord had seized for rent, and all they had belonging to them was not enough to pay him: and she, with her husband, then ill in bed with a fever, together with her three poor little babes, must be turned/ out into the road, destitute of a change of apparel, or a penny to buy a bit of bread. One look at her and the little innocents, with the idea of their sick and suffering father, sufficed to determine our conduct. The sum due to the landlord was not very large; we had sufficient about us for the purpose; so we paid it immediately; and received from the woman blessings and thanks in abundance. When the first effusions of her joy and gratitude had a little subsided, Mrs. Herbert said to her,

'I am greatly surprised to find you reduced to this situation; I have known you by sight a long time, and you always appeared to me to be industrious people, and to be doing very well.'

'Ah! lack a dasy! madam,' cried the woman, 'and so we *was*, but my poor Joseph was always a little *onprudent* all along; we had once, madam, a pretty snug farm *upo* 'Squire Grig's *'state*; but my husband did too much to make the house fine, and then *that there* tied his hands, and made us we could n't do no more good in 't; so the 'Squire made us quit, and we came to this/ here place, where we was doing very well. I took a nurse-child that brought us in a good bit o' money, and Joseph worked hard at his trade, while I *tended* customers at home, and we *begun* to lay up a small matter; and, moreover, could give a bit of *wittels* to a poor starving body, *now* and *tan*, and *seem none the poorer for't*. And we should ha' done very well yet, if Joseph had n't a loved a fine house so much; but, God bless him! he does like a bit o' *genteelity*, and so he thought as how it would *reduce* customers to come more to us if so be as he did up the place a bit *neatlyer*; so he whitewashes the walls, and paints the *winders* and doors, and puts in a bit o' new furniture here and there, and so spent all the money we had laid up; but that would n't ha' *sinnified* if he'd done no more, but what was *worser* nor all, he would make it complete; so he had *arter*wards the Goose new painted, and the chequers at the door; to be sure I did *demire* it, for it looked very pretty, that it did; but you know, madam, such *great* doings as *that there* must cost *sommat*, so it/ run us a trifle into debt, and then when Joe fell sick a fretting at it, I used to *set down* and cry and think as how no good never comed a making a *show in the world*. – But he did it all for the best, poor man! *Howsomdever*,' added she, 'as you two ladies has been so good to us, we shall do well again, and be bound to pray for you as long as ever we lives.'

The poor woman predicted truly; they have gone on comfortably, it seems, ever since. – Joseph got well, presently; works now at his trade as before; she has got another nurse-child; and they are both as happy as king and queen. – But their story, simple as it is, has a moral in it applicable to the situation of great numbers in this metropolis.

Our dear friend, Louisa Fitzallan, is much with me. Her brother is perfectly recovered, and looks as well as ever. He is still obliged to confine his arm in a sling, but his figure is not less graceful on that account. – He is elegant in every attitude; but he never appears to more advantage than when in company with his sister. The respectful tenderness/ of his behaviour to her creates universal admiration. He and Charles Montgomery have been quite intimate from their first meeting, and seem to have contracted a solid esteem for each other. I have the pleasure to tell you, that a week ago the family were made happy by the safe arrival of Mr. Fitzallan, of whom I have not now time to give you a descripton. Suffice it then to say, he possesses those qualities which insensibly engage the heart. He expresses great impatience to pay his personal thanks to Mrs. Martinius, whom he calls the benevolent supporter and protector of his deserted child. Tomorrow is fixed on for their visit to C— house. At their united request, I am to accompany them. Indeed, Harriet, I think you judged right about Louisa, for she does not yet seem completely happy, tho' I never notice that to her. However, I do not fear any ill consequence from her attachment. I consider that Sir Edward is a very young man; that *time*, as it blunts the edge of every sorrow, may, in a great measure, efface the fond remembrance of his late lady, and open his heart to receive a second impression, and I know none/ more likely to make it than Louisa; in whose form and features he already traces the resemblance of his Matilda. He was evidently pleased with her conversation. When he returns to England, be it your care to promote his frequent enjoyment of that. You and I are both sensible that she will not please *less* on being better known. – On the contrary, I am much inclined to think she will gradually and imperceptibly steal into his affections, and the happiness of both will be thereby made complete. – So, from this time, I intreat you to let all your concern about her vanish. I rejoice with you in the prospect of your brother's returning health, and ardently wish to see you both, as I do also to see the charming group of friends who surround you, and shall be impatient till you all arrive.

Remember me, affectionately, to good Mrs. Horton.

I am, ever, your sincere friend,
RHODA BERTILLS./

LETTER XLIX.

Charles Montgomery, Esq. to the Hon. Augustus Fitzmaurice.

FIR-GROVE.

YOUR recipe, Augustus, may be an excellent one for encouraging hope in a state of probation, as you term it, but thank my good stars, I have no occasion to have recourse to such means, and your recollection might have saved you the trouble of penning it for my advantage, if that was your motive, as I have had the honor to be elected, and have now only to take the vows of allegiance, &c. and my establishment for life is fixed. I left my angelic Rhoda a fortnight ago, and am come hither to give the necessary directions, that all may be in proper order for her reception. In the mean time, the lawyers are set to work in London, drawing up the writings; I therefore flatter myself with the hope of calling her mine shortly after my return to town. The generous,/ the noble-minded Mr. Bertills, gives her a most splendid fortune, far superior to my expectations or even my wishes; but he will not be opposed in it, and all my remonstrances were in vain.

I perceive I have again insensibly fallen into the error you so justly reproved me for in your last. I am treating wholly of my own concerns, and neglecting to say a word upon yours. Let me, then, retrieve myself in your good opinion, and rescue my character from the despicable appellation of selfishness, by declaring, that tho' the idea of my amiable Rhoda occupies a large part of my heart, there is still room in it for friendship. I am as strongly interested in your happiness as in my own, and shall rejoice equally in its completion. I firmly believe, Miss Melworth is calculated to make your felicity as perfect as human nature admits of. – She is the bosom friend of my Rhoda, consequently, must be truly good. I sincerely wish you would hasten your return hither, and complete the business. I think, Augustus, you and I shall then be the envy of the whole county; for our brides will surpass/ all the females in it for accomplishments both personal and mental.

Last week, I spent a few days at Westbrook-lodge, and have the pleasure to assure you Lord and Lady Lucan were both well, and earnestly wishing for your return; but not *more* earnestly I believe than *I* wish it. You cannot think, Augustus, what a scene of dullness Fir-grove, and, in short, every place in the county, appears to me now; Edward and you are absent. I did not miss either of you half so much when I had Mr. Bertills here, nor afterwards, when Miss Bertills was at Leeds; for, at both those times, their company was a most pleasing resource, and left me not a wish for the enjoyment of any other: but now deprived of *all*, Yorkshire is no longer Yorkshire to *me*. I shall make the utmost haste to leave it, and to facilitate my departure, I must attend closely to what I have to do here; therefore, shall spend no more time upon you than just to add, that your father and I went together to Melvin-park; where, to our surprise, we found the whole family in the utmost confusion and grief mingled with rage; the cause of which was,/ Lady Bab Stansfield had eloped for Scotland or Paris, they knew not which, with her father's chaplain; who, no doubt, thought *that* the readiest method to obtain a mitre. The pride of the family will secure him one, notwithstanding their present displeasure. Great as it is, it will very soon subside. Not one amongst them is endued with much *stability*; we have seen its want there, in many instances.

Yours, sincerely,
CHARLES MONTGOMERY.

LETTER L.

The Hon. Augustus Fitzmaurice, to Charles Montgomery, Esq.

NICE.

I CLAIM your gratulations, my friend! Harriet, the lovely Harriet Melworth, condescends to accept my vows! Mr. Watson and Edward express their satisfaction in words and/ looks; and the amiable Marchioness in smiles testifies her approbation; while the good old Marquess declares he will never give his consent to the match, because he has been, for some months back, wooing her for his second son. You will wonder, Charles, that I have deferred till now, so important a point, as that of declaring my sentiments to her: the reason was, I had really too much diffidence to venture till I could persuade myself that my assiduities had gained her esteem, and made some impression on her heart; but I believe even vanity's utmost exertions would not have flattered me into the belief that I had yet succeeded far enough to make such an attempt with safety, had I not been thrown off my guard by the visible attention paid to Miss Melworth by a young French nobleman. I could not bear the idea of yielding so valuable a prize without making some resistance, therefore seized a lucky moment, and in hesitating terms, confessed to her my love. The vermilion of unaffected modesty overspread her cheeks[18], and, at length, in return to my pressing intreaties, I brought the sweet maid to confess, in faltering accents, a preference in my/ favor. – This was enough to make me half wild with extacy; but my rapturous gratitude was presently interrupted by Mrs. Horton joining us. To her I related my success, and then flew away, for the same purpose, in search of Sir Edward, who, laughing, said to me,

'Really, Augustus, I now give you credit for a much larger portion *of modesty* than I thought you had possessed; since it could be *that* only which prevented your developing the secret of Harriet's heart long ago.'

'Very likely,' cried I, 'but you must allow that the modesty of my love is some sort of security for its constancy, and it tends to heighten my present joys.'

I shall write to acquaint Lord and Lady Lucan of my happiness; – they will rejoice with me in it. I will endeavour to prevail with our friends here, to hasten their departure to your happy isle. I feel my impatience for the completion of my felicity too strong to admit of any very long delay, and there will be much to be done, when we get to England, before that desirable event can take place.

Lady Gertrude has not yet been able to/ make any impression upon the heart of our friend Edward, but she is indefatigable in her attempts upon it; and tho' this speaks not much in favor of her delicacy, yet it establishes her reputation for the elegance of her *taste*. Her ladyship praises the goodness of his constitution; admires his altered looks; and tells him, 'he has lost the apology he once had for continuing single; since he may, now, with a good grace, offer his hand to any lady whatever;' adding, 'she thinks it next to an *impossibility* he should meet a refusal from any one.'

I was interrupted yesterday and obliged to break off abruptly; but am now returned to tell you how I have just been entertained.

The Duke of — is now at Nice; he brought the Duchess over to Aix to visit Lord and Lady Castleton, who have spent the winter there. His Grace staid with them a few weeks, when, hearing that some of his old friends were at Nice, he determined to come hither and join them; and learning, this morning, that I was here he called, *en passant*, to ask after my/ health. In a few minutes after his entrance, Lady Gertrude Carruther was announced.

'Heaven defend me!' – exclaimed she, as she entered the room, – 'I little expected the happiness of meeting your Grace in this part of the globe! – I hope the Duchess is well?'

'Perfectly so, my lady, when I left her;' replied he, 'she is now at Aix, with Lord and Lady Castleton; but,' continued his Grace, 'I think, Lady Gertrude, *this* is the only spot in the world to meet one's old friends in. It is not half an hour since I met General Hampden; he looks full as young as he did fifteen years ago, when he fought a duel in Hyde-park with Lord Kendrick: it was the most remarkable occurrence in his Lordship's life, I believe, for he was then just upon the point of marriage with the Honourable Miss Wellers; but being confined by the wound he received, near three months, the lady was out of patience, and would wait no longer; therefore, broke off the treaty by giving her hand to Sir Thomas Olney. You know Ferdinand/ Selby, my lady? he dined with them on the wedding-day, and from him I learned that, before the repast was over, they quarrelled about a grasshopper!'

'Bless me!' – cried Lady Gertrude, with an important gravity of aspect, – 'that was very extraordinary indeed! I declare I am quite at a loss to guess what they could find out in a grasshopper to occasion any thing of a serious quarrel.'

'Nothing at all, nothing at all, my lady,' resumed the Duke, 'only whether it should be spelled *with* or *without* an *h*. – But I have known many matrimonial *fracas* founded upon things equally insignificant. I remember hearing Lord and Lady Mowbray quarrel once about the beauty of Charles Fox;[19] one thought him *handsome*, the other thought him downright *ugly*. – I was appealed to, but who could pretend to determine a difference upon a point of that kind which depended entirely upon the fancy? Tom Wharton thought Charles Fox was –'

'Very true,' interrupted Lady Gertrude, your grace is quite right indeed; it depends/ entirely upon fancy to determine that point: but Lord and Lady Mow-bray have none of those considerations; they differ upon every subject that's started; the *one* never asserts but the *other* is sure to contradict; by which means they render themselves objects of ridicule, tho' they afford others a fund of entertainment.'

'Ay, ay, their disputes serve well enough to laugh at – well enough to laugh at,' rejoined he, 'I have been often diverted with them myself; but unfortunately, they have not so happy an effect upon every person. – Poor Mac-Arthur, for instance, is so highly disgusted by that sort of conversation, he would never go into their company I am certain if he did not depend upon his Lordship for preferment in the church. Apropos, Lady Gertrude,' continued he, 'you have, I suppose, heard of the philosophical dispute lately held between his Grace of M—, and Lord Lis-wold? The latter's chaplain was called upon to decide which was right, and he very wisely gave his verdict in favor of the Duke; who, as a mark of/ gratitude, next morning sent him a presentation to a living of eight hundred a year.'

'Really?' cried her ladyship, 'well, it was undoubtedly a very favorable dis-pute for *him*, and I am extremely glad of his success; I hope he will now fix his residence in the country; for I am certain the air of London was much against his constitution, and occasioned him quite a complication of disorders. – I prescribed for him very often but could only gain little temporary reliefs: – an evident proof to *me* that his complaints were of a very obstinate nature, as *my* prescriptions are in general attended with great *success.*'

'But the *living* – the *living*, my lady,' resumed the Duke, 'will, I believe, be of infinitely *more* service; his indisposition sprang entirely from the difficulty he found in providing for his family. Parsons act very ridiculously in marrying before they have got a good benefice. Harris was an instance of the folly of it. – He was chaplain to Lord Raysby, and tutor to his son; he married very young, and, when he had fourteen children,/ he found an hundred and fifty pounds a year insufficient for their support; so he got into debt, and at last died in the King's Bench Prison.[20] His eldest daughter, afterwards, married a chancery solic-itor, who went, when she lay in with her first child – no, I beg pardon, it was her *second*; I remember now; – yes, yes, it was her *second*, really: – he went, I say, to examine a will at the commons, for a client; and accidentally casting his eye upon one on the other side of the book, he saw there the maiden name of his wife; this raised his curiosity to examine it farther, and he soon saw that the testator was her godfather, Mr. Martin, who had put her name down for a legacy of two thousand pounds, which she had never heard of, tho' the old man had been dead near ten years. Martin had been a wholesale grocer, and died very rich, after being twice Lord Mayor of London; but his wife was not like the present city dames, she was very notable; made all her pies and puddings herself; for tho' indeed her husband was rich, *she* was descended from *nobody*. Her father/ was a butcher, and her mother the daughter of an innkeeper in Smithfield, who having money enough at command, used to lend it upon good mortgages, by which means he got some fine estates into his possession, which his grandson, Doctor Jackson, now enjoys. That beautiful spot of his, in Surrey, came to him in that way; it was, formerly the property of the late Sir Edmund Harcourt, the great florist, who almost ruined himself by his penchant for gardening. – He did not value how much he paid for a curious tulip-root. His life, at last, fell a sacrifice to his favorite pursuit. I was informed that he died of a cold caught by standing out in the garden during the fall of a heavy shower of rain, to observe what effect it had upon some of his favorite plants.'

'No; I beg your Grace's pardon,' – cried Lady Gertrude, eagerly, – 'indeed Sir Edmund died of a dropsy: – I was then down at his seat, upon a visit to Lady Harcourt; and, knowing an infallible cure for that disease, I took infinite pains to persuade him to try it, and, could I have prevailed, he/ would undoubtedly have been alive now; but he was too obstinate, and so fell a martyr to his own folly.'

'Give me leave, my lady,' said Mrs. Horton, 'to ask what your remedy is, which proves so infallible in such a dangerous distemper?'

'It is only the easiest, simplest remedy in nature, madam,' returned she, 'nothing more than *swallowing a live frog* every morning, fasting.'

Not one of us could contain our laughter at her very singular and curious prescription: but she was too full of her own consequence to be at all disconcerted by it, and only said,

'I see you are all prejudiced against my mode of treating that complaint; but, upon my honor, it is the very best thing in the world.'

'It may be so, madam,' rejoined the Duke, 'I'll not attempt to dispute with *you* on the subject, but really –'

'Well, I vow and protest,' interrupted Lady Gertrude, 'you lords of the creation are a most intolerably obstinate set of mortals;/ you would rather sacrifice your lives than that pride which you feel in your fancied superiority of mental endowments. Your grace is as strong an instance of this as any I have ever met with; you have been several years past under the care of Doctor L—, for a rheumatic complaint, and are not yet perfectly cured of it; but you still persevere in abiding by his directions, merely because you have an opinion that only *men* are capable of attaining to any degree of perfection in medical skill or judgment; yet, I dare say, if you would place confidence in me, I could convince you of the contrary, by curing you in less than six weeks, with a proper application of a little gum-guiacum mixed with snow-water and sal –'

'I would by no means,' – interrupted his grace, with quickness, – 'give your ladyship the trouble of prescribing for me, as I am, at present, totally free from *all* complaints; and, if I were not, I acknowledge myself too partial to Dr. L—, to try any thing that he does not recommend. Doctor L— is a great man, my lady, a very great/ man in his practice; he has had a fine education and is nobly descended. – I knew all his family well; they were not *rich* I confess, and that obliged the younger sons to take up different professions. A brother of the Doctor's is now in the army, but I fear he is not likely ever to rise very high, for want of powerful friends: without those, or money, few, I think, gain preferment till they arrive at old age. Colonel Hogard, notwithstanding his extraordinary bravery in several campaigns, lived till he was turned of fifty before he rose higher than to the command of a company.'

Lady Gertrude now rising to depart, I attended her to the carriage; as soon as we had quitted the apartment, she exclaimed,

'Lord bless me, Mr. Fitzmaurice! what a tiresome old man the Duke is! I declare I hate to sit in his company; he talks *me* to death; I am quite exhausted now with the fatigue of hearing him. – I verily believe he thinks himself wiser than all the rest of the world, for he is as positive as he is loquacious, and you know he engrossed almost the/ whole conversation; he scarce gave opportunity to any one else to put in a word. I am really glad Sir Edward Melworth did not happen to be at home; the Duke would quite overpower his spirits, he made *me* ready to faint two or three times.'

After seeing her ladyship drive off, I returned to the room where I had left his Grace, and had no sooner entered than he cried out,

'Well, Fitzmaurice! you have got rid I see of that antiquated piece of virginity, Lady Gertrude; and I'll answer for it, are not a little pleased! – What an everlasting tongue she has! it is no wonder she has lived single thro' all her best days, for none but a deaf and dumb man would think of marrying such a woman. – If she was not obliged to pause sometimes to recover her breath, there would be no possibility of taking any share in the conversation.'

I could not help being diverted to find they each blamed in the other what each was equally guilty of. I have no room for further remarks, therefore must subscribe myself, yours,

AUGUSTUS FITZMAURICE./

LETTER LI.

Miss Melworth to Miss Bertills.

CHATEAU DE RIVIERES.

WE are got back to this place some weeks sooner than the time fixed on for that purpose. – Our hasty return was occasioned by the unexpected arrival of the Marquess de Riviere's eldest son, who dispatched a courier to inform his parents, whose eagerness to embrace him would admit of no delay. I think I foresee that this will be a means of our returning to England earlier than I imagined we should. – I shall then have the felicity of again be holding my Rhoda, the friend of my earliest days. Mr Fitzmaurice does all in his power to accelerate that period, for reasons to which I presume you are no stranger; as he tells me, he has informed Mr. Montgomery of his present happiness, and future prospects; and the latter, knowing the friendship that subsists between/ you and me, has, of course, not withheld from you a piece of information which is generally esteemed so very important. – Indeed the circumstance itself *is* of the *utmost* importance to the parties concerned, since it forms either the happiness or misery of their whole lives. – But where the choice of the heart is approved by the judgment, there can be little reason to dread the latter consequence. Perfectly satisfied in this point, Rhoda, I scorn the paltry affectation of gravity and thoughtfulness which some deem necessary, and which I have often seen assumed even by women of sense, for a few weeks previous to their union. Yet when I say this, I do not mean to become an advocate for rash, inconsiderate marriages; on the contrary, I do most heartily concur in the idea of that elegant and fascinating writer, Doctor Watts, in a poem describing the couples who may or may not rationally expect happiness in that state, he says,

'Not the wild herd of nymphs and swains,
'Who *thoughtless* rush into the chains,
   'As *custom* leads the way;/

'If there be bliss without design,
'Ivies and oaks may grow and twine,
   'And be as blest as they.'[21]

I would advise every one to *think seriously* upon the subject; but let them do this *before* their affections are so far interested as to blind their reason, or mislead their judgment. – This was the method I pursued, and I can now look forward with a delight serene and tranquil. I scruple not to confess to you, that Augustus Fitzmaurice is *dear* to my heart. I believe the attachment to be *mutual*. On my side it has been gradually progressive; – I was not attracted by the first view. I remember, I then thought the *tout ensemble* of his *person* pleasing, and his *manners* something more than agreeable. As our intimacy increased, I discovered in him many amiable propensities. Time still kept unfolding fresh perfections to my observation. His particular attention soon shewed that on *me* depended *his happiness.* – On examining my heart, I found *mine* was little less dependent upon *him*. I set myself to peruse with scrutinizing attention the volume of his mind, again and again; and, after the most/ mature deliberation, my reason united with my affection to declare in his favor. At length he avowed to me his sentiments, and solicited a return of tenderness. I acknowledged a preference in his favor; he received the confession with gratitude; but has since presumed so far upon it as to extort from me, by repeated entreaties, a promise to give him my hand at the altar, as soon after our arrival in England as conveniency permits. Thus, you see, I am brought into the situation of *wife elect.* Yet no idea of all the matronly cares attendant upon that character, no fear that my Augustus may ever prove less amiable, or that my felicity may be less perfect or less permanent in the matrimonial than in the single state, has had sufficient power over my mind to add one line of gravity to my features. Conscious that my attachment is founded on a solid esteem for his virtues, I regard its basis as durable: I am therefore *proud* of my choice, and feel too much satisfaction in it for one uneasy apprehensive thought to find room.

To my infinite surprise, Rhoda, Mademoiselle de Cherville's heart has returned with/ ardor to its first possessor, and I am certain the Comte cannot guess it has ever wandered for a moment. The young man seems to idolize her; they are to be married very shortly; and I hope will be happy: but I confess their future happiness appears to me a very doubtful point, since the same instability of mind which she has already displayed may again become visible, and strike a poisoned dart into the felicity of both. She is really a beautiful creature, and in many respects extremely engaging. I can only wish she may henceforth possess more firmness.

Mrs. Horton unites in every affectionate desire for your happiness with
    your real friend,
        HARRIET MELWORTH./

LETTER LII.

Miss Bertills, to Miss Melworth.

CHATHAM-PLACE.

YOUR sentiments and mine, Harriet, perfectly coincide; I see no reason to be ashamed of a tender attachment, when founded on virtue, and the merit of its object. – This idea made me so unreservedly communicate to you my feelings towards Charles Montgomery. – You know him; I need not therefore delineate either his person or perfections: he is now in London; and I have promised to join my fate with his on Tuesday next. – To that period I look forwards without any disagreeable apprehensions of the consequence: my principal concern arises from reflecting, that I cannot have your company on the occasion. Lady Jane Selwyn and Miss Fitzallan will both be with me; yet am I so ungrateful as to feel dissatisfied that I cannot have my Harriet./ Immediately after the ceremony is over, we purpose setting out for Sussex, where we intend to stay about five weeks, and then go into Yorkshire. The Major and Mrs Herbert will give us their company during the time we stay at the *former* place; but the expectation of a speedy addition to their family prevents their going with us to the *latter*, which is indeed a disappointment to me. My father will be with us at both places. – He flatters me with a hope of his declining business, that he may be at leisure to devote more of his time to us than that would permit him to do; but I fear this is merely flattery; for I am sensible his commercial concerns form a large part of the pleasures of his life, and I feel less reluctance at his yielding himself up so much to them, from the consideration that he might not enjoy either health or spirits in so excellent a degree as he now does, if he were deprived of the employment and amusement which business affords him. My observation often leads me to think he manages his time much more advantageously than most other men I have ever known. Notwithstanding he carries on a/ very extensive business, and directs every thing respecting the conduct of it himself, yet, all his affairs are ordered with the utmost regularity; he never seems to be in a hurry. Family worship is constantly performed. The employment of the counting-house is never suffered to interfere with the performance of any duty, divine, moral, or domestic. I never yet knew my father plead business to excuse himself from an exertion of benevolence. I write you, Harriet, the genuine effusions of my heart; others, perhaps, who have less refinement, would be apt to ridicule me, or say my pen was guided by partiality; but I will give you a recent instance of the truth of what I have asserted; I could give you many, but this one will be sufficient; and the little, simple tale connected with it will operate forcibly on that tenderness and humanity which are the most distinguishing ornaments of your disposition.

I believe I have before told you that my father is a liberal benefactor to a public charity,[22] instituted some years back for the laudable purpose of maintaining and educating a number of/ poor female orphans, till fit for a state of creditable servitude, for which every proper care is taken to form them, that they may be useful in their stations, and become valuable members of society. Applications for the admission of girls are become at length so numerous, that it is impossible to receive all who stand in need of it; of course, those only are admitted whose *interest* is most powerful; thus, like many other charitable institutions, its rules are doubtless frequently infringed upon, and many children received into the house who do not come exactly under the description of those for whom it was originally designed. The concerns of the charity are all regulated by a committee, of which my father is one. – A meeting of them for the purpose of deciding upon some application for admission took place two days ago. – My father, having business of importance to transact, had no intention of joining them till awakened to it, as we sat at breakfast, by a short note from an old lady for whom we have long entertained the highest esteem. She only reminded him of the day; and, without assigning any reason, requested, as a favor, that he would not fail being/ present at the meeting of the committee. Her request determined him in a moment; he immediately transferred to his first clerk the business he had previously designed doing himself, then ordered the carriage, and went to the place.

As we sat at dinner, after his return, he said to me,

'Rhoda, my love, I hope you have no engagement for tomorrow forenoon?'

'None whatever, my dear sir,' I replied, 'but if I had I would chearfully decline it for any other purpose you may wish to engage me upon.'

'Thank you, my dear girl,' returned he, 'you will permit me then, at twelve o'clock, to introduce to you a new female acquaintance. She will not expect to be treated with any ceremonious forms. – Her situation in life is too low for her to entertain such a thought; it is, in reality, much too low for her *merit*, which is such as will compel you to esteem and love her.'

'Pray, sir,' cried I, 'who is she? where or how did you become acquainted with her?'

'I must beg leave,' – answered my father,/ with a smile, – 'to refer you to herself for a reply to your *first* question, my Rhoda; to your *second*, I answer, that my knowledge of her commenced in the committee-room. – It was upon *her* account that Mrs. Kelso wished me to be there. Every other point in which your curiosity desires to be gratified must rest till you see the object by whom it is excited, as I cannot enter into particulars now, because I have some hours employment in the counting-house; and if I enter into that subject it will derange my ideas too much. – I will only tell you, my dear, that Mrs. Brown will relate a simple story, the moral of which will inform you how to act; but you must *ask* her for it.'

I waited with some degree of impatience till twelve the next day, when Mrs. Brown was conducted into my dressing room, where I was sitting with Mr. Montgomery. Whether I was prejudiced by what my father had said in her favor, or whether there was any thing peculiarly inviting in her countenance, certain it is she captivated me at first sight; there was in her appearance something however *far* surpassing/ the vulgar. She was not *finely* dressed, but wore what was good of its kind; very *plain*, and very *clean*. Charles and I rose at her entrance, and observing she looked somewhat fatigued, I insisted on ordering some refreshment to be brought in for her. She partook of it with that easy gratitude which, while it avoids being meanly troublesome, expresses strongly the sense of an obligation. When the servant was withdrawn, she said,

'By the direction of Mr. Bertills, madam, I have taken the liberty to wait on you to –'

'My father prepared me for it yesterday,' interrupted I, 'and at the same time, Mrs. Brown, he dropped some hints respecting you, which have, I confess, raised my curiosity greatly: – I think there must be some extraordinary circumstance connected with his knowledge of you that contributes to interest him thus warmly in your favor. He has not yet told me for what purpose he made this appointment; but I am convinced it was with a view to my rendering you a service in some way; therefore, indulge me so far as/ to gratify my curiosity by relating as nearly as you can recollect all that passed yesterday in the committee-room, which had any reference to yourself; I shall then be able to judge what it becomes me to do.'

'I obey you with pleasure, madam,' returned she, 'and will endeavor to be as brief as possible, lest I engross too much of your time.'

'I beg you will have no fear of that kind,' cried I, 'for I am now perfectly disengaged and at leisure to attend to you.'

'I will begin then, madam,' said she, 'with the relation of some previous events which concurred to bring me under the observation of Mr. Bertills.'

'I had a brother a few years younger than myself; he was a journeyman carpenter; a very honest, sober, industrious man, and thought a very good workman. He had been married near twelve years, to a worthy, industrious young woman, when it pleased God to afflict him with severe illness, under which he lingered for the space of ten months, and then expired, leaving her a disconsolate/ widow with *four* young children. During the last six months of my poor brother's life, he was quite incapable of working at his trade; and, as it was not possible for his wife to do much more than take proper care of him and the children, they found it very difficult to procure the common necessaries of life, and had nothing to spare to pay for their lodging, which made them both very unhappy. My husband then proposed to me to let them come to our house, as we had two spare rooms. I readily agreed to his proposal, and they came, after which we did all in our power to help them, but *that* was not a great deal, for my husband is only a working carpenter himself, and of late years has been so much afflicted with sickness that he has been often obliged to lie by and get nothing for some time. – But, at those times, the money I got by taking in washing enabled us to do tolerably for ourselves, and we were willing to spare part of our little to my brother and his family. After his death, we made his widow and children stay with us, and she tried to the utmost to maintain herself/ and them; but, poor thing! she had caught the consumption of her husband, and in a few months that and her grief together carried *her* off.

'She left four poor little girls (the eldest not more than eleven years of age), destitute of every support but what my husband and I could afford them. When she lay upon her death bed, she underwent extreme uneasiness from her solicitude for the welfare of her poor babes. The day before her death, as I was sitting by her bedside with her youngest child upon my lap, she looked wistfully at the little creature – then at me – and bursting into tears, cried, 'Oh sister! my dear sister! I am going very fast; and alas! what is to become of my poor little innocents?' 'Do not, pray do not afflict yourself thus,' said I, 'forget not that you have yourself been the care of providence – God has wonderfully provided for *you* and for *me*, from our cradle to this moment: – commit these dear little-ones to *him*, my sister, leave them in his hands, with a firm dependence upon his promises, and he *will* preserve and provide for them.' 'I humbly trust/ he will,' returned she, 'but still it is very terrible to me to think they have no other means of being provided for but by going to the parish, where the care of their *bodies* will be but little attended to, and the care of their *souls* not at all. I know,' added she, 'you feel an inclination to do for them, but times are now very hard, and I fear –' I interrupted her by saying, 'Fear nothing; my husband and I have determined not to desert them, and I here solemnly promise you in *his* name and my own, that while it pleases God to spare our lives, your children shall not go to the parish; we will work to maintain them.' The poor thing clasped my hand in hers in token of gratitude, but her heart was too full to let her speak for some time, at length she said, 'You have now, my dear sister, set my mind at rest – I shall die in peace. I know I may depend upon your word. – May God reward you and your husband, for the care and tenderness you have already shewn to us all! *I* shall soon cease to trouble you farther.' After this conversation, madam,' continued Mrs. Brown, she/ remained perfectly composed, and died very easy. As soon as she was buried, my husband and I consulted together about doing for the children. We had only a son and two daughters of our own; they were all grown up, and two of them at service in very good places; and to make it easier to us we agreed to let our youngest daughter go out to place, which she did in a short time; and we managed very tolerably for the space of six months, when my husband had the misfortune to break his leg by a fall occasioned by the giving way of a scaffolding he was at work upon. This laid him up again for a long time, and we then found some difficulty to get necessaries. I began to wish the children too to have a little better learning than I could give them, for attending my husband and a nurse child, and looking after my laundry took up all my time, that I had no leisure to teach them any thing. The lady whose child I had to nurse felt for me, and proposed attempting to get the second girl, near eight years old, into the orphan-house. I was very desirous of it, and the lady was/ extremely active in the affair, and tho' she found it a much harder matter to accomplish than she had supposed, yet she persevered till she got introduced to Mrs. Kelso, who happened then to have a right of presentation, and readily granted the favor; after which, I was ordered to bring the child, and attend the committee yesterday. And I shall ever remember with gratitude, the kindness shewn to me by all the gentlemen present, but particularly by your father, madam. – In consequence, I suppose, of a letter Mrs. Kelso wrote and ordered me to send into the committee, I was presently called into the room, when Mr. Bertills said to me,

'Mrs. Brown, I find Mrs. Kelso interests herself warmly in your favor, in this instance; I suppose you are well known to her?'

'No, sir,' I replied, 'I cannot say I am; but I hear she is a very humane lady, and the peculiarly unfortunate circumstance of these poor little nieces of mine has excited her compassion both for them and me.'

'Then,' said Mr. Bertills, 'you can undoubtedly give a little account respecting/ those children, which will be worth the attention of this company; Mrs. Kelso, indeed, tells us so.' Observing me rather confused, he added, 'Be not embarrassed, take your time, and let us hear the story in your own simple way; from *your* lips I am convinced we shall have nothing but the truth.'

'I then, ma'am, told the gentlemen all the particulars I have just related to *you*.'

'Did you so, Mrs. Brown,' – cried I, eagerly, – 'and pray what effect had it upon them?'

'Oh, madam!' she replied, 'to the honor of their humane kind hearts I speak it, there was not a dry eye in the room. – They all praised my conduct much more than it merited; for I had done nothing more than my duty; but they were pleased to think very highly of it, and not only received the child into the house directly, but, in conformity to a motion made by Mr. Bertills, gave me strong hopes of taking in the two youngest as soon as they come to a proper age for it. Each of them gave me a handsome present/ of money, and I went home very *rich* and very *happy*.'

While Mrs. Brown was talking to me, Charles rose and went towards a window, where he stood with his back to us; but I observed him apply his handkerchief to his eyes more than once, and when she had ended he took up his hat. After making some slight apology to me for leaving the room, he turned to *her*, and taking her hand, said, with a smile,

'Mrs. Brown, you and I must be better acquainted; I reverence your benevolent spirit, and will learn from you the true use of riches,'

He then left us hastily, and, on opening her hand, she found he had put five guineas into it. She shewed it me with surprise, and requested me to speak her thanks to the gentleman. You may suppose, Harriet, I perfectly understood my father's meaning, in directing her to come to me; I therefore endeavoured to fulfil his wishes; after which, I made a memorandum of her place of abode, and promised to call upon her in a few days. I insisted on her staying to dinner, and recommended her to the/ attention of Mrs. Wiers, the housekeeper.

It is unnecessary to make any comments to you upon the goodness of heart so conspicuous in the conduct of Mrs. Brown; you will be as forcibly struck with admiration at it as I was. The worthy creature furnished us with a subject for conversation the whole of yesterday evening, when my father chearfully said, 'he was determined to have no more to do with her, he had transferred that care to Montgomery and me, and in our hands he would leave her.' We then agreed between us, that she shall, from henceforth, suffer no more from pecuniary distresses; but that the rest of her life shall be made easy and comfortable; to effect which, Charles proposes to place her and her family in a small farm, now vacant, upon his estate in Sussex, which being within a day's journey of London, will, of course, be most pleasing to her, as it will give her more frequent opportunities of seeing her children, who are in service. We are just going together to propose it to her. – The carriage waits for

yours, sincerely,
RHODA BERTILLS./

LETTER LIII.

Charles Montgomery, Esq. to Sir Edward Melworth.

CHATHAM-PLACE.

A FEW minutes are all I can, at this time, devote to the purpose of friendly communications; but that will be sufficient to inform you of my happiness, and its cause. Know then, my dear Edward, that I am just returned from church, where I have been paying my vows at the altar, and receiving, in exchange, those of my amiable, my beloved Rhoda. To add to my bliss, Mr. Bertills expresses the highest satisfaction at this event, and tells me, that the union had been concerted by my father and him while we were both children; tho' once they feared their views would be entirely frustrated by Fanny Elwood. Heaven be praised for its mercy in preserving me from such a connection! – but I have no time to dwell upon the subject, or express the/ gratitude I feel on *that* account. We are preparing to set out for Sussex immediately, where we purpose staying a few weeks and going from thence to Fir-grove. You and the rest of your party will, I hope, speedily add to our felicity by joining us there. – In the mean time,

I remain,
your happy and very affectionate friend,
CHARLES MONTGOMERY.

P. S. My Rhoda has just entered the room; – she desires me to convey her affectionate remembrances to Miss Melworth, whom she earnestly wishes to see./

LETTER LIV.

Sir Edward Melworth, to Charles Mongomery, Esq.

CHATEAU DE RIVIERES.

YOUR welcome letter has just now reached me. – May your conjugal felicity be equal to that which I once experienced, and may its duration be more permanent! Be assured, my dear Charles, that no one upon earth participates more feelingly in your happiness than myself. I must make nearly the same apology as you have done, for a short letter; namely, preparation for a journey. We are going, in a few hours, to accompany the Comte de Rivieres and his lady, who were married last week, to a beautiful seat he has purchased near Languedoc, where we think of staying a few weeks, after which we shall begin to prepare for embarking for England, and hope to be in Yorkshire a few days after your arrival there./

My sister and Augustus join me in cordial congratulations to Mrs. Montgomery, who, I hope, will remember that her friend Harriet is going to be immersed in scenes of festivity and dissipation, which will deprive her of leisure for any mental employment. This must plead her apology, if she writes no more during the rest of her stay, as I really fear it will not be in her power. Fitzmaurice says, he envies you for having arrived at the summit of human bliss – matrimony, so long before him; but he will exert all his rhetorical powers upon Harriet, to persuade her to facilitate matters, that he may follow your example in a short time.

I am,

    yours, with esteem and friendship,
      EDWARD MELWORTH./

LETTER LV.

Mrs. Montgomery, to Mrs. Herbert.

FIR-GROVE.

My dear madam,

A SUCCESSION of visitors has engrossed a large part of my time since my arrival here, which has deprived me of the pleasure of testifying my friendship and esteem by making an earlier enquiry after your health and that of your family. I hope and trust you got safe home, and suffered no inconvenience from the journey. I feel extremely anxious about you, and shall not be perfectly at ease till I hear you are delivered, and in a fair way to do well. May the Almighty be as merciful to you in this approaching hour of difficulty as he has been heretofore in similar instances! I have the pleasure to tell you, that our worthy friends, Mr. and Mrs. Clements, are both well; they unexpectedly did us/ the favor of meeting us at Ferrybridge, and came from thence with us, but talk of departing next week.

Lady Jane Selwyn is still with me, and I expect will continue for some weeks, as Lord and Lady Castleton do not talk of coming down to their seat for near two months. When they do come, the Duke, it seems, intends to accompany them for a short space; and Jane tells me, honestly, that his nonsense is so disgusting to her she is determined not to go home till he is gone back to London or elsewhere. I can assure you her ladyship makes herself very merry at the expence of her sister the Duchess, who she firmly believes would now be glad to return back to the appellation of Lady Charlotte and domestic comfort, which it is not possible she can enjoy while the Duke lives: and indeed I am of her opinion; for I think no woman of her understanding can be happy with such a companion.

I was obliged to break off abruptly yesterday, to receive the friend of my infant years, the dear Harriet Melworth; who, with her/ whole party, arrived at Melworth-hall on Tuesday evening. Her impatience to see me would not admit of delay; she therefore persuaded her brother and Mr. Fitzmaurice to attend her hither. Their stay was obliged to be very short; they left me early this morning, Lord and Lady Lucan having engaged to dine with them, that they may have an opportunity of paying their respects to their noble guests, the Marquess and Marchioness de Rivieres, Mr. Watson, &c. Mr. Fitzmaurice did not omit to inform Charles, that this day month is fixed for the completion of his happiness, and we are engaged to go over to the Hall, to be present at the celebration of the nuptials. A few days after that event has taken place, they are all to return hither with us, and spend a few weeks. By that time, I flatter myself, you will be up again, and in a situation to give us the agreeable addition of your company and the Major's. Apropos, to the mention of him you must permit me to congratulate you on the additional conquest you have gained over his heart. It is pretty evident, that by exercising/ the virtues of prudence and gentleness, you have, at length, wholly subdued all his wandering desires. His tender attention to you has charmed all who were witnesses of it. Mr. Montgomery was telling me to-day, that in a late conversation he had with the Major, when in Sussex, the latter expressed to him the deepest regret for his past conduct, and, at the same time, applauded *yours* very highly, attributing entirely to that the reform in his own. He knew, long ago, the amiable part you performed to the poor infant, whom its unnatural mother, Miss Elwood, so unfeelingly deserted. He wished to thank you for it, but declared himself absolutely ashamed to touch upon the subject yet; and frankly confessed, that when nurse told him the circumstance, his eye sunk even before *her*. – He felt humbled to the dust, at the idea it gave him of your superiority in every excellence; and at *that* moment he mentally vowed everlasting fidelity to his beloved Eliza. Charles and I both believe he will hold the vow sacred: his present conduct seems to promise it; and then your merit, my/ dear friend, will be rewarded as it deserves. Let me hear from you soon. Adieu.

 Yours affectionately,
 RHODA MONTGOMERY./

LETTER LVI.

Mrs. Herbert, to Mrs. Montgomery.

ADELPHI.

I THANK you, my dear, for the warm zeal you manifest for my happiness; I will heighten *yours* by adding, that my dear Major's conduct is such as confirms me in the idea of his heart being now entirely my own. A week ago he took an opportunity to converse with me upon the subject you mention. He then condemned his former errors in the strongest terms, and spoke with energy and feeling on the dreadful consequences attendant upon guilt./ I saw him affected by the discourse, therefore requested him to drop it. – He replied,

'I will, my love, if it gives pain to *your* feelings; but the event of this day has furnished me with an extraordinary fund for contemplation; which not being likely to afford any pleasure to my mind, I wished to avoid it by conversing upon the matter with you.'

'Do not mistake me, Herbert,' cried I, 'I was not afraid of you giving *me* pain; my fears were only for *you*; but if you think unbosoming yourself to me, without reserve, will, on the contrary, afford *relief* to your mind, I will be all attention.'

'Really, Eliza,' returned he, 'my mind is too much oppressed to refuse the relief which communication usually affords, particularly where there is a prospect of meeting the return of good sense and tender sympathy. I therefore accept, with thanks, your kind permission, and shall begin by telling you, that during the criminal intercourse I held with Fanny Elwood, now Mrs. Wilkins, she frequently mentioned to me a Miss/ Matthews, who, at that time, lived in London, and who, she said, was her most particular friend; and so strongly attached to her, that, to use her own expression, *she could wind her round her finger*: tho', at the same time, Fanny did not hesitate to ridicule what *she* termed her *folly*. This young lady, she fixed upon to be her companion during her weeks of retirement. She artfully effected it by giving her a pressing invitation to Leeds; and, adding, that being engaged to spend a fortnight in a family within seven miles of Grantham, she would meet her at that place, and they could go forwards to Leeds together. The proposal was agreed to, and the evening of Miss Matthew's arrival at Grantham was the first of my seeing her. A female servant who had been ordered to attend her till she joined Miss Elwood was then sent back and we proceeded to M—, where it became necessary to inform her of the *true* state of things. – The effect which that information had upon her, was such as convinced me she was really virtuous, and I sincerely regretted that she had been drawn into the/ snare. She wept bitterly, and it was long before our united sophistry could appease her, or gain the promise of her continuing at M—; at length, however, her youthful inexperience coinciding with her humane wish to preserve the character of her fallen friend, – by which means her return to the paths of virtue might be rendered not altogether impracticable, – she acquiesced; but when *I* visited, she never appeared voluntarily in my presence; and when her appearance was unavoidable, she behaved with such refined politeness as threw me at too great a distance to admit of the smallest approach towards freedom with her. I think it necessary, Eliza,' continued he, 'to say thus much in defence of Miss Matthews, lest her connection with that bad woman should in any degree prejudice your mind against her. I never saw her after that affair, till this morning, when walking thro' the Mall in St. James' Park, I observed on one of the benches a venerable looking old lady, sitting with an agreeable pretty young woman, of whose countenance I thought I had some knowledge, tho' I did not at first recollect/ who she was. Looking hard at her as I passed, the color rose into her cheeks, and, as I turned from them, I overheard the old lady say, in a low voice, 'Do you know that gentleman, my dear?' to which she replied, 'It is Major Herbert, madam.' The sound of her voice instantly struck me; I knew it to be Miss Matthews; therefore turned immediately, enquired after her health, and made my apologies for passing her without notice. She answered not, but the other lady said, 'I perceive, Major, that the sight of *you* has overwhelmed my niece with confusion, arising from the recollection of the disgraceful circumstance which first brought her into your company; but it is with infinite satisfaction that I lay claim to your good opinion of her, by assuring you, her acquaintance with the late Miss Elwood has been totally broken off for many months past.' I interrupted Mrs. Fleetwood by acknowledging my conviction of the merits of her niece, and my condemnation of my former conduct. 'Major,' resumed the good old lady, 'you must permit me to congratulate you on the conquest/ I am informed you have gained over vicious passions, and vicious habits. Had I not known of this alteration in you, a cool inclination of the head would have been all the return I should have made to your civilities; but, fortunately, Miss Matthews and I were visiting last night at the house of a friend of yours, where, hearing your name mentioned, I spoke of you with the detestation which I then thought you merited, and dignified you with the epithets of *libertine*, and *seducer*. I was, however, presently convinced I had mistaken your character. Your friend, Mr. Ackroyd, entered warmly into your defence, and assured me, that tho' an artful, abandoned woman had drawn you into error, yet, you were not the votary of *vice*, but, on the contrary, ever stood distinguished for possessing many *virtues*; and he added, that you had, for a long time past, made an unexceptionable husband to one of the most amiable of her sex, by whose gentle and prudent conduct *yours* was entirely reformed. In short, Major,' she continued, 'I was so much pleased with his account of your lady/ and you, that I requested Mr. and Mrs. Ackroyd to do me the favor of an introduction to you both.' There is, Eliza, a certain *je ne scai quoi*[23] in Mrs. Fleetwood which creates at once admiration and esteem; of course, I was much pleased at finding she entertained so good an idea of me, and I warmly expressed the pleasure I felt at it; but that pleasure was much damped by her telling me, afterwards, she had been credibly informed, that Mrs. Wilkins, as soon as she knew her husband was to be a bankrupt, had packed up all the valuables he was possessed of, and eloped with them. The creditors, on missing them expressed dissatisfaction at the account he gave, and very naturally supposing the poor man privy to the transaction, and to his wife's place of concealment, had him committed to prison till he should deliver up all, or account satisfactorily for the effects that were missing. – *He* well knowing it was not in his power to do either, nor even to supply himself with the necessaries of life while under confinement, in a fit of despair rashly terminated his distress and his existence/ at the same time. Struck with horror at this intelligence, and unable to speak, having now reached Spring-garden Gate, I silently handed the two ladies into their carriage, and we separated. Just as they drove off Colonel Atkins accosted me; we turned into the park again together, and I related to him what I had just heard. 'I am amazed' cried he, 'that you never heard that tragical story before; perhaps you are ignorant also that Hampden has turned her off, and she is now reduced to the lowest possible state of infamy.' – I was so much affected by these shocking accounts, that I came immediately home and retired to the library to indulge my reflections.'

'I fear, my love', cried I, 'they were not very pleasurable ones; for it is only the reflection of *virtuous* actions which yields delight in the hour of retirement.'

'True, my Eliza,' resumed the Major, 'and virtue shall henceforth be my pursuit.'

The entrance of company put a stop to our conversation at that time, and the next day I had the pleasure of observing, that my dear/ Herbert had regained his usual chearfulness. Early in the forenoon, came a polite note from Mrs. Fleetwood to enquire after my health, and to request permission to visit me when I was at leisure to receive her. I fixed the same afternoon; she readily complied; and we have since been often together. I am indeed quite charmed both with her and her niece. The latter is an elegant, lovely girl about two and twenty, and appears to me to have one of the sweetest dispositions in the world. Mrs. Fleetwood is pretty ancient, and of a very delicate constitution; but indisposition does not render her peevish; good nature, sense, and piety, operate upon her mind, and raise her superior to pain and weakness. I find they very seldom visit the metropolis; their constant residence is in a village a few miles on the other side of Stamford, whither they talk of returning shortly.

I am taken ill and must conclude. The critical symptoms approach, but this shall not be dispatched till all is over. I will then get the Major to enclose it in a few lines from himself.

Yours,

ELIZA HERBERT./

LETTER LVII.

Major Herbert, to Charles Montgomery, Esq.

ADELPHI.

Dear Charles,

THE intelligence I have now the happiness to communicate is such as affords a delight beyond all my powers of expression. My amiable, my beloved Eliza, has presented me with another son, beautiful as a cherub. She was delivered about two hours ago, and both mother and child are in a fair way to do well. – *As well as can be expected*, is the answer I have heard nurse give to half a dozen messages since the happy event; so, of course, I must be right in repeating the same. In all probability, my friend, you will one day experience, upon a similar occasion, feelings similar to mine at this moment. You will then be able to account for my being too much overcome by joy and gratitude to be capable of adding/ more than my best wishes to Mrs. Montgomery, to whom deliver the enclosed from her friend.

    I am,

      yours, sincerely,

        FRANCIS HERBERT.

LETTER LVIII.

Mrs. Montgomery, to Mrs. Herbert.

FIR-GROVE.

CHARLES and I have just received *your* letter and the *Major's*, informing us of your safety and the birth of another son. Accept our united congratulations, and be assured we rejoice in two events so pleasing to you both. May every addition to your family be a large addition to your happiness! This agreeable intelligence arrived very opportunely, since it affords some degree of compensation for the losses/ we have sustained. Mr. and Mrs. Clements left us three days ago, and some letters from London occasioned my father to depart thither yesterday morning. He talks of returning again in a very few weeks which removes the pain I should otherwise feel at the separation. He kindly assures me, too, that he will never be long absent from us. – Conversing upon this subject, he said,

    'I look to you, my children, for the comfort of my remaining days; your society will enliven my spirits, and help to alleviate those infirmities of nature which I must expect to approach as I advance farther in years.'

    We then entered into an agreement with him to spend our winters in Chatham-place; and he will devote the greatest part of the summers to us in either of our country residences. Upon this plan you see, my dear madam, we are not likely to be much separate. The evening before his departure, this dear, this excellent parent, took my beloved Montgomery and me into the library; where, taking a hand of each, he seated himself between us, and exclaimed, with joy,/

'What an enviable state has Almighty goodness seen fit to place me in! my most ardent wish accomplished, and my declining years crowned with delight! Thus situated, my beloved children, my happiness surpasses my powers of expression. – Heaven has not only given me peculiar success in my commercial concerns, but has, likewise, blessed me with a daughter, who has been hitherto the pride of my life, the delight of my heart. To these mercies is added the indulgence of living to see that daughter placed under the protection of a man whose tender affection combined with his excellent principles, renders him, in every respect, worthy of her, and gives me the strongest assurances of her happiness. Surely, then, my gratitude to God should demonstrate itself in every action of my future life. He has an equal claim upon your gratitude, my children, and I trust you will both endeavour to testify your sense of his kindness. Suffer me' he continued, 'to use at this time the privilege of a parent in giving you my advice, and reminding you of your *most* consequential/ duties. – You have entered into the most honorable of all human connections, and are beginning to act your part in the great theatre of the world. The charge you have taken upon you is an *important* one; time will, in all probability, render it still more so. – A *family* should be considered as a little *state*; to govern it properly requires as large a portion of discretion and policy. You must exert your wisdom, you must exert your benevolence. Gain the affection of your domestics, and the performance of their duty will then constitute their highest pleasure; while *your* felicity will be augmented by the diligence and alacrity of their efforts to oblige. Reflect, that *servitude* changes its name to *slavery* when *fear* is the predominating passion, and the only incitement to the performance of duty. – You are blest with affluence; let it not be a snare to draw you into indolence, but rather consider it as a loud call upon you to exercise industry in using it properly. Visit the abodes of sorrow; dispense your bounty, with a liberal hand, to the indigent. Consider all/ the sons and daughters of affliction as your kindred; and let them see you, as the delegates of heaven, dispensing blessings around you, comforting the sick, supporting the aged and infirm, clothing the naked, rewarding honest industry, liberating the captive debtor, wiping away the tears of the orphan, and making the widow's heart to sing for joy. These necessary offices of humanity, if properly attended to, will engross a considerable part of your time; the return of each day will provide its work; – be diligent in performing it. The pleasures of reflection will sweeten the succeeding night's repose: they will likewise smooth your pillow amidst the pangs of dissolving nature, when you are verging on eternity, and about to appear in the presence of God, to give an account of your stewardship. I am sensible you have both, hitherto, demonstrated the warmest pleasure in acts of humanity and benevolence; nor do I doubt its having proceeded from a principle of love to our divine Redeemer; consequently, there can be but little reason to doubt, that, under the influence/ of the same pious motive, you will still persevere. – But I have sometimes seen that a change of condition has caused a change of conduct in young persons, for which *avarice*, under the guise of *prudence*, has furnished them with plausible apologies; such as *increasing expences, incurred by an increase of family; supporting the dignity of their house; an attention to the future interests of their children, for whom they think it their first duty to accumulate wealth; &c. &c.* I wish you both to guard against being actuated by any such motives, – they are *all* ill founded. I will not believe that any one ever was the poorer, in reality, for the expence incurred by a benevolent or humane action. – There is,' continued my father, 'another *very* important duty which I think it necessary to remind you of, and upon this subject, my dear Charles, I must particularly address *you*. You have had the advantage of a religious education, and, I trust, have experienced its vital influence. – The *conduct* of your late father afforded you an example of practical piety which I hope you/ mean to imitate. Do not forget, my son, that, as the head of a family, you are accountable to your maker, for the *souls* of all under your authority. Be careful that those of your household pay a due attention to the sabbath day, by a constant and regular attendance on the public worship of God. I fear *family* devotion is not now very much practised amongst people in polite life; but it is nevertheless a duty. – You have been accustomed to it. Fear not the laugh of the profane for joining with your household in calling upon the Lord night and morning for his blessing, and he will bless you, and all that you have. Let me beseech you, too, not to omit secret prayer; nor to fail in earnestly recommending the constant practice of it to those under your direction. Let some part of the scriptures be daily read in your family; and endeavour, by explanations, suited to their capacities, to draw some improvement to your auditors from the passages you read to them; for, by such means, a lasting and advantageous impression may be made upon their minds. I am convinced,/ my Rhoda will chearfully assist you in fulfilling every domestic duty; let not, then, any engagements in company detach you from them. I will now, my children, drop the subject; I know you both too well to apprehend my advice will be disregarded.'

My beloved Charles received my father's instructions with modesty; and, with the humble gratitude of a christian, acknowledged the kindness of it, and his resolution, with divine assistance, to pursue the path he had marked out. As the first step towards it, we have been this morning examining for a proper spot to erect a school-house as there is no building vacant upon this estate, and we mean to establish a school here for a few poor children, upon the same plan as that in Sussex; but we cannot help regretting that we have not a Mrs. Brown to take the superintendence of it. That good creature will, I hope, prove a blessing to those at present intrusted to her care. If I could but find her counterpart here, I should be satisfied.

Neither Montgomery nor myself could avoid a sigh at the dreadful intelligence you/ gave of Mrs. Wilkins and her husband. What a load of guilt has that unhappy woman drawn upon herself! I do not wonder the Major was so much affected, since *I*, who knew neither of them, was depressed by the information; but I have no leisure to dwell upon the subject. – We are going to set out for Melworth-hall immediately. Lady Jane Selwyn accompanies us; she is to officiate as bridemaid. Adieu!

In the hope that we shall see the Major and you here soon after our return,

I remain,

yours, affectionately,

RHODA MONTGOMERY./

LETTER LIX.

Mrs. Herbert, to Mrs. Montgomery.

ADELPHI.

MY late state of confinement renders unnecessary all apologies for delaying to write till now. I shall, therefore, my dear friend, waive the subject, and give you instead, the pleasing information that I am perfectly well – have been out twice – and, next week, the Major and I intend setting out for Fir-grove, and joining your select social party of friends, to all of whom we wish much to be introduced. – But, my dear Rhoda, I must beg leave to take with me a stranger, one too for whose politeness I will not take upon me to be accountable. On the contrary, I fully expect he will be sometimes so rude as to cause a general disturbance to the whole company, and lay them under an absolute necessity of expressing their resentment by voting his expulsion from their/ presence. Yet, notwithstanding these disagreable circumstances, humanity forbids me to leave him behind, as he depends entirely upon me for support. To be plain, you know I am not so much the woman of fashion as to transfer to another the pleasing task of fostering my children; so pray let your nursery be put in order; it will only be preparing it a few months before its time.

The subject of the following part of this letter, will, I doubt not, affect your and Mr. Montgomery's feelings; as much as it has already affected Major Herbert's and my own. The wretched Mrs. Wilkins has, at last, suffered the natural consequence of her abandoned conduct; a conduct, it seems, shockingly depraved to the last moment of her existence. The Major, a few days ago, passing thro' the city, saw her taken out of an hackney coach, and carried into the Poultry-compter,[24] so totally unlike her former self, that if he had not heard her voice, he thinks he should not have known her. – Her face flushed with liquor; her person emaciated by disease; and reduced almost to a skeleton. – Her dress tawdry,/ ragged, and dirty. The offence with which she was charged, upon the Major's enquiry, was such as would subject her to the severest punishment of the law. Mrs. Fleetwood and Miss Matthews, on whom the Major called, in his way home, very humanely sent their servant from time to time with the means of alleviating, in some degree, the misery of her condition; but, on the third day of her confinement, a note from them informed us, that the servant was just returned from the prison with an account that Mrs. Wilkins died the night before, in a state of insensibility and intoxication too horrid to be described. Thus ended the life of that wretched woman, whose conduct procured her no one real friend while living, nor one sincere mourner to lament her loss. We often in novels, Rhoda, read of sickness and deathbeds causing very sudden transitions from vice to virtue, and even to piety, but I believe that such things exist chiefly in the fancy of authors, for it is very seldom we meet with such a circumstance in *real* life.

Mrs. Fleetwood is ready to return home; and, as we are all going the same road, we/ have agreed to travel together as far as her house, where I am to rest for two days. As it is possible fatigue may unite with her entreaties to detain us longer, I will not fix on any particular *day* for seeing you, lest I should disappoint you; but, with the permission of providence, we shall be at the Grove before the conclusion of next week; in the mean time, believe me affectionately yours,

ELIZA HERBERT.

FINIS./

Lately was published,

IN TWO VOLS.

price six shillings,

ELEONORA,

A NOVEL,

IN A SERIES OF LETTERS,

by the author of

THE CITIZEN.

EXTRACT
from the
Monthly Review, for June 1789.

These volumes are rendered interesting by a great variety of natural incidents, and are enlivened by an easy and often humorous delineation of characters. The former are, indeed, such as often happen in life; and the latter are chiefly taken from the middle or the lower classes of society: but the general effect is pleasing, and the writer certainly possesses a vein of comic humor. Her account of a Yorkshire courtship is particularly happy.

Critical Review, for August 1789.

ELEONORA is, on the whole, a work highly creditable to the good sense and the benevolence of the author. The story is not perplexed by an artificial plot, unravelled with skill, but an artless tale, told in an easy pleasing style; enlivened by the occasional introduction of humorous personages and laughable events; and rendered instructive by the excellent morality which pervades every page of these volumes. We heartily wish the author in her future attempts the success which she so well deserves.

EDITORIAL NOTES

Volume I

1. BY MRS. GOMERSALL: Gomersall published her first novel anonymously, identifying herself only as 'A Female Inhabitant of Leeds in Yorkshire' on the title page of *Eleonora*.

2. VISCOUNTESS IRWIN: Gomersall dedicated *Eleonora* and *The Citizen* to Frances Ingram, Lady Irwin, of Temple Newsam in Leeds. Lady Irwin was the natural daughter of the wealthy London politician, Samuel Shepheard, and the grand-daughter of the London merchant (also Samuel Shepheard). Despite her illegitimate birth, Ingram was accepted in the best social circles, perhaps due to the fact that her father openly recognized her and she was worth £60,000. She was well educated, beautiful and politically astute. See *Oxford Dictionary of National Biography*. (Hereafter, references to the *Dictionary of National Biography* will be abbreviated as *ODNB*). In her dedication to Lady Irwin, Gomersall states that 'The patronage of your Ladyship reflects a lustre sufficient to justify my ambition in publishing to the world the very flattering distinction with which you are pleased to honour me' (*Eleonora*, pp. iii–iv).

3. *SUBSCRIBERS' NAMES*: Publishing novels by subscription became less common toward the end of the eighteenth century. Jan Fergus notes that authors had four options for publishing: (1) by subscription, (2) by profit-sharing, (3) by selling copyright, and (4) on commission. 'An author solicited subscribers for a proposed book, collected money, and kept records so that a list could be printed in the book as a kind of advertisement for its virtues'; but very rarely did one make a profit as Frances Burney famously did with the subscriptions for *Camilla* (1796) totalling at least £1,000 (Jan Fergus, 'The Literary Marketplace', in C. Johnson and C. Tuite (eds), *A Companion to Jane Austen* (Oxford: Blackwell Publishing, 2009), p. 43).

4. *RIGHT HON. LADY HAWKE*: Lady Hawke was most likely Cassandra Turner (1746–1813), second cousin to Jane Austen and the author of *Julia de Gramont* (1788). Her novel received some favourable reviews, and she had enough of a literary reputation to be attacked by William Beckford in his *Azemia: A Descriptive and Sentimental Novel* (1796). Frances Burney called Lady Hawke's circle 'this terrible set'. See S. Brown, P. Clements and I. Grundy (eds), 'Cassandra, Lady Hawke', in *Orlando* (Cambridge: Cambridge University Press Online, 2006 [accessed 31 August 2011]).

5. *Dr. Lettsom*: The inclusion of Dr Lettsom's name points to the appeal Gomersall made to City contacts in London that included prominent Quakers such as John Coakley Lettsom (1744–1815). Lettsom was a physician practising in London. Born on one of the Virgin Islands, Lettsom later freed all his slaves and became actively involved in the

abolition movement. He was part of an active society of Quakers who were engaged in many philanthropic projects. See C. Newman, 'John Coakley Lettsom', *British Medical Journal*, 2 (1975), pp. 382–3; and *ODNB*, online version.

6.   LIST OF SUBSCRIBERS: The list of subscribers were mostly from outside of Yorkshire and concentrated in London, Portsmouth and Newport, where the Gomersalls seemed to have most of their family and business contacts. The topic of trade and the connections to merchants would seem to have been appealing to those from Jamaica and the City. Surprisingly, several prominent members of Dulwich College subscribed to *The Citizen*, although Raven found no copies of Gomersall's works in the college. See Raven, *Judging New Wealth*, ftn. 70, pp. 133–4.

7.   *he intended ... to visit the Continent*: Britain was not at war between 1783 (when war with America ended) and 1793 (when war with Revolutionary France began), allowing travel to resume to Europe. British tourism abroad involved both young gentlemen on the Grand Tour, as well as avid antiquaries in search of art. As Linda Colley notes, however, internal tourism became more popular from the 1760s, when war closed off the Continent as a destination. See L. Colley, *Britons: Forging the Nation*; R. Sweet, *Antiquaries: The Discovery of the Past in Eighteenth-Century Britain* (London and New York: Hambledon and London, 2004) and J. Black, *The British Abroad: The Grand Tour in the Eighteenth Century* (Basingstoke: Palgrave Macmillan, 1992).

8.   *thro' his optics*: The term 'optics' is unusual, possibly referring to Newton's *Opticks*, a work published in English in 1717–18, which G. J. Barker-Benfield cites as a work that shifted the paradigms of eighteenth-century thoughts about the body and the mind. The description of the 'vibrations of the ether' was highly influential in shaping ideas of sensibility. In this line, Gomersall interestingly opposes 'optics' with the 'eye of unprejudiced reason'. See Barker-Benfield, *The Culture of Sensibility: Sex and Society in Eighteenth-Century Britain* (Chicago: The University of Chicago Press, 1992), chap. 1.

9.   *Create an awe / About her, as a guard angelic plac'd*: John Milton, *Paradise Lost*, Book VIII.558–9.

10. *in the oratorio of the Messiah*: George Frideric Handel (1685–1759) led the 'way of the future' in English vocal musical performances with his oratorios after opera faded in popularity during the early decades of the eighteenth century. The success of his *Messiah*, first performed during the 1742 season, convinced him that 'his future lay with oratorios in English using native singers' and he produced an 'astonishing repertory of oratorios' in the next ten years. The decline of opera's popularity had nationalistic overtones as most opera was based on Italian *commedia dell'arte*. See J. Brewer, *The Pleasures of the Imagination: English Culture in the Eighteenth Century* (New York: Farrar, Straus and Giroux, 1997), p. 373 and p. 369.

11. *I was then convinced ... she was a perfect female Proteus*: The rake of Samuel Richardson's *Clarissa* (1747–8), Robert Lovelace, is called a 'perfect Proteus' several times throughout the novel. Jocelyn Harris views him as a 'very icon of the mutability that once meant man's paradoxical potential for creation and destruction in his similarity to the sea-god Proteus' ('Protean Lovelace', in D. Blewett (ed.), *Passion and Virtue: Essays on the Novels of Samuel Richardson* (Toronto: University of Toronto Press, 2001), p. 92). Lovelace, as a 'Proteus', embodies the dangers to virtuous women of men whose characters are easily changeable, something that Fanny Price also finds dangerous in Henry Crawford, in Jane Austen's *Mansfield Park* (1814).

12. *CHATHAM-PLACE*: Chatham Place was located in the borough of Hackney, a popular place for successful London merchants and 'noted for its pleasant, rural surroundings, and easy communication to the business district' (P. Gauci, *Emporium of the World*, p. 29).

13. *from Jamaica*: Gauci writes that 'long-distance international trade was more limited to certain times of the year' compared with the more recurrent traffic with Europe. Ships from America and the Caribbean tended to arrive in the summer. See Gauci, *Emporium of the World*, p. 68.

14. *at the Opera-house*: During the eighteenth century, the King's Theatre in the Haymarket was designed by Vanbrugh during Queen Anne's reign, was barred from producing plays after the Licensing Act of 1737, and became the Opera House. Masquerades were also held there. See Brewer, *The Pleasures of the Imagination*, p. 61 and pp. 369–70.

15. *my mother was carried off by a consumption*: Consumption is now known more commonly as tuberculosis. Susan Sontag's well-known *Illness as Metaphor* (New York: Farrar, Straus and Giroux, 1978) traces the association of this disease with 'heightened beauty, refined sensibility, and artistic creativity', (C. Lawlor and A. Suzuki, 'The Disease of the Self: Representing Consumption, 1700–1830', *Bulletin of the History of Medicine*, 74 (2000), pp. 458–94, on p. 458).

16. *the East India company*: The East India Company was incorporated in 1600 and was governed by a board of twenty-four committeemen, who were usually the City's top businessmen. See Gauci, *Emporium of the World*, p. 168. The Company was nearly engulfed in a credit crisis in 1772, which resulted in the Regulating Act of 1773. See P. Langford, *A Polite and Commercial People*, p. 532.

17. *nem con*: Shortened from the Latin, *nemine contradicente*, which refers 'Esp. with reference to a motion carried: (with) no one speaking (or voting) against' (*Oxford English Dictionary*, hereafter abbreviated as *OED*). The *OED* also notes that the only other use of this term in an eighteenth-century novel was in Henry Brooke's *The Fool of Quality*.

18. *I see you in danger of becoming a slave to your passions*: David Hume wrote in his *Treatise of Human Nature* that 'Reason is, and ought only to be the slave of the passions, and can never pretend to any other office than to serve and obey them' (2.3.3.4). While his *Treatise* was not as well-known as his essays, he was famous and well-known during his lifetime. See D. Hume (1739–40), *A Treatise of Human Nature*, ed. D. F. Norton and M. J. Norton (Oxford: Oxford University Press, 2004), p. 266. The novel focuses quite specifically on the passions of Charles Montgomery and develops the debate between passion and reason through his character.

19. *wool-stapler*: 'A merchant who buys wool from the producer, grades it, and sells it to the manufacturer' (*OED*).

20. *poshay*: 'Poshay' or 'po-chay' is a variant pronunciation of 'post-chaise', which was a four-wheeled hired carriage seating two or four persons, with the driver or postilions riding on one of the horses and often used for carrying mail as well as passengers (*OED*). This character speaks in a heavy Yorkshire accent, which Gomersall renders phonetically. William Enfield, in his review of *The Citizen*, had noted particularly that Gomersall 'has a happy facility in sketching familiar conversations' (*Monthly Review*, 3 (1790), p. 223). Tobias Smollett was one of the first novelists to render these verbal distinctions in speech, with the character of Winifred Jenkins in *The Expedition of Humphry Clinker* (1771).

21. *his Dulcinea*: 'The name given by Don Quixote to his mistress in Cervantes' romance; hence, a mistress, sweetheart, lady of one's devotion' (*OED*).

22. self-love: Alexander Pope makes self-love the topic of Epistle 2 of *An Essay on Man* (1733–4).

23. *tant mieux … tant pis*: *Tant mieux*: 'so much the better' and *tant pis*: 'so much the worse' (*OED*).

24. *my dear young master is an illegitimate son*: The issue of Charles's illegitimacy and the guidance he receives from his mentor, Mr Bertills, raises comparisons with the real-life

story of Philip Stanhope, the illegitimate son of Lord Chesterfield. Chesterfield's *Letters to His Son* were published in 1774, after his death, by his daughter-in-law who sold them for £1,500. The debates raised by Chesterfield's letters began as soon as they were published, with the *Monthly Review* dedicating space to the discussion in four monthly instalments from April to July 1774. See R. K. Root, 'Introduction', *Lord Chesterfield's Letters to His Son* (London: J. M. Dent & Sons; Everyman's Library, 1963). Samuel Johnson famously stated that the letters 'teach the morals of a whore, and the manners of a dancing master', but he later stated that the letters 'might be made a very pretty book. Take out the immorality, and it should be put into the hands of every young gentleman. An elegant manner and easiness of behaviour are acquired gradually and imperceptibly' (J. Boswell, *Life of Johnson* (1789), ed. R. W. Chapman, intro. P. Rogers (Oxford: World's Classics, 1998), p. 188 and p. 754). This issue of morals and manners in a gentleman is a central theme of *The Citizen*.

25. *the Citizen and trader*: Given Charles's prejudice against merchants, his understanding of 'citizen and trader' is probably that of Samuel Johnson's definition in his *Dictionary of the English Language*, in which he defines a 'citizen' as 'a townsman; a man of trade; not a gentleman' (London, vol. 1, 1786).

26. *we seem upon the eve of a war*: Britain did not enter the French Revolutionary War until February of 1793, but the signs of war were brewing for several years prior. Edmund Burke's *Reflections on the Revolution in France* (1790), written with the aim of showing that 'the Revolution was both destructive in its effects and dangerously contagious', sparked a massive public debate about events in France. See B. Hilton, *A Mad, Bad, & Dangerous People? England 1783–1846* (Oxford: Clarendon Press, 2006), pp. 57–64.

27. *the failure of two capital houses in the city*: As Raven noted, Leeds had experienced a series of bankruptcies in 1788, although he did not note that any repercussions affected London businesses (*Judging New Wealth*, p. 130). Gauci writes of the rise of finance in the City, with the establishment of the first Stock Exchange building in 1773. He notes that although finance became a central business of London, 'the vicissitudes of the market over the century had bred a healthy caution with regard to financial investments, if not outright hostility' (*Emporium of the World*, p. 163). Hence, many financial houses probably rose and fell during the century, particularly the second half when finance expanded greatly.

28. *my appointment at Lloyd's*: Lloyds Bank opened on 3 June 1765 in Birmingham, where its Quaker founder Sampson Lloyd II had built an impressive fortune in the iron industry. The bank was a great success and in 1770, Sampson Lloyd, Jr., formed a new partnership (Taylor, Lloyd, Hanbury and Bowman) and established a bank at 60 Lombard St. in London. This bank rapidly became one of the more important London banks. See A. Raistrick, *Quakers in Science and Industry* (London: The Bannisdale Press, 1950), p. 325.

29. *poor Miss Musgrave was seized with the small pox*: 'The one eighteenth-century improvement in practical medicine which decisively saved lives was the introduction first of inoculation and then of vaccination against smallpox. The "speckled monster" had become virulent throughout Europe, responsible in bad years for perhaps a tenth of all deaths' (R. Porter, *The Greatest Benefit to Mankind: A Medical History of Humanity* (London: W. W. Norton & Co., 1998), pp. 274–5). Lady Mary Wortley Montagu raised widespread awareness of the benefits of inoculation when she returned from Constantinople. Dr Lettsom, one of the subscribers to *The Citizen*, was active in his efforts to prevent smallpox among the poor.

30. *the memorable year of forty-five*: On 23 July 1745, Prince Charles Edward Stuart, the grandson of the exiled James II, landed on the Western Isles of Scotland. The 'Young Pretender' made surprising inroads on his march toward London and got as far as Derby.

The Jacobites were defeated at the Battle of Culloden. See Langford, *A Polite and Commercial People*, pp. 197–203.

31. *her consummate quackery*: The eighteenth century, often called the first 'modern' century, was fixated with health, and alongside the rising professionalization of physicians, was the growing prominence and success of mountebanks and quacks. Quacks peddled their remedies, guaranteeing cures and taking money from the more gullible members of society. Both the peddlers and the buyers were often ridiculed in the press. Selling quack medicines could be extremely profitable. A few of these nostrums were: Anderson's Scots Pills, Hooper's Female Pills, Dr Radcliffe's Famous Purging Elixir, Turlington's Pills, Bateman's Pectoral Drops, Daffy's Elixir, Stoughton's Great Cordial Elixir, etc. 'In just twenty years, some 1,612,800 sachets of [Dr] James's powders were sold' (R. Porter, *Bodies Politic: Disease, Death and Doctors in Britain, 1650–1900* (London: Reaktion Books Ltd, 2001), pp. 200–1).

32. *these nasty nervous disorders*: Nervous disorders and nervous sensibility became watchwords for hypochondriacs. Nervous disorders were, however, also considered to be very real illnesses. See Barker-Benfield, *The Culture of Sensibility*.

33. *the Bristol waters*: Spa towns such as Bath, Bristol Hotwells, Scarborough and Harrowgate were famous for their baths and their medicinal waters drawn from hot springs. These cities were fashionable resorts and places where both legitimate physicians and quacks had thriving practices. See Porter, *Bodies Politic*, pp. 164–9. Smollett famously excoriated the fashionable folly of those who visited Bath in *The Expedition of Humphry Clinker*.

34. virgin-tabby: Perhaps a reference, again, to Smollett's *Humphry Clinker*, in which the comical old maid Tabitha Bramble (also called 'Tabby' by her brother Squire Bramble) woos and marries Lismahago. According to the *OED*, a 'tabby' is 'an old or elderly maiden lady'. The sub-plot involving Lady Gertrude Carruther's pursuit of Sir Edward Melworth bears a strong resemblance to that of Tabitha Bramble.

35. *poor General/ Wolfe*: Benjamin West immortalized General James Wolfe in his painting 'The Death of General Wolfe' (1770) during the Battle of Quebec in 1759. Wolfe's career and his endeavours in Canada captured the imagination of the public and he was lauded as a hero of the Seven Years War (see *ODNB*, online version).

36. *the siege of Gibraltar*: In the European battles of the American Revolutionary War, 'Gibraltar was preserved against a final Spanish assault in September 1782' (Langford, *A Polite and Commercial People*, p. 556).

37. *I would rather turn author, and write any nonsense in a garret for a shilling a sheet*: In the early part of the eighteenth century, 'Grub Street' writers posed a threat to literary culture because they wrote what was commercially popular. See I. Watt, *The Rise of the Novel* (Berkeley: University of California Press, 1957), p. 54. Even respected writers such as Oliver Goldsmith were known as one of the more famous of the '"Grub Street hacks" – that growing breed of writers-for-hire whose work was to fill the pages of an ever-increasing number of newspapers, journals, and magazines' (R. L. Mack, 'Introduction', *The Vicar of Wakefield* (Oxford: World's Classics, 2006), p. viii–ix).

VOLUME II

1. he *is really* very *handsome for his years; ... and he looks, at least, twelve years younger than he says he is*: James Raven strongly suspects that Gomersall modeled Mr. Bertills on the 'self-made Matthew Rhodes, one of the most prominent of Leeds merchants in the 1780s' (*Judging New Wealth*, p. 116–17). He gives as supporting evidence the fact that Mr. Bertills's daughter is named 'Rhoda' and that the obituary to Rhodes lauds his 'boundless public spirit' (*Judging New Wealth*, p. 118).

2. *Mr. —, of the Old Jewry*: Jews had emigrated to England from Spain and Portugal during the mid-seventeenth century. 'Whitechapel and the Petticoat Lane area became the hub of the Jewish community' near the East End of the City (R. Porter, *London: A Social History*, p. 132). Restricted in many ways, Jews tended to work as stockbrokers within the City. Within the City of London, religious tolerance reigned, but patriotic prejudices were difficult to overcome and acts such as the Naturalization Act of 1753 failed (Gauci, *Emporium of the World*, p. 160). From Shakespeare's Shylock to Mr. Moses in Richard Brinsley Sheridan's *The School for Scandal* (1777), Jews were often portrayed in literature as moneylenders.

3. *the plain dress Mr. Bertills wore*: The wealthy merchants of London, regardless of religion, nationality or trading specialty, all prided themselves on 'their directness and honesty of appr oach', or their 'plain dealing', which was symbolised even in their dress (Gauci, *Emporium of the World*, p. 101–2).

4. *quondam*: 'Former' or 'one-time' (*OED*).

5. *Lord Howe*: George Augustus Howe, third Viscount Howe (*c.* 1724–58), was second-in-command to Major-General James Abercromby in the force against Ticonderoga during the Seven Years War. He was shot while attempting to find a route to Ticonderoga (see *ODNB*, online version).

6. *The General, Sir William Howe*: Sir William Howe (1729–1814) was a general in the British army who played a prominent role during the American Revolutionary War. He was the younger brother of George Augustus Howe, third Viscount Howe. See *ODNB*, online version and Langford, *A Polite and Commercial People*, pp. 540–1.

7. *while the British sceptre is swayed by a monarch like the present*: George III (1738–1820) ascended the throne in 1760. He suffered a bout of madness in 1788. Although he recovered, George III became ill again and his son, George IV, became Regent from 1811 until George III's death.

8. *the Brunswick line*: The Hanover line in England began with George I in 1714, when Queen Anne died. George Louis was the great-grandson of James I. His family had 'astutely promoted their Dukedom of Brunswick to an Electorate' (D. Greene, *The Age of Exuberance: Backgrounds to Eighteenth-Century Literature* (New York: Random House, 1970), pp. 16–17).

9. *the India House*: The headquarters of the East India Company was located on Leadenhall Street. Its 'traditional facade was "magnificently" rebuilt to a classical design' in the 1720s (Gauci, *Emporium of the World*, p. 35).

10. *THE ANCIENT VIRGIN'S LAMENTATION*: This poem appears to have been composed by Gomersall. She published only one poem, *Creation*, in 1824.

11. *the estate in Sussex, being entailed upon the male heirs of my family*: In the case of Mr. Montgomery, he did not leave a will and his property legally went to Mr. Bertills, hence the entail was the work of his predecessor(s) since 'If an estate was settled in tail male the contingency of the eldest son's failure to produce a male heir was covered by a long list of possible male successors, alive and unborn ... If a man died intestate (a very unusual occurrence) state law enforced primogeniture' (C. Jones, 'Landownership', in *Jane Austen in Context*, p. 271). Sandra MacPherson gives a very detailed history of entails in 'Rent to Own: What's Entailed in *Pride and Prejudice*', *Representations*, 82 (2003), pp. 1–23.

12. *to whom much is given of him will much be required*: Quote from the Bible, Luke 12:48.

13. *tho' I brought him a large fortune, ... no part of it had been settled upon myself*: According to inheritance laws, a wife had no legal claim to her husband's or her father's property or wealth unless it was settled on her. Ruth Perry argues that a woman's legal claim to property was seriously undermined during the eighteenth century (*Novel Relations: The*

Transformation of Kinship in English Literature and Culture, 1748–1818 (Cambridge: Cambridge University Press, 2004), pp. 124–5). Of course, there were stunning exceptions to this trend, as in the case of Frances Ingram, Viscountess Irwin, whose father left her a massive fortune and who worked shrewdly to secure an inheritance for her daughter (see *ODNB*, online version). Another exception was the case of Sarah Child-Villiers, Countess of Jersey (1785–1867) who inherited the massive Child's Bank fortune left to her by her grandfather Robert Child. Along with an inheritance that gave her a whopping £60,000 annual income, she also inherited Osterley Park, Middlesex. See *ODNB*, online version. Interestingly, both women were heiresses of City businessmen. Rhoda Bertills is also the sole heiress to her father's fortune.

14. *the war with the Turks*: This reference most likely refers to the Austro-Turkish War (1787–1789). See M. Z. Mayer, 'The Price for Austria's Security: Part I. Joseph II, the Russian Alliance, and the Ottoman War, 1787–1789', *International History Review* 26:2 (2004), pp. 257–99.

15. *They propose to us to winter at Nice*: As Lawlor and Suzuki noted in their research on consumption, warmer climes were beneficial for those suffering from that illness ('The Disease of the Self', pp. 470–1). Travel works were highly popular during this period, and many of the writers (of both fictional and true accounts) visited Nice. One example is Tobias Smollett's *Travels Through France and Italy* (1766).

16. *corrode and leaven all the rest*: Samuel Johnson cites these lines from Matthew Prior in his definition for 'leaven', meaning 'to taint; to imbue' (*A Dictionary of the English Language*, London, vol. 2, 1786).

17. baisemains: French, 'a kiss of the hands' (*OED*).

18. *The vermilion of unaffected modesty overspread her cheeks*: John Gregory had written in his popular work, *A Father's Legacy to His Daughters* (1774): 'When a girl ceases to blush, she has lost the most powerful charm of beauty. That extreme sensibility which it indicates, may be a weakness and incumbrance in our sex, as I have too often felt; but in yours it is peculiarly engaging. Pedants, who think themselves philosophers, ask why a woman should blush when she is conscious of no crime. It is a sufficient answer, that Nature has made you to blush when you are guilty of no fault .... Blushing is so far from being necessarily an attendant on guilt, that it is the usual companion of innocence' (quoted in V. Jones (ed.), *Women in the Eighteenth Century: Constructions of Femininity* (London: Routledge, 1990), p. 45).

19. *Charles Fox*: Charles James Fox (1749–1806) was the second son of Henry Fox, Baron Holland, a brilliant Whig politician and a main opponent of William Pitt, the Younger. He was also the grandson of Sir Stephen Fox, a financier who made a fabulous fortune. Fox was associated with Edmund Burke, Richard Brinsley Sheridan and Georgiana, the Duchess of Devonshire through his activities for the Whig party. His private life was one of luxurious excesses and pleasures. See L. G. Mitchell, *Charles James Fox* (Oxford: Oxford University Press, 1992).

20. *the King's Bench Prison*: The King's Bench Prison was one of the major prisons in London, along with the Gate House, the Fleet and the Marshalsea. Tobias Smollett often set scenes in prisons, using them as targets for satire and as vehicles to inspire sentiment, in *Peregrine Pickle* (1751) and *Ferdinand Count Fathom* (1753). See P. Wagner, 'Introduction', *The Life and Adventures of Sir Launcelot Greaves* (London: Penguin Books, 1988), pp. 7–28.

21. *Not the wild herd of nymphs and swains ... And be as blest as they*: Isaac Watts (1674–1748), 'Few Happy Matches' (1701).

22. *my father is a liberal benefactor to a public charity*: Paul Langford notes that the 'sentimental revolution' that overtook Britain in the third quarter of the eighteenth century led

to a popular belief in an 'age of benevolence' and an 'age of charity' and gives details on the number of charities and organizations that were founded in this period (*A Polite and Commercial People*, chap. 10: 'The Birth of Sensibility'). The reference to 'poor female orphans' might possibly refer to the Magdalen House, founded by Robert Dingley (a wealthy merchant) in 1758 for repentant prostitutes (Langford, p. 144).

23. je ne scai quoi: Literally meaning 'I know not what'; 'an indescribable or inexpressible something' (*OED*).

24. *the Poultry-compter*: A prison located at the east end of Cheapside in the City of London. It was demolished in 1817 (*OED*).

For Product Safety Concerns and Information please contact our EU
representative GPSR@taylorandfrancis.com
Taylor & Francis Verlag GmbH, Kaufingerstraße 24, 80331 München, Germany